FORGOTTEN REALMS®

Ed Greenwood

Swords of

The Knights of Myth Drannor Book I

Eveningstar

The Knights of Myth Drannor, Book I

SWORDS OF EVENINGSTAR

©2006 Wizards of the Coast, Inc.

Cover art by Matt Stewart (www.duirwaighgallery.com)
Map by Todd Gamble
Original Hardcover First Printing: August 2006
First Paperback Printing: June 2007

9 8 7 6 5 4 3 2

ISBN: 978-0-7869-4272-5
620-95938740-001-EN

U.S., CANADA,   EUROPEAN HEADQUARTERS
ASIA, PACIFIC, & LATIN AMERICA   Hasbro UK Ltd
Wizards of the Coast, Inc.   Caswell Way
P.O. Box 707   Newport, Gwent NP9 0YH
Renton, WA 98057-0707   GREAT BRITAIN
+1-800-324-6496   Save this address for your records.

Visit our web site at www.wizards.com

Ed Greenwood

Shandril's Saga
Spellfire
Crown of Fire
Hand of Fire

The Shadow of the Avatar Trilogy
Shadows of Doom
Cloak of Shadows
All Shadows Fled

The Elminster Series
Elminster: The Making of a Mage
Elminster in Myth Drannor
The Temptation of Elminster
Elminster in Hell
Elminster's Daughter

The Cormyr Saga
Cormyr: A Novel (with Jeff Grubb)
Death of the Dragon (with Troy Denning)

The Knights of Myth Drannor
Swords of Eveningstar
Swords of Dragonfire
August 2007

Stormlight
Silverfall: Stories of the Seven Sisters
The City of Splendors: A Waterdeep Novel
(with Elaine Cunningham)

The Best of the Realms, Book II
The Stories of Ed Greenwood
Edited by Susan J. Morris

Caveat lector. Non solum fumo speculisque, sed etiam tintinnabulis fistulisque factum est.

This one's for Andrew, Victor, John, Ian, Anita, Jim, Cathy, Jenny, and all who've brought the Knights to life over the years. May you always ride in glory.

Now in the time of which I have the honor to write, the fair realm of Cormyr was suffering from a dearth of adventurers, which is to say: an uncustomary shortage of fools . . .

Ragefast, Sage of Baldur's Gate
Gloryswords: An Informal And
Incomplete Overview of Adventuring
Bands in the Year of the Spur
published in the Year of the Gauntlet

MAP OF CORMYR

Prologue

Delyn Laquilavvar laughed in farewell and let the mists claim him.

Then he was falling, a brief and silent plunge toward an elusive brightness beyond the swirling blue endlessness . . .

His boot came down on soft moss, the great dark trees familiar and friendly around him. Sunfall soon; the shadows were already long as he crossed his glade. The unseen wards stirred at his approach, and amid their gentle caresses Delyn of the Seven Spells chuckled softly, remembering the merry jests Fluevrele and the others had just flung.

Most elf mages—if they disliked bullying apprentices or taking awed and fearful lovers—walked alone, and grew as wary as the ancient Horned Ones of the forests. He was fortunate to have such friends, and so escape tha—

His wards hummed serene and unbroken, nothing amiss. Nor had the ancient way he'd just taken, to cross half of Faerûn with a single step, been a whit different.

So why now, with his wards singing all around him, was something coiling—nay, *uncoiling*—sickeningly, deep inside him.

"What—?"

He'd time for no more than that before something gnawing, strange, and impossibly large surged up into his throat, chokingly . . .

Delyn reeled, clawing vainly at the empty air. His tree-cats, who'd been mincing unconcernedly to join him, now shrank back, arching and hissing.

Whatdoomcanthis*be*? Wherewhatracingoutofmyown*mindto*—to—

The elf swayed, face as white as winter moonlight, towering over Myrithla, eldest and longest of his furred companions, who watched in grim fear as her master's eyes went as dark and empty as the sockets of a skull. Even before they shriveled, she could see that he was no longer there behind them.

No one was.

Whatever had been Delyn Laquilavvar had been snatched—or drained—away, leaving behind a suddenly spasming, trembling body that flung wide its arms, dropped its jaw slack to drool a foamy river, and . . . started to flare at its fingertips.

Flare as in *flames*, licking and rising, as swiftly as if the elf were dry deadwood and not living flesh.

Myrithla hated fire, and sprang back, spitting in fear. The other rethren were already fleeing behind her, mewing their terror in loud unison.

Their cries were abruptly drowned out by a loud wail, a shriek that burst not from the elf mage's mouth but from his every orifice, air and juices boiling forth together as the flames built into their own roar.

Myrithla flung herself back, heedless of rough landing.

Her master was a column of flame, already shedding ashes, the air thick with the stink of scorched meat . . .

And like all rethren, Myrithla hated her meat cooked.

The scrying orb glowed brightly, lighting up a soft smile.

The column of flames in its depths was already beginning to shrink and flicker, the evening gloom of that distant deep-forest glade returning around its fading brilliance.

"Perfect," said the owner of that smile, in a voice soft with satisfaction. "And such spells, Laquilavvar! This one should give me just the key I need to open Dathnyar's wards. *Thank you.*"

Chapter 1
WEARING RABBIT STEW

Great things befall when one is brave enough to do something bold, strange, and unusual. Something off one's daily trail, apart from one's chosen character and station and presented-to-the-world mask. Great things—or terrible. Or merely pratfalls and troublesome chaos in their wake.

All of which proves one thing beyond all doubt: Whatever gods watch over us, they're starved for amusement, and richly reward those who entertain them.

Ulvryn Hamdarakh, Sage of Saelmur
Musings On Mortality
published in the Year of the Dying Stars

It had been a bright and glorious day of listening to the new leaves rustle around her every time the gentle breeze set them to fluttering.

Yet the late Tarsakh sun stabbed through them, eager and hot. The Purple Dragon was glad to doff her helm and step into the road-side shade when the gruff old lionar led a dozen fresh blades to her post and told her she was done until next sunrise.

Though the bustle of Waymoot was just around the bend behind her, she went the other way, striding straight to the smells that had been tantalizing her.

The farmwife who'd been selling apples and fresh bread whisked aside the fly blankets from their baskets at her approach, her smile widening.

"Tummy trumpeting?"

"And how," the warrior replied, fumbling for her purse. "Gods, I feel I could eat—eat—"

She stared past the end of the farmwife's cart at something in the trees beyond, her jaw dropping open and her words trailing away forgotten.

The farmwife peered—and grinned. "Him? Aye, I think half the folk hereabouts could, given the chance. The female half."

The Purple Dragon swallowed. "Who *is* he?"

They stood elbow to elbow, watching a tall, broad-shouldered man coming out of the trees as quietly as a passing breeze. His stride was long and liquid, his square-jawed face as handsome as—

"King Azoun," the warrior whispered. "He carries himself like a king."

The apparition's level blue-gray eyes had noted the two women several soft strides ago, but flicked a glance at them again now. Their owner added a firm smile and a nod—and then was across the road and into the trees on its far side, his dusty brown leathers vanishing among them in a few strides.

The farmwife chuckled. "Nay, he's not one of the king's brood. Or so his parents claim. Prentice to the armorer Hawkstone these last few seasons, but seeking the king's coin as a forester now, I hear. 'The Silent,' they call him hereabouts. You can see why."

The Purple Dragon licked her lips, cleared her throat, and blinked as if banishing daydreams. "Now that," she said almost regretfully, "was what a man should look like."

The farmwife turned to her. "*The Rebel Prince*. Chapter Three. Boldgrim the Outlaw!"

The warrior nodded eagerly. "You read Goldghallow too?"

The farmwife beamed. "Aye, I've every one of his at home— including the ah, Blackcovers edition of *The Nymph Said No*."

The Purple Dragon's jaw dropped open again. This time, one of the flies that had been buzzing around the food took a chance and flew into her mouth.

When she was done choking, the farmwife flung an arm around her and said, "Eat what you want for free, dear—and take latestew with me this night. Rhabran's gone to market these two nights, now, and we can talk all we want. *After* you read the naughty bits."

The shadows in the sun-dappled shade were deepening; sunset wasn't far off. Florin moved quickly, gliding through ferns like a ghost. Queen of the Forest, but he loved these walks. The deep green shadows, the magnificent trees, gnarled and vast and patient, sentinels that had seen dozens of passing kings of Cormyr, and stags beyond number . . .

He was *of* the forest, he felt at peace here. This was where he belonged.

And yet as spring quickened toward summer in this Year of the Spur, there was a restlessness rising in Florin Falconhand.

Not the weariness of hot metal and forge-crash and ringing, numbing hammerwork that had driven him here from Hawkstone's service, despite his passable skills, but . . . something else. Something that was riding him as eagerly as his fellow youngbloods of Espar were riding their lasses this spring, despite the peace of the forest. He gave the trees around him a smile. He didn't want anything more than this.

But somehow, he *needed* something more than this.

Soft-footed and sure, Florin strode on, along a ridge that would bring him back to the king's road again.

Unthinkingly, as he threaded his way around rocks upon rocks, he set enjoyment of the forest aside to wonder rather irritably what it was, this mysterious 'something' he yearned for . . . and abruptly became aware that a new sound had joined the whirring wings and chirping calls of the berrybirds all around.

A distant, faint, confused sound that didn't belong here, in the deep stillness of the forest.

A few long strides took him close enough to know that it was a human voice—a high, furious woman's voice, with the shrill, thin fluting accents of highnose Suzail. Someone rich, then, or even noble, but cursing like . . . like . . .

Well, like no one Florin had ever heard before. He was used to the snarled "tluin, sabruin, and hrast" of the exasperated, and everyone said "naeth" in surprise or dismay, but *this* . . .

This was something new.

Florin headed toward the voice as swiftly as he could soft-stride, leaves dancing in his wake. It was rising into a screech, like the cooks did at Tlarnuth's in Espar, savaging each other after emptying too many tankards, unfamiliar words coming out in a fluid rush, and

. . . yes, there, again: being answered by a deeper voice that spoke but little.

Florin ducked under a long-fallen tree cloaked in moss, slithered down a muddy bank beyond, and was close enough to hear properly at last.

"Lady, I—" It was a man's voice, low, gravel-rough, and to Florin's ear somehow familiar.

" 'Lady' nothing, sirrah! 'Oh, pretty lady,' you mouth, but your words are empty, *empty*—and your head emptier still! Deeds, not words, knave! Deeds! Treat me as a lady and I am one—but insist I am one yet treat me as any common trull, some prettily dressed *slave* of yours, and you make me that!"

"Lady," the man said heavily, "I have my orders. They're quite clear and em—"

"*Hah!* What care *I* for your orders, sirrah? You say I am a lady, and so I am—and that means *I* give orders, and *you* obey! O, watching gods above, *why* must I be saddled with such a hog-faced, slop-guzzling idiot *dog* of a miscreant?"

Florin winced, embarrassed by this venom almost into retreating back into the trees, yet fascinated.

The angry lady whooped for breath and went on. "Brutish in words and deeds and at your trencher, before all the gods! You call *this* food? Fare fit for dogs, aye, and for any passing hog, but not for a lady of the realm!"

The next word was a screech of pure rage, as if words had failed she who insisted so strongly on being a lady, and left her clawing the air in search of what next to say.

She found something.

"Villainous *traitor!* Seek to poison a Crownsilver? Sirrah, royal blood runs in my veins—I *am* Cormyr! When you seek to harm me, you harm all Cormyr! The next Purple Dragon I see, I'll inform of your treachery, and have you put to the sword! Keep me captive, drag me into this *horrible* wilderness, feed me chopped and stirred *offal*—why, I'll see you dead for it! Yet—yet—you'll suffer first!"

There followed a violent wet sound akin to a wet fish being

slapped on a riverside rock, a short, choked-off male growl of anger, and the furious feminine voice rose again, a little farther off.

"Whoreson! Rogue! You'll die begging for my forgiveness—and I'll not give it, and stand smiling as they lop off your head!"

"Lady—"

Florin had heard that tone of exasperated protest before, and knew who the man was, now: Delbossan! Horsemaster to Hezom, Lord of Espar, a man he'd known all his life. But who was this spitfire of the loud and murderous rage? Hezom had no daughter, to curse a man in the for—

"Oh, yes, *Master* Delbossan, you'll *die* for this! I will have it so!"

With a final shriek of outraged dismissal, the harridan—by the Dragon, the Lady Harridan!—fell silent.

A smirking Florin ducked around the last few trees, crouching low to avoid thorncanes, and peered out onto a pleasant view of one of the old woodcutters' glades beside the king's road, long ago gone to grass and much used for camping.

Its well-trodden grass was dominated by a grand pavilion tent of flame-orange hue that had been pitched at the far end of the glade. Several horses had been hobbled at the near end, and a dainty coach sat in its trail between, with two of Hezom's guardsmen wincing and grinning in its lee, not yet daring to peer around the conveyance at what sat glumly beyond.

Not far in front of the pavilion a tiny fire flickered on scorched stones, and sitting on a log before it was Irlgar Delbossan, wearing the remains of a—yes, a *large* bowl's worth of stew that had been dumped all over his head.

Florin slipped out of the trees so swiftly and quietly that he was halfway across the glade before the two guards saw him. They came around the coach in a hasty scramble, swords singing out—but Delbossan looked up, gave Florin a hard stare that turned into a sour smile of recognition, and waved the men back whence they'd come.

Flies were already buzzing around the horsemaster. There was—Florin sniffed appreciatively—rabbit stew, still steaming and thick with toasted bread-ends and a thick herbed gravy, all over Delbossan's shoulders and lap, and piled high on his head.

Some of it fell from brow to lap with a slow, inexorable *plop* as Florin came to a halt, trying *very* hard not to chuckle.

"New way of banishing baldpate, Del?" He couldn't quite keep a smile off his face.

Delbossan scowled. "I suppose your four friends are trailing along behind ye, to come and laugh at me, too."

"Nay, friend, Tymora smiles upon you: I'm alone."

"Good. I wearied of Jhessail's merry tinkling waterfall long ago."

"Her—? Oh. When she laughs. Aye."

Planting one boot on the battered strongchest the horsemaster had been using as a dining table, Florin leaned forward, chin in hand, and smiled down at his friend. "So give. Tell me why rabbit stew—*good* rabbit stew by the smell—ends up piled high on the head of Irlgar Delbossan, horsemaster bold!"

Delbossan sighed and leaned out to reclaim one of the discarded bowls. The loud lady who'd presumably flounced off into the pavilion had obviously slammed her own bowl of stew down over his head, flung it aside, and plucked up his own to season him a second time. Holding the bowl glumly under his chin, he raked a goodly amount of stew down off his head into it.

Florin fought the urge to laugh quite successfully this time.

With gravy running in rivulets down his face, Delbossan looked up and muttered, "I'm at my wit's end, lad. Yon flaming chit of a noble lass—ye heard her, I know ye did—Horns of the Hunt, half the King's stlarning *Forest* heard her!—has driven me half mad already. I can see why her parents have had it to *here* with her!"

"Nobles, aye? Who *is* she? And what're you doing with her out here, in the trees? Aren't her sort all 'prithee dance me around my great hall' types, all gowns and gaudy airs in heart-of-all-Faerûn Suzail?"

Delbossan grinned despite himself and licked stew from the back of one hairy hand. Then, as if remembering his manners, he held out the bowl with a dainty flourish. "Stew, lad?"

Florin almost choked, trying not to roar with laughter, but managed to wave the offer away.

Delbossan grinned and got up, stamping his feet to shake great clumps of stew from himself, and headed for the trees. To wash himself clean in the stream that looped and wandered back there, of course. Florin followed, even before the horsemaster's beckoning wave.

Delbossan sent the two guards out into the glade with a quick hand signal, waved away their grins good-naturedly, and strode along a little trail that led to a privy, and past it, toward the faint tinkle of moving water.

"She's a fair demon, lad," he said, wading out into the stream and sitting down. Fish glided away as the horsemaster winced—this creek ran fast and cold—and lowered himself onto his back. "As ye doubtless heard. Like I said, even her parents are fair tired of her high-handed, haughty-to-all behavior. 'Despairing,' was the word our lord used. She's a Crownsilver, and wants all the world to know it."

"That much I heard. One of the three 'royal noble' houses, aye? Yet I must confess, Del, I know nothing much about them. 'Proud Crownsilvers, fierce Huntsilvers, and Truesilvers bold/Give Obarskyr silver and trouble enough, but no gold.' Her parents sent her *away*? To Lord *Hezom?*"

"Sent her to be trained so she'll not shame them the more. And aye, Lord Hezom sent me down to throne-town to fetch her back up to Espar for his tutoring. The Lady Narantha Crownsilver, as charming a lass as ever kicked me, dumped my best rabbit stew all over me, slapped me, raked my face with her nails, and shrieked at me worse than any drunken lowcoin lass! Lad, it seems nobles don't bridle their younglings, these days!"

Florin shook his head in disbelief. "So this banishment is to be punishment for her?"

"Belike they want her temper trained in private, instead of before all Suzail—so 'tis the upcountry backwoods, where stride the likes of ye and me, and no highnose gowned lady goes!" The horsemaster raked the last of the stew out of his hair. Now that it was gone from his face, Florin could see two crisscrossing rows of fresh bloody scratches the Lady Crownsilver had left on Delbossan's cheek, by way of loving adornment.

Their eyes met, and both men shook their heads in unison.

"I can't believe I'm doing this, lad," said Delbossan.

"*I* can't see Lord Hezom taming her—not unless he's planning on using you, Tarleth, and all your whips and bridles to break her!"

"Ha ha, lad, tempt me not," Delbossan replied, rising and shaking himself like a dog to be rid of a dripcloak of water.

Florin waved an arm at the stream. "So, has she an oh-so-haughty servant to bathe her, or are you expected to do that, too?"

"Dismissed all her maids, or they fled," the horsemaster growled. "She half-slew the last one, I hear. And no, I don't expect to be plying any backscrapers or holding out any drycloaks this trip, young Florin! Don't be spreading word I have been, either!"

"*Del,*" Florin said reprovingly, "that's not my way."

"I know it, lad," the horsemaster growled, wading out of the stream and squelching past Florin. " 'S just I've got troubles enough, about now, without half the King's Forest thinking I'm *bedding* this dragon!"

"Dragon, is it? Face full of fangs, has she? Ugly as an old toad?"

"Oh, she's beautiful enough—if ye like ivory curves mated with the tongue, temper, and nails of a snarling wardog!"

The horsemaster turned, shaking his head, and added, "Must be rooted in being reared noble—no woman of Espar behaves thus!"

Florin surprised himself then. Without really knowing why, he found himself clasping Delbossan's forearms, leaning down over the older man in his urgency, blurting, "Let *me* do it, Del. Let me take her on a—a little foray through the forest, then back to meet up with you again. I can follow the Dathyl here up past Espar, and join you at Hunter's Hollow!"

The horsemaster blinked at him in utter astonishment.

"Wha—*why?*"

"I—I think I can break in yon highnose-lass a bit, *without* whips, lead-reins, bowls of stew, or Lord Hezom made miserable for a summer, with . . . well, a walk in the woods!"

Delbossan stared at Florin. His jaw had dropped open.

"Let the mud, the thorns, the stinging insects—and feeling lost, cold, and hungry, to say nothing of the little matter of having to *walk* a good distance," Florin said swiftly, shaking his old friend, "break her high-and-mightiness, or at least tire her out a bit and make her a shade more grateful for having shelter and riches. I could pretend to be a beast or outlaw after dusk, and chase her out of her tent—and then rescue her, as Florin the wandering forester, the moment she's in the deep trees."

"*Lad!* She's not to be touched! If—" Delbossan's voice was raw with horror.

"I can control my lusts, thank you, Master Delbossan," Florin said firmly. "And I believe you know me well enough to be sure I'm chasing no ransom here. Nor rescue-coin."

"But why by all the *gods* would ye want to get mixed up in this? She's—"

"Del, I've never even *seen* a noble, let alone talked to one! And beautiful, you say! Silks, velvet, facepaint, and airy graces—all *here*, not in stinking Suzail with me trying to peer past half a hundred glaring guards, to even get a glimpse of her!"

"But if she's harmed—if she even thinks ye've pawed her, whate'er the truth, lad, your life is forfeit and so's mine! I dare not—"

"Let her starve on the road to Espar because your bald head is so greedy for rabbit stew!"

The horsemaster shook his head and plucked himself free of Florin's grasp.

"Ye're wanderwitted, lad. Wild-crazed!"

"I'm . . . perhaps I am. Del, hear me! I—don't you remember when you were young? I'm like that *now*, aye?"

The horsemaster's look of horror deepened. "Ye want to bed half Espar, without any of them knowing about the oth—?" Then, as Florin's expression changed to one of amazement, Delbossan flushed a deep red, shut his mouth like a poacher's trap, shook his head violently, and whirled around to stamp back down the trail.

"Del!" Florin hissed urgently, grabbing at his arm. "Del, *listen!*"

The horsemaster kept walking.

"Del," Florin said quickly, into the older man's ear, "you trained me! As a little lad, with smiles, apples, and letting me ride: you trained me. I'm a steed you schooled and sent into the world seeing things your way. My parents told me what was decent and right, aye, but you made their words true by showing me they weren't just trying to sway me with empty speeches—just by being yourself, you showed me what it is to be of Cormyr. You know what I will and won't do."

The horsemaster swung around again.

"Lad," he said heavily, "ye're what they call 'handsome.' I'd hate to be the cause of the two of ye—both young, both headstrong—rutting because ye're alone together. What if ye get her with *child?* Hey? What then? I say again: her life would be ruined, but thine and mine'd be ended, short and sharp! If not by blade by the king's decree, then by bow or dagger, some night soon, on Lord Crownsilver's orders!"

"Thaerefoil," Florin said firmly, fingers busy at one of his belt pouches. He held out the leaves for Delbossan to see. "You know what it does."

"Makes even a stallion less than a man," the horsemaster murmured, bending to smell the leaves. "Fresh. Ye just gathered these."

"I did. Not with this in mind, but . . ."

Delbossan looked up at the young forester. "Ye'd drink a tea made with this—of my making, and with me watching?"

Florin put the smallest leaf in his mouth, chewed, opened his mouth to show the horsemaster its crushed paste on his tongue, swallowed, and opened his mouth again for inspection.

"Gods above," Delbossan murmured, "that much'll unman ye for days!" He gave Florin a long look. "And if she runs off and breaks her neck, or gets eaten by wolves?"

Florin drew his dagger. "This shall defend her. No harm will come to her, and I'll demand no coin of her family nor spread falsehood about her. I swear by the Purple Dragon and by the honor of the Falconhands. I swear by the Lady of the Forest I serve."

His last sentence seemed to roll away among the trees, echoing weirdly, and as Delbossan stepped back in amazement, leaves everywhere seemed to glow, for just a moment. The older man caught his breath as he watched them fade.

Florin seemed unaware of both glow and voice-thunder, but stood eyeing the horsemaster, his gaze steady. "Well?"

Teeth flashed in Delbossan's sudden smile. "Lad, I begin to feel delighted. Mind ye tell me all about it, after."

They clasped forearms, as one warrior to another, and the horsemaster leaned forward and muttered conspiratorially, "Do nothing until nightfall—and then wait 'til ye hear yon two jackblades snoring . . ."

Chapter 2
A HUNGER FOR ADVENTURE

Grand adventures are tales full of wonder, daring, and peril. They all began as slapdash accounts of some folk having a horrible time, long ago and far away, and found a little lace and glimmer along the way.

Thus do sages solemnly record all 'history.' Whatever gods smile upon you grant that storytellers favor your tale, so that it displays you brightly, and twists you not so much that your very name and face are lost.

Arasper Ardanneth,
Sage of the Road
Arasper's Little Book
published in the Year of the Prince

To the north of the scattered cottages of Espar, grassgirt hills rise west of the King's Road, rolling like half-buried green leviathans for a long way north ere the woodlots scattered across their humpbacks rise and join together into true forest again.

To the west, the hills find close-tangled trees more swiftly. The folk of Espar are not so numerous as to hew firewood enough to swiftly thrust back the woods.

On the crest of the highest hill, at the edge of that close and familiar forest, stand the tumbled foundation stones of a ruined, long-fallen cottage. No man alive in Espar can recall who dwelt there, or when it fell into ruin. All know it as 'the Stronghold,' though it was never a keep. For generations it has been the playground of the boldest youths of Espar.

Two such bold youths, young lads in dusty breeches, boots, and homespun, were lounging against its weathered stones, watching the sun descend toward the trees. One had just arrived, puffing slightly from his eager trot up the hillside, and had been greeted thus: "Ho, Clumsum."

"Hail, Stoop," the arrival replied calmly. He rarely sounded anything other than calm, which was unusual in a youngling—or anyone else—who bore the silver Ladycoin about his neck and sought to be ordained in the service of Tymora. His name was not 'Clumsum,' though few in Espar called him anything else. "Saw you down by the creek this morn. Much luck?"

"Much luck, thanks to your tireless prayers," came the gently sarcastic reply, "but not so much fish." As if to punctuate that statement, the speaker's stomach rumbled loudly. He added a sigh, tossed aside a tough blade of grass, and plucked another to chew upon. Though he was 'Stoop' to most of Espar, that wasn't his real name either. And although he bore around his neck not a luck-coin of Tymora but a sunrise disk of Lathander he'd painted himself, the two Esparrans were firm friends, and always had been. Doust Sulwood and Semoor Wolftooth: Clumsum and Stoop.

"Sit, Doust," Semoor said around his blade of grass, waving at an adjacent stone. "The shes will be late. As usual." His boots were propped on a rock before him, and his words came floating lazily past them.

Doust grinned and sat, saying by way of reply, "Well, they *do* have more chores than we."

His friend made a rude, dismissive sound halfway between a snort and a spit, and shifted his feet a trifle to give Doust room to prop his own boots up on the same handy rock. Semoor looked even more sleepy than was his wont. There was an easy smile on his rumpled face, and his shoulder-length hair was its usual dusty brown rats' nest. His overlarge nose jutted out at the world as it always did, giving him something of the look of a vulture.

Just now, he was waving a disdainful hand at the hillside below.

As usual, the sward was dotted with Hlorn Estle's flock of patiently grazing sheep—and as usual, Hlorn's three sons were sitting here and there on the slope, eyeing the two lads up at the Stronghold suspiciously.

" 'Tis *so* nice," Semoor said sarcastically, "to be wanted."

"Ah, I see the Morninglord's rosy glow doth suffuse thee, this even," Doust observed with a little smile, selecting his own blade of grass.

"Sabruin," Semoor drawled, choosing the least polite way of saying 'go pleasure yourself.'

"After you do the same, so I can watch and learn how," Doust responded, and then pointed into the trees across the road below and added in satisfaction, "Ah! Islif comes!"

"Jhess'll get here first," his friend replied, pointing across the hillside to where the sheep were gathered most thickly.

Doust scrambled to his feet. "Huh! Belkur'll set the dogs on her, if she goes walking right through the herd!"

"He already has—and she's worked some spell or other; they won't go near her," Semoor said delightedly.

Belkur Estle's snarled curses rose clearly into the evening air, amid canine whinings—and through them came a petite lass in long, gray skirts, striding as unconcernedly as if the field were hers and empty but for her strolling self. Fiery orange-brown hair fell free around her shoulders in a tumbling flood, and her eyes were large, gray-green, and merry.

"Ho, sluggards," she greeted them, lifting her skirts to reveal wineskins hooked about both her garters. She proffered them with a wide grin.

It was matched, with enthusiasm. Semoor plucked one skin and unstoppered it eagerly. "Ah, Flamehair, Lathander sent you!"

"No," Doust disagreed, claiming the other skin and sitting down again, "I believe Tymora—"

"And I rather believe *I* managed to bring myself here—*and* steal the wine from Father's end vat, too," Jhessail told them tartly. "Don't get drunk, now, holy men; I grow tired of slapping the both of you at once."

"Ah," Semoor told her slyly, "but we never tire of being slapped!"

"Sabruin," Jhessail told him in a dignified tone, settling herself between them. Both promptly laid hands on her thighs in hopes of being slapped, but she gave them withering glances instead. They grinned, shrugged, and applied themselves to emptying wineskins.

A young woman taller and more heavily muscled than anyone on the hillside—including the sheep—was striding up the hill now, clanking as she came. As straight as a blade and as broad of shoulder as the village smith, Islif Lurelake was in a hurry. Some of the Estle dogs barked at her, but none dared rush her, because a drawn sword was gleaming in her hand.

The clanking was familiar; it came from her homemade battle-coat, an old leather jerkin onto which Islif had sewn castoff fragments of old plate-armor in an overlapping array. But none of the three in the Stronghold had ever seen that splendid sword before.

"Heyah, Islif!" Semoor Wolftooth called, when the striding woman was still a good ways below. "Where'd you get *that?*"

The warrior woman lifted icy gray eyes that stabbed at him like two sword points and said flatly, "From Bardeluk."

Doust frowned in thought. "Uh . . . oh, Lord Hezom's new guard, aye?"

"Ho ho," Semoor said teasingly. "*Persuaded* him to give you his second-best blade, did you? Just like that?"

Islif Lurelake strode into the Stronghold and came to a halt, towering over them. When she was this close, broad-shouldered and buxom, her arms corded with muscles Doust and Semoor would have given much to call their own, the battle-coat lost all hint of the ridiculous. She was striking rather than beautiful, with a hard, long-jawed face that had caused her to be dubbed 'Horseface' more than once by unfriendly tongues, and her jet-black hair was cut short in a warriors' helm-bob. With those piercing, almost silver eyes, she looked as dangerous as the sword in her hand.

"I didn't sleep with him, if that's what you mean."

The would-be servant of Lathander lifted his sunrise disk and told it, "Oh, I never thought you'd been *sleeping*, in all those half-days —half-*days*, lass!—you've spent behind closed doors with, ah, *fortunate* Master Bardeluk."

Islif snorted, and nudged him with the metal-shod toe of a much-patched boot. "What a *small* mind you have, holynose! I've been shut up teaching him to read and write. This—" She hefted the long, slightly curved longsword, and they saw a blue sheen race down it—"was my price, from the beginning."

"Stop waving that about," Jhessail said quietly. "You're . . . impressing me."

Islif grounded the blade on the toe of one boot—and surprised them all by smiling broadly. "Well," she said, bright teeth flashing, "that's a start."

"You're certainly impressing the Estle boys," Doust observed. "Their eyes are like roundshields!"

Jhessail looked downslope. "They look less impressed than suspicious to me." She sniffed. "Afraid we'll pounce on one of their precious sheep and butcher it right here, belike."

"Huh," Semoor grunted. "More likely they're hoping we'll start kissing, and you'll take your clothes off. That's what *they* use the Stronghold for."

"Live in hope, don't you, Wolf?" Jhessail replied, her words dripping acid.

The priestling of Lathander shrugged and spread his hands—an elaborate gesture somewhat spoiled by the half-empty wineskin wrapped around one of them. "Lady Flamehair," he explained, as if to an idiot child, "that's what holy folk *do*. Live in the hope that the gods grant us, every day."

"Until, in the fullness of time, you die like everyone else," Islif commented, extending an imperious hand for his wineskin.

Semoor pretended not to notice, and declaimed, "Islif Lurelake, Jhessail Silvertree, Semoor Wolftooth, and Doust Sulwood— adventurers bold!"

Doust sighed. "I'm not so sure 'bold' is telling truth. Say: restless for adventure."

"And you neglected to mention the boldest of us all," Jhessail said, from between the two priestlings. "Florin, who's off somewhere tracking stags and exploring the King's Forest right now!"

It was Semoor's turn to sigh. "The man in whose shadow I dwell, day after month after season."

"Well, that's because you're not—in truth—bold enough," Islif pointed out, firmly plucking the wineskin from his grasp as a breeze rose at her back, setting the leaves rustling. "Florin is. Which is why he's elsewhere, whilst we sit here watching the last of the day fade, talking and dreaming—and no more than that."

"But we can't just go tearing off into the woods hacking at things and telling everyone we're adventurers!" Semoor's growl was as fierce as it was sudden. "Or 'tis the inside of one of the king's *jails* we'll be finding, soon enough! We need a charter—and charters cost coins none of us have!"

Doust looked at his friend, his eyes even darker blue than usual. "Coins we could scrape together, but we *still* have to convince someone we deserve a charter, and by all Tymora's holy kisses, I don't know how! Would *you* grant a bunch of restless younglings license to wander about the realm, hacking at things and *looking* for trouble?"

Semoor snorted. "Of course. Stupid question. Fortunately for the realm—and ill luck for us—I'm not King Azoun."

"Stoop, don't *say* that. Tymora frowns on those who speak of . . . ah, 'poor fortune.' "

" 'Tisn't Lady Luck's frown that makes me despair of ever managing to convince any court official to grant us a charter," Jhessail snapped, her face going red. "I mean, *look* at us! Bored, restless younglings, yes? Get apprenticed, they'll say! Learn a trade! Earn an honest day-coin! And send word back to us that you've done so, to save us the trouble of sending a war wizard by to peer at you as we serve all the malcontents!"

She stopped waving her arms suddenly, snatched the wineskin Doust was holding, and took a long, deep drink.

The two priestlings exchanged glances. Semoor spoke first.

"Let's just go to Sembia, and to the Nine Hells with a charter!"

Jhessail gave him a fierce look. "And bid farewell to *Cormyr?*" She waved down the hill at its ripples of waving grass, then swung around to indicate the gently dancing leaves in the great gnarled trees above. "Our home? Leave *this?*"

"Well," Islif said dryly, "I haven't noticed any great mustering of outlaws in Espar. Or heaps of treasure, dragons' caves, or evil wizards, for that matter. And if we walk around our neighbors' lanes and pastures trying to stir up adventure, there soon will be outlaws hereabouts: us."

"Aye," Doust said slowly, gazing out across the fields, "Espar's a fair and pleasant place . . . but watching sheep wander is about all the excitement any who dwell here can expect, most days."

"Most *years,*" Semoor corrected sourly.

Islif shrugged. "If we ever—somehow—become adventurers, staying dry and warm and fending off hunger may well become daily excitements."

"Always the cheery merry-maid, aren't you?" Semoor sighed, turning his sunrise disk of Lathander over and over in his fingers.

"I'm easier on the ears than some always-sharptongues I could name," the warrior-lass replied, hefting her sword meaningfully.

"Oooh," the priestling of Lathander gasped in mock-terror, recoiling with all the subtlety of old Laedreth the Lute playacting a frightened queen in the greatroom of the Eye, with a few tankards inside him. "You're so—*menacing!* Oooo!"

Islif sighed. "With just one good kick, holynose, I could *really* make you squeal!"

Semoor leered, "Ah, but I can do the same to you with naught but my tongue!"

Islif rolled her eyes. "Semoor, your mind outreeks a cesspit. It's a wonder to me your prayers don't make the Morninglord spew his guts out!"

Semoor's smile went away in an instant. "Don't jest about that. Holy Lathander blesses new ventures—and that's just what we'll be, if we set off adventuring!"

"Aye," Jhessail agreed grimly. "If."

"And if not," Doust said quietly, " 'tis temple-field farming for Wolf and for me, separate somewheres in the upcountry, while the two of you grow gray hairs here in Espar as farmwives, birthing calves, tilling fields, having babies, and cooking, cooking, cooking."

"*Don't* remind me," Islif snapped.

"Florin," Jhessail said wistfully. "We need Florin to show us the way clear of this."

The wind rose around them with a sudden howl, as if in agreement.

"Lad, both of the lord's jacks're deep in dreams," came the hiss out of the darkness on the other side of the tree. "Still game for this?"

"Of course, Del," Florin murmured, from his side of the great duskwood. "I'd not miss this for all Lord Hezom's gold."

The dark shape of the horsemaster moved in the still-faint light of the rising moon; Delbossan was shaking his head. "Huh. If she gets hurt—or if yon pair of jackblades wake—'twon't be Hezom's gold the two of us'll have to be worrying over! He already owns rope enough for our hangings!"

"They won't wake 'til morn," Florin muttered close by Delbossan's head. "Trust me."

"Oh. Another of your herb-powders in their tankards?"

"Now if you ask not, I'll not have to say, aye?" The ranger grinned. "Yet I've a strong hunch, somehow, they'll be unharmed when they rise . . . around highsun. Mind you pretend to have been affected, too—and scare them enough that they agree to help you search along the road to save all your hides, rather than running straight to Espar to cry the alarm. Somewhat south of Hezom's guardpost you 'find' a trail, and follow it through the woods around Espar to Hunter's Hollow. I'll meet with you there by highsun, three days hence."

"Done, lad. Don't make me rue this."

"Trust me, Del. Now take my place here behind the tree, and keep hidden. She'll probably run to where the moonlight's strongest, but who can say for sure?"

"With *that* dragon, lad, there's no surety—trust *me*."

They chuckled together, foreheads almost touching, and parted, clapping each other's shoulders in the nightgloom. In the words of the old song: 'Twas time to be taming the lady. . . .

The pavilion glowed like a bright jewel in the night, which surprised Florin not at all. A city-reared noble lass would want the warmth and reassurance of nightlamps around her, of course.

Filigreed screens inside the tent cast intricate, pleasing patterns on the pavilion walls, concealing shapely silhouettes from prying eyes outside—but Florin could see enough to know that the Lady Narantha Crownsilver was still up on her feet and moving around. Barefoot, by the soft gliding sounds, rather than shod. Probably—if she were anything like the wealthy merchants' wives who betimes stayed for a night at The Watchful Eye, Espar's lone inn—she'd be brushing her hair. Brushing and *brushing* her hair. Long and glossy it would be, in the lampglow. . . .

Florin swallowed, shook his head at himself for thinking such thoughts, and glided forward as silently as drifting night mist.

He grinned like a wolf as he went, lips drawn fiercely back from teeth. It might not be much, and was far from heroic, but Florin Falconhand was finally—after all these years of dreaming—having an adventure.

"Where's Florin right now, I wonder?" Jhessail asked, halting outside her door.

Islif shrugged. "Safely abed somewhere, if he has any sense."

Jhessail peered up at her and said softly, "But like me, you don't think he has, do you?"

"No." Islif's teeth flashed in the moonlight as she turned to go. "No, I don't. I think he's awake and about in the night, right now, having an adventure."

Florin Falconhand cast a last long look around, drew in a deep breath as he sank down into a crouch, and—face less than a handspan from the glowing canvas, gave throat to a horrible growl.

He heard a sudden intake of breath from inside the tent.

Grinning, he growled again, a long, bubbling beast-sound, trying to sound eager and . . . *hungry*. Then he made sniffing sounds, scrabbling with his knuckles along the canvas where it met the ground.

There was a tense silence from the pavilion, and he could hear the faint, close whistling of swift breathing.

He growled again, as horribly as he knew how—and there came the whisper of fast-moving bare feet, and a tremulous, "Delbossan?'

She'd gone to the front of the pavilion, and was no doubt standing just inside its door-slit now, staring at the hard-knotted lacings she'd so recently tied, and wondering whether to start untying them. "Master Delbossan?"

Florin put a gleeful chortle into his next growl, and clawed at the canvas with both hands, thrusting it inward. His reward was a little shriek followed by a full-voiced cry of Delbossan's name.

The ranger drew his sword and used its pommel to thrust hard at the canvas, denting it in and leaning his weight on it while raking and scrabbling with his other hand. A tent-peg lost its hold, the pavilion buckled slightly, and the Lady Narantha Crownsilver screamed.

All dignity gone, she gave vent to a throat-stripping howl of terror, gulped breath, and shrieked another.

My, but Horsemaster Delbossan was hard of hearing this night.

The young noblewoman cried Delbossan's name half a dozen times as Florin tugged out another tent-peg, and another, so he could bow the entire back wall of the pavilion inward, all the while clawing the canvas and snarling for all he was worth.

Sobbing in fear and rage, the Lady Narantha came rushing back across the pavilion, and Florin wisely ducked his head back from his outthrust sword.

"Oooh!" she gasped in effort, striking the canvas with something small and hard that set his sword to thrumming. He gave vent to a startled growl that began with a note of pain and rose into a terrible roar of rage—and the canvas in front of his nose punched and thrust groaningly at him, again and again, as the noble lady on its far side belabored it with—a gilded corner burst through the stretched and ravaged canvas—her jewel-coffer.

Lady of the Forest, she'd be through it and charging at him in a moment!

Between loud grunts of effort, young Lady Crownsilver was

wailing Delbossan's name repeatedly now, her voice growing steadily higher and more shrill in fury, leaving fear behind.

Then the canvas bulged with what was probably her descending head and shoulder, she made a startled sound, and Florin heard metallic slitherings and chimings. She'd overbalanced and fallen.

With the loudest roar he could muster he pounced atop her, clawing and biting at the canvas, trying to make sure she felt the hard edges of his pommel and belt buckle and still-sheathed dagger—and her next shriek was pure fear again, stabbing higher and shrill right through his eardrums, the canvas heaved under him frantically . . .

And Florin Falconhand, head ringing, was on his knees amid tangled canvas, his prey fled across the sagging pavilion and shrieking wordlessly as she tugged, tore, sobbed, and tugged again at its door-lacings.

He growled as he caught his breath and got to his feet, shaking his head to clear it—and he'd barely caught his balance and hefted his sword before something barefoot that streamed long, unbound hair burst out into the night, splendid nightrobe fluttering.

"Delbossan!" she screamed as she ran to the turf-covered fire and stared wildly around, clawing the air and stumbling in her haste. *"Delbossan!"*

Florin ducked back behind the tent and roared again.

The young noblewoman shrieked and ran away from him, toward the road. There was nothing in her hands, and nothing on her feet—so she'd not get far before she'd be limping and would look back.

Florin dragged his jerkin up and half over his head to conceal his face, waved his sword, and loped after her, growling and snarling.

Lady Narantha screamed again and sprinted down the road, in the direction of distant Suzail. Florin pounded after her, making sure she heard deadwood snapping under his boots, and she wept and shrieked and ran.

When the ranger reached the vast, moss-covered trunk of a long-fallen, rotten shadowtop that told every traveler the camping place was nigh, he sprang onto it and raced along it into the trees, outpacing his noble prey as she stumbled, sobbed for breath as her wind was jarred from her, and stumbled again.

Then he burst out of the trees right beside her with a horrible roar, a great hulking headless shape with a sword in its paw—and she shrieked again and fled blindly away, west off the road into the trees.

Toward the Dathyl, just as he'd planned. His tunic hid Florin's wolfish smile from the world as he ran after the fair blushing flower of House Crownsilver.

She was panting like a deer on its last legs—and he was almost choking on a delicious thrill. Adventure at last!

Cormyr had always been a safe place of warmth, good food, and scurrying servants, of beauty, fine clothes, and coddling, of bright banners, and of airy graces. Oh, it was the Forest Kingdom, of *course*—but its forests had never been anything more than a distant green line beyond Jester's Green, and the place where all the stags whose heads adorned more mansion and highkeep walls than she could count had come from. Narantha half-remembered fearsome nursery tales of outlaws, owlbears, and wolves, foresters simply vanishing in the dark leafy depths, and the fell magic of malevolent faeries and elves who saw humans as foes or even *food*. . . . Oh, why had Father *ever* fallen upon this foolish, nasty, *hateful* idea that she needed tutoring of some sort by some backwoods bumpkin? Hezom wasn't even a *proper* noble, but one of the king's appointed lordlings—why, he might be an old drunkard of a Purple Dragon, or an outlaw and stag-poacher given a title by Azoun to keep younger, wilder rivals in check!

An outlaw! But what mattered it, when she was going to *die* here, alone in the dark, with no one to even know she'd fall—*oooh!*

The Lady Narantha caught an ankle between two unseen branches and crashed through a thornbush to fall on her face in something scratchy that left burrs all over her as she rolled frantically, sobbing for breath, and scrambled to her feet again. It was the third time she'd fallen, and every step now brought a stab of pain—she'd have been weeping non-stop if she'd dared spare breath for doing so. Branches whipped across her face and breast often, some of them slashing her or tugging at her with their horns—and she'd left a lot of hair behind on them.

Yet she dared not stop, because not far behind her in the darkness there was always the growling *thing*, its footfalls, occasional crashings . . .

"Tymora deliver me," she gasped, "Torm defend me, Father Silvanus send away your . . . your . . . things that hunt—"

She ran hard into a horizontal branch that caught her low in the ribs. All the breath whuffed out of her, the night spun in a swirl of crazy yellow motes of light, and Narantha was falling . . . falling . . .

The moonlight went away, and the darkness that awaited hungrily all around her flooded forward and dragged her down. . . .

Chapter 3
A FORAY IN THE FOREST

Beginnings—beginnings are easy. Any fool with a sword or a shout or a moment's witlessness can start something. 'Tis finishing such matters alive, and getting home again whole—that takes bold heroism. And the luck of the gods.

Gornrel Murtarren
One Merchant's Musings
published in the Year of the Turret

Florin came to a cautious halt, his heart pounding. Was she—?

Cautiously, he circled the huddled shape, his own breathing hard and fast. Gods, she'd run like the wind! He bent closer, very cautiously . . .

Was that a hiss of breath?

He was a fool, a reckless young fool! She'd been leaving bloody footprints this last while, racing terrified and blind into a forest where unseen branches could serve her as eye-gouging, throat-piercing blades—through tangles where even wise foresters could turn ankles or break legs.

And now she'd collapsed, and if she were dead, he and Delbossan were worse.

Grimly Florin sheathed his sword. "Lady of the Forest, forgive me," he breathed, feeling an icy breeze rising to ghost past his cheek. Gods, if she *were* dead . . .

'Twas too dark here, in the shadow of a gnarled forest giant, for moonlight to tell him what he needed to know. The ranger's fingers ran along the carved wooden catches of his belt pouches until he found the right two shapes, got them open, and rubbed together a fingerdaub of moss and a particular mushroom. A faint, ghostly radiance arose from their mingling, and he thrust his glowing fingers at her still, white face.

The Lady Narantha's eyes were closed, and her mouth was

slack. He put his other hand to her mouth and nose, and felt a faint warmth. She was breathing.

Mielikki deliver me!

Florin bowed his head and muttered a silent prayer of thanks, feeling almost weak. Seeing a long stone amid the rotting leaves and fallen twigs, he smeared the glow-mix on one end of it, wiping away the last of it on some protruding bark that he then carefully tore away and thrust into his jerkin-pouch.

Going around behind the noblewoman, he hauled off his jerkin, did off the rough tunic he wore beneath it—and bound its homespun over her eyes, letting the loose end cover her face. He hoped she didn't mind the smell.

Her breathing deepened, but she didn't rouse, thanks be to Mielikki. Florin rolled the Lady Narantha onto her back and ran his fingertips lightly along her limbs. No weapons, nothing hidden—just the double-layered robe, all slippery silk and shimmerweave. Over bone-white skin, all soft curves and . . . well, enough of that. Seeing her displayed thus in the pale glow was unsettling, but somehow— the thaerefoil, of course—aroused nothing in him beyond a sort of restless, wistful hunger.

He rolled his catch onto her side, very much as he turned large game for skinning, and knelt astride her hip, feeling at his belt for the right pouch again—the one wherein rode the rawhide thongs every ranger carried when in the forest. Swiftly, now, in case his handling awakened her . . .

Five hard, fast breaths later Florin had bound two noble thumbs together, and served Narantha's big toes the same way. The next two thongs did her little fingers and her elbows, pulling her arms forward in front of her. She hissed and made as if to pull away as he finished tying them. Ah, just in time.

Plucking her off her feet and up over his shoulder—whoa, she was tall; this might prove tricky—Florin drew his sword and set off deeper into the forest, seeking the gentle glimmer and chuckle of the Dathyl.

Not striving overmuch for stealth, he hacked aside clawing branches as he went.

His noble catch was weightier than he'd expected, but not staggeringly so, yet apt to tip if he didn't stride carefully. He was a foolhead, and this venture not such a glorious thing as it had seemed in his fancy. Yet he was in it now, up to his neck . . .

His neck, indeed.

Florin swallowed and walked on. As he shouldered through the trees, Narantha heavy on his shoulders—and squirming now, definitely awake—small crashings in the night marked the flight of small animals, disturbed by his approaching boots.

The Dathyl seemed farther away than it should have been, but eventually he stumbled down a leaf-strewn bank onto its sandy shore, nearly blind in the deep gloom where moonlight could not reach.

The stream rushed merrily past, chuckling over stones, and Florin stood for a moment in thought. He must be a good ways south of the foresters' cache he needed, where there were boots, packs, bandages, and weathercloaks. It was back toward the road, and he thought he remembered the tangle where he'd have to turn away from the Dathyl. A big tree had fallen over in a winter windstorm, years ago, and left its roots standing up like so many bristling spears, aye . . .

Yet the stream was shallower hereabouts; he'd best cross right over. Decisions, decisions, decisions—so this was adventure. Huh.

He hefted the shapely burden on his shoulder and balanced himself, lifting first one boot then the other to make sure his heels hadn't sunk into the wet sand deep enough to throw him into a fall the moment he tried to spring forward. They hadn't, but one step told him there'd be no leaping the Dathyl dryshod here. He was going to have to wade hip-deep, or more, and that meant he'd best reach a hand down to lift the lady's head. Blindfolded or not, Crownsilver blood wouldn't keep the lass from drowning if he trailed her head underwater all the while he was trudging through the chill flow. Not quite the facing-what's-real training her parents had intended. And dragon, haughty foolhead or not, he'd brought her here.

His tunic was still in place over Narantha's eyes, though her upside-down dangle had bared her chin and throat. Cupping his hand around a trembling, hard-corded white neck so as to be ready to lift her head in mid-stream, he stepped carefully forward into the cold, cold water, slowly and deliberately finding footing.

One stride, two—then he gasped and almost fell at a sudden, unexpected pain in the fleshy heel of his hand. She'd bitten him!

Florin shook his hand free, wincing, heard her hiss a *very* unlady-like word after it, and fought to keep his balance. He was going to fall, he was going to—

Shrug, spread his hands for balance, and drop the fair flower of the Crownsilvers head-first into the Dathyl, with a satisfyingly solid splash.

She screamed, of course, or tried to—he could hear the shrill bubbling from beneath the water, faint amid her thrashings. Which meant she was now choking on Dathyl-water, and—Florin grabbed firm hold of one bound arm above the elbow, got a grip on a bare leg just above the knee, and hauled, hard.

She came up spluttering and sobbing, choking and spewing water, and squealing in rising alarm as he half-swung, half-hurled her ahead of him, onto the sandy far shore of the Dathyl, where an invitingly large clump of ferns awaited.

They crashed down into crushed ruin under her weight, uncomplainingly perishing under her retching, twisting arrival—and Florin plucked her up, made sure his now-sopping tunic was still serving as a blindfold, and dropped her down again, snarling, "There he is! Get *him!*"

He rushed a few strides up the bank, making as much noise as any dozen foresters, and drew his sword and dagger. Clinking them against each other, he snarled in the lowest growling voice he could muster, and rushed a few strides this way and then that in the damp underbrush. Twigs snapped merrily.

"I see him!" he cried then, in a much higher voice, as he raced side-wise between two trees and crashed to his knees, clashing his blades together again. *"Die,* outlaw!"

Growling, he rolled over and over amid dead saplings, old leaves, and more ferns, back toward where the helpless Lady Narantha lay. "The king's justice upon you!" he roared as he went.

A swift roll over a rotten log, and he was amid the ferns, where his captive was moaning softly now, sucking in air rather than water.

Rolling past her close enough that he could feel the warmth of her breath on his cheek, Florin shouted suddenly nigh a noble ear, in as rough a voice as he could manage, "Ha! Creep away, king's man? *Die!*"

He sprang up, stamping his sodden boots hard and clanging his sword and dagger together like angry bells. His shouts and grunts of effort sounded convincing enough, he hoped, fighting down a sudden urge to laugh. He ran right at her, springing over her at the last moment and making sure his jerkin trailed along her body. She flinched away.

Good. Florin applied himself with enthusiasm to staging his mock battle until the Lady Narantha was either quivering in terror or shivering from the cold.

"Hide her!" he gasped then, close by her head. "Quick, now!" He flung his jerkin over her shoulders and tore up armfuls of ferns to cover her legs.

When he was done, he walked away and let his breathing steady and grow quiet again. The forest was still around him, and bared to the waist, he was none too warm himself.

Florin shrugged. The bed that awaited him was of his own building. And its name was "adventure."

Smiling, he glided silently back to his captive, and sat down beside her in the moonlight, to guard her until she fell asleep. When her slumber deepened, he'd have to cut those wet thongs.

Obligingly, in a surprisingly short time, the Lady Narantha started to snore.

This was his favorite part of the garden. The little bower where his spells had shaped stone into smooth, unfissured frozen waves, sweeping up in graceful curls to seemingly enfold the flowers planted in them. Moonflowers, shining their pale grace back at the moonlight now touching them.

This was the first place he'd wrought after arriving in Evereska, and it was where he liked to linger and think. And if Erlevaun Dathnyar was far from being the most brilliant mage in the Hidden Realm, he was—he liked to believe—the moon elf mage most rooted there, where others traveled or used spells to spy afar to quell their restlessness.

Here he belonged, here he'd be quite content to perish, when—

Erlevaun stiffened, his eyes widening. He had just time to look up and stare his horror at the serene moon before gnawing darkness rose within him, racing through his very mind . . .

Mewing like a forlorn kitten, the helpless mage swayed, struggling to work a spell. Swirls of sparks came into being around his writhing, slowing fingers, he choked on an incantation that had never given his nimble tongue trouble before—then his staring eyes went empty and dark, and he started to topple.

Yet he never fell. His body took fire in midair, blazing up like a dry torch, bright flames roaring into a great ball of flame that sank in on itself and was gone into drifting smoke with terrifying speed.

By the time his two guards sprinted up, panting, there was nothing left but a few sharp-smelling wisps and a scattering of ash on Erlevaun Dathnyar's smooth-sculpted stone.

Swords drawn, they knelt to peer at the ash, then gave each other grave glances.

"One of Dathnyar's new spells, more spectacular than ever, that whisked him elsewhere?" the older one asked, tossing her head to banish long blue hair from her face. "Or did we just see him perish?"

"I . . . I don't know," the younger one replied, on her knees on the other side of the ash. "Yet there's something I *do* know: I have a bad feeling about this."

The two guards stared at each other grimly in the moonlight, their eyes large and dark in the curves of the scrying orb.

Above that enspelled sphere, the one who watched them broke into a long, soft chuckle.

"Ah, elves! So sneeringly superior—and beneath it all, just as helpless and hopelessly blundering as the rest of us!"

A deft hand swept across the orb, bidding it to go dark. Its radiance dwindled slowly, but had grown faint indeed before the softly exulting voice spoke again.

"Oh, even better spells! I'll need some time to work with these . . . so every mantled elf in Faerûn is safe for a few days more. A very *few* days more."

The soft chuckle began again—and promptly soared into full-throated laughter.

The moon was riding high and clear, scudding through a few thin, clawlike tatters of cloud. Jhessail lay awake watching it, alone in her small bed, as she had on so many restless nights before this one.

No matter what she wished or whispered, the sky-sailing moon paid her no heed. As always.

The window around it was her window, her place. Home. Not the grandest cottage in Espar, but not the smallest, either. And Espar's familiar, boring lanes and trees and muddy pastures were deemed fair, even by those from grander places in Cormyr; she'd heard some of them say so over the seasons, with the ring of truth in their voices.

Yet with the coming of every new spring, the restlessness grew within her. She needed *more*.

What, she wasn't quite sure, though "adventure" had proved as handy a word as any. She had to see other places, look upon the sea, behold the tall spires of the Royal Palace in Suzail, look upon nearby looming mountains, and someday—*some*day—set foot on soil that was not part of Cormyr. See a unicorn, perhaps even a dragon, watch a wizard of power hurl a spell that did something dramatic . . . and above all, find someone who would be her guide to learning the Art.

If Faerûn held anyone who would want Jhessail Silvertree to work magic, that is, or take the care and time to see that she did it well.

It was not as if she had anything of worth to give in payment. Her body and her hard work, aye, but backcountry lasses aching to follow their dreams dwelt in Cormyr by the caravan-load, and she could hardly hope they'd be scarcer elsewhere.

And she likely had things better than most. Espar was fair, and she had kind and keen-witted parents who loved her, good friends, and a rightful place.

Aye, a place—and a road ahead of her in life as sharp-hewn and high-fenced as a slaughter-chute to butcher sheep or hogs. She would be expected to marry a man of Espar, a longjack probably much her elder, and cook, bedwarm, sew, clean, and slave herself for him, until he died or she did. No matter how he treated her or wherever else he strayed. And if the gods took her longjack first, she'd be "Widow Longjack" the rest of her days, expected to live alone and be one of the local backlane crones blamed for all misfortune, never to remarry or even look at another man.

If she found no way out of Espar, such would be her lot. No choice and no escape. Her friends might dream large and dare little—but they were all she had. And, gods smile, they ached to get out of Espar just as much as she did.

Not to leave it behind forever, or shun its beauty. Just to have horse and coin and life enough elsewhere to ride in and out of it as she pleased, to go hither and thither, to make her own life and not be doomed only to being a man's drudge. Or a lass-lover dwelling in some abandoned steading or other on the edge of the Stonelands with other women too bitter or scarred to want any man, drudging together to farm the days and seasons through, to have enough to eat.

Never to have the Art that stirred betimes thrillingly within her, even to glowing and crackling at her fingertips, be more than untapped restlessness, a wild might-have-been that would earn her the mistrusting spy-watch of the war wizards, a fell reputation among respectable folk . . . and yearnings unfulfilled.

Jhessail sighed and whispered to the moon, "Lady of Silver, I beg of you, speak of me to Mystra, that she show me what to do about the Art that kindles in me! I am not worthy to ask this, yet must, for the Art stirs in me and has firm hold of my heart and hopes. I, Jhessail Silvertree, beg this."

It was an entreaty she had made so many nights before. And would again, for there was nothing so glorious as when the Art stirred in her and surged through her, and her mind and eyes flickered blue-white and alive with power . . .

She sighed again, a soft moan of longing that sent her plunging into memories of spell-sparks drifting from her, the cool fire coiling in her throat, the fear and awe on the faces of her friends as her first fumbling attempts to work spells did *something*, and ended their snorts and jeers forever.

She remembered the hope being born in their eyes as they looked at little Twoteeth—nay, at her paltry yet wondrous attempts to call up the Art—and saw in her their own road out of Espar. For if she could truly be a mage, they could truly be adventurers, and charter or no, dare to seek their fortunes across the Realms, through chance, daring, and drawn blades. 'Twas said adventurers earned high coin in Sembia, just the other side of the Thunder Peaks.

Jhessail closed her eyes against the moon, the better to chase memories of those moments of magic leaping through her . . . hoping, just perhaps, if she remembered vividly enough, the Art would stir again, or Mystra would send her a sign, or—

Spell-sparks and swirling blue-white flames roiled and eddied in her memories—then, astonishingly, slid aside to show her a face she knew.

Clumsum. Doust, his dark blue eyes twinkling at her, an unseen breeze stirring his brown hair as he said something silent and unheard to her. A memory she could not quite recall the where and when of, though 'twas probably the day he'd told her he was giving himself to Lady Luck. The quietest and kindest of them all, never terse like Islif, and lacking Semoor's nasty streak—except when word-dueling Semoor himself. Yes, there was his symbol of the goddess, held proudly up for her to see: a silver coin, large, heavy, and smoothly featureless as all novice priests' holinesses of Tymora were. He'd not be given one with the face of the goddess on it until he'd proven himself worthy in her service.

He was probably jesting, the dry, deadpan mirth that was incredible given all the beatings he'd suffered under his father's drunken fists. A shadowy line of whiskers across Doust's upper lip and along the line of his jaw told the world what a youngling he was—and warred with his eyes, that proclaimed just as firmly to those who bothered to look into them what an old wise soul he was.

Then Doust's face turned into Semoor, grinning at her. Nay, let's be honest: *leering* at her. It was he—Stoop, from the bent-over way he carried himself from so much time fishing, slumped bonelessly over his rod—who dubbed her 'Flamehair,' and first told her she was beautiful, and that he wanted her.

They'd both been all of nine summers old at the time, and Semoor was already a schemer and sneering cynic. She remembered him, grinning that same twisted grin, facing down a shouting drover with the bored words he used so often: "Impress me, cow the wind, awe yon dog."

Even more ox-beef of build than his best friend Doust, peering at the world past that unfortunately large vulture-beak nose. Dancing brown eyes to match his shoulder-length brown hair. Sly, loud, and quick where Doust was quiet and aloof, a natural to take the robes of a priest of Lathander—if he strayed not to the dark worship of Mask instead.

Sharp-tongued, always chuckling. Always telling her he'd not mind bedding "little Jhess Flamehair, fairest flower of all Espar." Never seeming to mind her refusals, but not ceasing his hints and outright requests, either. Surprisingly, fascinated by elves, and always having a smile and wave for any of the Fair Folk he saw.

And when Semoor looked at folk, he seemed to always see them as they truly were, staring past lies, deceptions, and grand talk.

Two friends who saw priesthoods as their roads out of Espar. Even if they never dared adventure, there were shrines and temples to Lathander and Tymora in cities and towns all across Faerûn, and holy service could take them far from quiet Espar.

As could the sword. That glorious blade Islif had waved under their noses today . . . the blue sheen of the steel, the longsword so heavy, solid, and deadly sharp as it flashed so close to her face, the sword that could do more to foes with one swing of Islif's brawny arms and shoulders than all her own halting cantrips and scraps of spells, with a day to fuss and prepare and hurl them in.

Yet every trudging Purple Dragon had a sword, and most every grown man in Espar, too. Battered old blades, most of them, dark and marred from use, probably most often used to hack vermin, slash stubborn knots, or poke fallen food out of the fire before the flames made it entirely ash, if truth be told.

Yet Islif's sword was different.

It was a glittering thing, sleek and made to deal death, with nothing "everyday" about it. Just like Islif.

Islif was more man than lass, with her broad shoulders and rippling muscles, her eyes icy gray, her brows dark, and herself always alert. Close-mouthed, strong enough to hurl men back or trade blows with them and stand tall as the victor, breaking jaws and showing fear to no man. Slow to anger, genuinely amused by most insults, and more like a striding sword-commander than any Purple Dragon Jhess had yet seen; when cottages caught fire or the winter wolves came raiding, Islif snapped orders at men twice her age, and was obeyed.

Jhess was a little afraid of her, and had admired her hunting skills and the way she stood up to men for years. Those large, raw hands could whittle a knob of wood with surprising grace, too, using a belt knife as deftly as any man shaving his jowls for a wedding, to make a tiny bear, or boar, or deer with its head raised. And then, silently, Islif would toss it away, or find a child's hand to drop it into. If

Cormyr ever needed a warrior-queen, it had Islif Lurelake.

Yet taller than Islif, and far grander of voice, manner, and looks—yet free of the superior pride that such god-gifts usually awakened in men who owned them—stood the best among them all, Florin Falconhand.

Florin *could* be a king, if Cormyr ever needed one of those.

Jhessail sighed, opening her eyes to gaze at the moon again.

She saw its glow, but somehow that glow was around Florin's square-jawed, handsome face. Blue-gray eyes, quiet yet forceful, curly brown hair and shoulders as broad and as muscled as Islif's. Kind, dignified, never saying anything remotely as rude or jovial as Semoor at his usual.

Not that he talked much. "Silent," they called him in Espar, and there were farmers who scarce knew the rest of them existed, yet respected "Young Silent" as a man among men, a bright hope for the years ahead, a man who'd lead and give wise counsel and end up an elder, a rock to stand against the storms.

Jhess sighed again, rolling over to clutch her coverlet against herself. She was a little in love with Florin, she thought, and a *lot* in awe of him. Tall, handsome—and there was something about his looks, his keen glances, that drew the eye.

The eyes of every lass, more like. She'd seen them watching him, just as she watched him. Florin came into her mind whenever she heard minstrels singing of heroes. Quiet of manner, never a swaggerer, but firm. And kind. And understanding. And probably not for her, ever, no matter how deeply she might long for it.

But did she? It was enough to call him true friend. Yes. No woman can ever have enough true friends.

She could see him now, standing in the Stronghold, saying firmly, "We must do what is right—and be very sure as to what 'right' is." It was one of his favorite sayings. Purple Dragons must revere the king as she—as they all—revered Florin. A man you'd follow to your doom, knowing it, because he'd ordered it, and you wanted his respect more than anything else.

Jhessail looked at the moon again, Florin's face suddenly gone, and asked it in a whisper, "And what will happen, if the king—if Florin—ever comes to know what power they hold over us? And ask us to follow? What then?"

In answer, the moon stared unblinkingly back at her, as silent as always.

Chapter 4
IN FOREST DEEP, A LADY FAIR

In forest deep
A lady fair
Her secrets keep
Though wolves dare
To hunt her down
To have her life
To taste a crown
Nobles have a certain spice.

Anonymous
Nobles Have A Certain Spice
minstrels' ballad, first popular in
The Year of Silent Steel

The world wafted back to her on woodsmoke. Sharp and thick, from a fire that was snapping a little . . . sloth of sleeping dragons, would she *never* find capable servants? Oh, but Khalandra was being unforgivably careless this morning! No bedchamber fire should *ever* snap like that, spitting sparks on what could be a priceless Athkatlan rug! Why, the room'd be ablaze in a breath or two, if—

Someone touched her feet, gently. The light, deft handling made pain stab through her, jolting the Lady Narantha Crownsilver rudely awake.

She blinked up at green leaves blazing emerald in bright morning sunlight, and a blue and cloudless sky above them, over her head. Where by all the watching gods—?

In a wild forest somewhere, it seemed, but how . . . ?

A forest stream was chuckling softly past, somewhere beyond her pain-wracked feet, the smoke she'd smelled was wafting from a small fire yonder, mingled now with smells of cooking meat and fish, and—and one of the most handsome young men she'd ever seen was washing and bandaging her feet.

Her bare, scratched, and *cut* feet!

In a sudden rush the night came back to her: the fear, the horrible growls, her frantic flight into menacing darkness, crashings close behind her, being cruelly bound and carried, blindfolded as men lugged her like a sack, pawing her—she was unbound now, thank the

Dragon!—and some sort of fight around her in the dark, between outlaws and the king's men . . .

Outlaws would be cruel, murderous rapists, unshaven and filthy, hardly likely to wash anyone's feet. Nor would they untie a captive.

So this man had probably rescued her, and must serve the king. Or did he?

He'd not looked up at her, though her sudden fast and hard breathing as she remembered it all must have told him she was awake. The Lady Narantha raised herself on one elbow, suddenly acutely aware that she was wearing only her crumpled and torn, once-splendid nightrobe, and a strange man was kneeling at her feet, where he could see more than enough of her!

Fear and fury surged in Narantha, and she wanted to kick him and shriek at him for being the lustful villain that he was . . . but he wasn't done binding her feet yet, and . . . gods, yes, her back *was* aching. Oooh. Worse, she was beginning to feel bruises and stiffnesses all over herself. Gods above, she probably couldn't even stand without his help.

Narantha clenched her fists until she felt the sharp twinges of her own nails digging into her palms, and choked down the furious words she'd been about to spit. She needed this peasant, whoever he was, just to find her way back to a road and some Purple Dragons to escort her to Lord Hezom—that thrice-cursed, stinking backwoods *lowlife* that Father had for some *insane* reason decided she needed to be tutored by! Why, the only tutoring she'd allow—

A particularly strong stab of pain brought her attention back to the here and now. Wincing, Narantha looked around.

She was lying on a fern-cloaked sandbar beside a forest stream. A snared—she sniffed; yes, rabbit and two river brownfin; those were smells she knew—were roasting on arched-over saplings, tied just above a small fire that had been lit on a bare rock.

Beside the fire lay the largest leaf she'd ever seen, heaped with fresh-picked buds of some sort that small brown birds were swooping and darting at. The man at her feet was shooing them away with long sweeps of one brown-tanned hand, without seeming to even look their way. A long white scar cut across the palm of that hand.

He wore dusty, dirt-smeared leather armor—foresters' garb—yet looked like a king. Not like a blood-son of King Azoun, Narantha told herself hastily. Rather, he had the same quietly commanding manner and air of alert intelligence as Duke Bhereu or Baron Thomdor . . . or the king himself.

Then he looked up at her, this dirt-smudged stranger, and Narantha was lost.

Fearless yet friendly blue-gray eyes gazed at her out of a square-jawed, quietly regal face—that split suddenly with a warm, welcoming, kindly smile.

A smile, somehow, that she wanted to earn again and again. Her heart started to beat faster.

"Well met, Lady Fair," he said quietly. "I am Florin Falconhand, son of Hethcanter and Imsra of that name, of Espar."

He looked aside, and made a swift lunge that sent a bird whirring away with a bud falling from its beak. Deftly he caught the little green orb out of the air, and put it back on the leaf. "Forgive me," he added, "but the wood-riskins are intent upon stealing our morningfeast."

"Where's Delbossan?" she blurted. "And where am I?"

Florin looked back at her and spread his hands. "As to your first, I know not, though if you mean the Master Delbossan who is Horse-master to Hezom, Lord of Espar, I know him. As well as any Esparran does; Espar is not so large a place. A good man. As to your second: here. In the forest. The King's Forest, to tell larger truth, hard by the stream called the Dathyl."

"Wherever *that* is," she snorted. "The King's Forest covers half the kingdom!"

"So it does," he agreed with a smile, reaching out one hand as swift as a striking snake to grasp a diving riskin, turn, and throw it out over the stream. The bird chirped shrilly, obviously astonished to find itself no longer racing at a tempting heap of buds, but headed in quite a different direction.

Florin gave it a bright chirp in return, and it answered him, sounding almost rueful, as it vanished across the Dathyl into a dark stand of trees.

Narantha stared at him. Could he speak with birds? Or was he crazed-headed, and—

Then this Esparran forester brought the same hand that had just caught a bird—the same *unwashed* hand—down on her own ankle. "You're fair cut up, and no doubting," he said, and shifted aside on his haunches, as graceful as any dancer, to reach behind himself and pluck something from a pack.

" 'Tis unwise," he added gently, "to go out into the forest—into any woods—without good boots on your feet, Lady. Yet fair fortune is with you this day: I never travel without a spare pair."

He was gently pulling boots on over her bandaged feet: great horrible heavy man's boots, made for feet half again larger than hers. *His* feet, of course. And what was he doing *now*?

Stuffing . . . yes, stuffing more bandages into the boots! Wadded roll after none-too-clean-looking roll, into the open, gaping tops of the boots, thrusting them firmly down around her feet (fresh pain). Whereupon he started *bending* her feet with his hands—

"Owww!"

—twisting them around, his fingers sliding past her aches and bandages like deft talons, shoving wadded cloth here, and there, and everywhere around her ankles and calves—

"What're you *doing?*"

"Pray pardon, Lady, but the boots are too large for your feet. They must be packed tight so you don't wobble as you walk, or they'll rub you raw and you'll probably very swiftly step right out of them, or turn an ankle and fall."

The forester shoved a last rolled-up bandage in, thrust it down with two firm fingers, and sat back, satisfied. She need never know that boots, pack, and bandages had all come from the foresters' cache. Not that there was much worry, that oh-so-high-and-mighty Lady Narantha Crownsilver would know anything at all about foresters' caches—to say nothing of foresters. Still, even if she'd already deemed him a faceless servant, that was no call for him to give her rudeness. "I must warn you further, Lady. Don't keep walking if your feet begin to hurt in one place repeatedly. We'll be stopping betimes; I'll have to wash and dress them often."

The Lady Narantha's eyes blazed. "You expect me to *walk?* With my feet all cut up?"

Florin shrugged. "You must," he told her quietly. "Once the wolves and owlbears catch your scent, they'll follow you. If you can't keep ahead of them, they'll eat you. Slowly, if it's an owlbear that catches you. They like cruel sport with their food."

"What?" Narantha shrieked, in a decidedly unladylike scream that must have been heard by owlbears in the most distant reaches of the kingdom. "Get me out of here! I am a Crownsilver, man—a *Crownsilver!* Oldest and highest of all noble families in Cormyr! Get me out of here at once! I *command* you, in the name of the king, whose Decree of Rights Noble obligates you to the very cost of your life: Take me forthwith back to Suzail! I desire to be out of this horrible wilderness without delay!"

The forester rose, as liquid-graceful as any sword-dancer Narantha had ever seen at any family revel, and stood tall and broad-shouldered above her. Frowning.

"I've never been to Suzail," he murmured, telling her plain truth—and then turned to look across the Dathyl in case his face betrayed his great falsehood as he added, "I know not the way."

Even a child would know that if he could find the road—that lay everywhere in *that* direction—he couldn't fail to reach Suzail along it. The royal roads were not so winding as all that. South through Waymoot to Suzail, following clear and well-maintained signposts all the way.

Even a child, aye . . . but a young noble lass?

Aye, she wasn't snarling disbelieving curses at him for being a liar, now. She was staring at him in dismay.

"I can and will get you to Espar," he told her solemnly, "but—"

"Villain! Sneaking, lying whoreson of an outlaw! Dung-faced

peasant! Disloyal, impudent dog of a thieving, maiden-ravishing dolt! How *dare*—"

"But it will take a few days," Florin continued, raising his voice effortlessly to override hers without shouting in the slightest, "because we're way out in the wilderness, out where the big beasts roam."

Another great lie . . . but the Lady Narantha was staring at him in fresh despair, aghast.

"A few *days?*" she echoed, disbelievingly—and then found her feet in a hobbling rush and started to hit him, slapping and pummeling his unyielding chest wildly with her small, pale fists. "Incompetent! Ignoramus! Wretched, slug-ignorant stonehead of a lazy, useless *fool* of a servant! Whoring, cheating, horsefaced (gasp) good-for-nothing—"

Ignoring her rain of blows, Florin shrugged and calmly turned away to lace up his pack, paying no heed when she belabored his backside, nor even when she kicked him hard up between the legs from behind, jarring her toes on what had to be a hard metal codpiece.

Straightening and swinging the pack onto his shoulder with a hummed tune, for all the world as if she weren't there at all, the tall forester strode away along the bank of the stream, his legs long and his gait eerily quiet.

"Where d'you think you're going? *Come back here!* Come back, I say, you worthless—"

The silent lout strode on, and with a snarl of outraged exasperation Narantha started after him in a wobble-booted rush, launching herself into a stumbling, splay-footed trot that carried her over one dead tree, caught and scraped her damp-gowned leg painfully on another, and hurled her through a thorny and thankfully dead and crackling-dry bush into a hard nose-first meeting with the ground.

The very muddy, reeking ground, all roots and hurriedly slithering leaf-worms and—

"Come back!" she cried, suddenly terrified of being left alone in this vast forest, lost and . . . and hunted . . .

"Please!" she sobbed. "You—man! Forester!" Frantically she fought to recall his name, and in tears shrieked, "Florin, I beg of you! A rescue! Succor! *Aid!*"

Weeping openly as she struggled up to her knees, blinded by tears and truly miserable in her helplessness, the Lady Narantha Crownsilver did not hear her departing rescuer half-smile and murmur *very* quietly, "What? All of those? Do I look like an army? Lazy, good-for-nothing peasant whoreson that I am?"

"Please come back," she pleaded, choking on her tears. "Good Florin, *please!*"

Good Florin grinned, took another long step as he carefully wiped away his mirth and assumed a stern look instead—and whirled around and stalked back the way he'd come.

Gods, he hoped he'd be able to keep this act up until he got her back to Delbossan. This was an adventure, all right, but . . .

His face was calm and his expression gravely unreadable as he walked right past her, back to the sandbar. "By the Queen of the Forest, where are my wits? I was so appalled at your lowborn rudeness that I almost forgot morningfeast."

Wallowing on her knees with fresh rage rising inside her, Narantha Crownsilver stared at the forester, dumbfounded. My . . . lowborn rudeness?

Lowborn?

Rudeness?

"All praise Mielikki, they've not yet started to burn," Florin said, plucking the sizzling fish away from the fire.

Narantha went on staring at him, open-mouthed. How *dare* he—

Was that really how she seemed to him?

Florin turned. "Lady," he said pleasantly, holding out a great green leaf with a slab of brownfin steaming on it, "morningfeast is served."

Narantha found her mouth suddenly flooded and aching. So hungry was she, really smelling the fish now, that she came crawling mutely back to him, almost clawing aside branches in her haste.

"Don't eat the leaf," Florin told her, "but use it as a platter, to keep the hot juices from scalding you or staining your gown. Hold its edge up—so—and nothing will run out. 'Tis safe to lap and lick at the leaf, to get all the juice. Eat merrily; there're no fishbones left."

Fearing being burnt, Narantha nipped tentatively at one end of the fillet. Ye *gods*, 'twas good! Overly hot, yes, and she found herself gobbling to keep her lips from searing, but . . . ahh, wonderful.

Long, strong fingers took her well-licked leaf away from her, and replaced it with another, this one cupped around a small handful of the green buds. Narantha peered at them curiously then looked up questioningly.

"Cavanter buds," Florin told her, pointing at a nearby bush, "from yonder shrub. Only pleasant to eat this time of year, when they're green and swelling. Truly mouth-watering if you've butter to pan-fry them in."

Narantha's mouth *was* still watering. She watched Florin bite into a bud as if it was an olive or radish, and did the same. Chewy . . . unfamiliar . . . a bit like carrot in texture, but fried bread in taste. Nothing so spectacular as the brownfin, but . . . pleasant.

The forester had made his fish and buds vanish in a trice, and was at work on the rabbit, pulling it apart on another leaf. Thankfully, his knife had already made the head disappear, and it seemed to have cooked so thoroughly that it came apart like custard as he pulled on the legs. In moments another leaf was held out to her. "Bones in this," Florin warned her. "Not to be eaten. Spit them onto this leaf; nowhere else."

Narantha had eaten rabbit many times before, usually covered in the choicest simmered sauces prepared in the kitchens of many high houses and even the palace, but this—sauceless and too hot, stinging her fingers as she bit and gobbled—this overmatched all. The best food she'd ever eaten.

It was gone while she still ached for more, and she never noticed that the forester had slipped his portion onto her leaf as she gnawed—nor that she'd been moaning softly, in sheer pleasure.

Licking her fingers hungrily, Narantha sat back and stared at the greasy leaves. In all the feasts she'd eaten, as far back as she could remember, she'd never tasted anything so fine.

Florin was washing his hands—and his chin too, it seemed—in the stream. "Come," he said gently. "We've a long way to travel before nightfall, to escape the beasts. Wash."

Narantha blinked at him, her moment of bliss gone.

"Are you suggesting," she asked icily, "I should go on my knees and lap up water like a dog?"

"Only a little. Drinking too much at once isn't good. Use the sand to scour your mouth and hands."

She made no move, but stared at him, eyes smoldering.

The forester calmly tossed handfuls of water onto the fire, dousing it amid puffs of smoke and loud hissings, until he could rake it apart and wet it down thoroughly. The largest twigs went into the water, thrust down into the submerged flank of the sandbar and buried there. The leaves they'd eaten from were served the same way.

Then Florin scooped up dry sand and cast it across the scattered ashes of the fire, rinsing his hands in the Dathyl once more. "Wash," he told her firmly, sounding for all the world like one of her child-hood nurses.

"And just who are you, man," she told him back just as firmly, "to give orders to me?"

Florin gave her the same sort of "old wisdom looking at her with grave disappointment" look that her long-dead uncles had favored her with. "The scent of the fish and meat on you will come off on every branch or leaf you touch, leaving a clear trail even a half-witted wolf or owlbear—and there *are* no half-witted hunting beasts—can follow. You'll lead them right to your own throat. To say nothing of the stinging flies and worse that'll find it much sooner than that, and buzz around your eyes day and night through. Wash."

Defeated, the fair flower of the Crownsilvers gave him a wordless snarl and went to the water, turning her back on him.

"Relieve yourself over there," he added, pointing off into the trees. "No thorns or stinging leaves. Yes, yon bushes are thicker, but you'll be burning or itching for days if you head that way."

Narantha's back stiffened, but she made no reply.

"If you wait to go later," Florin added calmly, "remember this: what you leave behind is like shouting your whereabouts to the hunting beasts."

Wordlessly Narantha went where he'd directed. "Use the big pale leaves, no others," he added—and suspected, by the manner in which the tangled vines she'd vanished behind immediately danced and rustled, that she'd made an immediate and very rude gesture by way of reply.

He looked all around for signs of their stay, scraping the sands with the side of his boot to do away with the prints of boots, knees, and hands.

When the Lady Narantha emerged from the bushes, glaring at him mutely, Florin murmured, "Please follow me"—and walked into the stream.

Narantha looked incredulous. "What are you *doing?*"

Standing knee-deep in the Dathyl, the forester replied, "Always do this when leaving a forest camp. Doing so makes it harder for the more intelligent monsters to track you from your cookfires to wherever you next sleep. Elsewise, they'll soon be biting out your throat."

The flower of the Crownsilvers looked down at the unfamiliar and overlarge boots on her feet, her lips drawn back in distaste. "It's going to be cold and wet," she snapped. "I hate being wet."

"Best get it over with quickly, then," Florin said briskly. "Always face what you mislike, do battle with it, and get it done: all the more time then for what you prefer, yes?"

Narantha glared at him. "You're enjoying this, aren't you? Humiliating me every chance you get, mocking my ignorance of forest ways, as much as telling me I'm utterly useless. I hate you. Gallant men of Cormyr—*true* men of Cormyr—never stoop to treat a lady so."

Florin glanced up at the sky. "The day," he told it conversationally, "does draw on. We have to cross an owlbear's hunting ground to get out of this forest; it'd be a real pity for us both if night found us when we were just passing its lair."

"*Stop* spinning dire tales!" Narantha spat. "You're lying! Just making things up, to try to scare me into obeying you! Well, I won't, so there! There must be a bridge across this stream somewhere—or you can chop down a tree and *make* me one! Yes, sirrah! Hear now my command: fell a tree, right here, and—"

Florin strode up out of the water, gallantly cupped her elbow in his hand, and escorted her—straight into the Dathyl. When she started to struggle, seeing where he was heading, his gentle grip turned to iron, and he towed her into the water until she was stumbling, flailing, and almost immediately shrieking as her foot threatened to come out of her right boot, leaving it behind, deep underwater.

"Stamp down hard," he commanded quietly, "or you'll be out of those boots—and crawling for days through the forest. If the beasts let you live that long."

He kept hold of her—which was a good thing, considering how many hidden holes and rocks she seemed to stumble over, unintentionally almost sitting down twice—and took her on a long and very wet stroll down the stream before climbing out onto some bare rocks, with a grimly dripping Narantha beside him.

Something seemed to shift, along the side of a tree ahead of them, and Florin called something soft in a liquid, shifting-sounds tongue Narantha had never heard before. She thought she heard the merest whisper of an answer before Florin dragged her back into the stream and walked on, around another bend.

This time she *did* fall, snatching her hand away from him and promptly losing her footing. She came up coughing, spitting, and very wet, and made no protest when he gently claimed her arm again. Her teeth were chattering by the time they stepped out of the Dathyl once more.

"What was that you said?" she asked, miserably, folding her arms across her breast to try to cover herself from him in the drenched ruin of her nightrobe. "And to whom?"

"A polite greeting, and assurance we meant no harm. To the one whose home we almost blundered into."

Narantha waited, shivering, until it seemed clear the tall forester wasn't going to say anything more. "I've never heard that speech before," she blurted, finally. "What was it?"

Florin gave her a raised-eyebrow look. "You've never heard Dryadic? With all the schooling nobles get?"

"We nobles do not," Narantha told him icily, "anticipate dealing overmuch with dryads when debating great matters of the realm. Now if you speak to me of Elvish, I can write *that*, and speak it . . . a little."

Florin merely nodded.

"Well, sirrah? Can you?"

Florin nodded again. His attention seemed to be on the trees around them, as if he were searching for something.

After a few breaths, he nodded in satisfaction, as if he'd been shown something by an unseen hand. Collecting her hand again, he set off through the trees in a slightly different direction, his strides slow and deliberate.

"Was that really a dryad?" the noblewoman asked, curiously, as he towed her along. "I—I didn't really see."

Florin nodded. "And that unseeing," he said gently, "is why you'd be dead before nightfall, if you took to wandering around this forest alone. Don't leave my side, if you want to see your grand houses again."

Narantha opened her mouth to say something really rude—then shut it again without uttering a sound.

Florin's sword was in his hand, and she hadn't even seen him draw it. "Ah . . . is there danger?"

"Always," he replied shortly, stalking on through the trees. Narantha tramped after him, her boots squelching.

"Why is your sword all dirty like that?" she asked, after they'd walked for what seemed an eternity. "My father's blades—*all* Crownsilver swords, and all those I see at Court, too—shine bright silver; they gleam like mirrors."

Florin nodded. "My life may depend on a foe not seeing sunlight— or moonlight—reflecting from my steel. So I rub it with a tree gum we use to quell rust, as well as shine. The swords you describe are meant to impress. I've never had a need to impress anyone, nor had anyone standing around to be impressed, come to that. Swords don't impress many Cormyrean farmers . . . nor rangers."

His words done, he fell silent again, leaving the noblewoman listening to silence—except for the thuds and crashings of her own clumsy progress—and expecting more. Didn't this lout know how to spout gallant converse? To pass the day away with clever words?

No. Of course not. He was an unlettered, graceless, backcountry lout who knew a trick or two and so thought himself better than—than his betters. The sooner she was out of his clutches and seeing him flogged for his impudence by a few furious Purple Dragons . . .

She turned her ankle for about the dozenth time, and slammed the side of her head hard into a sapling as she started to topple. Clawing her way down the tree until she caught her hands in enough branches to stop her fall, she gasped angrily, "Are you expecting me to *walk* all the way to Suzail?"

Florin gave her a puzzled frown. "Why not? How else do you usually move yourself around?"

"Horses," Narantha told him, seething, as she dragged herself back upright. "Coaches. River-barges. Palanquins. That's right: servants *carry* me."

They trudged on for a few more paces before she snapped, "Well? Aren't you even going to offer to carry me?"

Florin waved his sword. "This requires one of my hands. Moreover, this pack is already heavier than your entire body; can't you manage to carry *yourself* around?"

Narantha had no answer to that, and trudged along in silence as they crested a little ridge, still deep in the forest, and found a rather slippery way down its far side.

"I'm appalled," she announced, reaching more or less level ground again—and wondering why so many trees seemed to feel the need to fall over, and keep right on growing sidewise, in a tangle no forester could have nimbly won past. "Appalled, do you hear me?"

Florin did not reply, so she was forced to explain. "I'm appalled at the thought you expect me to walk most of the length of the kingdom!"

Florin turned his head away. She suspected—correctly, though she could not be sure—that he was hiding a grin from her, and snarled, "Don't you dare ignore me, ignorant, lowborn lout!"

Florin towed her along even faster, setting a swift stride that forced her to trot to keep up with him; when she tried to slow, he kept firm hold of her hand and started to drag her.

"You're hurting me!" she shouted, truly furious again. "You cruel, coarse ballatron! You titteravating cumberworld! You—you gidig nameless-kin *bastard!*" Florin made no reply, and the flower of the Crownsilvers abruptly fell silent, her panting telling him why: she'd run out of breath to curse him.

Keeping his face set hard to keep the widening grin within him entirely off it, he quickened his pace still more.

"Slow *down*, knave!" the noblewoman snapped. "I can't—can't—"

"Catch your breath while you're yelling at me? I'm not surprised. But we dare not slow down. Not while you're making all this noise. Every owlbear and wood-wolf for miles has heard—"

Narantha shut her mouth abruptly, pinching her lips into a thin, furious line.

"—all the crashings of your every footfall . . . and they'll be stalking us right now, following patiently, waiting until you weary and stop to rest."

"Oh, gods bugg-buh—*violate* you!" the Lady Crownsilver snarled, stumbling in her fury and almost falling on her face in a slimy hole of mud and long-rotten leaves.

Florin raised expressively reproving eyebrows, looking so much like her father when he did so that Narantha shrank back. The ranger turned his head away from her, jaw set, and her cheeks flamed with mortification.

They would have flamed with something else if she'd been able to see his face, and the crooked grin that now kept springing onto it despite Florin's best efforts to wrestle it down.

Laws, Schemes, and Dooms

In my days thus far, I've observed three things that beset all kings: laws that trip them up or are used against them; the plottings of traitors, scheming to weaken and shame them and bring them into the dark regard of their subjects ere the plots turn to their bloody removal from the scene; and those very same murderous fates that befall them. Yet do they not deserve it? After all, the dooms of kings are always a lot more bother for all than the killings of mere bakers, foresters, and cobblers.

Havandus Haeratchur
Musings of an Ale-Seller
published in the Year of the Lion

The floating scrying orb darkened and sank a little as Horaundoon passed his hand over it, banishing a scene of one more elf mage lying dead with doomed astonishment stark on his face.

Humming a jaunty tune, Horaundoon strolled past a table on which rested a neat row of three human skulls, to another table where several old and massive metal-bound tomes lay waiting. At his approach, the air in front of his nose roiled briefly, presenting an intricate glowing sign in warning.

He slowed not a step, and the sigil promptly vanished again—without the thunderclap of unleashed Art that would have slain any other man.

The archmage reached out with a hand that shimmered with enspelled rings for the darkest, most battered book. Galaundar's Grimoire should hold what he was seeking, somewhere in the pages just after the section on preparing dismembered limbs to be spell foci . . .

A sound as of tinkling bells occurred in the room behind him.

He drew back his hand, and turned. "Yes?"

The sounds came again, more liquid this time, ascending in different notes. In time with them, a glow flickered in midair like a passing flame leaping out of nowhere, a little glowing scene dancing above the central skull of the three.

Horaundoon peered at it closely. The hargaunt was showing him his last slaying: the elf mage crumpling down his own garden steps, to sprawl limp and lifeless, forever staring.

Its bubbling, bell-like speech came again.

"Yes," Horaundoon agreed gravely, "the spell *is* dangerous—but only if I'm actually caught in the act of using it. It leaves no trace behind, no link to me or to this place."

Bells cascaded like water, and another scene sprang into brief existence where the first had danced only moments ago. The hargaunt, it seemed, was unimpressed.

One of the earliest slayings, this time, the elder elf who'd raced in vain to reach his ward-spells, and died clawing the air well outside their crackling reach.

The archmage nodded patiently. "No magic is foolproof—with the Art, we steer and shape energies that betimes have intent of their own, in a world full of old, hidden spells that can flare into life without warning. Yet consider how safe, in something as rife with uncertainty as sorcery must needs be, this crafting of mine is. Mages are given to grandiose claims and boasts that far outstrip their true talents, yes, but this is not only my masterwork, but a masterwork by any solemn measure of spellcrafting."

He strode back through the protective ward, waving a hand to call up a vision of his own, much larger than those the hargaunt emitted.

The air between them was suddenly full of yet another elf mage, this one life-sized and battling something that swirled half-seen around him, dread on his face as he came to know that there was nothing he could do against this attack, and that his doom was come upon him at last.

Horaundoon stepped right through the image even before it began to fade, as he strode to stand over the skull. "My master-spell can detect any mantle and move toward it, drifting across half Faerûn if need be. When it impinges upon the mantle, I am made aware of this—and at my command, the spell conquers the mantle and turns it against its user! From the mantle's focus gem it lashes into the mind of he who wears the mantle, emptying his spells into the gem and feebleminding him as it does so. This, too, I am made aware of, whereupon it sends those spells to me. The weight of that mind-burst can be staggering, yes, but—behold—I'm still standing. I then command my spell, intermingled with the mantle, to immolate itself, gem, mantle, and mantle-wearer—or merely his mind, turning his brain to ash, and 'tis done."

The hargaunt belled anew.

"Ah, but it has worked *every time*. I've slain elf after elf, though I'm going to have to work very swiftly indeed, now. Word is spreading, and Fair Folk are abandoning use of their mantles from Evereska to the Dragonreach shores. I've been stealing the spells of the most powerful mages I can catch alone, avoiding only masters of the High Magic—and with each mind I empty, the spells at my command grow richer."

The hargaunt made its querying whistle, accompanied by that wisp of pink that meant, as clearly as if it had shouted out the word in Common: "Why?"

Horaundoon shrugged. "The ranks of the Zhentarim grow steadily unfriendlier, the schemes and betrayals and false blamings crowding in hard and fast, one upon the other. If I remain, with the wits and standing all know I have, I continue to be a target. Sooner or later, most probably sooner, some rival or cabal of rivals will inevitably slay me."

The archmage raised a hand, and the air around him sang, briefly and faintly, reassuring him that his shielding spells—that blocked all scrying, and warned of attempts to intrude, or to shatter or alter them—remained intact.

"So I must grow powerful enough to make myself a way out of the Zhentarim. That's why I tolerate apprentices. Already my magics have made them my slaves, though they know it not. When the time is right, I'll force one of them to take my shape and seeming. The others, just as spellbound, will slay this false Horaundoon. Leaving me, in a new guise fashioned by you, to vanish from the notice of the Brotherhood. Free once more."

The hargaunt trilled, throwing up a scene that flashed briefly blue.

"Already? Haularake, where does the day go?" Horaundoon hurriedly loosened the sash of his robes and shrugged them back off his shoulders, letting them fall to where his arms held them up at his waist. "I know, I know," he added, before the hargaunt could interrupt him. "Spellcrafting always takes longer than I think it will. Naed, we'll have to really hurry now."

He extended his other hand to the skull. It promptly bulged, coiled, and became an ivory-hued, sightless snake, oozing up his arm with purposeful speed, and leaving no sign of the skull it had been.

"Naed, naed, *naed*," the archmage murmured impatiently, the last word muffled by the hargaunt flowing over his lips as it molded itself to his face, giving him quite a different visage. A woman's face, strikingly beautiful.

Below Horaundoon's newly pointed chin, the bulk of the hargaunt had molded itself into a pair of decidedly feminine—and decidedly attractive—breasts.

He was breathing hard in his haste by the time he reached the wardrobe mirror, and cast the spell that turned him from a rather gaunt and hairy man with an incongruously smooth and beautiful woman's face and front, into a shapely and curvaceous woman. Blowing himself a mocking kiss, he whirled into the wardrobe, snatched out a suitable gown, thanked the watching gods (and not for the first time) that the current fashions in footwear were low-heeled and the current jewelry simple, and hurried to pin up his hair.

He was staring into a mirror, three of the pins in his mouth and one in his hand, when a hollow chant arose from whence he'd come. He slammed the hairpins down on the table and hurried back to his study.

"An intruder!" the remaining two skulls chanted in unison, jawbones wagging. They were still rising up from the table as Horaundoon slid to a halt in front of them. "An intruder!"

"Blast him down!" Horaundoon roared, "and trouble me no more with such trifles!"

He was two running strides back toward the mirror when the floor under him shook slightly, there was a long and rolling booming sound, and the skulls ceased their chanting in mid-word.

Duly blasted. Good.

Horaundoon snatched up the pins and grimly set to work again pinning up his hair. With all the war wizards infesting this oh-so-peaceful Forest Kingdom, beautiful and wealthy merchants' widows could get *far* closer to king's lords than archmages widely suspected of being Zhentarim could.

And there was a lord or three in Cormyr he wanted to befriend. They might well come in *very* useful when the time was right. Soon.

"We . . . we're following the stream, aren't we?" Lady Narantha gasped, clambering up to join Florin beside an overhanging tangle of exposed tree roots and boulders.

The forester gave her a sharp look. "We are. Well spotted. 'Tis the best way not to get lost."

"Won't the bears and the . . . the hunting beasts follow it, too?"

"Yes."

"But—" Narantha started to scramble up a stairlike tangle of roots, to look over the boulders. Florin's hand shot out and caught hold of her elbow—and Narantha found herself struggling to climb but not moving one fingersbreadth forward. "What're you—?" she gasped.

Florin drew her close and murmured sternly, "Never show yourself over the top of a ridge like that. Haven't you been watching me? Cautious, duck low, show as little head as possible as you take a good look; that's the way. Now, you just used one of my least favorite words: 'but.' What were you going to say after that?"

The noblewoman blinked at him, as they stood nose to nose, then frowned as she remembered. "*But* if the beasts follow the stream, they'll find us—and what then?"

"Ah." Florin nodded. "Then this." He held up the sword Narantha had all but forgotten was in his hand.

She looked at it, then up at him. He asked, "You've never been trained to use one of these, have you?"

Narantha frowned. "Well, of *course* not."

" 'Of course' *nothing*. What were your parents thinking? Or not thinking? Lord Hezom will likely have you swinging steel—something light enough for to suit your arm, mind, not this."

"Crownsilvers," Narantha said haughtily, waving an airy hand to indicate phantom legions of retainers in lace and livery, "need not swing swords. We have servants enough to do that for us."

"Oh?" Florin crooked an eyebrow. "And if the person who seeks to slay you is one of those servants? What then?"

The noblewoman looked incredulous. "No servant would ever *dare*—"

"And yet I do—constantly, it seems—and again and again you exclaim that I wouldn't or shouldn't. I think you'd be unpleasantly surprised at just what some folk of Faerûn will dare, if ever they catch someone as beautiful and as important as you alone."

Narantha stared at the forester, eyes widening and face going pale, then took a swift step back from him. Unfortunately, a root was right behind her.

A moment later she was blinking up at him, flat on her back and winded, with Florin reaching down a helping hand.

She gazed up at him for a long, hard-breathing moment, face unreadable. Then, slowly, she reached out and took that proffered hand.

Gently but firmly, the ranger pulled her upright. "Lady Narantha," he said, "I don't mean to give you orders or offer you rudeness. Yet understand this well: doing the wrong thing, out here in the forest, can get us both killed. Please do as I suggest until you are safely in the hands of Lord Hezom—or your family. *Please.*"

The flower of the Crownsilvers was breathing fast and her face was set, her eyes hard and unfriendly. But she nodded, curtly, and snapped, "I'll try, man—what was your name again? Hawkhand? Falconhand? I'll try."

"Florin Falconhand thanks you, Lady," the handsome forester said, his manner almost humble.

Narantha inclined her head regally. *"That's* better," she declared, starting to climb the ridge again.

This time, Florin let her go, merely snaking swiftly around a boulder to look at the forest ahead before whatever might be lurking in it got a good look at a wild-haired young noblewoman of Cormyr with a dirty, once-translucent nightrobe plastered to her, and large, flopping mens' boots on her feet.

A bird took startled wing at Narantha's appearance, but nothing more sinister seemed to be lurking in the trees just ahead.

"Coming, Falconhand?" the Lady Crownsilver called imperiously. "I grow tired of seeing nothing but rocks and trees. Is all this corner of Cormyr endless rocks and trees? No wonder no one ever goes here, or thinks of it. My father must be mad."

Florin rolled his eyes. So much for terrifying her. So this was a high noble of Cormyr.

And this was an adventure.

Florin rolled his eyes again. Ye gods.

"I will see the crown princess *alone,*" Vangerdahast said, cold iron in his voice. The royal magician was making it clear that he'd grown unused to having to repeat orders—and that this was not one of his patient days.

The two most senior highknights of the Bodyguard Royal hesitated. "Our orders—"

"Were given to you by *me*, as I recall," Vangerdahast almost snarled. "Now, to a *thinking* man, wouldn't that lead rather readily to the conclusion that having given them, I can also countermand them?"

The knights nodded reluctantly, turned and saluted the princess between them, turned again, and marched out of the Greatgauntlet Audience Chamber, bootheels clicking on the tiled floor. Just before the two war wizards outside the doors closed them, to leave the royal magician and the crown princess alone together, one of the highknights remarked to the other, his voice carefully pitched to carry clearly back into the audience chamber, "Well, old Thunderspells is certainly having one of his bad days!"

Vangerdahast turned away before the Princess Tanalasta could see him smile. Better that she thought him furious, and sat still to *listen,* for once.

Fourteen years old and turning into quite the Lady Wildnose; he should have squashed her rebelliousness long ago. Of course Azoun and Filfaeril had spoiled her. Nevertheless, his duty was clear. Well, he could make a good start on it today. He casually turned back to the princess—and found her looking away, down to the dark and empty end of the room. Obviously she did not want to be here, and was trying to pretend, for a few breaths more, that she was elsewhere.

Tanalasta turned her head away in case wily old Vangey could tell she was fighting down a smirk. It wouldn't do to give him something to pounce on as evidence of her "wild, wanton waywardness" he was so fond of complaining to Mother about. He wanted to have a free hand in disciplining her—short of chaining her up and flogging her with a whip, the way they broke wild horses, or perhaps *not* short of that—and would seize on just about anything to achieve that.

And in Cormyr, what the royal magician wanted, the royal magician got. Well, doomed or not, she was going to make him work hard for *this* prize. She was going to be as solemn and as regal as she knew how, all stiff formality and words chosen with care.

Vangerdahast clasped his hands behind his back and strolled toward her. Just as he swept out a hand to point at the lone high-backed chair he'd ordered set in the center of the room, and before he could order her to sit down on it, Crown Princess Tanalasta folded her skirts gracefully under her and sat down unbidden, as if assuming a throne.

"You requested audience with me, Magician Vangerdahast," she said in neutral tones, looking not at him but up at the giant's gauntlet for which the room had been named, a long-ago battle trophy hung high on the opposite wall. "Your request was couched in terms that the queen my mother termed 'just shy of a command,' and I concur with her. I find it highly . . . *unusual* to find myself unescorted by my maids or my knights-of-presence, meeting with you in private." Her hands went to her half-cloak and drew forth the Fire Tiara. She donned it with slow deliberation, ere raising her eyes to meet his gaze directly. "As this must be a matter of state, I have come prepared, yet uninformed. So, Royal Magician: why am I here?"

So, Tana was playing her I-can-be-very-solemn-and-grownup-look-you act, determined to be regal, and cleaving to stiff formality. Halting in front of her, Vangerdahast kept his wry inward smile off his face. *She's shaking with self-importance; how long before her manner breaks, I wonder?*

"You are here," Vangerdahast told her flatly, "because you are the crown princess. Ceremonially anointed with that title or not, from the moment your brother Foril perished and you were confirmed as a child of Azoun and Filfaeril Obarskyr, you have been the crown princess. The next ruler of all Cormyr."

The royal magician started to pace. "Being a princess—*any* princess—of the Dragon Throne is not a matter of wearing pretty gowns and murmuring diplomatic nothings, of smiling and waving. Cormyr needs princesses who can *think*. All too many princes and noble lords conduct their reasoning only with their codpieces, so you lasses who lack them must do their thinking for them."

"I am unaware that any of my tutors have thus far discovered or reported any deficiency in my reasoning," Tanalasta said stiffly, her face an expressionless mask. "My judgment may be lacking, but it must needs be informed by my experience, which thus far has been scant. May the gods grant that the king my father sit the Dragon Throne for decades to come, and keep my experience meager—for the good of the realm, which flourishes so under his wise and just rule."

Vangerdahast found himself chuckling. "Ah, as smooth as any adroit courtier, and better than most! Well said, Princess!"

Tanalasta gazed once more upon the great gauntlet on the wall.

"Are you mocking me, Royal Magician? I confess I am unused to hearing your mirth, and may misjudge you."

"I never mock any citizen of Cormyr. Their lies, yes, and their foolishly founded opinions, on occasion—and all of those occasions are in debate, in open court, for all to hear. Yet no matter, Princess; I confess that I am more than used to being misjudged. Hear me well: I mean you no harm, nor seek to coerce you by menace. As you must be aware, I often counsel your royal parents, separately and together, in private; it is my most important daily duty. As Heir Royal, it is important that you receive my counsel too. My wisdom may not be great, but—scourge the gods—it is better by far than any other advice you are likely to find in our fair realm."

"I hear similar sentiments from Alaphondar, and Dimswart, and nigh twoscore highknights, heralds, maids, and courtiers, too. Yet I do not intend to debate the quality of your counsel with you, Royal Magician, but merely move forthwith to its content. The day draws on, and this tiara is heavy. I ask again: what do you desire to tell me?"

Vangerdahast inclined his head as if acknowledging a shrewd point, hooked his thumbs through the belt that gathered his severe robes together at his ample waist, and said, "Rulers may in the end rule by force, but frequently swording subjects soon leave a king ruling empty land—and a land without farmers is a land wherein a king and his knights starve. So rulers enact daily justice and order through rules: laws. Cormyr is no different, and our laws, royal decrees, treaties, and records of legal disputes and their resolutions fill vaults beneath us, scribes' workrooms all around us, and secure chambers in four other places in the realm: fortresses in Arabel, Marsember, and High Horn, and in a secret forest location. Of the specifics of such laws you have hitherto no doubt remained blissfully ignorant, but it is high time that you, as heir, were made aware of the boundaries outlined by a few of them, so—for the good of the realm as well as yourself—you set no foot wrong in time to come. You must know your rights and responsibilities, so no false advice nor claims of those who seek to do harm to Cormyr can lead you astray.

This learning will take some years, and we will have many meetings like this one. However, we must begin with a matter you must be informed about before another day passes. I speak particularly of the laws of succession, beginning with royal life and death."

"Surely those are matters I have no control over? I do not recall, mage, being consulted beforehand about my birth."

"Jest if you feel the need, Tanalasta. I won't be forcing you to read over legal documents this day or any other for some months to come; it is more important that you understand what the laws—the rules all Cormyreans live by—are and what they do, in simple terms. So I ask you: what would happen, gods forfend, if your father and mother had died this morning? What are you obligated to do? What would you *try* to do?"

"Summon the overpriests of Chauntea, Helm, Torm, and Tyr to have my father and my mother brought back from the dead, to rule on. Not only is this my desire, it is my obligation."

"Not so. In seeking to do so, you would be breaking the law and dooming the realm."

"What?"

"When this realm was founded, the first Obarskyrs to dwell on these shores entered into agreements with the elves who held this land, just as the elves had with the dragons who ruled here before them. Down the years, there have been many disagreements as to just what happened back then, and what was agreed to—and to quell ceaseless civil war using such pretexts as its banners, solemn treaties have been written, and laws devised and passed pertaining to those treaties. In short, no matter what really befell, Cormyr has agreed to commonly accept and abide by a certain version of events and rules tied to them. If this agreement is broken, we are taught (and so the heads of households grand and rude all across this kingdom believe) the Dragon Throne will shatter, the dragons will return in great numbers to hunt humans, and the realm will be swept away."

"So a *treaty* dictates what will happen, if my—if the king and queen die."

"Indeed. Simply put, in Cormyr, nobles of the realm cannot be magically restored to life, it is expressly forbidden to resurrect ruling monarchs and regents, and all other members of the blood Obarskyr will only be brought back if they agree to this before death, and do not principally follow a faith that forbids such customs. Heirs cannot be recalled to life and still remain heirs; no one who has died and been returned to the living can inherit the Dragon Throne, or even sit upon it by right of conquest. Even if the royal family is extinguished, and the succession passes to other houses—a process that almost certainly will plunge the realm into bloody civil war."

The eyes of Princess Tanalasta had grown very large and dark. "Why—" She licked dry lips, swallowed, and tried again. "Why can't my father just change this inane treaty? Why can't any Dragon King name a clear sequence of successors, to head off war?"

"Ah, I fear not, Lady Highness," the royal magician said gravely, pacing away from her with his hands clasped behind his back, "for there's a law—another law, relatively recent but just as strong as any law in our code—forbidding that. Laws, I fear, inevitably pile up like a beaver's dam, a great untidy intertwined heap one must traverse with care."

Tanalasta frowned. "But my royal father is the king! Surely he can ignore a law that stands in the way of his will? His justice? Do his decrees not *make* law?"

Vangerdahast whirled around to face her, robe swirling, and leveled a finger at her—and despite all her training, despite all she'd schooled herself to do and not do ere entering this chamber, Tanalasta flinched back from a spell that never came.

She'd have fled in tears if the royal magician had sneered then, or even crooked his mouth in amusement.

But instead he stood looking sternly at her, as if she'd been *very* bad.

"Laws and rules," he said firmly, "*must* be observed at all times. Even by kings. For if a realm is a bright-armored knight, every rule broken is a piece torn away from his armor that a traitor's blade can thrust through later, with its wielder crying, 'But in days gone by, so-and-so set aside this rule; why then cannot I?' "

Tanalasta trembled for a long, pale-faced moment, then blurted, "But *you* break rules. All the time. I've heard Father say so, and nobles and Alaph—" She fell abruptly silent, afraid to say more, trembling in shoulder-shaking earnest.

The royal magician took a slow stride forward.

"So I do," he replied, his voice calm. "For the good of the realm. That is my duty—and my doom. For the great engine that is the court to work at all, someone must kick and tug and heave at it nigh daily, breaking the rules when need be—the rules that all others must follow. I am that rulebreaker."

Tanalasta's tremblings were almost shiverings, now, but she lifted her chin almost defiantly to meet his eyes. "And if you are ever wrong in your breakings? What then makes you not a traitor? Nor someone who should be hounded as an outlaw?"

Vangerdahast *was* smiling, now, and it was a thin, mirthless, unwelcoming smile. "I have been wrong in my breakings, as you put it. Many times. Yet kings have forgiven me."

"Why?" Tanalasta whispered. "Have you . . . enspelled them?"

"Their wits, to compel them? No. Though most of the realm believes otherwise. Nor do kings leave me unchained out of fear, or hatred. Can you see your father fearing me?"

"Yes." The crown princess was as white as her favorite snow-fur robe, her lips bloodless, but her whisper was firm.

The royal magician regarded her, smile gone again to leave his face old and expressionless, for long enough to make her quail, and said casually, "Well, perhaps he has grown wise enough to do so by now, at that. We'll leave such considerations for another time, Princess, and return to the matters you must know and understand before another night comes. It is needful for you to know these things, that you be fit to serve the realm properly, when the day comes that you're called upon to do so."

Uncertainly, one of Tanalasta's hands rose to her mouth. "When— when Father dies, and I . . . become queen?"

Vangerdahast's face became severe again. "It is sincerely to be hoped that any princess of Cormyr will serve the realm fittingly, in many, many ways large and small, before she's called upon to actually rule. There are other ways to serve than giving commands."

"As you would know well," Tanalasta murmured, the graceful verbal slash so like her mother that Vangerdahast, far from being angered, had to quell a grin. Ah, but the lass *was* an Obarskyr true, under that stonefaced mask and haughty starch! Best to ignore her comment and simply—

"Mage, why are you telling me this now?" Tanalasta was frowning at him in real concern. "What are you really trying to tell me, with Father off hunting more than a tenday, now; he's all right, isn't he?"

Chapter 6
DECEPTIONS WITHIN DECEPTIONS

Most of us fall afoul of the tangles our tongues make for us when we trade in falsehoods too seldom and too clumsily. Yet there are courtiers, peddlers, seers, and moneylenders who lie adroitly, and can spin deceptions within deceptions deftly, rather than desperately or unintentionally. They court discovery as do clumsier liars, but flirt also with another danger: weaving deceptions so well that they lose sight of who they are, and without perceiving it are themselves transformed by their own falsity.

Tarth Ammarander, Sage of Athkatla
World of Coins: Musings On Merchantry
published in the Year of the Saddle

We halt here," Florin murmured, going to his knees in another place of rocks. Narantha had been clutching her arms and shivering for some time, and her face showed him how heartily sick she was of trees, trees, and more trees. She sank down beside him without a word.

"See, here?" Florin asked, reaching out a finger to trace a roughly scratched symbol of two ovals joined by an arc on a head-sized stone in front of him. Narantha nodded wearily.

"Remember it: this is a foresters' cache. There are hundreds of them in the King's Forest." He rolled the stone aside to reveal a stone coffer set into the ground, a mossgirt cluster of other stones heaped around it. Florin had the coffer lid off in a trice, plunged a hand into the dank interior, and drew forth a leathery bundle that stank of mildew.

Inside, when he shook it out, was another pair of boots, a belt, a tunic, breeches, some rope, and a weathercloak. There was also a sack of something right at the bottom of the coffer, beside a scabbarded knife that was dark and sticky with something oily, and some arrows.

Florin drew out the sack, poured a handful of nuts onto a stone, and handed a smaller stone to the noblewoman. "Crush some of these and eat them."

She gave him a glare then nodded and set to work. Nuts bounced and flew under her clumsy attack, but Florin paid no heed. As a breeze rose and rustled through the trees around them, he shook and laid out the clothing.

Narantha had just managed to crack her first nut without reducing it to powder, and was chewing and finding it pleasant enough—her mouth flooding with a sudden rush of hunger—when the forester said, "Stand up, and face yon tree."

Wearily she rose, still chewing, and he drew her boots off. When she looked down at what he was bringing to her ankles, she started to protest—then threw her hands wide in exasperation, choked off whatever she'd been going to say, and cooperated as he drew the breeches up her legs. They were of stiff, stout hide, smelled a little of mildew, and gaped at the waist, twice the size of her own.

"Hold them up," Florin murmured, sliding rope through belt-loops. Plucking her nightrobe up out of the way, he ran the hemp rope up and around her neck.

"What're you—"

"Patience. Take off your robe."

"*Sirrah*, if you think I'm—"

"That's why you're facing that way, and I'm around here behind you. Take it off."

With a weary sigh, her shiverings nigh-constant now, the Lady Crownsilver obeyed. Florin swiftly drew the rope tight into a suspender harness, plucking the robe from her hands and winding it around the rough-haired hempen to pad it and keep it from sawing at her skin. Cutting off the excess rope, he put the tunic over her head and the weathercloak over her shoulders—more mildew—and gathered the cloak at her waist with the belt. Getting her to sit down, he put her boots back on and carefully repacked them, massaging her feet where they'd rubbed raw. Narantha was mortified to discover that they'd acquired a faint but lingering smell.

"There," Florin said, drawing her upright again. "That ought to—"

Narantha snatched her hand away. "Ought to, *nothing*. I look like a vagabond who's stolen a floursack and tied it around herself. I'm not wearing this!"

Florin shrugged and stripped weathercloak and tunic away with a flourish. Untying the rope, he tugged twice—and the breeches fell in a tangle around shapely Crownsilver calves.

Shivering in her cloak of goosebumps, Narantha shrieked and sank down hastily, more out of discomfort than out of modesty.

"Gods naeth, the *cold!*" she spat, her lips blue and trembling. The breeze quickened around her, almost mockingly.

Florin's firm hand took hold of her neck and raised her upright again—for all the world as if he were a farmer, and she his chicken, Narantha thought savagely—to swiftly reclothe her. Mutely furious, she didn't try to resist.

Smelling of mildew, hide hissing against hide with every step, the reclad fair flower of the Crownsilvers took a few tentative strides, a trifle warmer but no less miserable, sighed, and went looking for the nuts.

Florin was munching a handful of them, and holding a handful more—already shelled—out to her.

As she took them, the forester commanded, "On. Now. Eat as we walk. I don't want to be anywhere near here when the light begins to fail." He pointed at some fur caught in the bark of a nearby tree. "Bear," he said darkly.

Narantha shook her head and looked down at herself. "I look like—like—" Words failed her, and she bit her lip and turned her head away, shaking it.

"A beautiful woman," Florin replied, "whose beauty shines forth no matter what she's wearing."

When she looked at him disbelievingly, he winked.

"Oh, I hate you!" she snarled feelingly, giving him a glare.

Florin shrugged. " 'Tis one way to get through life. Though too much hating eats away a person, inside. You'd do better to turn all that . . . verve . . . to loving, aiding, and helping. Young bride-hunting lordlings'll be swarming all over you, swift enough, if you do."

Narantha snorted. *"Those* fops! Swaggering emptyheads, the lot of them! I doubt any of them can light a fire, or catch food, or—"

She stopped abruptly and looked away again, her face flaming. Florin carefully said not a word.

The spell flickered, fading noticeably—but not enough to obscure the scene its caster was intent upon.

A lone lady in a dark gown smilingly traded jests one last time with a overloud and rather tipsy Derovan Skatterhawk, then gracefully descended the wide flight of steps toward the long line of coaches gathered under the mansion lamps.

"Another *highly* successful feast, I see," the watcher murmured, toying with a favorite—and loose—unicorn-head ring.

The scrying-spell was wavering on the verge of collapse; only by the bright favor of the gods had it lasted this long, through all the wards and watchspells laid on Skatterhawk House by Laspeera and her enthusiastic underlings: the young, avid dregs of the Wizards of War.

The watching wizard hissed in anger, thinking of them—then shrugged, smiled, and waved the unicorn ring-adorned hand dismissively. "Ah, but set aside such harshness. I must never forget I was one myself, once."

The lady was handed into a coach. She waved airily to Derovan—who almost fell on his face on the steps, waving back as he leered through mustache and monacle—as her conveyance rumbled away.

"So Horaundoon of the Zhentarim is taking she-shape and courting randy elder nobles of Cormyr now, is he? Why, I wonder?"

'Twould be an elaborate scheme, unless Horaundoon had changed greatly in two summers . . .

"More importantly," the watching wizard mused aloud, as the spell collapsed into a cascade of winking sparks, "can he be convincingly blamed for what I'll do, when I strike at last?"

"Jhess? You're sure you want to try this?"

Jhessail gave Doust a withering look. "I didn't drag you all the way out here at this time of night to dare nothing. Douse the lantern."

Her friend frowned. "Why? 'Tis hooded well enough—"

"I don't want it interfering with my spell," she hissed, holding her cloak wide to form a shield over him.

Doust blew the lamp out quickly, without leaking overmuch light into the darkness around them. Backing carefully away from it on his knees to avoid toppling it, he turned, patted Jhessail's arm, and whispered, "Do it."

She nodded, handed him her cloak, and on hands and knees crept to the edge of the dell.

As she'd expected, it was flooded with moonlight—and, sure enough, two nightbeaks were down there, tugging and tearing at the huddled bony heap that had been one of Hlorn Estle's fattest sheep before it had stupidly strayed over the cliff.

Her lip curled back in disgust; the vultures of the Stonelands were cruel, rapacious things that hunted day and night. Doust had brought a cudgel, but she hoped it would not be needed. A nightbeak could easily kill a person, and they shed maggots and lice even more copiously than they voided.

Shuddering at the thought of fighting one fists to talons, Jhessail backed carefully away from the cliff edge—'twas a killing fall for her as surely as for a sheep—and found her feet again. Drawing a deep breath, she started to pick her way along the lip of the dell, Doust trailing her. She had to get to where she could see the nightbeaks, for the spell to work.

If she could make it work.

Here. This spot would do.

She could see them picking at the carcass. Big and dusty black, their heads like fire-scorched helms, their beaks like . . . like . . .

She shuddered again, and shut her eyes to banish such thoughts. Breathing deeply, she tried to settle her mind on the image of blue fire roiling vigorously in darkness.

My first big spell. My first battle spell, that deals harm to others. Blue fire, seething and leaping . . .

If I can't cast this, I am no spell-worker.

By Lady Mystra and Lord Azuth, the working was simple enough. So if this Art was beyond her, then all Art was.

She swept that thought away, seeing blue fire in her mind and plunging into it.

When she had its image bright and strong in her mind, she opened her eyes again to give Doust a quick smile and nod. He stepped carefully back, getting well away from her.

Jhessail looked up at the stars, brought the blue fire foremost in her mind, and when she was gazing at it and feeling a part of it, she looked quickly down into the dell, glared at a nightbeak, flicked her fingers in a swift circle, and with that hand pointed at the vulture.

Blue fire trembling inside her, she snapped, "Ala*vaer!*"

Unleashed, something wonderful raced along her arm, coiling and surging arrow-swift, thrilling her though it left emptiness behind. It burst forth from her pointing finger as a deep blue bolt that streaked down into the darkness with the faintest of whispers.

One nightbeak looked up at the sudden flare of light. *Approaching* light, streaking—

Alarmed, it tried to flap its wings to leap into the air—

And died before it could even unfurl them, snatched off its talons and blasted, fire that wasn't fire scorching through it, to bounce and flop among the cliff-bottom weeds and stones in loose-necked silence. Dead silence.

The other nightbeak looked up and squawked questioningly, expecting an answer that would never come.

"*Yes!*" Jhessail cried exultantly, shaking her fists in the air. "I *did* it!"

The sound of her cry sent the surviving nightbeak into the air, flapping heavily out of the dell in search of quieter meals.

Laughing, the delighted Silvertree lass raced to Doust and embraced him, whirling him around and around in the night shadows.

"I believe," he observed with a grin, "it's considered bad form to sound surprised that your spell worked. Wherefore: of *course* you did it. Well done!"

Ecstatic and drenched with sweat, Jhessail hugged him, relieved and delighted laughter bubbling over him in a flood. Nose buried in her bosom, Doust managed to say gruffly, "Careful, now. You'll start giving me unholy ideas."

"Hah," she laughed, clutching him even tighter, "and you'd dare to do something about them, when I can blast you with magic? Hey?"

"A compelling point," he said to her stomach, as her wild mirth made him slide downward, his voice muffled by warm and smooth Jhessail.

An instant later, his chin struck her knee, which was *very* hard, bouncing him back up to behold the stars for a crazed and whirling moment—before his chin met the stony ground, which proved even harder.

"Oww," he said. "Aye, most compelling."

"What was that?" Narantha hissed, as the strange hooting call came again.

"Owl," Florin said, his voice just a murmur above a whisper. "Successful in its hunting."

The noblewoman rolled onto her side to look up from the rough pillow of his pack. The forester—*her* forester—was sitting just as before, back to a tree and drawn sword across knees, staring into the night. Stars glimmered over his shoulder.

"Are you going to sit there all night?"

"Yes."

She waited for him to say more. Waited for breath after breath, until the chirping night insects started up again. Then she sighed in exasperation. "But when will you sleep?"

"On the morrow."

"But you said we're going to walk through the forest all day. So when?"

"I'll find plenty of time to slumber," he replied, "while you're talking."

"What?" she sputtered, nettled.

"You talked more than half the sunlit day just past," the forester observed serenely. "Don't you ever get tired of talking?"

"You," she hissed back at him, "are *impossible! Such* rudeness!"

"The curse of our generation, I'm told," Florin told the night. "Wherefore Cormyr sinks sadly from what it was in the golden days of our grandsires."

His mimicry of a gruff old whitebeard sounded so like her uncle Lorneth that Narantha found herself giggling. The giggle built inside her, into something that burst out and had to be muffled by biting her knuckles and rolling over to put her face into the ill-smelling pack.

Above the shaking bundle that was Narantha wrapped in her weathercloak, Florin smiled up at the stars.

"Father, I—"

"Not a word, Torsard," Lord Elvarr Spurbright said quickly, in the tone of voice that meant he would brook no defiance. "Not a *word.*"

He held up an admonishing finger, and his son was astonished enough to blink at it mutely for the few moments Lord Elvarr needed.

Plucking up the great polished wooden ball that crowned one of the low footposts of his bed, the head of House Spurbright plucked a fine chain out of a hidden recess in the post that the root-peg of the ball had been sitting in, like a giant tooth, and dropped the ball back into place.

Torsard's mouth fell open. His eyes bulged in fresh astonishment as his father undid a fine silver clasp at one end of the chain and reached out to snap it around Torsard's wrist. Closing the clasp at the chain's other end around his own wrist, Lord Elvarr nodded toward the balcony.

Mutely Torsard trotted after him. It was not until they were out on the balcony, with the great bedchamber doors closed behind them and the night breeze ghosting past under the moonlight, that Lord Elvarr spoke again.

"Yes, the chain is magic. And it cost me more than our tallhouse in Suzail, so don't pull away from me suddenly and go breaking it. It cloaks our speech from everyone. Your mother could step between us right now and we could put our mouths to both her ears and talk—and she'd not hear our words, only squawks and gruntings. Nor could a war wizard, with all his spells. This is a family secret, mind: not even Thaelder knows of it. Keep things that way."

He walked to the stone rail, Torsard following. Together they gazed out and down at the night. Rolling wooded hills and verdant pastures stretched north into the night and the not-so-distant mountains, under a sky glittering with stars. Below the balcony, on the lawns and in the orchard garden, there were no signs of anyone still up and about. "Now, you wanted to ask me something?"

"Yes, Lord Father. Ah . . . at the Fallingmoon feast I heard Lord Delzuld talking with some of the older lords—Gallusk and Illance among them—about the king. He said the Obarskyrs are corrupt and it was high time we were free of them, and that they had no stronger claim to the Dragon Throne than any of us! Is this true? Why does he hate the Obarskyrs so? And why were so many lords agreeing with him?"

"Steady, son, steady. Ask, receive answer, then ask again, not this flood of why, why, and why! As to the first: Lord Delzuld—'twas Lord Creion, aye? Head of his house? I thought as much—says many things. Most aren't true, but he believes that if he says them oft and loud enough, those who listen will begin to think they are true. For so it has worked before, on many folk in diverse lands. Truth is a surprisingly mutable thing."

Lord Spurbright smiled wryly. "As to the second: the Delzulds are the wealthiest nobles in Arabel, and would swiftly become far richer if they paid no taxes to the Dragon Throne, and could crush trade rivals without the annoying hindrance of Crown law. More that that: most folk of Arabel—commoners as well as proud houses—would fain be free of Cormyr if they could. They were once a free city, and hunger to be so again; that will never change, in either of our lifetimes."

Lord Spurbright turned to face his son directly. "As to why

he's gaining so much support: very few nobles are pleased with His Majesty at the moment. Nor have they been since the mage Vangerdahast rose from being just court wizard to also being royal magician, head of the war wizards and—in all but name—the real ruler of Cormyr."

"Vangerdahast. They hate him, I know," Torsard Spurbright said. "But why? Just fear of his spells?"

"That, and his use of the war wizards as his spies. More than one who's spoken out against him—remember Lord Lorneth Crownsilver?—has vanished, probably permanently silenced by our beloved royal magician. It should come as no surprise to you that we hate anyone and anything that seeks to curtail our powers—just as farmers hate tax collectors, and outlaws hate Purple Dragons. Well, King Azoun and his Royal Magician Vangerdahast have steadily been making new laws, these last few years, that increasingly restrict the power of all nobles to do as they please with those who dwell on their lands. Dissatisfaction with Azoun's rule is widespread, and growing."

"So why don't we all act together?"

"Lad, have you ever known more than three nobles to agree on anything?"

"Yes: that the king's rule is bad! So the Obarskyrs are few, and I've heard the war wizards really serve Vangerdahast, not the king—"

"Correct."

"—so if enough of us make common cause, and call on our house wizards . . ."

"To do what? Blast the palace in Suzail to smoking rubble? Torch cows in the fields? Melt the banners of Purple Dragons as they come riding to arrest us? Talk sense, boy!"

Nettled, Torsard Spurbright slapped the balcony rail, stared away into the night, and said petulantly, "Well, I *don't* see why we don't just use the spells of our house wizard to get what we want! I've seen Thaelder—"

Lord Elvarr rolled exasperated eyes. "Know you *nothing* but hunting and hawking, Torsard? Every titled family in Cormyr has a house wizard—and every last spellhurler of that sort in all the realm is a war wizard, or has their minds reamed by the war wizards nightly. House wizards are here to keep *us* in line, and report back all talk of treason, and everything else interesting we do, to old Vangerdahast. Remember that, if you'd like to keep your head a while longer." He raised his hand and rattled the fine chain meaningfully. Its magic glowed obligingly.

"So we can do *nothing* to stop the Obarskyrs? And old Thunderhast? While they do just as they please to us?"

"Gently, son, gently. I did *not* say that."

"Well, then?"

"Well, then, you'll learn in good time. News will spread at revels and in marketplaces and taverns—news that comes as great astonishment to all of us, who know nothing and had no part in what befell."

"No part in it all? We're *noble!*"

"Precisely. And the essence of being noble is getting what you want without seeming to take any direct action to get it. Leaving your reputation unstained and your hands clean. Remember *that*, if you remember nothing else."

Florin smiled.

Yon hillside was familiar; they were right where he'd planned to be. They'd already passed Espar well to the west, and must now circle back north and east to strike the road at Hunter's Hollow where he'd agreed to meet Delbossan. It was time to slow their pace, so they'd not reach the road until that third day.

Behind him, trudging up to join him, Narantha groaned. Florin turned, lifting an eyebrow in silent question.

"My feet hurt!" Narantha hissed. "These stlarning boots!"

Florin nodded. "You can do them off now; we'll halt here awhile. 'Tis past time we bathed."

The Lady Crownsilver lifted her head to give him a startled glare. "Bathe? *Where?*"

Florin pointed at the stream. Just here, the waters of the Dathyl looked placid—and green, as they slid lazily over scum-covered rocks. Narantha regarded the water with disgust, and rather predictably hissed, "I'm not getting myself wet in that!"

Florin turned and pointed through the trees in another direction, to where a swarm of tiny insects danced above a muddy patch of leaves. "There's the alternative."

The Lady Narantha Crownsilver drew herself up and said in her most frigidly haughty manner: "Falconhand, if you think I'm bathing here at all . . ."

"We'll both be washing," Florin said flatly. "One at a time, while the other stands beastwatch. We both stink enough that beasts can readily scent us, now, from a good distance away. Your long hair and reluctance to get wet have left you smelling a lot worse than I do, and if we wait much longer, so much of our reek will be in our clothes that we'll attract beasts—and stingflies—just as readily as if we blew war horns with our every step."

"I *stink?*"

"Yes."

"I see," Narantha said icily. "And just how do you expect me to wash in . . . that?"

"Take off your clothes, sit down there—there's a sandbar under the water, see?—to scoop up sand, and scrub yourself with it. Stings a bit, but you'll be done soon enough, and I'll crush some ardanthe sap into your hair. It has a nice smell."

"And how will I dry myself?"

Florin pointed up at the sun then through the trees at a large boulder. "Lie down on that and bake until you're dry enough to get dressed."

"While you leer and look. And you seriously expect me to do that?"

"I hold no expectations, Lady, but I've been given to understand that many nobles of our realm are from time to time sensible. I'm hoping you're one of them."

Eyes flaming, Narantha clenched her fists and stepped up nose to nose with him—she had to look up to do it, which made her even more furious, and she was already seething. "Do you know who I am, knave? Do you know who I *am?*"

Florin's blue-gray eyes bored into hers. "Lady, increasingly I am learning what you are: a bone-idle, arrogant, spoiled chit of a girl. You seem to spend most of your labor in tirades and cursings, berating me because you find fault with my service—the service I tender out of kindness and my duty to the realm, not out of any obligation to you, or coin-hire. There's an expression about 'only a leucrotta being crazed enough to bite the hand that feeds it.' Well, Lady, you're a leucrotta."

"How *dare* you speak to me so! Why, if it weren't for the nobility—nobles like me—Cormyr would be all backcountry louts starving and grubbing in the dirt, bedding their sisters and mothers and having no law but that of the fist, and no tongue but gruntings! How dare you!?"

"Someone should have dared, long ago, and done so as often as it took to break you of this serenely *wrong* view of the ways of the world. Hear this, Narantha, and hear it well: Faerûn is *not* going to change to your will. Either you must change to dwell in it, or it will break you."

Florin slid his pack off his shoulder and added, "You've been doing this for so long that your tirades are almost a habit: the way you always deal with anything that displeases you. Count yourself favored of Tymora that I'm not the backcountry lout you see all of us common folk as—or I'd have silenced you forever with the back of my hand, or at least until you woke up with your head still ringing, and started crawling around looking for your lost teeth. We *are* schooled and taught courtesies, we commoners, and one of them is never to hit a woman—for women are the nurturers who keep families strong and therefore the realm strong. However, just now, my schooling is on the very sword-edge of slipping."

Falling abruptly silent, Florin whirled around and stalked away to the stream, tearing off his clothes as he went.

Leaving Narantha staring at his back, open-mouthed.

His *bare* back. She blinked.

She closed her mouth, firmly, and turned her head away. How dare he speak thus! Why did he refuse to know his place, and keep to it? Why—

She looked toward the stream, and hastily turned away again. Gods, he *was* using sand.

She shuddered, tramped to the high boulder, and started watching for beasts. Ones that weren't wet and hairy, and cheerfully sporting right over there in the stream.

Chapter 7
TO LOVE CORMYR

Far from being a traitor, I do love Cormyr. Deeply. Which is why I intend to raise an army and go back to the fair Forest Kingdom, slaughter every last Obarskyr, war wizard, king's lord, and Purple Dragon in it, and claim every stride of its soil as my own.

Sorn Merendil
The Obarskyrs Must Die (pamphlet)
published in the Year of Moonfall

Ready?"

Jhessail nodded, and Islif brought the cudgel forward from her shoulder in a hard, fast throw that sent it end-over-end across the meadow, to crash down into the midst of the tangle of briars.

As expected, a rabbit shot forth, racing like the wind. Jhessail murmured, pointed, and a vivid blue bolt of magic lashed out, racing arrow-swift—

The rabbit changed direction, very swiftly. In a few moments it would zag again, then stop to—

Just as sharply, the magic missile turned in the air to follow its racing quarry—and lanced home.

The bunny turned a cartwheel in the air and thudded back to earth, where it lay still.

"Rose of Moander!" Islif gasped, growing a broad grin. "You did it!"

Jhessail's answering cry was lost in a sudden chorus of barks and bays. Over the shoulder of the meadow came an all-too-familiar torrent of teeth and loping legs and burr-bedecked, flea-ridden coats. Hearing their voices, though they weren't on Estle land, Belkur Estle had loosed his dogs.

Islif growled her annoyance and ran for her cudgel.

Jhessail took an uncertain step back—then stepped forward again, looking determined. She had but the one missile, but if she could down Old One-Eye, their leader, the others might well draw off in confusion.

Or so she hoped.

Islif waded into briars, cursing, but turned as One-Eye's rising growl of menace suddenly turned into a yelp—and just as suddenly fell silent, as if cut off by a knife.

Or a spell.

The lead dog of Estle's pack, it seemed, would never be a belligerent terror in the Esparran fields again.

The others were barking furiously at Jhessail—but they were doing so stiff-legged, leaping back and forth in a line of not-daring that confronted her, their headlong charge broken.

Islif laid hands on her cudgel and burst out of the briars in a roaring charge of her own.

To the dogs, she was a familiar foe, and they had bruises and stiff-nesses of broken ribs a-plenty to remind them of her prowess. Their barkings rose higher and more fearful, marking their hasty retreat.

"Well done!" Doust called in cheerful greeting, as he and Semoor came out of Rorth Urtree's woodlot together.

"Ah, the two holy men. Arriving just too late to be useful, as usual," Islif replied. "Saw you the spells?"

"Of course. We're foolish, not blind. Shall we start a fire to cook the bunny, or did Jhess's spell cook it for us?"

Islif reached for her belt knife. "We'll have to find out. Yet, look you, we can be true adventurers now: We have our wizard!"

"True adventurers," Jhessail echoed thoughtfully as they gathered around her. "I wonder where Florin is?"

"Mother Mielikki, that feels better!" Florin said, stretching. Water pattered on leaves as he clambered onto the boulder. His rippling muscles were magnificent, and he gave Narantha a bright smile as he joined her.

She broke off staring at him and looked away quickly, blushing.

"Your turn," he announced, and when she looked up at him

again, she discovered he'd assumed a hero's pose: exact mimicry of the balled fists and sternly lifted chin of the famous statue of King Dhalmass Surveying The Realm. Oh, yes, there was supposed to be a copy of it on Espar's village green, wasn't there?

The effect was hilarious, and she had to bite her lip to keep from giggling. Florin moved one eye sidelong to give her a wink, and she looked away again, knowing he could see her suppressing her mirth.

When she looked back at him this time, their gazes met, and she blushed a deep scarlet, but kept her eyes on his and asked curiously, "That scar on your hand; how came you by it?"

"Dragon breath. Back when I was young, I was foolish—rather than the wise elder of the realm I am now. A caravan merchant had a pet red dragon he was taking to sell in Sembia, where the *real* fools live. It was about the size of a large dog—a wolfhound—and I made the mistake of trying to pet it."

"*What?*"

"You're terribly fond of that word. What merchant? What dragon? What happened next? Or d'you mean 'I can't believe you'?"

Narantha stared at him. "I . . . I guess I really mean 'I don't believe it.' No one—no one's ever talked to me as you do."

Florin dropped his pose and stood casually facing her. "And are you going to have me horsewhipped for it, when we reach Espar?"

"No." She looked at the ground, and said almost petulantly, "You must think I'm some sort of dragon. I—" Almost reluctantly, she looked up again. "No, of cour—no, I'm not."

"Well, that's a relief. Your turn in the Dathyl; 'tis not exactly warm, but it'll be colder later on."

Narantha looked at the forester thoughtfully, as if judging him, then blurted out, "Don't stop doing it. Even when I scream at you. Please. You're like the older brother I've never had."

Florin smiled. "Have my thanks, Narantha. Those words are . . . nice to hear." He reached out to pat her shoulder, and said not a word when she flinched away from him.

Swallowing, she deliberately stepped forward again to meet his hand.

"So," Florin asked lightly, unhooking the catch of her weather-cloak, "will you let your older brother help wash your hair?"

Horaundoon frowned over his scrying orb. The hargaunt belled questioningly.

Without taking his eyes off the glowing orb, the Zhentarim replied, "Echoes. I've never felt *echoes* before. I wonder . . ."

He stroked his chin thoughtfully. "They could just be wards, or detection spells responding to my magic . . . or they could be something more dangerous."

Horaundoon went on staring into the orb. The hargaunt trilled and chimed again, but he made no reply.

"He knows," Horaundoon said suddenly, one of his hands closing into a fist. "The elf *knows* my magic is drifting into his mantle. He keeps looking over . . . ah, *there* it is. A scepter of some sort, probably his strongest battle-magic. Yet he casts nothing, makes no adjustments to his mantle at all. Restless, though, as if he wants to. Yes, he's itching to. So why the echoes, if he's not—?"

His eyes narrowed, and he scratched at his jaw as if at an agonizing itch. "Once my spell conquers the focal gem and the spellstealing begins, the link back to me is strong. Yet if I hold back from the gem, and trace all spells linked to *it*, I should be able to see if our elf mage has some waiting friends."

Horaundoon closed his eyes and let his hands fall to his sides, concentrating hard. "Yes," he whispered, after a long moment. "Yes, there's a second link . . . and a third. Tracing spells. Nigh a dozen."

He opened his eyes as he ended his spell, letting it collapse and take the distant elf away from him. "And other mages at the end of every one of them! A band of wizards waiting to spring their trap on the mysterious Eater-of-Mantles. Not a mantle among them, but I daresay they'll have minds brimming with murderous spells and eagerness to use them."

The hargaunt spoke, and the Zhentarim smiled a wolflike smile. "Not ended, just halted for a time, until I can craft a spell to plunder mages' minds when they're *not* wearing a mantle. In the meantime, I can attend more revels and learn about a few more magical baubles in the collections of old and foolheaded Cormyrean nobles. While their house wizards probe at me in vain, finding minor cosmetic spells but not the shapeshifting magics they're expecting. Thanks to *you*."

He grinned at the hargaunt almost fondly, and its chiming reply was intricate and enthusiastic.

The Lady Narantha Crownsilver came out into the glade and stopped in wonder. Florin strode on in his nigh-soundless way, but seemed to sense she wasn't right behind him. He whirled around, saw that nothing menaced her, and came back to join her, moving as quietly as ever.

Narantha no longer felt sticky and dirty, and for the first time her boots felt familiar and almost painless. The sun was bright and warm, birds were calling in the trees around, and looking down the length of the glade she could see the land ahead rising in a great shoulder of pines and duskwoods, to a rocky ridge. Beyond, purple in the distance, great mountains rose like so many eternal fangs against the cloudless blue sky: the Storm Horns . . . and somewhere at their forefront, probably hidden behind the nearby ridge, rose the bright fang that was the great castle of High Horn.

Narantha looked long at the scene before her, breathing deeply of the clear air. The merest ghost of a breeze was bringing her the sharp scent of bruised needles, and just a hint of unseen, distant woodsmoke. She had never really looked at a sky before, or wild and magnificent Cormyr laid out in a vista before her. The green glory of trees and rolling hills. . . .

Narantha pursed her lips and shook her head. She had gazed, but she had never really *see* before. So much time wasted, so many petty nothings and empty fripperies crowding her life.

Florin was standing beside her, looking down at her. She looked up at him, not knowing how to say what was in her mind.

He caught hold of her hand with his own, and squeezed. "Memories are treasures," he murmured. "Lock the best of them in your mind forever, the most splendid moments, and throw away the rest. Any day when you gain such a treasure is a day well-spent."

She nodded, her throat tight on the edge of tears, and they walked on in silence together, still holding hands.

Jalander swallowed. Vangerdahast was looming over him, having appeared as unexpectedly and disconcertingly as always. He could not avoid that commanding gaze; bristling eyebrows lifted in a silent question, the eyes beneath them hard and keen.

Jalander was not a junior war wizard, and so could—just—control his awe and fear at such close attention from the Royal Magician of Cormyr. " 'Tis these new ward-spells you've had us working at. They work well enough when cast on Jester's Green or a back pasture somewhere, even when guarding someone who's moving. But they keep collapsing—and going wild, too, in little outbursts here and there—whenever we cast them anywhere near the palace. Even up at High Horn we had problems. Too many other magics—"

"Indeed," Vangerdahast said. "Wards upon wards, old enchantments underlying those we know about, some slumbrous and many awakening without warning. They all interfere with each other. I feared as much. So the gaps in our armor must remain."

Jalander Mallowglar dared much, then. He dared to sit back in his chair and observe, "I thought you'd be more upset than—than you seem to be."

"Lad, if I let Cormyr see how upset I am most of the time, they'd lock me up as a madman. If I showed all Cormyr *why* I'm upset, they'd flee the realm so hard and fast, screaming their terror to the skies, that most of them would probably drown in the Dragonmere before they noticed they'd run right off the ends of our piers!"

There was a sudden shriek from the deep words to their left, and Narantha tensed, wide-eyed. "What's that?"

The shriek rose wildly and broke off suddenly, leaving an ominous silence. Florin strode on.

"Aren't—aren't you going to go see?" Narantha asked, aghast. "That was a woman, frightened and in pain! Something just *happened* to her! Don't foresters care—"

Florin spun around, looking grave. "That was a wolf, not a woman—and it was dying. Under the claws and jaws of something large enough to kill a wolf at a pounce, without much of a fight."

He shrugged, and added a little sadly, "Whenever you hear that sort of noise, 'tis too late to do anything."

Narantha stared at him, her face white, and Florin added, " 'Tis the way of things. The forest is fair to gaze upon—but cruel."

"Gods," she said, her voice almost a sob ere she steadied it. "Even here. I thought—I thought . . ."

"You thought that out here, because 'tis beautiful and you've lost your first fears of it, that things are, ah, gentler than the games of verbal and social dagger-hurling nobles play at?" Florin's voice was soft. "Ah, now, that *would* be a world. . . ."

He drew his sword again, and reached out his free hand to take hers.

"Come, Narantha. The light will fail soon, and we must find a good place to camp—or yon wolf's fate may yet be ours."

Narantha shivered. "I . . . Florin, I've been horrible to you."

And I far more so to you, Lady, did you but know it, Florin thought, guilt jabbing at him through his relief that playacting at being both square-jawed hero and veteran forester was largely done. *Oh, you'd* never *forgive me, if only you knew. I wonder how long it will be, before I dare to tell you I chased you out here just for sport?*

"No," he said soothingly, "you were just being . . . what you thought nobles should behave like. And you may have done so very properly; you're the first noble I've ever met."

Narantha shook her head, smiling ruefully. "No, we don't all have my temper. If we did, there'd be very few nobles left in the realm now. Just a lot of crypts full of nobles who killed each other."

"Oh?" Florin gave her an innocent look, but arched a by-now-familiar eyebrow. "I thought there *were* lots of crypts full of—"

She dealt his arm a friendly blow, her smile going wry, and said, *"Please* don't make this harder for me. I—I'm not good at apologies; I've had little practice." She drew in a deep breath, and pulled Florin to a halt, to look up at him squarely.

"And . . . and I find I very much want to apologize to you."

He looked down at her in grave silence, and she added in a rush, "I'm sure my tongue will get the better of me again, but I see you as a friend now, not a servant—and I want to have you as a friend."

Florin started to smile, and Narantha swallowed again and asked, "Please? May I?"

"If you'll trust me," he told her, raising her hand in his grasp to his lips, "I'll trust you—and if we do that, we'll be better friends than many who hail, jest, and gossip together."

Narantha blinked, then whispered slowly, "I have never trusted anyone, in all my life."

It was Florin's turn to blink. "Gods above and below," he murmured. "No wonder all nobles are mad."

He put his arms around her, and Narantha hugged him tight. A few breaths later, Florin realized the noble lass in his arms was crying against his chest. He stroked her hair and rocked her in his arms, looking warily about at the darkening forest.

Overhead, in the reddening sky, the stars began to come out.

Tathanter Doarmond happened to be one of the most handsome Wizards of War in all the realm, blessed by the gods with an impressive, mellifluous voice. It was for that reason that, despite his junior standing and comparatively paltry mastery of the Art, he was often called upon to speak for the war wizards when old Thunderspells wanted a courtier impressed—or a citizen scared right down to the soles of his boots.

Just now, he was busily frowning his best "I fear you're in serious trouble" frown as he stared again at the two letters lying on his desk.

They contradicted each other so flatly that even a child would have been forced to conclude that one of these two merchants was lying.

Yet was this a matter for the Wizards of War, or merely a trader—perhaps both—saving himself a few coins in taxes? Not that even a single deception should pass unchallenged in the Forest Kingdom, but among merchants there were so many thousands upon thousands of them that no mage could hope to catch every last one. Moreover, Tathanter had been instructed to consult War Wizard Ghoruld Applethorn whenever he found himself uncertain . . . and Tathanter was more than a little afraid of coldly smiling, dagger-eyed Applethorn, master of wards and crystals. Perhaps—

His office door squealed open and his closest friend and fellow war wizard Malvert burst in, bending close to his ear to hiss, "Tath! Remember you Garrlatus? And Sonthur, the one who was blasted to bits in his first tenday as a war wizard? Well, old Thunderspells thinks he knows what they were killed with now!"

"Oh? Killed by whom?"

"That he doesn't know—or if he does, isn't saying. Garrlatus and Sonthur were both spell-blasted when seemingly alone in warded chambers, studying their spells. Apparently whatever felled them was the same thing. Well, Thunderspells got to thinking what it might have been, and remembered the Arcrown did that sort of slaying. He thought he'd better try its powers to make sure, went to get it, and sure enough: the Arcrown's been stolen!"

"The Iron War Crown? From the vaults?"

"The vaults. They say Vangey's frothing, for to get it out of there without triggering all of his personal warning-wards, the thief must be one of the Obarskyrs—or one of *us.*"

Tathanter whistled. "Oh, *that's* going to be sweet! Tantrums of Mystra, if he's going to be mind-reaming every last one of us, the kingdom'll go to the rutting dogs!"

"Pretty much," Malvert agreed bitterly. "I caught just a touch—a stray edge—of one of his mind-probes once, that time he came after Talarla to find out who she'd been sneaking out at night to kiss and cuddle—remember?—and I thought I was going mad. My head hurt for *days,* and every few paces I took, memories kept tumbling out of nowhere and flooding my eyes. All I could see was them, not what was really around me. Couldn't sleep, kept seeing Vangerdahast smiling, skeletons tumbling out of shadows or reaching for me, their grinning skulls always looking like Vangerdahast . . ."

"Mal! *Enough!* Say his name that often and you'll have him down here reaming us for real!"

Malvert nodded quickly. "Sorry. Shouldn't have . . . you really have no idea how horrible it was. I only have to think of it . . . Now, after all this time . . ." He clawed the air in a great sweeping away of something unseen, and added briskly, "So, would your wagered coins be on one of us, a bored Obarskyr playing at pranks or a parlor cult for nobles . . . or a sinister Obarskyr?"

"One of us, I'm afraid—though any of your royal alternatives sound far more entertaining."

"Huh. No disagreement here. Remember the last scandal? Queen Fee's mysterious stalker?"

Tathanter chuckled. "Aye, and I remember who it was, too. Alusair the toddler, spying on Mummy to learn how to be a queen! How humiliating for our Imperious Leader! I thought he was going to vomit up a litter of kittens on the spot, all down his royal magicianly robes!"

"Well, Vangey evidently remembers that too. For now, he's not mindbursting all of us, but setting us all to hunt for the Arcrown. He seems to think it may have found its way to Arabel, so accordingly, I bring you your bright new orders."

"The Dragon you do! What about our morrow-night card game?"

"If we're lucky, we'll be playing it with the Acting Captain of the Watch of Arabel, a—"

"A *watch* officer? They've got us working with guilty-if-I-don't-like-you watch stoneheads now?"

"Well, he's really a Purple Dragon ranker: the king gave secret orders a few years back, it seems, that thanks to the everlastingly rebellious tendencies in Arabel, all watch officers in that fair city be Purple Dragons, and so right under his thumb—"

"Huh. And we know which cunning royal magician was behind *that,* don't we?"

"Aye, I doubt not. But Vangey's cunning hand or not, this acting captain's hight Taltar Dahauntul, and I'm told he—"

"Ah, yes, the stalwart Dauntless!"

"Hey?"

" 'Dauntless,' everyone calls him. He seems to like it, and uses it himself now, too. Duke Bhereu once called him that: 'dauntless in pursuit' or some such thing, and the name stuck. *He's* all right. A little grim and 'it be against my sworn duty to laugh at anything,' but then they all are. Old Thunderspell's orders say anything about what wands and such we're supposed to take?"

"No," the inkwell under Tathanter's nose said with some asperity, in a voice that made both war wizards freeze into instant gape-mouthed silence, their faces going pale, "but I'm on my way down to you two mirthful gossipers, to rectify that. Remain right where you are, though if you feel the need to wet yourselves, the potted plant by the window is quite dead; you can use its pot. Oh, and Doarmond: both merchants penned untruths into their little missives to you, but Harmantle is the one who should see a dungeon cell before the night is over. I'll see to that. Both of you are going to be rather busy."

"Sometimes it seems as if I've been walking in the forest with you forever," Narantha mused, "yet it's been just a few days. And this is our last? I don't want it to end, now."

"I'm afraid this must be our last," Florin said. "Delbossan will be mad with worry—he's probably been searching day and night since he lost you, and must be raving and reeling by now for lack of sleep. If he's dared to tell Lord Hezom, there'll be scores of men out searching for you, and if he hasn't, Hezom will probably have sent riders south to see what's delayed Delbossan. And if any war wizard has got wind of what's befallen, your parents will know by now, and they'll be tearing the Royal Court apart chamber by chamber getting

Purple Dragons out of their barracks and onto horses and up here at fast gallop!"

Narantha made a face. "I don't *want* Lord Hezom's teachings. I want . . . oh, I don't *know* what I want. I—"

Florin whirled and put two fingers over her mouth. "Be silent," he whispered, and cocked his head to listen.

"Wha—" Narantha shut herself up and strained to hear whatever Florin was so intent on hearing. They were in deep forest, carpeted in dead leaves and great green ferns, with the huge trunks of shadowtops and duskwoods soaring up all around them like dark columns. There were ridges ahead, and beyond them the forest seemed lighter, as if more sun reached down through the trees there.

There came a very faint clink of metal on metal, and Florin turned to Narantha with a fierce warning to keep utterly silent blazing in his eyes. Then there came a slightly louder, lower rattling and whirring noise. Florin sank down to his knees, drawing the noble lass with him.

"Hear that?" he whispered into her ear, his breath as warm as a candle flame. "That's a windlass: a crossbow is being winched ready to fire. No forester around here uses crossbows, nor do Purple Dragons."

"Outlaws?"

Florin nodded grimly. "Most likely. Yon sunlight ahead is Hunter's Hollow, where the Way of the Dragon runs through the forest, 'twixt Espar and Tyrluk. Well suited for an ambush." He wagged a stern finger in her face. "Stay here and keep quiet. *No* screaming, unless someone or something is rearing over you, about to take your life."

"You'll leave me undefended?"

Florin slapped a dagger into Narantha's palm, his eyes as iron-hard as its steel, and said grimly, "I must. *This* is what it means to love Cormyr. Above all else, serving the realm before oneself . . ."

And with that fierce whisper trailing behind him, Florin crawled ahead, swift and nigh-soundless on his hands and knees. Trotting, then slinking, then trotting again. Just like the panthers Lord Huntsilver liked to loose in his gardens, to keep thieves away from his revels—and to keep his guests inside his mansion, rather than slinking out into the night to tryst and make shady trade deals, or depart early with some of his more handsome candlesticks and painted cameos. Narantha stared open-mouthed at Florin; he seemed, right now, more beast than man.

She watched him rise up like a vengeful shadow on her side of a tree, just this side of the first ridge, and peer cautiously around it in the lee of a low, leaf-laden branch. At that moment there was a sharp snap, then another. A horse screamed. There were shouts of angry alarm, the ring of swords being drawn in scabbard-nicking haste—and Florin took off around the tree like an arrow, sword in one hand and dagger in the other, all stealth abandoned.

Narantha stared at where he'd vanished, over the lip of the ridge, then hefted the dagger he'd put into her hand, set her mouth in a determined line—and hurried after him.

Chapter 8
BLOOD AND GLORY

Glory always has a price, and that cost is almost always paid in copiously spilled blood.

Harbunk Jhelliko
One Halfling's Wisdom
published in the Year of the Wanderer

Narantha ran hard. *Outlaws.* Gods above, she and Florin might both be dead a few breaths from now!

"Mother," she gasped aloud, "Father . . . forgive me for all the upsets I've caused you, all the disappointments I've occasioned, all—"

A stone turned under her foot, she slipped wildly, and her chin glanced off her knee, cutting short her speech and coming within a painful instant of biting off her own tongue. She winced, spat blood, and ran on, saying no more.

A thunderous rumbling—a coach or wagon, moving in dangerous haste—rose ahead, moving to the left and dying away into distance, only to end in a thunderous crash, and more screams, this time of horses in pain.

Panting, Narantha reached the crest of the ridge in time to see Florin, almost at the lip of the second and last ridge before the sunlight, fling himself flat on his face to avoid eating a war-quarrel.

Almost before the bolt passed over him to hum harmlessly off into the trees, he was up again in a sprinting charge, the crossbowman cursing and snatching out the longest dagger Narantha had ever seen—a knife as long as her own forearm. Two other crossbowmen in dark and tattered leathers were clustered at the ridge-lip with the one who'd just fired. The tallest was grimly advancing on Florin with one of those overlong daggers in each hand and his crossbow lying in the leaves behind him, and the last was working his windlass like a madman, glancing betimes over his shoulder at Florin but keeping most of his attention on the unseen road beyond.

Unseen crossbows snapped, farther away—probably across the hollow—and there were more shouts.

Narantha started to sprint in earnest, sobbing for breath, as the forester reached the three outlaws. His sword rang off the long knife of the one who'd fired at him, driving the man back on his heels—and Florin sprang aside from him to confront the man with two fangs, leaping high.

The man stabbed with one, raising the other as a guard—but gutted only air as Florin came down into a froglike crouch and launched himself like a hurled hammer at the man's ankles.

The outlaw toppled helplessly face-first into the leaves, burying one of his blades almost hilt-deep in forest loam. On the far side of him Florin rolled over and up and slashed at the third man, taking him in the back of the neck as he was still crouched over his bow.

The bowman fell sideways, head jerking loosely as blood spurted, but Florin had no time to even look at what his blade had done; he was whirling to slash the outlaw he'd toppled, moving almost as frantically as that man rolled and twisted around to face him.

One-Knife was hurrying around his fallen comrade to get at Florin. Running hard, Narantha shrieked, "In the name of the *king!*"

Her cry brought One-Knife's head snapping around to look at her, as Florin slashed the downed outlaw across the chest. His sword skirled across unseen armor there, and its owner hacked viciously at Florin's swordarm with his remaining knife. Florin let go his sword to avoid losing his arm at the elbow—and crashed down on that knife arm with both knees, driving his own dagger into the man's throat.

Narantha threw her dagger at One-Knife's face. It whipped past his cheek harmlessly, but kept him staring at her long enough to give Florin time to roll aside and out of reach.

Giving Narantha a sneer, the last outlaw turned and raced after the forester, stumbling across the bodies of his comrades as Florin wisely gave up trying to scoop up his sword and kept on rolling, hard and fast, to find his feet among the roots of a duskwood.

The outlaw's charge came with lightning-swift back and forth slashes of his knife at the fore, and Florin ducked behind the tree to use its trunk as a shield.

The outlaw stumbled on roots in his haste and Florin raced around the tree and tackled him from behind, the pair of them crashing and bouncing in wet leaves as Florin drove his dagger home again and again.

Into unyielding mail. Narantha was almost upon them now, winded and panting, but she started the raw, strangled beginnings of a scream as she saw One-Knife twist around and drive his long knife backhand at Florin's shoulder—

The young forester flung himself away, off the outlaw, who rolled over with a triumphant snarl and scrambled to get up. Whereupon Florin arched, shoulders on the ground, and lashed out at the man with both boots, catching him just at that crouching moment when the forester's feet were gathered under him and his balance was shifting. The man flew backward and sat on roots, bouncing and cursing—as Narantha ran up, scooped up a fallen knife, and stabbed clumsily at the nearest part of him she could reach, his shin, right above his boot.

The dagger spun out of her hand, not seeming to do much harm, but One-Knife roared in pain—and Florin landed on him hard, stabbing ruthlessly. The outlaw's cry sank into a long groan that trailed into silence.

Florin whirled around, letting the dying man slump against the tree. "I gave you a *command!*" he snarled at Narantha, eyes ablaze and bloody dagger in hand.

"I don't take orders from you!" she hissed back just as fiercely.

They glared at each other, breathing hard. Then Florin whirled away from her, jaw set, and ran to retrieve his sword.

Without another word he plucked it up and raced over the ridge, down into the sunlight beyond.

Leaving Narantha standing over three very dead men, sprawled on the leaves in their blood. She could see bright new mail through the slashes Florin's steel had cut in their leathers; where would outlaws get such?

A matter for later. If, when "later" came, they were still alive to ponder outlaws who were not outlaws . . .

The fair flower of the Crownsilvers snatched up the only long knife she could see that wasn't spattered with blood and ran after Florin, plunging down a tree-girt bank into the narrow vale beyond.

Hunter's Hollow was a battlefield.

It was a pretty place where the forest rose in two tree-cloaked hills, and in the space between them curved the king's road—a wide and high-crowned dirt way flanked by ditches. As Florin had said, a superb place for an ambush.

Two horses were lying dead in the road, and a man was lying in the dust where he'd been flung off the saddle of one of them, a heavy war-quarrel through his body and his face white and staring fixedly at nothing. There was astonishment on his frozen face—and it was an expression he'd worn often enough while Narantha was cursing Master Delbossan that she recognized him right away: the taller and quieter of the two guards Lord Hezom had sent to escort her to his home.

The other guard lay in a huddled heap in the road well off to the left, several crossbow quarrels standing up out of his body, and a dark lake of blood spreading around him.

More quarrels studded the road north of that corpse, to where a coach lay smashed and canted on its side in the ditch, two weakly thrashing horses tangled in a welter of harness and more quarrels— beasts that no longer screamed in agony, but coughed and bubbled blood from their muzzles, drooling out their lives. Narantha's stomach heaved.

Off to Narantha's right, along the road, Master Delbossan still seemed to live. He was crouching, a light crossbow bolt standing out of his shoulder above an arm that hung limp and useless, in the lee of a dead horse bristling with half a dozen bolts.

Florin was bounding down to Delbossan, sword held high—and

a crossbow bolt came humming out of the trees on the far side of the hollow, flashing past his hip before he could even hope to dodge.

Narantha tried to scream, and succeeded only in choking on her own sickness. Spewing her guts out, she slipped and slid down the bank into the hollow, another quarrel thudding into the earth close beside her.

There came a sudden thunder of hooves from the north, then around the bend and down into the hollow came three riders—men dressed in new and clean flamboyant hunting leathers, astride magnificent horses.

"I *thought* I heard shouting," the foremost called back to those behind, a silver hunting horn in hand. "Look ye: Here's a coach down, and—"

A crossbow cracked, and the man with the horn gave a queer sort of sob as a crossbow bolt tore out his throat and hummed on its way. Swaying in his saddle, already starting to topple, he galloped on, dead or dying, until another crossbow fired, and his snorting mount took a bolt in the withers, squealed, and reared, lashing out at the sky in pain.

The dead man fell to the road dust like a grainsack, windlasses whirred madly in the forest—and Florin changed his mind about running to Delbossan, and swerved to leap a fallen guard and race up the far bank of the hollow, shouting something incoherent.

"Back!" cried the second rider to the third, hauling on his reins so hard that his mount reared, bugling in fear.

Crossbows cracked in unison, a quarrel snatched the sword he was frantically drawing right out of his hand, blood spraying—and a second quarrel laid open his ear and spun him right out of his saddle with a shout.

The third rider—a tall, broad-shouldered, bearded man—was already out of his saddle and racing up the slope into the trees that held the crossbowmen, gleaming sword in hand.

Narantha cowered away from the wildly dancing, riderless horse of the man with the horn, ducking away as deadly hooves lashed out in all directions. Maddened with pain, it raced off south, bucking and twisting. Gods above, Narantha thought, losing her footing again and clawing at bushes and weeds to try to keep her balance, what next?

A moment later, she found herself thinking: What superb horses! Who are these men?

The rider with the wounded hand and copiously bleeding ear had drawn his dagger and was staggering up the slope whence the deadly quarrels had come. White-faced and reeling, Delbossan staggered after him.

There were shouts in the trees, and violently dancing branches. Steel rang on steel, someone shouted, and someone else burst out of the trees and flung a crossbow full in the face of the man with the bleeding ear. The wounded rider fell over, losing his dagger, and was promptly pounced upon and stabbed. Delbossan lifted his sword awkwardly, in his off-hand—then retreated, cursing weakly, as a second man joined the first, followed by a third, fourth, fifth, and sixth.

Then Florin sprang out of the trees in an explosion of leaves, sword first, and slammed into the rearmost two, sending them all tumbling down the slope and taking the legs out from under the other "outlaws."

Someone screamed hoarsely, back in the trees, and the third rider loped out of them, blood all over his sword and a ruthless smile on his face, and came leaping down to join the fray.

Florin rose up out of the tangle hacking like a madman, and Delbossan lurched forward to chop whoever he could reach. Bouncing ribbons of slashed leather revealed more bright mail as the crossbowmen struggled to their feet, cursing and shouting. The moment they saw the bearded third rider, they ignored Florin and Delbossan, crowding forward to slash and stab at this new target.

Who had both sword and dagger, and wielded them with deadly skill, crafting a wall of ringing steel that brought death to the first two who tried to wade through it. Fighting furiously, Florin took down a third, and in the frantic swordplay that followed Narantha saw Delbossan grunt and grapple a man from behind. They struggled together, snarling, and beyond them one outlaw sprang forward to bear down the bearded rider's sword arm, the last outlaw lunged, thrusting hard over it at the man's face—and Florin slashed that thrust aside, wielding his steel in wild and frantic parries that took him reeling aside entangled with one outlaw. The bearded man's superb blade lashed out so flickering-fast that the second outlaw was going down, head wobbling atop his slit throat, before he truly realized he was dying.

"No! Not supposed to—" he said plaintively, blood bubbling forth at his every word, and he fell on his face.

The bearded man reached over him to slice the throat of the crossbowman struggling in the horsemaster's grip, turning to snap at Florin as he did so: "Take him alive! It makes the questioning easier!"

Somewhere behind them all, Narantha gasped.

Florin, however, was gasping too, doubled over and clutching his ribs with bloody fingers as if he could stop the welling blood. The slash was deep; he was touching one of his own ribs through the slippery stickiness . . .

The last "outlaw" spun away from the faltering forester, grinning savagely, and flung his blade full in the bearded man's face.

The parry was swift and hard, but sent the bright blade clanging out of its wielders hands, and the grinning outlaw sprang forward, drawing a needle-blade dagger that glinted bright purple in the sunlight.

"Poison!" Delbossan shouted hoarsely, as the bearded man reached for his own dagger, the "outlaw" leaped, and Florin flung his sword, sobbing in pain. End over wobbling end it flashed, to bite deep into the hand that held the poisoned dagger, and snatch it away, trailing a finger.

The "outlaw" shrieked in pain, and the bearded man brought his empty hand up in a roundhouse blow that lifted the man off his feet, scream ending in a clattering of teeth clashing together, and let him crash limply to the ground, senseless.

"Well fought!" the bearded man boomed, striding forward to ease Florin to the ground. "What's your name, lad, and where hail you from?"

"F-Florin," Florin managed to gasp, shuddering. He barely saw a gleaming steel vial being unstoppered under his nose, but it flooded down his throat cool and soothing, and the pain ebbed instantly. "Florin Falconhand," he gasped, "of Espar. What's yours?"

He was still too pain-dazed to lift his head and look around, and so did not know that Delbossan and the Lady Narantha were already kneeling in the road, but he did hear Narantha gasp at his blunt asking.

"Azoun," the bearded man said with a smile—a smile that broadened as a stunned Florin gaped at him. "Azoun Obarskyr, of all Cormyr."

If the glare that Lord Crownsilver leveled at the war wizard whose hands cradled and gave life to the speaking-stone sizzled with searing fire, the look with which Lady Crownsilver favored that same mage held deadly ice.

He met both dooms with an urbane smile and the words, "I'm not listening, lord and lady; you may continue to speak freely, in utmost confidence."

Narantha's father glanced mistrustfully around the chamber, deep in the Royal Court of Suzail—and her mother snapped, "Piffle! You're hearing every word, varlet!"

"True," the War Wizard replied solemnly, "but I'm not listening to them."

Narantha's tinkling laughter rose out of the speaking stone at that, causing the Lady Jalassa to wail, "My *baby!*" once more, which turned Narantha's laughter into a despairing, embarrassed, "Moth-*er!*"

"Well, you're safe," Lord Crownsilver said gruffly, "and so's the king. And you played some small part in foiling the mysterious assassins. We're proud of you, lass. Now you just sit tight, right where you are—never stepping out of sight of Lord Hezom or his chatelaine for an *instant,* do you hear?—until we see you again. Whoever sent those slayers will be furious, and will try for you next, so no more gallivanting around the woods with young commoners! I absolutely *forbid* such conduct! Do you hear me well, daughter?"

"Daddy!" Narantha protested. " 'Twas not like that at all! We did no 'gallivanting,' if that's your clumsy euphemism for rutting, and whatever his birth, he's a fine and loyal subject of the king!"

"I'm sure," Lord Crownsilver said curtly. "Just remember what I said—if you're a *true* Crownsilver, and would like to remain so in our eyes."

He wagged an imperious finger at the war wizard, and added, "This converse is at an end."

The two Crownsilvers rose together, ignoring both the nodding war wizard and Narantha's faint and fading farewells as the speaking-stone lost its glow of operancy, and strode into the innermost chamber, closing the door firmly.

The war wizard (they had not troubled to remember his name) had earlier assured them it was shielded to ensure utmost privacy—from war wizards and great archmages half Faerûn away, not merely lurking servants—but Lord Crownsilver trusted no wizard. He tapped the great crystal that topped his cane and murmured a word over it, saying nothing more until its kindling glow became a steady radiance. Then he held it out horizontally, and his wife sat herself with deft dignity in one of the waiting chairs and took hold of the other end of it.

"Gods above," Lord Crownsilver hissed, leaping in before his wife's tongue could rule their converse, "but I am more furious than I have ever been, in all my life! Our daughter—*our daughter*—bedded by some unshaven backwoods lout! And now she wants to *wed* him, too!"

"Don't be *silly,*" Lady Crownsilver hissed. "We won't allow her to do anything of the sort, and after she's raged about it for a tenday or so and smashed enough things over the heads of loutish servants who frankly deserve it, she'll be tired of him and be on to someone else, as she always does. Someone more suitable! We'll see to that, and so will the court, after I say a few of the right words to the right people!"

"But Nantha is *ruined*," Lord Crownsilver said angrily, "and our reputations with her! How can we expect anyone to believe she's untouched? Anyone who *matters?*"

"Maniol, stop bellowing foolishness." Lady Jalassa's voice was as iron-hard as usual, but it held a cold commanding note her lord had heard only once or twice before. "We will not have to convince anyone of any social standing to believe in anything—because we *will not tell* them what befell our Nantha. So they will never know."

"But Kim—"

"Your mother will know nothing if you say nothing, Maniol. For once." Now Jalassa's voice was like a stone dungeon door grating shut.

For the first time in his life, Lord Maniol Crownsilver looked at his delicate, diminutive wife with something akin to fear.

"So who is this 'Florin Falconhand,' anyhail?"

Highknight Arglas Duskeldarr shrugged. "Some backwoods bumpkin with a fair face, the luck of loving Tymora Herself, and a quick blade. Too clever by half, so he'll doom himself within the month, and end up dead behind some tree with a dagger in his vitals, black-tongued with poison in some noble's private feasting room because he refused to join in treason—or we'll be dismembering him, ye and I, on Vangey's orders. That's what befell the *last* half-dozen lads Azoun liked the look of, anyhail."

Highknight Malustra Thaurant sighed, cleaned already-perfect fingernails with the point of her belt knife, and uncrossed her long legs in a way that never failed to make Arglas swallow. She winked, just to watch him blush, and rose with sinuous grace, her every move a wanton beckoning. "Can I have some fun with him first?"

Arglas sighed in exasperation, and pointed the highcoin lass to the door. "I don't for the life of me know why His Majesty ever made you a highknight!"

"Oh?" She crooked one cool eyebrow and purred, "I do."

Her strut, as she went out, left Arglas swallowing repeatedly, his throat very dry. Which made him thankful he was the king's cellarer, with the duty to sample every last bottle and decanter.

He very much wanted to sample several of them, right now.

War Wizard Andreth Thalendur had safely returned the speaking-stone to its thrice-locked coffer long since, and was oh-so-casually commencing to dust the ornate container's lid for the third time when a door opened and the words he'd been expecting came to his ears.

"You, man! Sirrah!"

He made no reply and declined to look up, and so collected a sharp prod in the ribs with the gilded nether tip of Lord Crownsilver's cane, wielded by Lady Crownsilver, who accompanied her polite greeting with the words, "War Wizard, we're speaking to you!"

Andreth looked up, smiling the faintest of smiles. "Yes? I hear your words, but I've been trained not to listen to them."

"Oh, you'll listen to *these*, all right!" Lord Crownsilver snarled, reaching out a hand to dig iron fingers into the knave's robes at the throat, to haul the smug byblow right off his feet so every Crownsilver word henceforth could be spat right into his face.

"Maniol!" Lady Crownsilver snapped, but whatever else she'd been going to say died unspoken as tiny blue-white arcs of lightning sprang from the war wizard's robes to Lord Crownsilver's reaching fingertips, causing the noble to shout in astonished pain.

"Ah. Sorry. I'm wearing something new that *High* Lord Vangerda-hast is testing," Andreth said pleasantly. "Seems to smite foes of the realm very well . . . doesn't it?"

"Enough of this effrontery, knave," Lady Crownsilver said coldly. "We demand an audience with Azoun—His Majesty to you! Kindly take word to him at once!"

Andreth bowed to them, smiled, and wordlessly withdrew.

The Crownsilvers scarcely had time to exchange glances and for Maniol to receive a hissed, "Stop holding your fingers like a child about to cry! *Look* like a lord, stlarn you!" ere the war wizard returned, bowed, indicated the man who'd followed him into the room, and departed again.

The man was not, however, the King of Cormyr.

The Royal Magician Vangerdahast gave the Crownsilvers his all-too-familiar half-smile, along with the words, "I regret to inform you that His Majesty is in the countryside, shielded from converse by magics even *I* cannot break. Rest assured that he will be informed of your polite request as soon as it is possible to inform him of anything, and that he will grant you an audience shortly thereafter, as the pressing needs of the realm allow."

Lady Crownsilver said coldly, "Spare the glib-tongued emptynesses, Vangey. You're not performing before all the court right now. I'd have much ruder things to say to you if we didn't need your cooperation and candor—for the good of the realm, of course. So speak plain and true. Did this commoner Falconhand rut with our daughter?"

Vangerdahast did not hesitate. Looking Jalassa straight in the eye, he said, "No. Your daughter is, ah, untouched; you need fear no unexpected heirs."

Glowering, Lord Crownsilver snapped, "You're certain?"

"We've cast some spells to see into their minds, while they were dreaming," the royal magician said soothingly, "searching for memories of intimacy, and that alone. There were no such memories."

"Aye, but she's smitten with the lout! What if he—?"

"The king is well aware of your concerns. You might say that as a father and as a monarch concerned with inheritance and lineage, he anticipated them. More than that, he shares them. Wherefore His Majesty is going to grant this Florin Falconhand and his friends a charter—so as to have ready pretext to send them all away."

"*Far* away," Lady Crownsilver snapped.

"Where?" Lord Crownsilver snarled.

Vangerdahast smiled, spread his hands like a conjurer discovering a gift for a small child in his palm, and replied, "To the Stonelands, of course. It's needed conquering for years."

Slowly—very slowly—Lord Crownsilver nodded, a grim smile

spreading across his face. "So it has." His smile grew, as he echoed in a satisfied whisper, "So it has."

As the door closed behind the royal magician, busily ushering the Crownsilvers out before him, the speaking-stone glowed once, ever so faintly.

There was no one in the chamber to see it, but someone else did. Someone whose hand, adorned with a striking unicorn-head ring, waved into nothingness a scrying-spell linked to the stone. And smiled.

Sometimes, the watcher mused, it's very handy being a war wizard entrusted with enspelling scrying crystals.

When the time comes, and he's staring right into one, Vangerdahast won't know what's hit him.

Chapter 9

ADVENTURERS AVAUNT!

There is no greater plague upon the lands than the chartered adventurer. Crown-sanctioned mischief makers, brigands whose thefts, casual murders, rapine and pillage are excused where the same things done by a cobbler or a milkmaid would be answered with severings of hands or other appendages, plus brandings—or all of those and hanging or death by drawing between four horses.

Yet there is no more necessary plague. Adventurers make even kings think twice about cruelly oppressing all who pass within reach, teach prudence to high priests and even rogue wizards, and are almost the only curb upon the numbers of dragons and other large and monstrous beasts.

On the whole, I think the balance comes out about even. What makes us keep adventuring charters instead of burning them along with their bearers is the entertainment adventurers afford the populace. In hamlets and at waymoots, after one's grumbled about the weather, taxes, the latest rumors of war and orc raids, and the all-too-paltry gossip about the indiscretions of royalty and nobility, there's little else to talk about but the foolish escapades of adventurers.

Thundaerlel Maurlatrimm
Four Decades of Innkeeping
published in the Year of the Highmantle

Royal Scribe Blaunel, did you eat something bad?"

"No, Royal Scribe Lathlan," came the somewhat weary reply through the garderobe door. "I ate something at highsunfeast that disagreed with my patrician bowels. However, I'm hrasted sure they're empty now!"

"Good to hear. I'm not doing this new charter alone."

The door opened and Blaunel emerged, waving his hands to shake away the last few drops of rosewater. "What is it? Those dolts in Arabel haven't finally managed to agree on a name for their rushcaning guild, have they? Or run out of dissident rushcaners to knife in alleys?"

"No such luck, Tymora forfend. 'Tis our bold Azoun-saving adventurers, claiming their royal reward whilst their deed is still on everyone's tongues!"

"Huh," Blaunel grunted, sounding profoundly unimpressed as he slid back into his seat and reached for his favorite quill. "What are this lot calling themselves? No more 'Flaming Banners of the Valiant Valorous,' I trust?"

"Ha! These are upcountry hay-noses. They've not the learning to spell 'Valorous,' nor 'Valiant.' No, they just wanted 'Swords of Espar.'"

The senior scribe sighed. "Know they *nothing* of the lore of the realm? Some of the Swords are still alive—and dwelling right here in Suzail!"

"Aye, I saw Mlaareth a ride ago, striding along the Promenade like he owned it with a lass on each arm. And to answer you straight: no, I guess not. You'd think, growing up in Espar, they'd at least have *heard* of the Swords of Espar—minstrels only tell the tale of the Dragondown Slaying once a month or so!"

Undermaster of the Rolls and Scribe Royal Blaunel belched delicately, raising the back of his hand to his mouth more out of habit than politeness, and shrugged. "Mayhap they have. If they're as simple as all that, they may not know they can't name themselves after an adventuring band that still holds a charter, retired or not."

He fell silent to finish shaping an elaborate swash, did so with practised skill, and grunted, "So what'd they pick, when told they couldn't be Swords of Espar?"

Lathlan smiled. "Swords of Eveningstar."

Blaunel snorted. "Strained their wits hard, didn't they? Surprised they didn't call themselves the Trollblood Blades!" Shaking his head, he began to shape the first fanciful "S" of "Swords." Then another thought struck him.

"Still, I suppose if they *had* wits, they'd not be adventurers. They'd be merry-swindling merchants instead."

"And dwelling in Sembia, awaiting daggers in their backs," Lathlan replied promptly.

The two scribes exchanged grins, dipped their quill pens in unison, and bent their noses to the charter in unspoken accord.

The sooner done, the sooner off to the Swan for a tankard. Or three.

When it grew late and the back room of the Watchful Eye crowded with tired, well-slaked farmhands all too easily irritated into swinging their fists, the oldest topers of Espar were wont to drift outside for a last pipe and a word or two in the moonlight, ere ambling off home.

Under the moonlight, the usual six or seven old hardjaws were leaning against Dammurth Talgont's back stable wall, across the street from the inn, trading comfortable jests and the latest gossip.

That clack for once concerned not just highborn doings in Suzail, the latest flareups of those flamebrains in Arabel, unfolding schemes of the murderous and serpent-tongued smugglers of Marsember, and most recent flamboyantly coin-wasting idiocies of the legions of gold-for-brains gaudy prancing dolts who dwelt in Sembia. This night, talk touched on Espar itself!

On every tongue hereabouts, in the wake of the swift-racing news of the great Battle of Hunter's Hollow—wherein a lone local lad had singlehandedly hewn down a sinister and mysterious invading army lying in wait to ambush the king—was the name of Florin Falconhand.

Old Durrust the miller took his long clay pipe out of his mouth long enough to say, "Oh, he's a pretty one. The ladies all agree on that."

"More'n'that," Barth the Barrelhead put in, "plenty of lads look to him, too. He'd make a good Purple Dragon commander, he would." The local cooper was one of the few men adorning the wall who'd not been a Purple Dragon—and so of course considered himself an expert on all matters, large and small, of warfare and the Cormyrean military.

Thorl Battlestorm spat thoughtfully into a nearby clump of weeds. "Ah, but would he? What if he's a clevershanks, all selfish—or a real bad 'un? We don't know that, now, do we? I'd be fair surprised if he doesn't get up to some of the same foolishness all young lads do. Some come out of it, but some go on to greater and greater folly, and come to bad ends . . . usually long after the gods should've served them with what they deserved."

"That's just it," Durrust agreed. "He's young, yet."

"Aye," agreed the horse breeder Nornuth, "and as young bucks go, those looks and knowing the forest and all, bid fair to make him better at charming the lasses than most."

Durrust tapped out his pipe. "Sound not so rueful, Norn. I hear you did all right in your day, in such—*hem*—valorous pursuits."

There were chuckles, but Battlestorm overrode them with a stern, "Let's not ride down *that* road, lads; my ears have heard more than enough chortling memories of lasses long gone and how soft and splendid they were. 'Tis this Florin lad, late of Hawkstone's forges—where he acquitted himself well, I'm told—who's on the brink of knighthoods and royal favor and riding off to Suzail in mirrorbright armor and all. We've chewed over our elder days oft enough, and can again when other fancies falter. What I want to know is: Is he a shining hero sent to Cormyr by the gods, or a dullard who just happened to do the right thing when excitement landed atop him, or something in between? Is he really a brilliant bladesman, and a swift-as-a-hawk fearless strategist, and truly noble of heart and character? Or do we just want him to be?"

"Those are thoughts every loving mother wrestles with." A calm, quiet woman's voice came out of the night, from the shadows nigh Tarreth Oldhall's back shed. "I'm no different than most, Thorl."

The men fell silent, abashed, as Florin's mother stepped out into the moonlight. Imsra Skydusk's spells and the regard they all held for Hethcanter Falconhand, whose name still held weight in Purple Dragon barracks ten years after he'd last worn the king's armor, had kept her from the bother of any man of Espar trying to romance her, or even leer and wink at her over tankards. Yet her every stride was liquid grace, and she was the darksome half-elf beauty many local men thought about, when lying in their beds seeking sleep that would not come. Cloaked in moonlight, she was throat-tighteningly beautiful.

"I . . ." Thorl Battlestorm tended to dominate any gathering, and men of Espar looked to him. He felt he should say something now, and rather uneasily continued, "owe you an apology, ma'am. We—ah—meant no offense, but merely—"

"And you've given none, Thorl. None of you have. Every mother loves her son and wants to see him rise high and far in life, to be happy and looked to by all. Yet I very much fear my Florin will put a foot wrong—and the more exalted the company, the harder will be his fall. More than that, I can't and won't chase after him and spy on him every day, and so see not all that he does. Though I've seen nothing to make me worry, I'm afraid he may have put a foot or two wrong already."

Semoor spread his hands. "Why 'Eveningstar'?"

Florin shrugged. "The king suggested it. He said I'd learn why when he presented the charter to us."

"He's giving us a mission," Islif said flatly. "Go and get yourselves killed in the Stonelands, and mind you report in to Lord Winter along the way."

Jhessail rolled her eyes. "Grimtongue! A little cheer, *please!*"

Islif drew herself up, strode over to Jhessail, loomed over the flamehaired mage—and put a wide, idiotic smile onto her face, all teeth and oh-so-wide eyes. Then she let it fall right off her face again, leaving her looking as stern as ever.

"Soooo," Semoor drawled, regarding the ceiling. "What *really* happened between you and the lovely Lady Narantha Crownsilver during your little walk in the woods? It gets cold out there in the dark night, I'm thinking . . ."

"You're thinking? Does divine Lathander know? He might just change his mind about having a dangerous thinker among his ordained priesth—"

"Sabruin, gallant Falconhand, and answer my impertinent question."

Florin wrapped his arms around the back of a vacant chair, leaned his chin on them, and told his friends, "Nothing romantic or lustful happened between us. Nothing. And you can cast spells on me to be sure of that, if you'd like. Beauteous she may be, but she was a raging spitfire most of the time we spent trudging through the trees—and I'm not so addled by raging lusts that I want to have my pisspipe sliced off and my neck stretched in a hangman's noose, for all to watch. I can't think noble lords and ladies are too pleased with anyone who ruins one of their daughters."

"Unless they happen to be King Azoun," Semoor murmured.

"Silence!" Islif snapped. "All the realm may know about that, but 'tis surely the act of a death-welcoming fool to talk about it!"

"Yes, Semoor," Jhessail said reprovingly. "*Try* to behave yourself for the next day or two until we have the charter. Then, being an anointed adventurer, you can revert to your usual charmingly discreet self."

"*After* we get over the border into Sembia," Islif growled. "Where we can all walk away from you if your overclever mouth gets us into real trouble."

Semoor gave her a quizzical look. "You're worried about 'real trouble'? When we're going to be *chartered adventurers?* Just what do you think chartered adventurers *do,* anyhail?"

Then he looked pained. "Behave myself for an entire day or two? Whatever will I *do?*"

"Hear ye! Hear ye all! Good people of Espar, His Valiant Majesty Azoun, King of all this fair land of Cormyr, is pleased to grant a right royal charter this day, upon this spot and before all your eyes! Attend, all!"

The herald of Espar was in fine form, his voice rich and loud without seeming harsh. Effortlessly it rolled out across the crowd—a close-packed throng that filled the village green shoulder to shoulder, and extended right back to the inn and smithy walls, entirely blocking the Way of the Dragon.

The Watchful Eye had gained a splendid new porch for the occasion, hurled up by High Horn's best carpenters in a day—and standing on it beside the herald, sweating a little uncomfortably in the sun, stood four young Esparran, the friends Doust Sulwood, Semoor Wolftooth, Jhessail Silvertree, and Islif Lurelake. Idle younglings of scant regard a few days ago, but objects of intense curiosity and bright if fleeting fame, now. Semoor gave many winks and grins, and Islif glowered out at the crowd as if she'd happily hew the lot of them to the ground, while Doust and Jhessail kept their hands firmly behind their backs, so they could fidget largely unnoticed.

On the other side of the four friends stood Lord Hezom, the King's Lord of Espar, resplendent in a new greatsleeves doublet, half-cloak, and bright bold hose. He smiled out across the crowd in genuine pleasure, and many goodfolk of Espar shared his feelings, for the king was paying for the feast they'd soon share and the mead and ale they'd soon down, and royal coins had already given many of them—whose homes fronted on the green—bright new roofs and balconies, where Purple Dragon bowmen were stationed watchfully. Others had rented out their every last room and slept in their own stables, and were thanking the gods—and Florin Falconhand—fervently for the windfall of much-needed coins.

More Purple Dragons, out of uniform and trying not to look uncomfortable about it, stood among the sea of faces, striving to look like merchants or drovers. They shared space in the throng with war wizards trying their best not to look like war wizards, some with the aid of shapechanging spells. Undercloak or just what they seemed to be, the onlookers were many: curious wagon-merchants halting on their travels, peddlers, outlying crofters, the scores of bright-cloaked courtiers who followed the king whenever possible—and every last person in Espar who could walk, totter, or be propped up on sticks or in a chair to see the wonder of the season.

"You have all heard," the herald began, "how your own Florin Falconhand, a young forester of this place, came upon a lost noble-woman of the realm in the forest not far from here, and gallantly guided her in safety, days and nights through, to be restored to us. And how, when at last they reached the royal road not far north of here, in the place called Hunter's Hollow, they came upon a large force of murderous men who'd shot down Horsemaster Delbossan's honor guard—sent forth from here by your own gallant Lord, Hezom—"

The herald knew his job, and indicated Lord Hezom with a flourish, allowing time for cheers. The Purple Dragons and war wizards in the crowd knew their tasks, too, and provided those cheers lustily—but were pleasantly surprised to hear themselves drowned out by the very real acclaim of the folk standing around them. The local lord stood high in the regard of the folk of this backwater, it seemed; he must be more than just a haughty nose and a hand that smote with the king's authority.

"—and did battle with them, seeking to rescue the wounded horsemaster. The gods saw fit to send His Majesty the king thither at that moment, while riding out to a royal staghunt, and boldly did the Purple Dragon charge into the forest to slay the miscreants—whom, it now appears, had come creeping into Cormyr for the sole and most base purpose of slaying *him*. Florin Falconhand was already harrying these dastards, armed with but a sword and a dagger, and he and the king and the wounded Master Delbossan did great battle upon them, slaying all but one of the foe, whom the king graciously spared. In that affray, saith His Majesty, did Florin Falconhand personally save the royal life!"

Espar's voice had risen into an impassioned shout, and it was answered with a mighty roar. Purple Dragons on the rooftops rapped dagger-hilts on their breastplates in ringing chorus, to keep the applause from falling into vigorous chatter, and the herald rushed in to recapture the attention of all.

"So now, in recognition of this valiant and loyal bravery, His Majesty has seen fit to grant—free of charge—a charter founding a new adventuring company this day! For this was the one reward your modest Florin desired, to lawfully pursue a dream he hath nurtured to his bosom lifelong: to adventure with these his fast friends who stand here with me now!"

There was brief applause, which the herald overrode by calling out on high: "Some of you are wondering why these fine, upstanding young men and women of Espar have chosen to take the name of *another* place than this the fair cradle that reared them. Some of you have demanded to know why they have turned their backs on Espar!"

The herald fell silent just long enough for talk to begin and swell, then cried, "Yet, know ye all, they *have not* turned their backs on Espar! It is royal law and long tradition that no band of adventurers, no matter how noble, can take the name of another, earlier-founded adventuring company—and Espar, cradle of lions, hath already spawned the brave Swords of Espar who so memorably defeated and slew the rogue dragon Azazarrundoth, whereof minstrels sing the 'Dragondown Slaying'! Aye, there are still Swords of Espar alive in the realm today, so there cannot be a second company of that name. The king himself suggested Eveningstar be a part of their calling, and they have gladly accepted that wise royal advice!"

"Because to do otherwise would be muttonheaded self-slaying," muttered one Purple Dragon on a rooftop, unheard amid the roar of applause.

When it started to fade, the herald continued, "By tradition, every charter must have a sponsor. A royal charter is, of course, sponsored by the Crown, but as a mark of royal favor, the monarch always personally appoints a ceremonial sponsor. His Majesty smiles upon Espar, upon those who have served the realm loyally, and upon those who have fought at his side, and for all of those reasons hath named Irlgar Delbossan, your own well-beloved horsemaster, sponsor of this charter!"

More applause greeted this, and rose into shouts as Delbossan, white-faced but smiling, and apparently healed of his wounds, came striding out the front door of the Eye onto the porch, and took his place at Lord Hezom's shoulder.

He and the herald exchanged smiles and nods, whereupon Espar told the crowd, "Master Delbossan, mindful of the young man who saved his life as well as that of the king, desires to share his sponsoring duties, and has named—"

The man who strode out onto the porch then wore black armor, as smooth and as supple as velvet, that made no sound—and one of his hands was held out before him, palm up, with a faint glow flickering and skirling around it. Wary mutterings arose from the Purple Dragons and from the war wizards among the crowd, who'd known of the man but not expected the obvious magic, awake in his hand.

"—Hawkstone, ranger and swordmaker of some fame, who from his wanderings in the wild forests of Faerûn has come hither to mark the importance of this charter!"

Astonished applause, that sank away in eager anticipation when

Hawkstone flung out his empty hand to halt the herald, and in a voice deeper and yet louder than Espar's, that echoed off the fronts of houses across the green, said, "Witness all, that I bear the favor of Holy Mielikki here this day, to confer upon him who has pleased her well: Florin Falconhand!" He held up his glowing hand, and the applause this time was a storm of excited and awed talk.

Then Hawkstone cradled his hand to his breast, and nodded to the herald. The herald gave the famous ranger a look of wonder, but resumed his speech undaunted: "A noble lady of the realm in whose veins runs royal blood, a maiden Florin Falconhand also rescued from beasts in the forest, hath requested the right to bear witness to the granting of the charter. Folk of Cormyr, I present to you the Lady Narantha Crownsilver, flower of her house!"

Out of the inn door came marching a gleaming row of splendidly plate-armored knights, their spotless armor polished silver-bright. They split to right and left in succession, forming two lines—and between them appeared the Lady Narantha Crownsilver, smiling, in a gown of white a-sparkle with silver glister. More applause, sinking immediately into a great hissing of excited whispers. Narantha was blushingly and yet serenely beautiful, and knew it, yet seemed humbled by that knowing—and men's hearts broke all over the green as they gazed upon her.

The herald from Espar let the babble continue for a few breaths, almost smiling, then let out a sudden bellow, "All hail the valiant hero of the Battle of Hunter's Hollow!"

The crowd bellowed back, in a great roar that broke into wild cheering when Florin Falconhand, smiling a little uncertainly, strode out of the door of the Eye and lifted a hand in greeting.

When Hawkstone stepped to meet him and touched that glowing hand to his chest with words murmured too quietly for others to hear, Florin was visibly astonished—then moved to tears. Wet-faced, he gaped at his onetime tutor, as loud cheers rose in the green.

Espar waited until they had just begun to subside a little, then cried in a voice that rang out like a trumpet: "Folk of Espar, I give you: your king!"

No blare of horns followed, but none could then have heard them, even had all the warhorns in the realm winded at once.

Espar rocked with the din as Azoun, fourth of that name, *the* Purple Dragon, strode out onto the porch, and everyone there, led by the herald on one hand and Lord Hezom on the other, smoothly turned to face the king, and knelt to him.

"*What* did this Hawkstone just pull?"

Vangerdahast's glare seemed sharp enough to split the scrying crystal asunder. The largest such crystal in the realm, it floated before them, a bright, glossy oval as wide as an armchair.

Laspeera laid a comforting hand on the royal magician's arm. "I doubt he planned it, Lord Vangerdahast. I heard awe in his voice, though he tried to hide it. Divine favor is . . . divine favor."

Vangerdahast nodded, and clapped his free hand over Laspeera's, patting it in silent thanks. The young lass always said the right thing. Always. Thrice as graceful a lady as any of the other nobility he'd seen at court, strong in her Art and growing stronger with astonishing speed, she was a treasure.

He'd mind-reamed her, pouncing without warning, at least twice a tenday since taking her into the Wizards of War, and seldom let her stray far from his side. Thus far he'd found nothing save that he both amused and awed her, and she saw him as the true ruler and savior of the realm.

Oh, and that she'd started to *enjoy* being mind-reamed. He blushed even now, at the thought—and blushed still stronger when the slender fingers of her free hand came down atop his, patting him soothingly.

Neither of them said a word, but stared into the scrying crystal together. In distant Espar, the charter had just been granted.

The herald's glad cry of, "And so the charter is done! Behold your Swords of Eveningstar!" was almost drowned out by a thunderous cheer—a cheer that a blinking, smiling herald hadn't had to lead. He had to wait some time for it to die away enough to be heard again, whereupon he grandly directed everyone "up the Way of the Dragon, to where feast tents await!"

There were fresh cheers, and the crowd started to move. Free food and drink can move men who'll stand their ground against armies.

King Azoun's own hand had signed the charter, under the watchful gaze of Hezom, Lord of Espar, and his herald, as Delbossan and Hawkstone held the parchment flat, and three war wizards who'd quietly stepped out of the Eye had stood behind the king with wands at the ready.

Now, cleaving through the crowd streaming north, Purple Dragons in full armor were converging, standing close to form a solid shield-wall curving all around the porch.

Florin, Doust, Semoor, Jhessail, and Islif stood close together as if facing a foe. They were all a little overwhelmed as they blinked at their king, almost nose to nose, and Azoun clasped their hands in his own and spoke words of congratulation.

"I have every hope," he was saying, as Jhessail fought down a sudden urge to burst into tears, "that together you will stand and prosper and go on to greatness, becoming every bit as successful and famous as the Company of the Manticore Cloaks"—there were awed murmurs from those who heard—"and the Company of the Trollblood Blade!" More murmurs swelled; the king had named adventurers still famous all across the Sea of Fallen Stars.

"The Crown," Azoun added then, "expects you to—"

Ah, thought Semoor a little sourly, here it comes.

"—make at least one foray into the notorious Haunted Halls of Eveningstar, and report whatever you may see there to my Lady Lord of Eveningstar, Tessaril Winter. She can give you directions to the halls, and be your guide in matters ethical while you are within her writ." Azoun smiled. "I wish you fair fortune, and therefore warn you that you'd best recruit more members if you hope to stay alive for long. By giving my name and the word 'Tathen' you may compel Tessaril or other officers of the Crown to without fee add any such members to your charter, in griffon ink."

Then Azoun dropped his grand manner, grinning at them like the reckless lad he must once have been, and added, "And now that all the bellowing's done, we can go back in and eat!"

He turned to stride back into the Eye—and almost fell over Lady Narantha Crownsilver, who flung herself to her knees before him. "Your Majesty, a boon if you will!"

"Oh?" Azoun asked, gazing down into a face that looked humbled and windblown, far indeed from the haughty brightlass he remembered being presented at court. "What desire you, Lady?"

"I . . . Your Majesty, may I join the Swords? Ah, as an envoy, or something of the sort, for I must confess I'm useless in a fight."

"Oh, I'd not go quite *that* far," Delbossan muttered from close behind her, amid the general amazement. "Not when armed with rabbit stew."

The king gazed gravely down upon Narantha, and shook his head almost sorrowfully. "My heart leaps at the thought," he said, "just as I'm certain yours does. Yet duty of birth has a stern call that falters not, and must always be obeyed. I must, by blood and the needs of the realm, forbid the name of Narantha Crownsilver from appearing on this or any adventuring charter. The Crownsilvers lack an endless supply of daughters, to be hazarded on the wings of adventure!"

Azoun reached down and drew Narantha to her feet, kissing her gently on the brow. Then, still holding her hands in his own, he turned to the Swords. "Yet in the Cormyr *I* reign over, friend may freely ride with friend—so keeping this precious lady safe and away from you or safe in your company is entirely your affair."

What was left of the crowd gaped in unison, and the king winked at Narantha and gave her the tiniest of shoves toward Florin.

A moment later their arms were around each other, they were kissing each other, and a ragged cheer was rising around them.

Florin's parents stepped through the shield-wall with their own Purple Dragon escort before and behind them, and amid the happy chatter as the king led the way in to table, Florin's mother drew her son firmly aside and asked pointedly, nodding at Narantha, as she laughed in the arms of both Doust and Semoor, "Is she now a *close* friend of yours, my son?"

As the last lingerers by the now-empty porch became aware of the increasingly flinty glares of the Purple Dragon guard and started toward the tents whence a happy hubbub was already rising, a tall and plain-faced woman in the robes of a priestess of Chauntea walked among them.

No war wizard had detected disguising magic about her person, for the robes covered her from chin to booted ankles, and her breast and hooded head were all hargaunt.

Beneath its warm flowflesh, Horaundoon was thinking. Yes, he could make very good use of these Swords. War wizards were all around him now, but later he'd start scrying them.

'Twould be simple enough to prepare a mindworm to ride the mind of one foolish young Sword or another . . .

Chapter 10

New Blood for the Old Game

The chances and mischances of human folly and the whims of the gods hurl some of us high in life, and have some of us buried before we get any chance to leave our mark. The Year of the Spur saw the founding of a fellowship that was to shake thrones all across Faerûn. And it also saw the beginnings of some moderately successful adventurers, such as the Company of the Cleaver, Setesper's Shields, and what was to become the Knights of Myth Drannor.

Thardok Duirell
Cloaked Whispers Behind Doors:
Cabals, Cults, and Fellowships
published in the Year of Wild Magic

It's all been so . . . sudden." Jhessail shook her head. "These horses—gods, what splendid beasts!—a gown, dagger and boots that're finer than I ever hoped to own, and a belt full of lions from the king's own hand; bestowed with a kiss, no less!"

"Nice to know your bed-price, in his eyes," Semoor said.

"*Some* day, Stoop, that far-too-clever tongue of yours is going to get you—"

"Raised to exalted rank and showered with appreciative wenches, yes. Lathander smiles brightly on those who dare new roads, new views, and—"

"Wilder follies," Islif grunted. "What's wrong, Lady? What're you staring at?"

Narantha Crownsilver smiled and waved at a grassy roadside verge in the trees. "My pavilion was pitched just there. It seems like an age ago, now . . ."

"So you're feeling it, too," Doust said. "A touch of bewilderment, a feeling of emptiness. Such sudden splendor, followed by—a letdown."

"Nay. For me, it has been . . . I am different now than I was then. Before I met Florin, and knew what a forest was."

Riding beside her, the tall ranger kept his eyes calmly on the road ahead, turning his head only to look behind them, as he'd been doing since they'd started out, but Semoor cleared his throat loudly and meaningfully. "Aha. So what *exactly* did the pride of Espar show you, out in the green fastnesses?"

The Lady Narantha turned in her saddle to fix him with a direct and serious gaze, and said, "What it is to be a man."

She let Semoor's smile broaden and his voice begin a whoop of delighted derision before she added icily, *"Not* a lover, dirtyminded priest! Really, Master Wolftooth, your tongue is more suited to the tavern—or the gutter—than the cloisters of the Morninglord!"

There was applause from the riders all around them, to which both Doust and Islif added the same words: "Well said!"

Semoor tried to look innocent, raising an finger like a mild-mannered tutor seeking to make a point. "Priests must say what others dare not, in their ceaseless task of delving into morals and inner truths and—"

"High-heaped ripe verbal manure," Islif snorted. There was more applause.

"Yet if he can win past his fascination with beds and lovemaking in the woods," Jhessail said ruefully, "Semoor has a shrewd point. We chased bright adventure in our dreams for *so* long, seeing it as glorious freedom, and yet"—she indicated the horse beneath her, then the Way of the Dragon under its hooves—"our road ahead seems to have been rather firmly chosen for us."

"By the king," Semoor said darkly, "heeding *certain* furious parents." He glanced meaningfully at Narantha.

Who sighed, shrugged, and said, "The king *is* the king. He does what he believes is best for Cormyr. Would you want adventurers with blades and spells looking for trouble in Espar? In Marsember? Arabel? Suzail? Well, neither does he. I . . . I hope I'm not going to just scream and run, when the first orc I see is coming at us. Hungrily." She shivered.

"Dathen Brook," Islif interrupted, pointing ahead. "Time to stop and water the horses."

"And that's what successful adventuring is about," Semoor said brightly. "Taking the time to stop and water the horses."

The innkeeper had called this his "neither my best nor yet my worst" room, but it was little better than a closet. No window, two narrow bunk beds—Horaundoon undid his carry-coffer's shoulder-slicing harness with relief, and tossed the heavy burden onto the lower bunk—and a rickety chair drawn up to a small, scarred table. A shelf with a towel and a cracked water-ewer. A candle-lamp with scrips and a striker. A chamberpot under the bed, with a mouse scurrying past it. Doubtless bugs in the bed.

So this was upcountry luxury.

The Zhentarim closed the door. It fit loosely; the floor was warped. At least there was a wooden toe-wedge to hold it shut. Horaundoon augmented it with three wedges of his own and tacked up the black blanket he'd be sleeping in tonight over the door, to block all curious eyes. Then he cast a scrying-shield that was much better than the ring-stored sort sold to wealthy merchants in Sembia, and waited until it turned the air its ghostly gray.

So he was a merchant with secrets. That shouldn't be so rare in Waymoot as to upset local war wizards enough to call in superiors. He'd already planned to hide his orb inside the hargaunt, and hide the hargaunt as part of himself, whenever he set boot outside this oh-so-cozy chamber.

Horaundoon unwrapped his smallest scrying orb, set it on the table with the inn towel beneath it, laid his fingertips on it, and murmured the words that brought it to glowing, floating life.

It was time to go hunting foolish new adventurers . . .

Once dismounted, reins wrapped around her arm, Islif turned to Florin and embraced him. "Thank you," she said huskily. "I meant to do this earlier, but those war wizards were determined we'd not get any chance to talk together before bedding down, without them eagerly taking in every word. I'm surprised they didn't bed down with each of us; they *did* lock us in, you know."

Florin nodded. "I discovered that."

Islif kissed him. "Thank you. I don't know how you did it—you must have had Tymora's own shining luck, not to get killed!—but you got us our charter, and handed us all our dream!"

"Let's hope it doesn't become a nightmare." Florin sighed. "This may be a huge mistake. I made a terrible blunder a few days back, and if I go on making them, I may well get us all killed."

"Excuse me," the Lady Narantha said firmly, putting a hand on Florin's arm and giving Islif a beseeching look—who nodded and let go, allowing the noblewoman to drag Florin a few strides away.

Keeping her voice low, Narantha bent her head close to his and murmured, "You guided me in the forest; there, I was little better than a child. Please heed me when I say this now: forests may be unknown realms to me, but leading people, winning arguments, and manipulating folk high and low are where I can guide you, a little."

"Lady," Florin agreed, "I will. For as they say of the Blue Dragons, I'm all at sea in this. I can bark commands and look imperious—my father did that very successfully, and I can ape him easily enough—but when I ride with my friends, and their lives are at hazard . . ."

Semoor sidled a few steps closer to them, cocking his head with an exaggerated flourish to eavesdrop.

Narantha gave him a dirty sidelong look and moved around Florin to face him squarely—and be able to look past his arm and watch Semoor.

Putting her arms around Florin's neck, she drew his head down and murmured, as they stood nose to nose, "I must give you stern warning. *Never* appear indecisive or less than confident. Even if you quail inside, or feel bewildered, be firm, give orders, and make others *think* you are in command of what befalls—and you will be. You *must* do this, Florin!"

Sober blue-gray eyes met hers, and relief was growing in them. Florin let out his breath, smiled, and told her, "Thanks, La—"

"Nantha," she said firmly, kissed the tip of his nose, and stepped back out of his arms, catching hold of his hand to lead them back to the road.

Semoor was holding their horses for them, and at their approach he observed loudly, "So you *are* a couple. Sidling off by yourselves for kiss-and-cuddle moments, embracing whenever you get the chance—"

"Master Wolftooth," Narantha said crisply, "I'll tolerate much from the friends of the man who saved my life. Yet a woman's reputation is her all—for the nobly born, at least—and if you cast many more unfounded aspersions my way, be aware that you'll soon be doing so without teeth! Or what are vulgarly referred to as your 'family jewels,' or both teeth and jewels, as my outrage moves me. Hear me, upstanding servant of Lathander, and guide thyself accordingly."

"Oh, well said," Islif applauded. "Semoor, spare us any attempt at a clever rejoinder. Tell the lady: 'Yes, Lady Narantha. Thank you, Lady Narantha. Sorry, Lady Narantha, and it won't happen again, Lady Nar—' "

"Hey, now!" Semoor protested. "I can manage all of those courtesies but the last. Lathander looks not favorably on falsehoods."

Narantha wrinkled her forehead in the deepest of puzzled frowns. "And so you chose to serve him why, exactly—you being what you are?"

The Waymoot roadguard gave them a smile and a wave; evidently their fame had preceded them. The Swords took rooms at The Old Man after Narantha told them it was the quietest inn in town, ate a good meal, then strolled down the street.

Doust was bound for evening prayers at the local temple of Tymora, but the others sought the doors beneath the hanging signboard of The Moon and Stars.

Flanking the entrance, four watchful rangers with swords at their sides stood waiting, leaning against the jambs and side-panels with crossed arms and carefully expressionless faces.

"Down blades," one of them ordered.

"Goodman," the Lady Narantha replied politely, "you may guard my dagger." As she calmly hiked the skirts of her glittering flame-hued evening gown to unsheath it, raising all the eyebrows the four doorwardens possessed, she added, "These my companions have a charter, newly given them by the king himself, that permits—"

"Oh, you're the bright heroes from Espar! Be welcome!" The man glanced back over his shoulder, to where a sudden swell of noise had marked the appearance of a jowly man with a mustache through an inner door. The new arrival looked at the Swords, then nodded to the senior doorwarden—just as Narantha laid her dagger across the man's palm and said to the jowly man, "Fair even, War Wizard!"

The mage blinked at her, stepped back to survey her from head to foot, then said hastily, "And good even to you, Lady—?"

"Crownsilver," she answered, sweeping past him. "War wizard training is slipping, I fear; Vangey should have thoroughly acquainted you with all of us, from our faces to our indiscretions."

Still blinking, the surprised war wizard gave ground as the Swords followed her, emerging into a huge, many-pillared taproom whose dark wooden tables were crowded with cheerfully noisy drinkers. It was a splendid, warmly lit room, awash in the smells of fried cheeses and more exotic platters, and it stretched from the gleaming bar before them to the booths along the far wall of the room, a long spearcast away.

Out of long habit Narantha paused just inside the doorway to make a grand entrance—and Islif, who'd taken shrewd measure of Florin's new friend, threw out her arm like a door-bar to keep the rest of the Swords from walking right into Narantha's shapely back.

The noisy room hushed for a moment as the noblewoman clad in eye-catching flame was noticed, then talk returned all the louder. Through it, Narantha called to the tavernmaster, "A booth or table for six, if you have one!"

"Six?" Semoor asked, from behind her.

"Doust will no doubt be thirsty when he gets up off his knees," she replied, without turning. "In the meantime, it might keep the war wizard—who'll see it as his duty to eavesdrop on us—from *hovering*; he can just sit down with us, and join in."

At the rear of the Swords, Florin and Jhessail looked with some amusement at the jowly mage beside them, who harrumphed and blushed.

The duty tavernmaster looked Narantha up and down just as the war wizard had done, then hastened out from behind the bar to lead them down the room, beckoning them with a flourish.

The Lady Narantha glanced neither to right nor left as they threaded through the tables, but the Swords behind her were acutely aware of interested stares from dwarves, tattooed dusky-skinned traders from the South, dozens of merchants, and almost as many fighting men—probably guards, though they wore little or no armor, and not one of them bore scabbarded blades or any other sort of weapon. The Swords' sheathed weapons drew some curious looks.

The tavernmaster bowed and swept out his hand at a table almost at the end of the room. "Will this do, fairest Lady?"

"Admirably," Narantha replied. "We thirst."

The tavernmaster smiled. "As it happens, we solve such problems here. Ale, mead, zzar? Or shall I call the cellarer to acquaint you with our wines?"

"But of course," the Lady Crownsilver replied, seating herself.

Islif rolled her eyes and cast a glance back at Florin. He was smiling, and mouthed one silent word to her: *Adventure.*

"No. Not to my liking, I'm afraid," the tall trader said politely, setting down the boot. "Those I sell to rarely prefer anything practical—or used."

He strolled out of the shop and across the road to the Moon, where the doorwardens accepted his belt knife and admitted him. Striding to the bar for a tankard, the trader carefully neglected to glance down the room. The polished brass and finemetals on the wall behind the bar would afford him reflections enough to know where the Swords of Eveningstar were seated.

He had plenty of time. The evening was yet young.

As usual, the hargaunt itched.

Semoor peered mournfully at the empty bottom of his tankard, and Islif sighed and lifted her arm to signal for more ale.

As he turned to grin at her, the large-nosed priest of Lathander asked, "Why'd they take away the salted nuts? And then bring them right back again?"

"To give the war wizard a chance to enspell the bowl," Narantha told him, "so he can listen from afar rather than standing over us."

"Ah," Semoor replied. Scooping up the nut bowl, he put it to his lips and made a loud and rude sound. "I wonder what he'll make of that?"

"That Master Semoor Wolftooth is with us," Jhessail told him, "and being his usual self. Stoop, how are you *ever* going to keep your standing as a priest? If you behave like this inside a temple . . ."

"Dusking," Semoor cursed. "Am I going to go on being reprimanded even *now?* When I've escaped from Espar, charter-anointed, into a life of fabled adventure?"

Islif snorted. "The 'fabled adventure' part, good Stoop, may well be what swiftly befalls you if you ignore such reprimands. Ah, here's more ale."

As two smiling serving wenches in gowns with very low-laced corsets brought platters of drinkables, the talk at the table behind them—merchants from Sembia, if the shimmerweave and cloth-of-gold were anything to go by—rose in volume excitedly, so the Swords couldn't help but overhear:

"Ah, but every last war wizard in the realm'll be searching for it afore they're done, mark you! The thing can slay them—and has! I've heard six have been fried alive already! Heads blown off and innards sizzled like spitted boar!"

"Six? I heard eleven, and more who'll join them in graves right soon, if all the hired healing fails. Whoever wears this Iron War Crown can see active magics from afar—and from the thing hurl deadly bolts at anyone who has that magic!"

" 'Iron War'? What war's that? Something dwarves got mixed up in?"

"I know not. All these magic things have overblown and oh-so-mysterious names; didn't ye know?"

"Well, I know that magic in Cormyr means war wizards, and

that they're all frantically searching for this thing!"

"Well, I haven't got it—and if I did, I'd sell it right quick to someone who wants to fry mages and is willing to pay handsomely for the power to do so!"

"The Witch Queen? So she can snuff out Red Wizards even faster?"

There followed a chorus of raucous laughter, then a sudden hush as several burly men rose from divers tables and went over to the Sembians.

"So, what's all this about wanting to fry war wizards?" one of them asked, a shade too casually, and the richly garbed merchants looked up at him suspiciously.

"You look like a Purple Dragon who's left his armor at home to me," one Sembian replied, cleaning out one ear with a ring-adorned little finger. "So why don't you sit down here and tell us about war wizards? *We* only know what we hear."

"And what might that be?"

Another Sembian shrugged. "What all Cormyr is talking about— in the taverns, leastways: that something called the Arcrown's been stolen, and your Wizards of War want it back."

"Desperately," a third Sembian added.

"Before 'tis too late for them all," a fourth merchant put in, setting his tankard down hard.

The man who'd been bidden to sit down did so, fixed the loudest Sembian with a cool eye, and said, "Why don't you tell me more about what you've heard of this crown?"

"Oh? Such as?"

"What it does . . . that sort of thing."

The Sembian shrugged. "Arcrown or Iron War Crown, some are calling it, though most say it's a plain circlet. Wear it and you can see magic at work—and you can choose to send slaying bolts out of it, at whoever has those magics . . . that sort of thing."

"And then what?"

"And then they're dead, that's what, unless they throw away their magic or end their spell or whatever, right quick."

The Purple Dragon, if that's what he was, glanced up at some of the other burly men, and shrugs were exchanged.

Another of the Sembians looked down the table at the Cormyreans and added, "The rest is all rumors about how many war wizards have been slain already, by whom, and what it's all going to lead to—and being as you're all not-very-well-hidden agents of the Dragon Throne, suppose *you* tell us the truth about all of those things, hey?"

By way of reply, the man sitting at the end of the table favored him with a very cold stare, and without a word got up and went back to his own table, the other burly men drifting away as the Sembians chuckled.

When they spoke again, however, their voices were lower, and they seemed to be discussing prices and shortages and "how many barrels."

The Swords traded looks with each other.

Semoor, of course, spoke up first. "So would this make our reputations, if we found this crown and presented it to His Majesty?"

"That's a very large 'if,' " Florin commented. "First, we have to have the faintest idea of where to go looking."

Jhessail nodded. "And unless the spells the Morninglord grants you are more powerful than the spells of the war wizards—and remember, Stoop, some of them can split a castle keep in twain from top to bottom, with but a word!—we've not much chance of finding anything they can't. Certainly not with my paltry castings!"

Semoor plucked up the nut bowl again, and asked it brightly, "Any advice? Places you might like some enthusiastic, newly chartered adventurers to go look? Some noble's winecellar, perhaps? Or—ahem—pleasure chambers, where huffing and puffing monacled lords of the realm hide their hired harems?"

"*Semoor,*" Jhessail said reprovingly. "I deeply doubt the royal magician will find you either clever or funny."

"Oh? Why would he find me at all? And for that matter, *how* would he find me?"

The Lady Narantha leaned forward to look down the table at Semoor. "Well, by the choruses of exasperation, for one," she said, eyes twinkling. "And by the charter itself, for two: there're spells buried in all of those fancy inks, you know, and Vangerdahast can find out *exactly* where our charter is, whenever he wants to. Any war wizard can—and they can also, just by touching it and uttering the right word, know right away if it's a real charter or a forgery."

"Darkrose!" Semoor cursed. "Well, there goes my scheme for a wealthy retirement: go to Sembia, make dozens of charters that look very much like this one, and sell them to anyone who wants to traipse around Cormyr waving a sword!"

Jhessail sighed, turned in her chair, snatched the nut bowl out of Semoor's grasp, and told it fiercely, "He's jesting—jesting! Believe not a word!"

"Pray pardon," a voice purred by her ear. "I couldn't help but overhear mention of a charter. Am I correct in assuming you're lawful adventurers? And if so, are you looking for new members?"

The Swords of Eveningstar blinked at each other—then at the sleek young woman in dark leather who was leaning over Jhessail. Short and slender, with glossy black hair cut short in the same sort of "helm-bob" cut many warriors favored, she fixed them with large, liquid dark eyes.

"My name is Pennae," she added, "and this is Martess." She shifted a lithe shoulder aside to let the Swords see another slender, dark-clad and dark-haired lass standing behind her. "She casts spells out of books. I procure specifics when needs arise."

Florin stared at them, then around the table, not missing Narantha's look of encouragement.

Take command, it said, as clearly as if she'd shouted.

Clearing his throat, the man who'd rescued the king remembered one of Azoun's last bits of royal advice.

"Well, now," he began. "Well, now . . ."

"Lord Vangerdahast!" The war wizard's swift hail was high and shrill in excitement. "Someone has just approached them, and—"

The royal magician held up a quelling hand. "So I hear and see for myself."

He shrugged, the glow of his scrying crystal dancing across his face. "Let every jack and lass at loose ends in the upcountry join them, and ride hearty. It'll take most—mayhap all—of their lives, just to poke their noses into the Haunted Halls."

The Swords were still staring at the two women when two men wearing empty scabbards, easy grins, and the looks of muscled warriors came to the other end of their table.

"We'd also like to ride with you, if you'll have us," said the taller and more handsome of the two: a blond charmer who outshone Florin in looks. "Agannor am I, and this is my friend Bey. We swing swords . . . fairly well."

The Swords found themselves staring at the two newcomers, then back at the two women, then at the grinning men again.

The Lady Narantha raised her eyes to the rafters and asked disbelievingly, "What *is* this place? A branch of the Society of Stalwart Adventurers?"

"Nay, Lady," the tavernmaster told her proudly, arriving with a platter crowded with goblets and flasks on his shoulder. "Better than that: this is The Moon and Stars, finest tavern between Teflamm and splendrous Waterdeep!"

The tall trader nursing a tankard not far from the Swords' table glanced their way with casual indifference at the tavernmaster's merry boast—then stiffened in anger and surprise as his gaze fell upon a tall woman in forest green, who'd risen from where she'd been sitting alone, at a table against the wall, and was striding toward the Esparran adventurers.

Thinking silent curses, Horaundoon turned back to his tankard, taking care not to do so too swiftly. Dove Silverhand might be the most feeble in Art of the Seven—but just how feeble that might be, he did not care to learn.

No sane wizard challenges the goddess of magic, and expects to win.

+ + ✳ + +

Someone *else* was coming to their table. Florin glanced up.

And froze, heart pounding, as he met her dark blue eyes—and fell into them, plunging into endless wise depths . . .

He swallowed and shook himself like a wet dog, tearing himself out of whatever reverie—had he been caught in some sort of spell?

Was this a fell sorceress?

She had long brown hair, that swirled unbound about her shoulders—shoulders as broad as his own, and outstripping Islif in bulging build. She was as tall as him, too, and clad in the vest, tunic, breeches, and high boots of a man. A stylish man able to afford the best weaves and leathers, and have even his boots dyed forest green.

She was all in green, this woman, and strode up to them with casual grace, as one deft and strong who knows her power but assumes no airs of rank or mincing affectation. Narantha might have a title, but *this* lady was truly noble.

The very sight of her stirred and unsettled him; Florin looked down, certain he was blushing. Her image remained bright before his eyes even as he stared into his tankard. He *had* to know her, to speak with her—yet he felt none of the swift, strong lust that lush feminine beauty or flirtation was wont to stir in him. She was . . . she was . . . gods, was this what minstrels sang of, "love at first glance"?

He was lost . . .

"Well met, adventurers," she said, voice low-pitched and husky. "I happen to be an officer of the Crown, and perceive a possible need. If you desire to amend your charter—to add to your ranks, say—I can ply the pen properly, so the nearest Purple Dragon, Wizard of War, royal magician, or even the king himself will pronounce it proper."

"Uh—ah—t-that's very kind of you, Lady . . . ah?" Florin flushed crimson. Gods, he was gabbling like an awestruck village idiot! He was deathly afraid Semoor would erupt in a acidic comment about "lovestruck Florin" or some such, and yet . . . and yet he cared not.

"I am known here as the Lady in Green," she said warmly, and her eyes seemed to flare silver, just for a moment. None of the Swords saw war wizards and Purple Dragons all over the room stiffen and stare vacantly at nothing for a moment, silver flames dancing in their eyes—then return to their tankards and mutterings, all notice of a lone woman in green gone. "You can trust me."

Leaning close to Florin—who fought furiously with himself to keep his gaze from plunging into her bodice, and just barely won—she murmured, "As Azoun told you: 'Tathen.' "

Hearing her, and looking again at the four other visitors to their table, the Swords traded arrow-swift, excited glances, looking at last to Narantha. Who smiled at them in wry amazement, shook her head, and said, "Truly the gods *do* smile upon you, friends!"

Take command, Florin reminded himself. "Are we all agreed to accept four new companions? I know 'tis swift, and they're strangers, but the king . . ."

"The gods!" Semoor said firmly. "The hands of the gods have provided them!"

Islif spread her hands. "We need the strength. I'm for them all."

"I, too," Jhessail put in. Semoor, Narantha, and Florin found themselves nodding at each other.

"Done, then," Florin said, shuddering in relief, and clawed at the buckles of the breastplate he wore. Azoun had given it to him, and he hadn't wanted to leave it in his room, in case . . .

"Pray excuse this disrobing," he muttered, swinging the breastplate open and plucking the precious charter from between the inside of the plate and its inner lining. He held it out to the Lady in Green.

Who smiled at him and shook her head. "You'd best find another place for it. Your sweat will rot it away in a month or so if you keep it there; believe me, for betimes I wear steel in battle; I know."

Out of the inside of her vest she produced a plumeless, tapering quill and a vial of ink that sparkled through its confining glass. "I'm going to need four names," she said calmly, "with their proper spellings . . ."

Horaundoon brooded, the hargaunt shifting restlessly as it felt his fury. Not six places from him, she was, and the Weave fairly crackling around her. Sark her!

She was more than a creature of Mystra—though by all the eye tyrants Manshoon could name, wasn't that *enough?* She was a Harper, and this room could well be crawling with them . . .

Nay, almost certainly *was* crawling with them. Which in turn meant sarking Vangerdahast was probably scrying this place, right now, with half a dozen of his most senior Wizards of War.

Which meant Horaundoon of the Zhentarim dared do nothing. Nothing at all.

If any of the war wizards and out-of-uniform Purple Dragons in the taproom had happened to notice the tall trader, all they would have seen then was his eyes narrow, and his expression grow thoughtful.

And what trader doesn't get that look, a time or six each day?

The mindworm would have a new target. One of the four new Swords: Pennae, Martess, Agannor, or Bey. Which one, though? Who would be best to subvert?

Well, the answer to that would take *more* watching and waiting.

Praise Bane, watching and waiting were tasks Horaundoon excelled at, and was even beginning to enjoy.

"Agannor Wildsilver. Alura 'Pennae' Durshavin. Bey Freemantle. Martess Ilmra," Florin read aloud. "Welcome to the Swords of Eveningstar!"

The cheer that went up then rocked the taproom of The Moon and Stars, echoed as it was from many tables.

In the moment of silence that followed in its tankard-clinking, ale-swilling wake, before the chatter could resume, Doust Sulwood burst into the room, and hurried toward his fellow Swords.

"Did I miss anything?"

Chapter 11
AN EVENING STAR IN HAUNTED DREAMS

To see a steadfast star in your dreams is to behold a sign of favor from the gods. The trick, as usual in life, is to determine just which god, and what the sign means. Before, of course, 'tis too late.

Aundrammas Hulzondurr
Collected Sages' Sayings
published in the Year of the Fist

Something moved in the moonlit cottage. Something dark and serpentine. Malevolent, Jhessail knew a moment later, as it reared up, faceless and flowing, and somehow *looked* at her.

Somehow the wall was gone, between her room and her parents' bedchamber, and she was seeing their moonlit bed, holding the two of them asleep together, peacefully entangled.

Jhessail screamed, but nothing came out of her mouth. Nothing at all.

Faceless yet somehow sneering at her, the thing, wraithlike and dark, turned to rear over her parents.

Jhessail screamed again, screamed and tried to leap from her bed to wake her mother and father before it . . . before it . . .

Fell on them like a great endless wave, as black as deepest night and as cold as all winter, to slide into their sleeping mouths and noses, in at their ears, escaping into them like smoke as Jhessail burst free of whatever was holding her, sprang down from her bed atop the wardrobe, and raced to snatch up lantern and fire-poker and run to—stand above her parents, terrified and shivering, not knowing what to do.

Craegh and Lhanna Silvertree lay in the moonlight, murmuring in their slumber as they finished flinging aside the quilt and covers, their faces troubled and pale as the moonlight itself . . .

Then, as Jhessail stood over them helplessly, their faces went calm again, and they froze into peaceful stillness.

Leaving her with nothing to do, after long and fearful gazing, but trudge back to her wardrobe, feeling a dark and mocking gaze between her bare shoulderblades, and soundless laughter rolling uproariously around her . . .

She started to shiver and couldn't stop, ending up doubled over with her teeth chattering violently, trying to keep clawing her way up the wardrobe to her bed in her shudderings, deathly afraid whatever it was would reach out its flowing darkness for her . . .

Abruptly Jhessail became aware that the room around her was not her own, and held no moonlight nor parents. Instead there was someone in bed beside her whose shiverings were every bit as violent as her own, and whose breathing was sharp with fear. Jhessail rolled away, against the wall, and stared up into the darkness. Ah, yes: this was a room at The Old Man inn in Waymoot, and the woman wrapped in a close-bundled sheet beside her was—

Martess. Martess Ilmra, who called herself "Lowspell." Who was whimpering now, and—

Thrusting bolt upright in bed, gasping. "Where—"

"Martess?" Jhessail asked, trying to sound calm and gentle. "It's me, Jhessail. One of the Swords of Eveningstar you joined, earlier this even. I'm right here beside you. Rough dreams?"

"Y-yes," Martess whispered. "Gods, I was so frightened! Something dark and shapeless, that I could never quite see clearly. It moved by flowing, Jhess—oh, I'm sure I sound like a silly little lass!—and I watched it pounce on—on some sleeping folk, and flow into them, somehow, leaving them asleep as before. It was so . . . *vivid*; I—I can't quite believe 'twasn't really happening!"

Jhessail reached out her hand in the darkness, and Martess started and gave a gasp that was almost a cry at that touch. Jhessail stroked her side soothingly, through the sheet, and whispered, "You don't sound silly to me. I had the very same dream. I was sleeping at home and woke up, and saw the wraith-thing go into my parents. It laughed at me."

"Yes!" The answering whisper was fierce. "Exactly!"

There was a little silence, then Martess whispered, "The same dream—and if meddling mortal magic played no part in this, then shared dreams are sent by the gods. Who sent ours, and why?" She drew in a deep, shuddering breath and asked, "And what does it mean?"

"We're both dedicated to Mystra, above all others," Jhessail whispered back. "Even if this was not her sending, it is to her we should look for guidance."

"Yes," Martess agreed, and rose from the bed. The room was small, but she shrugged the sheet from around her and knelt on it, to give Jhessail room to slide out of the bed with the quilt, and do the same thing.

Side by side, able to hear more than see each other, they knelt together in the dark and prayed to Mystra, the simple Plea for Guidance that is taught to anyone who cares to learn it, and is muttered by many to the nearest candle flame or visible star when confronted with magic.

Their whisperings ended in perfect unison, and they were both drawing breath to speak to each other about what to do next when a sudden sound made them both freeze.

Just outside their door, in this upper-floor passage of The Old Man inn, whose aging timbers creaked betimes but was in the main quiet (the noises of persons striding briskly would have been clearly heard), they had both heard the ever-so-faint scrape of a boot on the floorboards.

Jhessail put her hand out to Martess and felt her way to the woman's ear. Putting her mouth against it, she whispered as quietly as possible, "I've a magic missile. What shall we do?"

She turned her head aside, to let Martess find her ear, and say into it: "Oh. A battlestrike, you mean?"

Jhessail patted her fellow mage's hand to signify "yes."

"Then get you to the wall by the door, ready to hurl it, and I'll use my 'servant unseen' to open the door and unhood our night-lantern. Forget not to shield your eyes."

Jhessail put up her hand, found and shaped the chin of her fellow mage, and murmured, "I'll go pour water from ewer to bowl and back, to cloak your incanting. Tap me with your spell, to let me know when to cease."

Martess whispered agreement, and they did those things.

Jhessail set down bowl and ewer the moment she felt the spell-touch, and scampered for the wall by the door, bruising the fingertips of the hand she flung out before her to keep from crashing into its boards.

There was a faint squeal from the floor beside her as the servant-spell tugged out the door-wedge. Then it snatched the door open.

As the battered old planking swung into the dark room, Jhessail clapped her hand over her eyes—and Martess magically lofted the lantern across the room at the passage, unhooding it as it went. Its swift flight made it flare up into roaring brightness.

The man outside blinked then squinted, raising a hand to shield his eyes that held a holy symbol of Tymora. The blank coin of a novice, on a chain that Jhessail recognized.

The lantern halted right in front of the novice's nose, close enough to keep him from seeing anything beyond it—and to be thrust full-searing into his face if he tried anything sudden or menacing.

What they could see of that face was grim, and belonged to Doust Sulwood.

"Jhess? Martess? Are you both well?" His voice was the quietest of murmurs, and was grave. "I've had a most disturbing dream . . ."

Maglor checked the two slow-coal braziers. Overnight heating was essential for these concoctions, but he didn't want to find them charred waste come morning—or half his workshop gone to ashes, either. Even if he hadn't served the Zhentarim, every village apothecary had ingredients and concoctions difficult to replace, and secrets his fellow villagers had best never see, even as smoking remnants.

His windows were already firmly shuttered against hopefully sleeping Eveningstar, for it would go ill indeed for him if anyone witnessed the moot he was here to attend.

Under orders, of course.

Why Old Ghost felt the need to meet every seventh night. . . . Unless, of course, it really *was* just to enjoy terrifying him.

Maglor's thin, cruel mouth tightened, and he shook his head. Some day he'd be mighty enough to destroy Old Ghost . . . somehow . . .

He felt a sudden tingling, as if every hair of his body was standing up on end. Well, they probably were, because the faint, dead-white glow that followed, tinged just for an instant with green, meant only one thing: out of empty air, by fell magic, the eerie, flowing wraith-like *thing* known as "Old Ghost" was joining him in his workshop.

From where, he knew not, nor could he do more than speculate as to how; the word "magic" was an explanation so broad as to be meaningless. He wasn't even certain what Old Ghost was. A fell intelligence that could speak, yes, and probably once a solid, mortal human wizard.

Probably.

Now, Old Ghost was Maglor's all-too-familiar Zhentarim superior, and Maglor wasn't sure if he hated it more than he was terrified of it—or whether his terror outstripped his hatred. The latter, he supposed, as he'd never dared try to—

"Maglor," Old Ghost said, in that hoarse whisper of a voice that never began with any greeting, "I have a task for you."

Maglor bowed his head. "I willingly serve."

The glowing, drifting presence made a sound that might have been a snort. "You remain a poor liar. Save your breath, and heed well. You are to deal with the upstart Swords of Eveningstar before they endanger our profits."

"Who or what are the Swords of—"

"Adventurers, who just personally received a charter from King Azoun—along with his order to undertake an exploration of the Haunted Halls. They will be here soon, and are bidden to report to Winter. Their very presence may disrupt our caravan traffic, for even if they haven't been ordered to report anyone they see in the Stonelands, some war wizards will have been ordered to spy on *them*, and so will be where we don't want them to be."

" 'Deal with'?"

"Eliminate them. *Without* attracting Purple Dragon attention to our smuggling activities in Eveningstar."

"I'll see to it at once."

"You will indeed. Or else."

And Old Ghost faded away, making this the shortest moot Maglor had ever "enjoyed" with it. The Zhentarim upper ranks must be busy.

Nonetheless, as he snuffed the last of the candle-lamps and headed for the stairs up to his cold and lonely bed, Maglor was trembling.

The sickening chill of Old Ghost's nearness—a bone-deep cold that stole his strength and left him retching on the weak brink of unconsciousness, on the rare occasions when Old Ghost swept *through* Maglor—always left him trembling.

Agannor snored like handfuls of gravel sliding down a shield.

Bey was slower and deeper, like the call of a distant and melancholy war horn.

Florin, however, lay silent, because he was awake. Again.

Too full of that strange tingling to get back to sleep. It was with him always now, a faint singing by day but a louder whispering by night. He couldn't make out the words, no matter how hard he strained, but somehow felt no evil, nor threat to him. "The favor of Holy Mielikki," Hawkstone had murmured, just for him to hear. "Given to you, lad, to blaze within you until Our Lady of the Forest comes to touch you herself."

And that was all the great ranger had said. He'd gone in with them to the table, but a bare two breaths later, when Florin—who very much wanted to talk to his former tutor, about the tingling and so many other things—had looked for him in all the scrapings of chairs and the king's jovial words and servants scurrying to set out dishes, Hawkstone was simply gone.

Vanished, as if the very air had swallowed him, without anyone else seeming to notice his absence or even remark on his being there in the first place. They'd said nothing, any of them, about Florin receiving the favor of Mielikki. Whatever it was.

The tingling was growing inside him now, as if responding to his attention. What *was* it?

Oh, he'd talked to Doust and Semoor about it, and even Jhessail for a moment or two. When he mentioned it, they remembered it—vaguely, speaking words without interest or emotion, as if discussing something overheard about someone they knew not—but had nothing useful to say. Or even to suggest, beyond going to see a cleric of Mielikki. Which obvious deed he was already eager to do—if he ever found one. Those who'd come to Espar had been wanderers, as was the way of rangers and druids, and he'd never met a "treecloak," as the druids called the clerics of all the woodgods in Cormyr. Yet it sounded very much as if the goddess herself was going to visit him. And "touch" him, whatever that meant. It must mean some sort of change or awakening in him, though, or why would Hawkstone have brought this power that now tingled within him to wait for it?

Unless he was entirely wrong, and it was something unknown.

Florin's long sigh of bewilderment roused Agannor to snorting confusion, but the son of Hethcanter Falconhand and Imsra Skydusk slid down it a long, long way, deep and dark, until morning.

"Get *in* here," Jhessail hissed, hauling Doust into the room. "We'll have half the inn up if you stand out there—and they're sure to want to know why you've come visiting and we're so upset. One *word* spills out about wraith-nightmares and half Cormyr will be telling the other half that we're cursed, and should be turned away from their doors, shunned, and all the rest of it."

"Wraith-nightmares! S-so you dreamed the same thing!" Doust stammered, as they bundled him inside.

Martess set the unhooded lantern down on the wide shelf that crossed the back of the room, plucked up the sheet to cover herself again, and gave the priestling of Tymora a level look. "We did. Now just why did your dream bring you here, to the two of us? Or rather, to come as silent as a thief, then just stand there? Were you planning to hold up yon passage wall until morning?"

Doust blinked at Jhessail, suddenly aware that aside from her boot socks, she wore very little. Jhessail spread her hands unconcernedly, then pointed at Martess. "There's only the one sheet, and I have my socks, so she has it."

Doust sat down hastily on the floor and turned his back on them. The two women exchanged glances then got back into bed; the air was cold.

"I'm waiting," Martess said. "How long does it take you to invent answers?"

"I'm not . . . forgive me. I dreamed that a wraith-thing—shapeless but it could see me, and rear up, and it was *evil*—was slithering like a snake, and, well, *flowing* some of the time, too. It came into my room, slithered around Stoop, then reared up and looked at me. It gave me a sneer, then went out under the door again. I put on my boots—our room is so cold that we both slept in our clothes—and went after it, but in my head I could see where it was going. It came here, and I reached to take down the passage-lamp and burned my hand on it. That's when I realized I was awake. I left the lamp and hurried down to your door as swift as I could, and was standing there wondering what to do when you . . . opened up."

Jhessail looked at Martess, who said slowly and distinctly, "Tluin. Gods-hrasting, stlarning—tluin. *Tluin.*"

Jhessail sighed. "I feel the same way, but cursing's going to help us not at all. What was it? And did it do anything, to any of us? I don't want to ride into danger thinking one of my friends, riding beside me, is really an evil monster inside, just waiting for the best chance to slay the rest of us."

"Is that what it really was, d'you think?" Doust asked. "What if it was, say, a sign from the gods?"

"Surely the gods, being so greater than mortals, could craft a sign we could understand," Martess said sharply. "Otherwise, what good is it? Do they think we're going to go running to a random priest and ask what it meant? We *know* we'd only get his guess, and might not follow it, so what good would that do the god? If a dream isn't a means of shoving us into doing or not doing certain things, why go to the trouble of crafting it?"

Doust nodded. "And which god sent it?"

Jhessail sighed. "None of this talk of ours *matters*. We've no way of knowing it's to do with the gods or not. What if it's a ghost that haunts this inn? Or a prowling monster? Or spell-sent by a wizard to hunt for something? It could be none of these things; we just don't know. Now, if the gods want us to do something, they can tell us. Plainly. Otherwise, all this guessing is just that: our guessing. Or a priest's guessing—and hear me well: I'm *not* spending the rest of my life wondering if I should do thus and so in accordance with someone else's guesses. Guesses that could very well be wrong. And they will be someone else's guesses, because I'm not wasting any time trying to guess anything."

She ran out of breath and fury at the same time, and stopped abruptly. In the silence that followed, Doust and Martess said the same thing, in untidy unison: "Well said."

It was a far later time than Tessaril Winter, the Lady Lord of Eveningstar, was accustomed to dining. Or to receiving smiling young Wizards of War alone in her bedchamber, for that matter.

Nevertheless, her room at the top of her tower was the most private and secure place she knew of in Eveningstar, and Vangerdahast's spy was obviously starving. She filled his tallglass again—glowfire, and a particularly fine vintage—and earned a bright smile of thanks.

The cheese, nutbread, and spicy pickles were delicious. Peasant fare, but she liked them, and kept them to hand in jars and stone coffers in her closet. Her cooks had taken to sleeping in the kitchen and pantry, and she'd rather they not know of young Malbrand's visit. The food gave their little chat something of a blanketfeast air, as if they were gallivanting together in a forest. Like a certain young noble lady and a handsome local forester, it seemed.

"These Swords must be something, if the Zhentarim are *this* worried about them," Tessaril commented, helping herself to cheese and shaking her head ruefully. She'd known she'd be unable to resist, once the viands were out and she could see and smell them.

The war wizard nodded. "They won their charter by saving the king's life, and ride now with the young Lady Narantha Crownsilver, much against the wishes of her parents."

"Hmm. Am I to detain the lady?"

"Neither the Crown nor the royal magician have sent instructions. Lord and Lady Crownsilver *will* send instructions, likely howled loudly—but they don't know she's still with them. Yet."

Tessaril smiled. "I *like* adventurers. Matchless entertainment."

Malbrand rolled his eyes.

Tessaril snorted. "Stop that. And tell me of this saving of Az—of His Majesty's life."

The young mage was beginning to get over his awe of her and embarrassment at being served a meal by a lady lord of the realm clad only in a nightrobe, not two strides from her bed. He leaned forward eagerly. "Of course."

Sipping glowfire and lifting his brows to her in appreciative salute—which she returned, silently raising her own glass—he asked, "Now, where to begin? Ah, I suppose with . . ."

The next morning dawned slow and chill, a reluctant sun slowly brightening an Eveningstar beset with the drifting smoke of thick ground mists. The dew had been heavy, and most folk busied themselves indoors, awaiting the warmer full sun.

Apothecaries, however, are desired in haste or not welcomed at all. The wooden box of his satchel rode heavily on Maglor's hip, its shoulder strap creaking, as he strode along the village roads. Old Mother Naura wanted clearthroat syrup for her ailing youngest, Beldrak's old wounds were stiffening and needed deepfire liniment, and—

Two rose-robed figures came striding out of the mists toward him, talking together in low tones. Ah, yes. The other brave farers forth in any sort of weather: priests of the House of the Morning, on holy business bent.

"Fair morning," Maglor greeted them heartily. He was not loved at the temple, he knew. Though the priests of Lathander weren't known for selling little bottles that soothed and healed, he was probably seen as a major reason for their lack of that particular source of easy coins.

"Fair morning, Master Maglor," one replied briskly, deep-voiced. Hamdorn the Hand-Wringer, that would be, the large, florid, balding man who comforted grieving folk of Eveningstar with empty platitudes and soothing nothings.

Which meant the other priest would be Hamdorn's nigh-constant companion, Claerend. The two conducted much of the temple's daily dealings with the village, and so would be a good way to begin darkening the reputations of these Swords. Right now, before they'd even been seen in Eveningstar.

A few fell falsehoods, hints of "involvements" and "they say that," would be a solid beginning. When he was done delivering bottled comfort, a visit to the Lady Lord of Eveningstar to impart similar tidings—as a frowningly troubled apothecary, passing on what he thought she should know, overheard from gossipy passing merchants—would be a second step of even greater solidity. Solid coin, solid progress; Maglor liked solid things.

He rubbed his hands as the priests drew nearer and a plume of wet mist slid away to confirm their identities, and asked, "Have you heard the latest? Seems the king's decided to rid himself of some troublesome sorts and have another go at the Haunted Halls, at one stroke. He's granted a charter to a band of younglings who call themselves 'the Swords of Eveningstar'—not that they've ever set boot in our fair village yet, mind—and ordered them up here, to play at being adventurers! I'm thinking we'd all best be alert, lest more than a few chickens start to go missing, if you catch my drift . . ."

Hamdorn and Claerend stopped dead and leaned forward, interest clear on their faces.

Maglor hid a grin. Solid progress.

✦ ✦ ✦ ✦

Jhessail was starting to get used to the constant creak of saddle-leather and jingling of bits and bridle-rings, but she suspected the ache in her thighs was only going to get worse. By the furrows on her roommate's brow, Martess was feeling the same pain.

"Not used to riding, hey?" Agannor had asked with a friendly grin, spurring past her on his way to the front, back when they'd been leaving the inn yard. In his wake, Bey had looked away and muttered something that sounded suspiciously like "Strengthens the thighs!" Well, at least he hadn't delivered those words with the delighted leer Semoor would have wrapped them in. Dhedluk was a full day's ride ahead, halfway to Eveningstar, but the road ran through deep forest and the sun seemed in no hurry, so the mists would cling and roll along it for most of their way.

" 'Ware outlaws," the grizzled leader of a patrol of king's foresters had said, coming into Waymoot as they were riding out. The mist had beaded the ranger's beard with water, droplets that hung along his jaw like jewels. "This—and full night—are when they're at their worst. Show those swords of yours, and wear the shields."

Agannor and Bey, looking seasoned and formidable in the best armor and weaponry among the Swords, had gone to the fore. With a silent jerk of her head and firm hand on the bridle of his horse, Islif had taken Semoor with her to the rear—largely to keep him away from all the lasses and so curb his tongue a trifle, Jhessail suspected.

The rest of the Swords were strung out between, riding in pairs . . . though, as she'd expected, Doust was falling back now, to join Semoor. Those two were as thick as—

Hmm. Now, was or was not Pennae a professional thief? And if she was, what sort of trouble would that land them all in, and how soon? Islif had firmly chosen to room with Pennae last night, and hadn't said anything much this morn, but perhaps a word or two . . .

Alongside, Martess was riding quietly. Jhessail liked her, thus far at least. She kept to herself, but watched the world alertly from under those arresting black brows. Just as eye-catchingly ivory skin—she seemed to own only high-collared gowns and tunics of black, dark blue, and purple, that made her look bone-pale. Black eyes, that ink-black long hair; if she'd been aggressive or insolent or acted sinister, she'd be the sort folk would be quick to call a "witch." Slender, petite, child-sized—and still largely a mystery.

Not that many of the Swords would give much thought to who and what Martess Ilmra really was, when they had Pennae purring and jesting all over the place in skin-tight black leathers, with a coiled whip riding one of her hips. Just now she was riding with Florin, and when she wasn't leaning close to say something tart or chuckle, she was running nimble fingers along his thigh, or striking poses in her saddle that best displayed her to his polite glances—small but nicely curved bells of which much could be readily seen, as she seemed to have forgotten to lace up most of the front of her leathers this morn. Oh, yes, *that* one was going to be trouble.

Jhessail sighed. Then she shrugged, smiling a little. A few days ago her troubles had been rooted in trying to think of a way out of Espar, and a waiting life of marriage into drudgery; at least she now had a fresh new set to ponder.

Chapter 12
TROUBLE TRAVELS NORTH

And when at last Prince Rarvarrick came to the Dread Door and struck mightily with his fist upon it, setting up a great storm of boomings and crashings, a tiny door within the door did open, and out from it thrust a head with no body, that floated in the air where most severed heads would have fallen, and spake unto him: "Thou art too late by a night, puissant prince. For, behold: the foe you seek hath flown. I am bid to say unto you: 'Trouble Travels North.' Make of this what you will, for being but a lonely head with no body, all that befalls is as one to me."

Thaele Summermore
The Roisterings of Bold Prince Rarvarrick
published in the Year of the Grimoire

"Let the favor of the Morninglord touch us all," the patriarch of the temple intoned with dignity. Then Charisbonde sat back in the tallest and most ornate of the chairs in the rose-hued alcove, and asked less formally, "Now what occasions such haste, you two?"

"News of adventurers, soon to arrive in Eveningstar," Claerend began.

"From Maglor, to us, just now," Hamdorn put in.

Charisbonde glanced at the man who sat beside him. Myrkyr, Bright Banner of the temple, returned that look, then leaned forward in his chair to ask, "The Swords of Eveningstar?"

"Yes!" Claerend sounded relieved, rather than startled, that the two priests who led the House of the Morning knew of the adventurers already. "The apothecary said they were . . . less than trustworthy. That the king had chartered them to be rid of them, and sent them here to scour out the Haunted Halls."

"And that all in Eveningstar had best beware thefts and worse, once they were here," Hamdorn added.

Charisbonde and Myrkyr exchanged looks and nodded.

"Brothers," Patriarch Charisbonde told them gently, "I would ask you not to place any credence in words said by the apothecary. He serves Zhentil Keep, and whispers at their will."

Hamdorn and Claerend blinked at him, clearly astonished.

"Then—" Claerend cleared his throat, visibly steeling himself to dare to say what he asked next. "Then why haven't we denounced him long since? So dark is *that* brotherhood that he'd be hounded out and away from our midst, and so much the better. We can physic all Evenor at half the prices Maglor charges—without worry that this ointment or that pain-quaff might be poisoned, to do dirty Zhent dark-work."

"We have at least reported his allegiance to the Crown?" Hamdorn looked anxious. The patriarch nodded.

Myrkyr rubbed his mustache in the back and forth manner that meant he was choosing his words carefully. "We await the right time," he told Claerend. "Violence always births new things, but the Morninglord is best pleased with splendid new beginnings."

Patriarch Charisbonde Trueservant stirred in his chair. "Of one thing I can promise you," he said, rising to signify that this interruption of his midmorning prayers was at an end. "By our hands or others, Maglor will be dealt with very soon."

" 'Twould be best," Islif said firmly, "if you two bosom chortling holy men did *not* ride together this day, dispensing your usual jests and airy comments. Not until we know our new friends rather better."

"Agreed, Liff," Semoor said quickly. "Clumsum here just wants a swift word with me."

"And I'd prefer you listen in, too," Doust told Islif, in a low murmur. "This concerns us all, and prudence, and—"

"Just say whatever you came back here to say," Islif said curtly, in a voice as low as his.

"Well, then: I think we two should pray to our respective gods for guidance."

"Regarding?" Islif's voice was cool. "You're not going to try to decide where the Swords go and what we do in accordance with what you claim the gods want, are you?"

"No, no! Guidance concerning the real aims and natures of our . . . new four."

Islif and Semoor nodded in unison, even before Doust added, "For the safety of all our hides!"

"Eveningstar has one of the foremost temples of Lathander in all the realm," Semoor said slowly. "I would have presented myself there for prayer and advice anyhail. Some say the House of the Morning is too sleepy a backwater, no longer a-kindle with the 'true fire' of Lathander—whatever *that* is—but worship there is led by Charisbonde Trueservant, and Holy Lathander hasn't allowed many of the Anointed to take so bold a consecration name."

Islif looked grave. "And how will you seek his advice without informing him you have your suspicions about our new members? Bearing in mind that even if those doubts are baseless, letting a high priest hear of them—if he takes note at all of anything said by a mere novice from the dust of Espar, wearing a homemade holy symbol—may make them real? If he and his flock treat any of us with suspicion, damage is done. Based on nothing, and nigh impossible to wash away. Be *very* careful."

Semoor nodded. "Yet you dispute not our underlying concern?"

"No," Islif murmured, giving both priestlings long and level looks. "No, I don't."

"So, lass? Have you come to scold me for not taking to my bed last night? Or to tell me someone's prepared me a meal? A royal pet's gone lame? Or is it something important?"

"No, Lord Vangerdahast." Laspeera gave the royal magician a rather pert look. "Merely reporting in, as you ordered me to."

Then she brought her hand out from behind her back. There was a handwheel of onion-and-mushroom cheese in it.

"Stolen from the kitchens for you. To keep you from falling flat on your face with hunger until you get yourself down to the Unicorn Chamber—where Samdanthra will shortly be serving you a meal you *will* eat, if I have to stand over you with a bullwhip."

Vangerdahast gave his favorite aide a bristle-browed look. "Stealing food? Bullwhips? Have you been talking to Queen Filfaeril again?"

"No, Lord. What befalls behind closed palace doors is none of my affair," came the oh-so-innocent reply, delivered by a Laspeera who was carefully studying the ornately molded plaster ceiling overhead.

"Ah, but it *is*, lass. It is. As you well know." Vangerdahast sniffed the cheese, bit into it cautiously—then started to devour it like a starving lion. "So," he managed to say between bites, "report!"

Laspeera inclined her head politely. "I have the pleasure to inform you that the Hammerfall affair seems to be moving to a satisfactory conclusion. The Goldsword situation remains very much as before, but we're working on a stablemaster right now, hoping he'll confess. You were right about Ruirondro; Vaelra and Straekus are working on some suitably horrifying dream-visions right now, to scare him appropriately. We thought you'd prefer that to any trial."

"You thought correctly," Vangerdahast grunted. "Blood of the Dragon, I busy myself for half a day watching just one of the usual traitors, and you get up to all this! You know I prefer to have a hand in everything."

"Yes, and we worry about you losing fingers, thereby."

"Ha ha. The trouble with clever-tongued lasses is that they too seldom resist being either clever or wagging their tongues about it. Anything *else* you've been up to?"

"Yes, Lord Vangerdahast. You set Braelrur and Daunatha to watching the Swords of Eveningstar. Well, as of last night there are four new Swords, duly written in on the charter and riding with the king's chosen heroes."

"Dragon! Who? Any sign of this being prepared beforehand?"

"None at all, as far as the Esparran are concerned. However, we worry that any or even all of the four may be members of, or agents for, various noble cabals, the Zhentarim, or Sembian sneak-coins."

" 'Sneak-coins'? Lass, I've chided you before about using cant. What are 'sneak-coins'?"

"Since Royal Undertreasurer Aliss Thondren invented the term—some two centuries ago, Lord—sneak-coins are Sembian cabals or even formal syndicates who covertly try to gain control of businesses in Cormyr, and all too often attempt to secure influence in the realm by bribery, blackmail, and otherwise influencing officials. Or nobles."

"Huh," Vangey grunted, inspecting his fingers and licking the last of the cheese from them, "as if a Sembian would behave any differently. We called those cabals 'cabals' in my day."

He got up from the chair he'd been slumped in. "I agree we should know more about them. Get Belthonder and Omgryn onto this; their current work can wait." He strode to the door. "The Unicorn Chamber, you said?"

"Yes, Lord Vangerdahast." Laspeera bowed, but Vangey spun around.

"Stop that," he snapped irritably. "You'll have me thinking I'm one of those popinjay nobles. Who are these four arrow-swift opportunists?"

"Lord, all youthful humans, two men and two women. The men are Agannor Wildsilver and Bey Freemantle, hireswords, and the women are Martess Ilmra, commonly known as 'Lowspell,' and Alura Durshavin, commonly known as 'Pennae.' You'll not have heard of them—"

Vangerdahast sighed. "Ah, such a dolt is our royal magician, waddling through life oblivious to the business of the realm and all the folk who throng it. As it happens, I *have* heard of the two lasses—and some time ago assigned Delavaundar and Marlegast, quite separately, to learning all about them."

Laspeera gave him a sidelong, challenging look. "And?"

"They're still learning, but as I recall, have told me thus far that this Pennae is a Mask-worshipper and an accomplished thief: acrobatic upper-balcony work, for the most part. Born in Arabel to a pastry cook, now passed on. Father unknown, probably a codloose Purple Dragon of the garrison. Martess is one of those lasses who came to Suzail with a feel and a hunger for the Art but no spells or tutor, and tried to make a living on her looks while seeking both. 'Lowspell' for her lack of spells, of course, though I hear she gained a handful from lonely old mages who wanted their limbs warmed;

she probably fell in with Pennae in a tavern somewhere in the city. So, clever lass, what can *you* tell *me?*"

Laspeera smiled. "As to the women, you're far ahead of Braelrur and Daunatha. They did ask a few folk in Waymoot about the men, this morn. Hearsay, nothing more, suggesting Wildsilver and Freemantle are just swordswingers. Easygoing, a trifle brutal but not 'mad slayers,' and apt to be lazy and prefer the flask over vigilant patrolling. Came out of upcountry Sembia and bounced around here and there doing short-coin work, never for long with one patron: caravan-escorting, valuable-package-protection, and bodyguarding."

Vangerdahast grunted. "Inform me when they truly learn something. I'm for the Unicorn Chamber." The door banged, and his voice came back through it: "Oh, lass?"

"Yes, Lord Vangerdahast?"

"Thank you."

+ + ✳ + +

Teasing fingers slid along his thigh again. "Lord Florin?"

Florin blinked, unsettled again. "I'm—I'm no lord, nor ever likely to be. I'm a forester."

And favored of Mielikki, which sounded wonderful. If only he knew what it really meant.

Had—had Mielikki been the Lady in Green?

He stared again into those dark blue eyes, flaring silver just that once. He'd be seeing that gaze until his dying day. There'd been no sign of her this morn, and no one at The Old Man or The Moon and Stars knew where she'd gone, though they all said this wasn't unusual for her . . . none even knew where she dwelt and what she did.

"*Flor*-in," an impish voice, close by his ear. "Strike me down, but you're half asleep this morning! Anything on your mind you want to share? Anything at all?"

Florin blinked again. Firmly thrusting aside—for now—memories of dark blue eyes he could fall into forever, he turned to look down at Pennae with his full attention—and found himself gazing down the unlaced front of her smoky black leathers. Again.

Blushing, he dragged his gaze back up to where it should be, and found himself gazing into eyes that were very dark brown—and laughing at him. Above a smile that could only be described as catlike. She was actually purring, reminding Florin amusingly of the tressym that betimes rode Lady Lord Winter's shoulder. "You seem . . . quite flirtatious, Alura," he said carefully.

She pouted. "Oh, now, call me *Pennae*. Please."

Florin glanced into the forest, put his free hand back on his sword hilt where it should be, checked that he had a firm grip on the reins with the other, lifted his chin, and told the ears of his mount, "You still seem quite flirtatious, Pennae."

He waited for a reply, and when all that he got was a low, husky chuckle, he added, "Why?"

"Oh, Florin, don't you know how you look? What they're saying about you: the man who singlehandedly fought off dozens of outlaws to save the life of the king?"

Florin wondered whether to roll his eyes or just give this elf-faced little temptress a cold look and tell her to leave off the verbal dung. He was still wondering when someone made a loud retching sound nigh his elbow—the elbow closest to Pennae.

The loud groans of mock vomiting were followed by a familiar feminine voice inquiring brightly, "Do thieves in Arabel specialize in clumsy seductions? Or comedic minstrelry? That is the most unsubtle, hilarious to hear 'come hither, large lad' blandishment I've heard in *months!*"

The Lady Narantha Crownsilver had deftly slipped her horse between Florin's and Pennae's. She left off ridiculing the Arabellan just long enough to give Florin a wink, then clapped hands to hips, rounded on Pennae—who was white with anger, but open-mouthed in indecision—and continued, "As you've heard so much about Florin Falconhand here, are you not aware that he's the beloved of a *goddess?* Do you truly think you can outshine the Lady of the Forest? Because if you do, I think your sanity is much too far gone for you to be a Sword of Eveningstar! If, on the other hand, your little performance has been mere teasing to amuse the rest of us, I apologize unreservedly, for it's been brilliant! Florin may personally find it a trifle tasteless, but the rest of us have been nigh wetting ourselves with mirth!"

Whatever reply Pennae might have been considering was lost in the wild, whooping applause of both Agannar and Bey, enthusiastically supporting Narantha's contention from the front of the Swords—and of Semoor, standing up in the stirrups of his snorting mount at the rear of their procession, to guffaw and drum his shoulder as Purple Dragons do when clanging blades against their shoulder armor.

By the time the clangor died away, Pennae had mastered her ire enough to give Narantha an apparently genuine smile, and ask lightly, "So you liked it?"

The Lady Crownsilver answered her kindly, and offered up some silly noble jokes that soon had the two women laughing easily together. Florin, however, noticed Pennae flicking some thoughtful glances his way in the converse that followed, and when there came a lull in the chatter, she quickly peered across Narantha to ask Florin directly, "Are you truly the beloved of Mielikki? That is, what does that mean, exactly?"

Florin looked at her, wondering what to say. If he told truth, that stripped away the defense against her that Narantha had just given. Yet if he lied, he risked Mielikki's wrath, and who knew what darkness *that* might bring. Oh, hrast. He would have to choose his words very carefully, to lead astray and thus deceive without actually uttering falsehood.

And he'd better begin with a prayer to the goddess, just in case. "Oh, Lady of the Forest," he murmured, "forgive me . . ."

The Dragon Queen of Cormyr shut the garderobe door behind her and drew its bolt. That bolt—old, ornate, and heavy enough to stop a dozen Purple Dragons for a snarling breath or two—was one of the reasons this cold, gloomy, marble-lined garderobe was the queen's favorite, of all such facilities in this wing of the palace. Not that she discussed her preferences with anyone.

In truth, she hated the garderobe's tall, spider-haunted ceiling and hard seat. However, she *really* liked the other reason this room was her favored place of relief: the secret door in the wall right beside the seat, that opened right through the thick stone outer wall of the palace, into the rear of a tiny litter-yard hidden in the high-hedged depths of the Royal Gardens. A place where the cracked and leaning statues and urns of yesteryear stood crowded together, leaning against the palace walls for the birds to bespatter and the dead leaves of a hundred seasons to blow through. A labyrinth of discarded stone seats and bird-baths, all hidden away behind the oldest, most ruinous growhouse. In all the years Filfaeril had been visiting it, she'd never seen so much as an undergardener. She'd heard their voices from several growhouses away or on the far side of tall, impenetrable hedges, but none of them disturbed their queen here, or even knew of her presence.

And if she could trust the Blackstaff about the powers of the necklace she'd slid from an inner pocket and donned before slipping out the secret door, neither did Vangerdahast, or any other war wizard. She was temporarily invisible to all their spells and scryings.

She strode a few soft paces to a particular cracked stone seat, settled herself on it in a graceful shifting of skirts, and laid her hand on the head of a reclining stone lion that flanked the seat, half-lost to view in weeds.

Almost immediately Filfaeril felt a familiar stirring tingling under her hand, and from half Faerûn away Khelben Arunsun's voice spoke in her mind.

Yes, Lady of Cormyr?

"Word has come to me of two wizards in the north of the realm I'd fain know more about. Who is Amanthan of Arabel?"

A good man. One of my apprentices, not so long ago. Too shy and kind to ever be a leader, or have much to do with power or politics around him. He'll keep behind his high walls and work on spells for as long as Faerûn lets him.

"Right. Who's Whisper?"

A Zhentarim who dwells in hiding underground, in the Stonelands.

He has wits, ambition, and malice, but his Art is middling at best. He's charged with overseeing Zhent-controlled trade through your realm and past it to the north, through the Stonelands and Anauroch. Vangerdahast is aware of him, and your Wizards of War keep rather inattentive watch over him. He bears watching, of course.

"Of course. As do we all."

Indeed, Lady. As do we all.

Horaundoon had wasted most of the morning waiting for a wagon-merchant in a sufficient hurry to get to Arabel that he'd not stay over in Waymoot, nor turn at Dhedluk down to Immersea, and buck flatter and safer country but much heavier traffic to take Calantar's Way from there to Immersea.

However, one had come at last, in the person of Peraegh Omliskur, dealer in scents and sundries. It seemed a new fragrance was all the rage among wealthy would-be-noble ladies in Cormyr, and the matriarchs of Arabel wanted to be as enraged as everyone else. More than that: no lady can ever have enough silk scanties, facepaints, and nailbright, and Omliskur had been waiting for a valuable cargo to pay the costs of running another wagon or two of such luxuries—pardon, necessities—north. That was why he was here now, his great dray-horses breathless and blown, enriching the horsebreeder Tirin by selling his drays at a loss and paying top coin for twice as many, so as to make lighter, swifter work of a fast haul through Eveningstar.

Not that the Zhentarim had waited in idleness. With the help of the hargaunt, Horaundoon had spent the morning in the shape of a wrinkled old man, quaveringly seeking a means of getting to Arabel "by way of the House of the Morning in Eveningstar, where I must pray at the grave of my grandmother, the Morninglord keep her!" He offered coins enough to more than make up what the wagon-merchant Omliskur had lost on the horses, so that wheezing worthy was delighted to take him as far as Eveningstar—and give him privacy in a crowded-with-coffers, rocking and pitching wagon, besides.

Horaundoon was crouched among strongchests and carry-coffers, hunched over to avoid having his skull split by the high stacks as their tiedown straps groaned and stretched at every bump and yaw, casting the only sort of scrying spell he dared try with the war wizards doubtless peering at the Swords constantly with their own spells.

Rather than try to find and watch the adventurers, riding on the road ahead of him, he'd set about watching a spot on the road he knew, waiting for them to reach it.

And here they were now, riding right into his view! He—

Around them, rainbow hues swirled.

Horaundoon cursed and banished his spell in an instant. Someone was watching the Swords from afar, and someone else was using magic to watch for anyone trying to scry them. That someone had become aware of Horaundoon's scrutiny, but hopefully had lacked the time to trace it or identify him.

Hopefully.

"To Eveningstar," he growled. Restlessly, the hargaunt shifted across his face, literally making his skin crawl.

Horaundoon sighed and settled down to, ahem, *enjoy* the long, bumpy ride to Dhedluk. Then on to Eveningstar, without using a trace of magic along the way.

And as usual, the hargaunt was starting to itch.

The sun was starting to lower in the west, near the end of a day later, when the Swords of Eveningstar reached the little bridge that marked the edge of Eveningstar, where a lone roadguard stood under a lantern, challenging all travelers.

"Swords of Eveningstar?" that Purple Dragon asked, peering up past the noseguard of his old-fashioned helm at the riders in the road. "Is this all of you?"

Bey Freemantle, who happened to be closest, was a man of few words, but Agannor smilingly bowed in his saddle and assured the guard that before him were indeed all the Swords of Eveningstar Faerûn had ever held.

"Right," the guard replied. "Go you right along this road, and tie your mounts up at Tessaril's tower. Stone building, big porch along the front, rises to the closest thing to a tower Eveningstar has—until you get to the temple, that is. The tower's two buildings this side of the Tankard, that's the Lonesome Tankard Inn, standing in the corner where this road meets, and ends at, the High Road 'twixt Tyrluk and Arabel. Go nowhere else, for the Lady Lord of Eveningstar has pronounced summons on you."

Agannor blinked. "Pronounced what?"

"Under Crown law, you must go straight to see her, tarrying not and turning aside nowhere else."

"Right," Agannor mimicked him, and rode on, the rest of the Swords following.

Two guards awaited them on the tower porch. They took the saddle-weary Swords' reins and pointed them inside with the words: "Audience room. Now. Expected."

Inside, yet another Purple Dragon stood facing them, at the back of the entry hall. There was an open door beside him, and he was pointing at it. The Swords tramped forward.

"I feel like I'm being herded," Jhessail muttered to Martess, as they went through that door—and found a lone woman sitting behind a desk. She stood up to greet them with a smile, ash-blonde hair falling free over her shoulders, and proved to be as tall as Islif, though more slender of build. She dominated the room just as the king had dominated the inn when they'd dined with him.

"They're all the same," Narantha whispered to Florin, as they shuffled in to stand in an uneasy cluster, facing Tessaril. "Eyes like drawn daggers."

The lady lord folded her arms across her chest, gave the Swords a smile that never quite reached her eyes, and asked pleasantly, "Your charter, please?"

Florin undid his breastplate again to proffer it, and Tessaril took it and read each name aloud in turn, raising her eyes to see who answered. When she was done, she looked to Narantha and said, "You seem unaccounted for."

"I am the Lady Narantha Crownsilver. I am not a Sword of Evening-star, but travel with them at the king's personal suggestion."

Tessaril smiled. "As I recall, His Majesty's precise words regarding me were: 'She can give you directions to the Halls, and be your guide in matters ethical while you are within her writ' and his precise words regarding you were: 'I must, by blood and the needs of the realm, forbid the name of Narantha Crownsilver from appearing on this or any adventuring charter' and 'in the Cormyr *I* reign over, friend may freely ride with friend—so keeping this precious lady safe and away from you or safe in your company is entirely your affair.' Somewhat less strong and firm than suggesting you travel with the Swords. Wherefore, as a noble who might some day lead the Crownsilvers and therefore is of great value to the realm, you must bide with me, in the guest chambers here in my tower, and not stay with the Swords at the inn or for that matter in the open, nor enter the Halls with them."

Narantha drew herself up, eyes blazing, and Tessaril added in the mildest of voices, "And I am certain that, understanding your duty to the realm as you do, your own reputation, and what it is to be truly noble, you would not dream for an instant of disobeying, rebuking, or even arguing with one of the king's lords."

Someone among the assembled Swords snickered—someone who sounded suspiciously like Pennae.

Tessaril gave no signs of having heard that mirth, but looked from a simmering Narantha to the rest of them to say gravely, "As the gauntleted hand of the Dragon Throne here in Eveningstar, I must keep order. This involves being always aware of perils and disputes in my domain that may in time, like fires, flare into something greater. Wherefore it should come as no surprise to you that I'll have my eye on all of you. Please come to me for advice, aid if you need it, and to report anything you see fit that I should know." She spread her hands. "Will you share your immediate plans with me, please?"

Narantha looked at Florin, who took a pace forward, met Tessaril's gaze steadily, and replied, "Lady Lord Winter, we've no desire to gain your disfavor. I tell you in truth that we plan to forthwith enter the

Haunted Halls north of the village, as I'm sure you're aware the king requires us to do. If we can, we'll scour it out, though I fear that may prove more than we can handle. You recommend we take rooms at the inn?"

Tessaril gave him the ghost of a smile. "I do. You are expected."

She strolled toward the door. "I wish you good fortune. Report to me if you intend to leave the vicinity of Eveningstar, or if you witness anything that might be of great interest to the security of Cormyr."

"Dragons, massed troops, that sort of thing?" Semoor asked impishly.

"That sort of thing," Tessaril agreed, with the slightest of smiles, and waved them out the door.

Chapter 13
In halls dark and haunted

But deep in halls dark and haunted
Even heroes bold, high-vaunted
Twice and thrice, to end up daunted
Think of loved ones deeply wanted
And much safer places to be.

Thalloviir Vaundruth,
Bard of Beregost
Ever A Hero Be (ballad)
composed in the Year of Moonfall

"I mislike the look of yon doors," Bey Freemantle said, breaking his habitual silence.

A few paces to his left, Martess wrinkled her nose. "What's that *smell?*"

"Troll," Islif said shortly. "Mate-rut: the stink they make to tell other trolls they're ready to breed." She tramped back and forth. " 'Tis stronger in that direction."

"So," Semoor said brightly, "we'll go the other way!"

Around him, several Swords looked uneasily about.

"I'd not want to come stumbling out of the Halls, weary and perhaps hurt—only to find half a dozen trolls waiting for me," Doust said grimly.

Islif shrugged. "Then get you to yon temple and embrace new prayers as the 'adventure' in your life."

"Our lanterns won't burn forever," Agannor snapped. "Let's get going."

Pennae looked to Florin, who nodded. Then she strolled forward, keeping close to the left wall of the square opening in the rockface. In one hand she held her own small lantern; in the other, a long, thin sapling she'd had Florin cut for her.

The Swords watched. Starwater Gorge seemed to have fallen very silent around them.

Holding her lantern high, Pennae peered at the stone wall, the ceiling, and the floor. She prodded all of them with her wooden pole, stepped forward, and repeated the probings. The Swords drifted forward a pace or two.

Pennae probed on, reaching a back corner beside the doors. She played her lantern back across the passage, peering at the far side, then turned her attention to the doors. Pressing herself right into the corner, she reached out to touch the nearest door with the sapling, letting its blunt end trail along the panels. Then she probed the floor in front of it and the ceiling above it. Nothing happened.

"Gods," Semoor muttered. "I'm going to die of old age just standing here watching."

"You *could* be praying," Martess told him tartly.

Pennae paid them no attention at all, other than to look up at Doust and firmly point out at the gorge, to remind him he was supposed to be watching for approaching beasts or outlaws, not staring at her. Guiltily, the priestling of Tymora swung around.

The rest of the Swords watched Pennae step cautiously forward to take a 'ready to spring' stance right in front of one of the doors, peering at it as if she expected it to lunge at her. Never taking her eyes off it, she ducked down and bobbed back up again, in a single graceful movement, to pluck something long, dark, and thin from inside her right boot.

"She's good at this," Semoor muttered. "I wonder how much practice she's had?"

The "something" proved to be a long rod with a small hook at one end and an eyelet at the other. Pennae undid a clasp at her belt, hooked that clasp around the eyelet—it fastened there with an audible click— then began to turn herself around and around while standing in the same spot, walking widdershins. Coils of dark cord that had been tight around her waist fell around her ankles, until she reached what looked like a slender, flat, miniature version of a ship's turnbuckle. This she undid, hooking the end still wrapped around her onto to her belt buckle. Taking up the free end of the cord now separated from her, she knotted it around one end of the sapling and swung open her belt buckle to reveal a palm-sized bundle of heavy thread.

Islif moved forward, watching with narrowed eyes, as Pennae lashed the hook to the other end of sapling with expert speed. Kicking the coils of cord to one side, she stepped back toward the corner, carefully keeping her feet just to the flagstones she'd probed, until she could just reach the pull-ring of the nearest door with it. Ducking down and lifting one hand as a shield in front of her face, she couched her other arm around the sapling as if it were a knight's lance, and deftly dropped the hook over the ring.

Nothing happened, though Pennae tensed, peering and listening, for two long breaths.

Then, careful to keep tension on the hook so it wouldn't slip off, she backed away, keeping to the route along the wall she'd probed earlier. When she reached the end of the sapling and had to let go of it, she'd already wound the cord thrice around her arm, so as the wood sagged, the cord stayed as taut as a ready bowstring—and the door started to creak open.

Pennae stopped to frantically wave the Swords away to either side. After a moment, all of them obeyed, moving to right or left of the passage-mouth, and she nodded grimly and resumed her retreat, dragging the door open.

The doors proved not to be latched to each other, or secured in any way. They were old, thick, and heavy, but hung a thumbwidth or so clear of the flagstones, and so didn't stick against the floor.

Beyond them was dark stillness. With one of the two doors fully open, Pennae crouched, aiming her lantern up high inside. Then, cautiously, she advanced along the wall, retrieving her hook and placing the sapling as a prop to hold the door wide.

She was restoring the cord to around her waist when Agannor stirred, sighed, and growled, "I'm not standing out here all *day!* Let's be about this!"

A moment later, he'd drawn his sword and was striding forward, approaching the doors square-on as if traversing a long hallway in purposeful haste.

"Wait—" Pennae blurted, throwing out one hand.

Ignoring her, the fair-haired fighter ducked through the open door, glancing quickly to the right, then up at the ceiling. Then he stepped back. "Dark in here," he drawled. "Lass, that lantern of yours?"

Pennae sighed in exasperation, took up her sapling, and joined him. He reached for the lantern, but she deftly ducked away behind him, snapping, "No. Bladesmen with lanterns make superb targets. Get yourself killed on your own time."

Agannor glared at her for a moment, his eyes two hard points—then relaxed, laughed, and waved Pennae forward with a grand flourish.

Uneasily the rest of the Swords moved forward.

Take command, Florin reminded himself, hastening to their forefront. Behind him, Semoor asked the listening world, "So we've poked our noses into the Haunted Halls, yes? Fulfilled our promise to the king, and can go elsewhere, right now, heads high and—"

"Stoop," Islif snapped, elbowing the priestling in the gut as she passed, "belt up. Now."

Walking in her wake, Jhessail sighed. "I wondered how long it would take before we happy merry adventurers ended up at each other's throats."

Behind them, Doust cleared his throat tentatively. "Uh, do you want me to stay here on trollwatch? Or . . . ?"

Islif swung around. "Come *on*, Clumsum. Stride on up here and get killed with the rest of us."

Jhessail rolled her eyes.

Two tunics tied around his shoulders and his old and patched weathercloak shrugged on over them, plus the hargaunt arranged just so, made Horaundoon seem a huge-headed, bulbous-nosed giant of a man. As he lurched down from the wagon to have his things carried into the Tankard, feigning being far stouter and shorter of breath than he truly was, his gaze fell upon a slender, black-haired man striding along the road toward him with a satchel on his shoulder. The satchel was probably full of vials, being as its bottom was something rare in satchels: a wooden box.

So this would be Maglor the apothecary, Whisper's spy and obedient fingers-in-the-dark in Eveningstar.

Their eyes met, and Horaundoon gave Maglor the disinterested stare of a total stranger and turned away. If he needed this darkjack in times ahead, he'd doubtless be wearing a different guise when they met.

The apothecary made a wide birth around the caravan wagons, and Horaundoon trudged up onto the inn porch. It looked a nice enough place.

'Twas almost a pity he was going to have to kill or mindmaim most of the folk here, before he was done.

"Scream if you must," Florin told his fellow Swords, as they peered around the room, "but no yelling or making loud noises. I'd rather we surprise whatever lurks here, rather than the other way around."

"Yes, O King," Agannor muttered.

"None of that," Islif told him sharply. "Florin's valor won us this charter, and he bears the favor of the goddess Mielikki. If he desires to lead us, he leads us."

"*I* have no problem with that," Pennae said, looking at Florin in clear invitation. "So whither now, Falconhand?"

The room they stood in held only a puddle of water and a heap of weapons, surmounted by a shield. Pennae had already warned everyone fiercely not to so much as approach the pile, let alone touch it. The passage that had brought them to the room continued out its other side, west into the solid rock underlying the high sheep pasture—the southern edge of the wild, dreaded Stonelands—that was somewhere above their heads.

The air was cool, and gently moving. It smelled of damp stone and earth. When Florin waved his hands for silence, the Swords could hear nothing but their own breathing.

A pair of rust-orange metal gates, firmly chained together, barred the way on, where the passage opened out of the center of the innermost wall. Through those close-spaced vertical bars, their lanterns showed that the passage ran straight on into the rock, intersecting with a cross-passage and continuing, to open out into a larger chamber or cavern. Partway down the farther run stood a wooden tripod surmounted with a crossbow too large for most men to lift.

It was loaded and ready—and pointed along the passage right at the Swords.

Florin borrowed Pennae's lantern (the only one they had that shone a beam, rather than illuminating blindingly in all directions) to peer at the crossbow. "It doesn't look in good shape," he murmured.

"Neither do these gates," Islif put in. "Why don't Agannor, Bey, and I try to break or bend just one bar, off to the side here, while everyone else clears right over to that side wall? Then, if it fires . . ."

" 'Tis only us who'll embrace sudden ventilation," Agannor growled—then grinned. "Let's do it."

"Should I hook at it, first?" Pennae offered. "It looks solid, but that mass of chain *might* collapse into dust. I doubt it, but 'tis worth a try—and if the crossbow fires, we'll learn how it's aimed, and if its firing brings someone to reload it."

"Or some*thing* to reload it," Semoor remarked.

"Yes," Florin said firmly. "Pennae's hook-and-pole first, then work on the bars."

Semoor sighed loudly. "I feel swindled by the gods! Thus far, 'adventure' seems to be almost all 'work.' When does the fun start?"

Islif hefted her sword. "When the first monsters find us."

"They're inside the Haunted Halls," Laspeera said, pointing at the scrying crystal.

Vangerdahast clapped her on the shoulder. "Thanks. Watch them closely until I return. It shouldn't take me all that long to have a mere merchants' delegation wetting themsel—"

A deep chime sounded in the next room.

Laspeera looked at the royal magician, and the royal magician looked back at Laspeera and told her, "Stay right here and keep scrying. The merchants will wait; I'll see what His Majesty wants first."

He strode out and down the passage, taking the swiftest route to the Chamber of Charts. For anything less than royalty, Gordrar would have sent a junior war wizard to fetch him; the chime meant the presence of Azoun himself, in anger or at least impatience—or Azoun was dead and another Obarskyr was standing there very upset about it.

Now, *that* would be dark disaster indeed for the Forest Kingdom. And he'd had quite enough dark disas—

Passing through a curtain, Vangerdahast opened a door into a tiny cubicle where the air sang with mighty magic. There he pulled the door firmly closed before he opened the door on its far side, bustled through that door and down a thickly carpeted ramp into the back of a wardrobe, thrust its well-oiled doors open, slipped out, and closed it again. He peered quickly around the deserted Chamber of Treaties to make sure it truly *was* deserted, crossed to its far wall, and went through a concealed door there into the servants' passage that ran behind the Chamber of Charts.

A bare breath later, he was smiling at Azoun and making the deft little gesture that told Gordrar he was to withdraw. "Yes, my king?"

"Vangey! My new adventurers—how fare they? Where are they, and what are they up to?"

The royal magician put on his best mildly puzzled face. "Adven— ah, yes, I recall. The 'Swords of Eveningstar.' I must confess I've spent neither spell nor time watching them, thus far. Yet if you deem it needful—"

"Nay, nay. When you've time will do. I was merely . . . curious."

"Ah." Vangerdahast looked up at the king in the manner of a kindly but disapproving tutor. "You were merely . . . curious. A flaw, I fear; rulers should—"

"Leave such character failings to their wizards?" Azoun's voice was dry. "Pray tell me, Vangey, which particular flaws do you think I should cultivate?"

Oh, naed.

Naed, naed, *naed*, naed, naed.

"Your Majesty," Vangerdahast began, in his most cajolingly hurt voice, "I hope you believe not for a moment that . . ."

The gates proved to be fused solid, the Swords heard no alarm raised, the crossbow didn't fire—and the assault on the gates began.

Rust fell in flakes, specks, and a fine dust that had Islif, Agannor, and Bey swearing, ducking away, and shaking their heads to try to get it out of their eyes. Finally, a snarling, sweating Islif, tendons standing out on her neck like the edges of daggers, managed to force her shoulder between two bars. She pulled with all her gasping, growling might.

When she fell back, panting and shuddering, two of the bars were bowed visibly apart—and the rest of the Swords were regarding her with new respect, Agannor and Bey gaping in disbelief. They looked at each other, nodded, and strode forward to the two bent bars, hauling and tugging on them with growls of effort and hissed oaths.

Agannor's bar bent visibly, but Bey's suddenly broke free of its frame at the top, and leaned out a handwidth. He threw himself shoulder-first against it, groaning at the bone-numbing impact, but managed to shift it only a fingerwidth or so more.

"Break off," Florin told the three, "and catch your wind." When they did, gasping and shaking their numbed hands, Florin waved Doust and Semoor forward.

Their struggles made no appreciable difference to the positions of the bars, but when they retreated, wincing and wringing their hands, they took most of the rest of the scaly rust with them, and the Swords could clearly see there was now an oval opening in the gates that someone tall, or someone who hopped in just the right manner, could traverse sideways.

"Behold," Semoor gasped, waving his hand at it. "Valiant victory."

"Our first," Jhessail agreed wryly. "Indeed, yon gates fought hard."

"I'm growing *older*," Agannor complained, striding to the bent bars with Doust's lantern in his hand.

"Wait," Pennae snapped, but he waved dismissively and shouldered his way through the gap in the barrier, into the passage beyond.

Going straight to its south wall, Agannor strode briskly along it to where he could shine lanternlight along the cross-passage to the north. Then he played his light for some time on the crossbow. It stood dust-covered and slightly askew atop its dark wooden tripod, with a widening room behind it that seemed to end in two temple-tall, bronzen double doors, with two statues of the same hue flanking them. The southern statue was of an armored warrior woman, staring endlessly at the Swords with one hand on scabbarded sword hilt and her other arm indicating the doors behind her. The northern statue was a similarly armed and armored man who was looking at the doors he was pointing at, his other hand also on sword hilt.

Agannor peered more closely at the sagging crossbow—then chuckled, strolled unconcernedly into its line of fire, and looked the other way along the cross-passage. Nothing erupted at him.

"Nothing to see but some old bones strewn all over the place," he said back over his shoulder. "So old they've gone brown."

He waved his hand back and forth, to indicate the cross-passage. "Both ways look the same: they run ten paces or so and open out into rooms that look the same size, and stretch on to the west beyond where I can see. I'm going to—"

" '*Ware!*" Pennae shouted, pointing.

Agannor whirled to regard her, then back along the line of her pointing arm, in time to see brown bones rising into the air beyond the tripod.

The bones drew together into two eerily silent whirlwinds that built with frightening speed into two human skeletons, brown and tottering.

He took a step back, cursing and reaching for his blade. They danced forward, their finger bones lengthening into long claws and cold lights whirling into being in the dark depths of their eye sockets.

Pennae was through the bars like a racing eel, with Islif right behind her.

"Stoop! Clumsum!" Florin snapped, following her. "Can't priests drive undeath down?"

Doust and Semoor looked at each other, swallowed in unison, and reluctantly started toward the bars.

"I don't know how 'tis done, exactly. Don't we need—"

"We're not real priests, yet—"

Bones were slithering along the passages, gathering into untidy brown heaps, and whirling up into more skeletons, swaying and dancing. Florin blinked. Dancing?

The bones weren't quite touching each other, and none of the skeletal feet were touching the stone tiles. The bones were all floating in the air, like biting flies swarming in clouds above ponds, rather than joined together.

Agannor snarled and slashed crosswise with his blade, shearing claws into bony shards. He ducked away wildly as that skeleton raked at him with its other hand—and Pennae crashed into it, hacking furiously with her daggers.

Islif smashed aside one claw with her own arm and swung her blade like a woodsman's axe, hewing through ribs and spine. Her skeleton tottered but did not fall, its severed upper part bobbing in midair, apparently unaffected.

Doust swallowed, facing a skeleton, and in a trembling voice said, "By the luck of the Lady, I abjure thee! Go down! Go—"

Claws raked the air in front of his nose, and he stumbled back, something that was almost a shriek rising in his throat.

"They've triggered my spell." The words were as cold and as calm as a crofter agreeing that the next village indeed lay in that direction. "You're ready?"

"Aye: bows, windlasses, one quiver each."

"Good. Maglor says there are nine of them. Two she-mages and two he-priests, both novices, Lathander and Tymora. Strike hard and then get out. Get clear before they can hit back, don't tarry to do battle so they get good looks at you. Any of you who get wounded or worse *must* be brought out with you. Meet back here, this side of the stone. Understood?"

"Yes, Master Whisper."

"Good. Go."

The skeleton reached for him again, and Doust almost fell, windmilling his arms to keep his feet.

Bey Freemantle lurched in front of him, snarling, "Don't *talk* at it, priest! Hack it to shards!" The warrior proceeded to do just that, plying steel vigorously in both hands as bone shards tumbled in the air, forming a cloud around him.

Florin, Islif, and Agannor hacked separate paths through it, cleaving skulls and shattering shoulder blades—and still the bones came slithering, hissing along the floor in their scores and dozens, ere rising up in whirling spirals to form new skeletal foes.

Semoor stammered a long and impressive prayer against "walking undeath" as he waved his hands at the skeletons.

Without effect. Bones rose up before him, eyeless skulls grinning behind long fingerbones that came reaching . . .

Dove sipped. "Ahhh, nice broth. Thanks, Old Mage."

"My pleasure, lass. Now ask thy questions."

"Questions?" Dove gave the Mage of Shadowdale her most innocent look.

"Lass, *that* hasn't fooled me since ye could toddle. Ask."

"Right, then. The Zhents, in and about Eveningstar. Maglor's just eyes and ears, yes?"

"Aye. Reports through intermediaries to Whisper, who reports to Sarhthor—when he must."

Dove nodded. "Those two I know. I've been sensing others this last month, scrying and prying."

Elminster shrugged. "Zhents crawl out from under stones by the score when they sniff opportunity. One—I know not who, yet—just found a way to strike at mantled elf mages."

"So *that's* what befell Arlathna. Know you a wraith Zhentarim? Or any entity that drifts about wraithlike, possessing living men?"

"I know of many such. Setting aside brief skulkings or fleeing in wraithform, only one Zhent, though: Old Ghost, he calls himself. Acts as a go-between for the lowliest Zhents and those just above them—Maglor and Whisper—yet serves Manshoon personally."

"Standing—right, drifting—outside the Zhent chain of command. The sort of being you usually strike down."

"Aye. Mystra has ordered otherwise."

Astonishment made Dove's eyes flare bright silver for an instant, and Elminster smiled and topped up her tankard.

Pennae drew back from the fray, winded, to watch these new dooms rise up, and saw something that made her eyes narrow.

Farther down the central passage, right in front of that menacing crossbow, a circle of finger-sized somethings whirled around and around above a particular floor tile: brown, dancing somethings.

She watched those tiny skeletons for a moment—then hefted one of her daggers, ducked a reaching skeletal claw, and threw her steel fang, hard and fast.

Her dagger crashed through the center of the whirling ring, bouncing and hopping with a flash and clang of steel, scattering tiny bones in all directions.

And all around the battling Swords, the remaining skeletons flew apart, shedding bones in all directions.

Pennae never saw them. She was watching her dagger skitter on across the tiles. It struck one of tripod's feet and bounded into the air, heading for those tall bronzen double doors and the two figures on their pedestals before them. It was going to fall short, strike the stones, and skirl to a stop.

Unless her suspicions about those overly grand statues were

correct. This had been an embattled lord's hold, once, if that garrulous tavernmaster in Dhedluk had spoken truth—and not a man along the aleboard had disputed with him. And what lord spends good coin on such fripperies, unless he's a madman who thinks himself Lord Emperor of All, or they're part of a trap—

Sudden blue-white light cracked, lashing out from the male statue to strike her dagger aside. Tiny crawling lightnings hummed and snarled after it, their roots playing briefly across the breast of the statue.

They were answered from the female statue, deadly pale twisted fingers reaching through the air toward its crackling male counterpart.

Most of the Swords stood gaping at the lightnings, but Pennae took two swift steps sideways, to where she could clearly see her dagger. It had stopped just in front of the northernmost of the bronzen double doors, a tiny wisp of smoke drifting lazily up from its scorched hilt.

The watcher leaned forward to stare hard into the crystal, the fingers of one hand pausing in their usual stroking of the unicorn-headed ring on the other hand. Was this a magic that could in time be used to fell the mighty Vangerdahast?

Or could these adventurers become the weapon that would slay the royal magician, and leave Cormyr unguarded, for the taking?

The last lightning bolts leaped and snapped, and the Swords gave each other grim smiles.

"This will come as a deep surprise, I'm sure," Islif said gruffly, "but I'm not in favor of proceeding to yon doors."

The answering chuckles were dry. Amid them, Pennae leaned forward far enough to peer up and down the cross-passage, and Agannor grinned and came over to her with his lantern.

"Doust, Semoor, Bey, Martess," Florin said gently. "Mount you a rearguard right here, while the rest of us go south down this cross-passage, to see what we may see."

Agannor gave the forester a challenging glance, just for an instant, then shrugged and started down the cross-passage, Pennae right beside him and Islif trotting to catch up. Jhessail rolled her eyes and followed, Florin with her.

A bare ten paces on, the passage opened out into a room, a dark doorway yawning in its western wall—and another passage branching off through its east wall.

"Halt," Pennae told everyone, in a voice of iron, before she ducked low and leaned out to shine her beam-lantern down the passage. It ran on a slant, back toward the rooms and passages they'd already been in, to end in a bare, angled wall. Pennae's eyes narrowed again.

She prowled along the short, doorless passage to its end, where she peered at the stone wall, running her fingers along cracks and tool marks and—aha!

"A secret door," she called back, her voice shrill with excitement. "And I can open it!"

Her fingers had already found two hollows wherein something clicked under her fingertips—and the door trembled, grating ever-so-slightly.

Agannor and Islif came hurrying along the passage, blades drawn. "Not before we—"

Pennae gave them both an "oh, *please*" look, and thrust the door wide. Though it proved to be thicker than her own body, piercing a wall of the same girth, it made no further sound, nor opened with any difficulty. She could push its ponderous weight with a fingertip.

The three Swords peered together into the room of the puddle and the heap of weapons. It was very much as they'd left it, holding no sign of lurking beasts, spies, or anyone but themselves.

Pennae studied the exposed doorframe for a moment, then the balance of the hinges and the frame behind them, too. Then she peered at the door-edge, looking for locks and catches and finding just the one she'd opened. She threw up a hand. "Wait here a moment."

Then she was through the door and across the room like an

arrow in flight, fetching up in front of the far wall with narrowed eyes and searching fingers. After a moment she nodded in satisfaction and thrust her fingers into two widely separated tool gouges.

Another concealed door promptly clicked open in the wall, its outlines appearing out of the weathered stone as if by magic. It was just as thick as the first one, but moved even more quietly. Recently used.

Pennae peered quickly into another slantwise passage, a mirror image of the one she'd just traversed. Seeing nothing but stone walls and an utter lack of marauding beasts, she hooked her fingertips into two other handy hollows to pull the door closed again. Its click was barely audible.

"Another slantwise passage, running so," she told the others, gesturing to indicate its position, as they hastened to rejoin Florin and Jhessail.

Jhessail greeted them with a frown. "Is it wise to go running off in twos and threes?"

"No," Islif agreed. "A mistake we'll not repeat." She gave Agannor a glance. "I hope."

"We must never leave some area unexplored, that could conceal a man—or even a biting snake—between us and the way out," Pennae warned them all, "lest we get trapped in here by a monster—or a band of outlaws."

Her fellow Swords, up and down the passage, nodded soberly.

"So, shall we continue?" Agannor asked, waving at the empty room before them, where the passage ended and that dark doorway awaited.

"Yes." Florin turned to look back at the rearguard. "All quiet?"

They both nodded, and the forester added, "Pennae and Islif to the fore. Agannor right behind, ready to charge in. Then you, Jhessail."

Pennae quickly circled the empty room, peering at the walls and ceiling. When she reached the doorway, she stepped well back to shine her lantern inside.

The Swords saw a table and chairs, some of the latter overturned or hacked apart. Bunk beds around the walls, some hewn and splintered. Strongchests under the lower bunks, their locks and hasps smashed. A door—ajar into darkness—in the middle of the south wall, with something odd huddled on the floor in front of it; something of a stonelike hue.

Pennae moved closer, shining her light everywhere. No other doors, no corpses or brown bones. No tools or weapons lying anywhere. "In," she told Islif and Agannor, "and watch that door. *Don't* push it open. I'm for the chests."

They proved to be empty, and their damp wood crumbled at a touch like badly made nutbread. By the time Pennae was finished looking at all of them and behind them, at the underside of the table and all around the bunks, Agannor and Islif had looked long and hard at the stony mass on the floor, prodding it with their swords and shifting it aside to make sure no hole or anything else was concealed beneath it. The rest of the Swords watched from the doorway. Pennae thrust aside chairs and the remnants of chairs to clear a wide path from doorway to where Agannor and Islif stood.

"Look at this," Agannor told everyone, pointing at the stone heap with his sword.

From the doorway, Jhessail did just that. When she spoke, her voice sounded uneasy, on the edge of disgust. "What is it?"

Even curled up as it was, it was a little thing, all stumpy legs and long, gangly arms, with a malicious face, flat-nosed and fang-mouthed, glaring down at the broken short sword it held. Its ears were pointed like a cat's, and it wore armor made of random plates of salvaged, battered human armor tied together in an untidy, overlapping array.

"Never seen a goblin before?" Agannor's voice was bleak. "This is—or was—a goblin. Something's turned it to stone."

Chapter 14
DARK DAYS FOR THE REALM

Find your swords, ye who still have eyes to see them, hands to wield them, and wits enough left to search for them. Polish them if it heartens ye, and drink a last goblet to those who have already fallen. Then gather ye with sword and shield by the old oak, and await my coming.

We are fated to die, and may as well do it together, achieving some small vengement upon our foes, as do it apart, falling alone beneath the blades of laughing foes.

So strike as one, for Cormyr, and go down into darkness with savage smiles, and the blood of dying foes on your blades. Seek not to flee or hold aloof from the fray; 'tis too late for that.

The dark days are come at last.

Andrath Dragonarl,
Knight of Cormyr
A Call to Arms
pinned to trees throughout the realm
in the Year of the Floating Rock

"Dark days for the realm, indeed," Blundebel Eldroon growled, set-ting down his gigantic tallglass. It was now half-full, but had been sparkling to the rim with the very finest of glowfire a moment ago. "I know old nobles always say something of the sort, but this time, as the gods bear witness, Cormyr truly—"

"Ah, Lord Eldroon," Prester Yellander said, his interruption as firm as the snap of a lash, "but that's just where your words fall into misadventure. Cormyr does not 'truly' anything. *That* is our problem, lords: we are so fallen into deceit and deception, with a royal magician insanely unable to tell the truth about the weather, the color of his own robes, and even his own name, let alone affairs of state, leading us daily farther and farther astray!"

"Strong words, Lord Yellander," Sardyn Wintersun observed. "As Lord Eldroon intimates, is this slide into untruth not a dark doom decried by every generation of nobles and sages—and Obarskyr kings, for that matter? Does the realm truly totter on the brink of savagery, civil war, and a shattered throne? We may dislike the manner and even particular stratagems of the royal magician, but many a crofter of the realm—and merchant both Cormyrean and outlander—likes well the stability his vigilant war wizards, and the king's well-trained Purple Dragons, have wrought. The realm pros-pers, the people multiply and are largely content, the—"

"Cowdung being spewed in this chamber near reaches my

eyeballs," Lord Eldroon growled. "Have you a head of solid *stone*, Wintersun? Canst think at all? Try looking past the smiles of the fool-headed rabble and underlings beyond counting, to hear and see the ire among those of us who matter: we nobles, who own much land, sponsor many mercantile ventures, pay good coin to all of the rabble of the realm who happen to toil for us—and pay a lot of *bad* coin, too, taxed from our hands into the court vaults."

He drained his glass in a single great sip, to snarl, " 'Tis *our* contentedness or lack of same as should be measured, not the views of some toothless old retired dragonard who's happy if his downsun tankard comes to his lips every night, and is served with some juicy gossip to chew over with his goodfellows!"

"Speaking of which," Lord Yellander told his own fingernails, "I've heard some interesting news, my lords. I chanced upon the Lady Jalassa Crownsilver yestermorn, and she seemed anxious to show me her new magecloak earrings."

Lord Wintersun wrinkled his brow. "Your juicy gossip concerns *earrings?*"

Prester Yellander sighed and steepled his fingertips, regarding Wintersun pityingly over them. "Your holdings *are* rural, aren't they, Sardyn? The term 'magecloak' is obviously unfamiliar to you, so my duty is clear. Magecloak items—be they rings, earrings, anklets, or false beards—are works of magic that foil magical scrying. While you wear one, no war wizard can see or hear you from afar. Perhaps not even the oh-so-awesome Vangerdahast."

"Made—or at least sold—in the cities of Sembia, for *far* too much," Eldroon growled.

Lord Yellander shrugged. "The price will fall when someone duplicates their magics and offers them for less than the price of a good keep." He slid back his sleeve to display a thin gold band. "Rest easy, Wintersun, mine should keep our converse relatively private, so long as you stray not far from me, and say nothing *too* imprudent."

Eldroon tapped a large jargoon ring on his fat and hairy left little finger. "I go nowhere without mine, these days."

"Yet be not led astray, Lord Wintersun, by our little displays," Prester Yellander said, "for Lady Crownsilver's baubles were merely her excuse to tarry and converse with me, not the choice gossip that was the weightiest part of her words to me. Nay, Lords, I'd hardly waste your time informing you that this or that high lady now goes about magecloaked."

"So what juice did she spout?" Eldroon asked, reaching for the decanter of glowfire.

"That the king has just chartered his own adventuring company, the Swords of Eveningstar, and sent them off to Eveningstar for a little training. When they've become seasoned killers, he intends to unleash them on nobles he sees as his opponents. So now Azoun Loosecods has his own private little slaying force—and 'tis a blade about to be thrust at *us*. Beware!"

Wintersun sighed and swirled his glass, to watch the dregs swirl like amber fire as they caught the light. "As if we didn't have *enough* to worry about."

"You're sure?" Eldroon asked. "This isn't just wildtalk? Jalassa had this from someone reliable? If so, who? And how?"

"She pieced it together, she told me, from three court scribes, an overly talkative war wizard too young to keep in mind that others in the realm besides his kind know how to use spells—and something she heard from the lips of Vangerdahast himself."

"Then he wanted all of us to know it," Eldroon said darkly. "That man says nothing unguarded. Nothing at all."

Lord Yellander shrugged. "He's just a man. I could hire a mightier mage on the morrow."

"Oh? Then why don't you?"

"The war wizards are too splendid a blade to shatter. Better by far to find the way to take hold of their hilt."

"Kill Vangerdahast, you mean."

"*Replace* Vangerdahast, by something that looks just like him. And obeys me."

"And is there such a 'something,' in all the world?"

"Oh, yes. I found it long ago."

"And yet we kneel not to King Prester the First." As if by magic, Eldroon's tallglass was empty again.

"Not yet. Certain matters stand unfinished."

" 'Certain matters'?"

"Yes. Regarding the 'obeys me' part. I may finish them in a tenday. Or never."

"Ah. Like the rest of us."

" 'The rest of us'?"

"The rest of us, Yellander. All the other nobles besides yourself who've glanced at the Dragon Throne and thought: That could be mine, and I'd ride it better than Azoun Obarskyr. Some of us set aside such thoughts and learn contentment. Others achieve little, and chafe and snarl the seasons away. A few dare ventures not shrewd enough, and lose their heads or the right to set boot in Cormyr. And more than a handful nurse schemes, working slowly toward a savage moment that may never come. In short: you're not the only one."

"Are you such a one, Lord Eldroon?"

"Once I was. Now I think the prize not worth the hazard. Let Azoun worry and work, while we watch and sip wine and cavil at the quality of entertainment he provides us. Speaking of which, more glowfire, Wintersun?"

"I believe I will. Lords, you've both given me much to think about."

"Think silently. The war wizards do one thing *very* well: listen to folk who think their talk is private. Get yourself one of these mage-cloak things. More wine, Yellander?"

"Forget not yon stone goblin," Pennae snapped, "and watch that door. If it moves, even a little, shout and then get out!"

"Shout and then get out," Jhessail echoed. "Not much of a war cry . . ."

"No," Florin agreed. "Pennae, what have you found?"

Pennae had been swarming all over the ransacked room, peering under things and over things, and running her hands over the walls.

She'd frozen at a spot on the wall by the head of one of the lower bunks, and was now frowning at it, and drawing her dagger.

"What is it?" Agannor asked.

She furiously waved for silence then probed with her dagger at a spot on the wall. Nothing happened. She probed again, a fingerwidth above—and a hand-sized panel in the wall appeared, pivoting open. As she pushed her dagger deeper, it swung open more. She stepped well back, keeping behind the door, until she could pluck up her lantern again and shine it into—a niche hollowed out of the rock about as deep as her forearm, which was empty except for a small, mildewed piece of folded parchment. Pennae drew it out balanced on the blade of her dagger, set it on the table, and opened it, reading its simple message aloud: "The rest are hidden in the door."

"The rest of what?" Jhessail asked.

Pennae shrugged. "Who knows? Yon door looks like solid stone to me. Anyhail, there's nothing else here. Do we go on through it, given that?" She nodded her head at the petrified goblin.

Florin shrugged. "There's mold on it—see?—so it's been here some time. If a wizard or cleric turned it to stone, I can't believe they're still standing guard somewhere beyond the door. If 'twas a curse magic left waiting here—on the doorway, say—then did it exhaust itself doing that to the goblin . . . or does it lie in wait still?"

"One way to find out," Agannor drawled, stepping over the goblin, shoving the door wide, and striding through it. Pennae's snarl of helpless anger followed him, as she started around the table like a storm wind—then stopped, shaking her fists in futility.

Agannor stuck his head back in the door and grinned at her. " 'S'all quiet here, little battlemaster. No beasties, just a jakes."

Pennae shook her head, still seething. "One day your luck will run out, Agannor! Tymora will shake her head and let Beshaba have you!"

"One day soon," Islif echoed, also shaking her head.

Agannor shrugged and waved his hand airily behind him. "Call of nature, anyone?"

Pennae strode to the door and examined it and its frame *very* closely, ignoring Agannor.

Then she stepped into the passage beyond, Islif right behind her. They pushed past a grinning Agannor, and peered along the passage. It ran a few paces and then turned sharp west, to end at a wooden-seat-over-pit privy, that smelled very faintly of—

"Wait," Pennae said flatly. "It doesn't end there. Look, off to the left: there's been a roof-fall, or they stopped digging. 'Tis all tumbled stones."

Florin, Agannor, and Islif walked with her, Jhessail staying behind in the doorway of the bunkroom.

In the beam of Pennae's lantern, the place where tool-marks ended in the solid stone overhead could clearly be seen. No collapse, then, but an end to delving through solid stone.

Pennae turned back to the privy, aiming her lantern upward. "A shaft—up as well as down. Islif, I need your blade here." She pointed. "Thrust it up, hard, as I duck in here under you and look down. I'd prefer not to have some biting beastie pounce on my head."

Islif nodded, and as soon as Pennae had slid in front of her, hunched low, the warrior woman brought her blade up, from knees to straight out over her head, in a hard, fast upward lunge.

The steel struck something solid, and Islif cried a warning as she felt her sword bite deep into it—as it *moved*.

She hadn't even formed the first word when a flood of iridescent gold and purple liquid showered down on Pennae's head.

The thief ducked blindly back, spitting, as something that squalled and scrabbled against the shaft walls in a frenzy descended, black fangs—if that's what they were—chattering in agony. Florin hurled himself over a rolling, snarling Pennae to add his steel to Islif's, driving his sword hilt deep into—

A spider the size of a Purple Dragon's shield, sagging into view with faltering legs, purple gold shimmering fluids streaming out of it as it died.

The thing was surprisingly heavy, and slammed into the privy-seat with force enough to break that lone board. Dying spider and splintered wood fell together into the privy-pit with a wet, solid crash.

Pennae had plucked her waterskin from her belt, and was sluicing spider juices out of her hair and off her face. "It stings," she gasped. "Make sure there're no little spiders higher up the shaft."

She thrust her lantern in Florin's direction. Agannor slid past the forester, hip to hip, to put his own blade up the shaft beside Islif's sticky, empurpled steel, and grunted, "Florin, shine the light along my arm—this shaft might be a way up to somewhere . . ."

It proved not to be, rough natural stone drawing together a tall man's height overhead, and the Swords retreated to the bunkroom to get a good look at Pennae. Her skin was bright red in two places, but the fluids seemed not to have harmed her otherwise. She pronounced herself, "Just fine."

"Back the other way," Florin said, relief bright in his voice, "to rejoin our rearguard, and go on north together. I'm thinking now that splitting up was more foolish than guarding our way out. If either group meets a strong foe, 'tis darker days than if we'd stood together."

They hastened, shining their lanterns on themselves and waving. The four Swords at the passage-moot waved back.

"What happened to you?" Semoor asked as the Swords drew together. He was peering curiously at Pennae's gold and purple hair.

"A tale for later," she said tersely, just as fresh lightnings hummed and crackled between the two bronzen statues. Pennae gave the crawling, stabbing bolts a disbelieving look. "Still?"

"Oh, yes," Doust told her. "They've been doing that, betimes, ever since you left us."

"Myself," Martess put in, "I wonder why they never veer to the doors. Everywhere else, yes, but all that metal standing there so broad and high, and the lightnings *never* go that way."

"I know," Pennae said sarcastically, holding up a finger in a mockery of delighted discovery. " 'Tis magic!"

"Gods," Jhessail muttered under her breath, just loud enough for everyone to hear, "another Semoor Wolftooth! Truly, the gods weave in mysterious ways!"

Islif chuckled, tapping Florin's arm to warn him to say nothing, and waved them on. Rolling her eyes, Pennae led the way.

The north end of the passage was a room with a westward archway and a slantwise passage back to the room of the barred gates that was a mirror image of the south end—except that the inner, westerly room lacked all furniture, damaged or otherwise, and had two doors in its walls, both firmly closed.

Pennae played her lantern-beam around the room and down at its floor, then up at its ceiling—which glistened.

Her eyes barely had time to narrow before something very small fell from that ceiling, to star across the floor with a wet *splat*.

She trained her lantern on it, seeing a leaf green color that darkened to bright emerald where her beam of light was. Deliberately, she sprang into the air and came down hard, stamping with both feet.

Splat, splat.

"Nobody get *any closer* to this," Pennae warned the Swords behind her, her voice like iron—even as she disobeyed herself, sidling sideways from the doorway as she stepped cautiously closer to it. "That means you, too, Agannor, unless you want to die right here and now."

"What is it?" Florin asked, as more drips fell from the ceiling to spatter the floor. Their lanterns were all trained on that floor, now—until Florin told Bey to swing around, and Jhessail with him, to watch their rear—and they could see the green, glistening wetness *moving* across the floor, creeping slowly but tirelessly toward the walls.

"Green slime is its name, bless all bards," Pennae told him, without taking her gaze from it for an instant. "Its touch dooms you. It turns you into itself, and eats through . . . many things. Our lights and our footfalls are making it fall."

She stepped back. "We dare not enter yon room, unless we can build a fire out here large enough to scorch the ceiling, and push it in there, and keep on moving it carefully around, so as to get it all—and

I don't want to be trying to breathe in here while a fire of that size is raging. See it moving? Every droplet that falls will spend almost a day—or more—oozing to the walls and up them, to rejoin the rest of the slime it fell from."

"Charming," Martess commented.

"I don't like the look of this," Doust said.

Just then Agannor pushed past him, gave Pennae a disdainful glare, and told the halls around him, "I don't heed warnings and I don't cringe and creep through life like an old farmwife a-quiver over ghosts. And I'm not going to start now!"

His first stride into the room brought a small rain of falling slime. His second caused fist- and head-sized pieces to plummet, spraying the room.

"You *fool!*" Pennae snarled. "Get out of there!"

Agannor whirled and leaped back through the door.

"Grab him!" Pennae snapped, snatching a candle out of a belt pouch and thrusting it into her lantern. "Hold him—he's got some of it on him!"

The Swords tussled with a cursing Agannor. The moment her candle was properly alight, Pennae thrust it at the warrior's arm then low on his breeches, holding the flame to the glistening spots there until the leathers started to smoke.

The reek was unbelievable—and very different from burning leather. It smelled of swamps and earthy decay and . . . *eels*. Martess and Jhessail gagged in unison.

Slime was falling like slapping rain beyond the doorway now. In unspoken accord the Swords drew away from it, gathering at the east wall of the passage room, at the mouth of the slantwise passage.

"So one way ends," Semoor began. "The grand 'way onward' bids fair to fry us with lightning bolts, and this route looks to be a death-trap, too. The only road that seems relatively safe is the way we came in. Any opinions? Have we done enough brave foraying to satisfy the king? Or Lord Winter, anyhail?"

"Hah!" Bey's laugh was more of a bark than anything else. "My bet is he's looking for us to scour out these halls completely, so he can use them for a Stonelands stronghold. He'll be satisfied if we do that—or die trying!"

"And holy Tymora would want us to take chances," Doust put in, spreading his hands.

"By doctrine, yes," Martess said, "but have you prayed to her for a sign?"

There sounded the tiniest of distant gratings from behind them, then a sharp crack that Florin knew all too well.

And Doust received his sign.

The crossbow bolt that hummed through the Swords caught him solidly in the shoulder, spinning him around like a child's whirl-top as he gasped in astonished pain.

Agannor was the first to move, and Bey was but a half-step behind him.

"There!" the most impetuous of the Swords roared, charging down the slantwise passage. The door at its end was ajar, and someone was standing in it. Someone helmed, armored, and holding a fired crossbow.

As the two men raced along, their swords flashing in their fists, that distant someone stepped aside—and someone else whose face was hidden behind a helm and whose body was battle-armored took a stance in the doorway, hefting a loaded crossbow.

Agannor and Bey pelted on, bellowing war cries.

The crossbow cracked.

There was a solid, meaty *thunk*, Bey grunted, and Agannor was suddenly running alone.

"The Crowned One's getting anxious. Scrying them yet?"

Laspeera gave Vangerdahast a withering look. "You know very well we can't scry into the Halls. *How* long have you had Narbridle and Rortaebur working on unraveling that webwork of spells? And it's not as if I have nothing else to do but keep watch on His Majesty's pet adventurers for him! Lord Goldfeather's secret little meeting in Marsember should be starting very soon, and—"

Vangerdahast winked, chuckled, and strode on. "I have every confidence in you, Wizard of War Laspeera Naerinth. When you're furious with everyone, all the time, you'll have reached where I am now—and my long hunt for a successor will be done."

Laspeera stared at the royal magician's dwindling, departing back, her face going pale and her mouth hanging open.

Nothing came out, so after a time she closed it.

Beyard Freemantle looked down at the bolt quivering in his gut. It had pierced his armor neatly, going into him about the length of his forefinger.

So I'm dead, he thought, as he doubled up around it, feeling wet looseness rather than pain. That was fast.

His legs seemed to be bending under him like storm-wet flowers. Then he found himself bouncing on very hard stone, his arms and legs loose and flopping and his sword clanging away somewhere.

Then the pain hit.

Bey struggled to find breath enough to scream ... and struggled ...

He couldn't even writhe. He was lying on his side, probably looking very dead—and fervently wishing he was dead. Anything to take away this stabbing, burning agony.

Tymora and Tempus, be with me now ... gods, the *pain!*

Irlgar Delbossan was red-faced and sweating, hay still trailing down over his head from the tines of his fork, but his smile held genuine pleasure. "Very good, milord. I'll—"

Then the horsemaster's face changed. Lord Hezom turned to follow his gaze.

Behind him, the War Wizard Marsteel had stepped soundlessly into this inner room of the stables, face as unreadable as ever and clad in the same black robes he always wore. "King's Lord," he said proudly, "I've news."

"Yes?"

Marsteel kept silent, shifting his gaze meaningfully to Delbossan. Hezom swallowed a sigh and asked, "Concerning?"

"Matters of state, Lord."

"Involving any or all of the Swords of Eveningstar, Lord Tessaril Winter, or Lady Narantha Crownsilver?"

"Yes," the wizard said.

"Then speak freely," Lord Hezom said. "Master Delbossan has every right to know whatever you desire to share with me. The Wizards of War have entirely too many vital secrets of the realm to keep, to fall carelessly into the habit of trying to make *everything* a secret. Have you by means of magic heard from Tessaril? Has she detained Narantha, to keep her from getting killed in the Halls alongside the Swords?"

Marsteel flushed. "I—yes, Lord Hezom, that is the heart of my news. We have and she has."

"Good to hear," Delbossan blurted. "I was fair worried over that. The lass—ah, from what young Florin said, she was . . . far from ready to taste adventure. If ye know what I mean."

"Yes," the war wizard said gravely, "I do know what you mean. The Lady Crownsilver is now in residence in Tessaril's Tower, with several Wizards of War watching to see she remains there. Her father rides north to Eveningstar right now to reclaim her. I know not if he still intends to bring her here to you, Lord Hezom; when last we spoke with him, his temper was less than serene."

Delbossan chuckled. "I'd love to hear *that* moot at Lord Winter's tower. From safe hiding, of course. The Haunted Halls are probably the safest place in the realm for the Swords, about now."

"I hardly think," Marsteel said, "that it would be proper to eavesdrop on such a reunion, and in any event—"

"The Wizards of War are going to do it anyway," Lord Hezom said. "I stand with Master Delbossan in this, Marsteel: I'd like to listen in on that meeting, too. You can arrange that for both of us, can't you?"

The war wizard flushed again, opening his mouth to snap a firm denial.

Then the voice of the herald from Espar, from right behind his ear, startled him: "Of course he can—and should, so the king's Lord of Espar and the king's Herald of Espar can best administer local Crown affairs. Lord Crownsilver's conduct and state of mind are vital knowledge. Horsemaster Delbossan may as well hear things firsthand, too; after all, his will be the task of rushing a mounted escort across the realm if the need arises. Shall I speak to Vangey about it for you?"

War Wizard Elgaskur Marsteel's face was a deep crimson, now, and his mouth was opening and closing like that of a gasping fish. He looked, in fact, distinctly ill—and as he instinctively stepped away down the stables so as to bring the faces of all three men into view, he was terribly afraid he'd find them all smirking at him. " 'Vangey'? Mystra and Azuth be with me," he muttered to himself. "For if I displease Royal Magician Vangerdahast, I'll need all the favor and protection of the both of you."

"Bey!" Agannor roared, running full tilt down the passage. Ahead, the door was closing.

He ran hard, his boots pounding and his own breath roaring in his ears. "Don't you die on me, you motherless bastard! Don't you—"

The door was seven running strides away, then six, and not quite closed yet. He bent his free arm in front of him to bring that shoulder up, to crash into the door and drive it wide—

The door swung wide open, leaving him stumbling onward as he looked right into his own death.

His shout going wordless, Agannor Wildsilver sprang, his sword flashing.

Chapter 15
DEATH ALWAYS SO CLOSE TO US

It is wise to remember always that no matter how grand our realms rise to be, how plentiful our coins, and how exalted our station, death is always so close to us that it can reach out a bony hand to our throat and drag us down in an instant. The trick is to fill our lives with splendid instants, so that when death does come, we'll at least be enjoying ourselves.

Dhammaster Dauntinghorn
The Young Stag: Memoirs of the Splendid Years of One Noble
published in the Year of the Behir

The helmed, armored warrior standing just inside the door had a long sword in his hand, held low. He was ready to lunge up and under Agannor's gorget, belt, or cod for a gutting thrust—and he had two fellows flanking him, the sharp points of their blades glittering.

As Agannor burst through the door, something large and dark smashed into the side of his head—a hurled crossbow, rattling as it crashed home and sent him reeling.

He'd barely begun that stagger when the first blade slid into his guts like an icicle, deep and very cold. Agannor grunted, waving his sword vainly.

The second blade sliced him like fire, riding up under his breastplate, and in. He sobbed as it lifted him off his feet—then somehow fell back and away and off it again, blind and breathless in his agony.

Agannor was dimly aware of falling back through the door and bouncing on stones, retching blood. His world exploded into roiling red mist, and he had no idea at all that the three warriors had snatched up the crossbow and fled, or that he was lying with his boots across the threshold, kicking wildly and feebly in his agony.

Horaundoon sat on the edge of his bed in the Tankard, sniffling through the part of the hargaunt that shaped his bulbous nose.

Anger was burning dark and slow at the back of his mind to match the prickling sensation in the gorget hidden under more of the hargaunt—the prickling that told him that some busynose of a war wizard was still scrying him.

That scrutiny had latched onto him on his first lurching climb of the inn stairs, and hadn't let up since.

He was *so* tempted to lash out with a spell that would snuff out the spy's mind in an instant.

Yet he dared not. That sort of death would bring a mustering of war wizards, and draw the attention of Vangerdahast himself. Too many even for Horaundoon of the Crawling Doom to spellblast. In such a battle he might manage to slay many, but the inevitable death would be his own.

So here he sat, twiddling his thumbs and feigning weary boredom. With every breath he took, that attitude became less and less an act.

Stlarning war wizards.

Islif Lurelake ran like the wind, her armored coat clanging and clashing, with Florin and Pennae right at her heels. South down the cross-passage, to come at the crossbowmen from another way.

She skidded to a stop at the passage-moot, expecting to eat a volley of crossbow bolts when she turned the corner. Gasping for breath, she balanced herself—then ducked around the corner, just as quickly dancing back.

A crossbow cracked. Its bolt hummed past, shattering against one of the statues amid a burst of lightnings.

Their foes were ready and waiting.

She traded glances with Florin, trying to think what best to do next—and Pennae hissed in the forester's ear: "Stand still and let me climb you."

"Yes," Florin replied, tensing.

Islif watched the thief swarm up Florin to his shoulders. Pennae crouched there for a moment, froglike, the passage ceiling close overhead—then launched herself forward in a great springing leap that sent Florin staggering back but hurled Pennae high across the passage-mouth, to strike the floor in a forward roll.

Two crossbow bolts sought her life. The first hummed past well in her wake, to crash into the old crossbow on its tripod—and send it toppling from its mount to clatter harmlessly on the floor.

The second missed her heels by a fingerwidth and raced on, collecting crackling lightnings as it passed between the statues. It shivered noisily against the bronzen doors, fragments pattering to the floor.

Pennae landed, rolled, and ran on into the darkness.

Islif and Florin were already moving, ducking around the corner again, trusting that not even the swiftest windlass-cranker could have wound up a crossbow to fire again, so soon after five shots. They were trusting their lives, of course, on the hope that there wasn't a sixth crossbowman, or more.

They'd trusted well, it seemed.

No bolts came humming at them, and they could see no foe in the light of Islif's bouncing lantern. The room beyond the rusty bars held no foes.

Panting from their sprint, they ducked through the bars—and almost hacked at Pennae, who burst through the open door from the southern slant passage.

"Where'd you—?" Islif gasped, waving her sword.

"The stone goblin. I tried to pick it up to be a shield, but—too heavy. *Much* too heavy," Pennae gasped back. "Hoped to catch our attackers here."

"Whoever they are, they'll be waiting for us outside," Florin said. "With their bows ready."

"So we find shields," Islif told him, "somewhere in here, before we try to come out."

"And let Doust, Agannor, and Bey *die?*"

"And just how many of us d'you want to join them in their graves?" the warrior woman snapped. "If we go out there while they're waiting, bows aimed at the d—"

"Be *still!*" Pennae snarled fiercely, clutching and shaking them both ere flinging out one arm to point. "Look! 'The rest are hidden in the door,' remember?"

They looked where she was pointing. Agannor's feet were still kicking feebly across the threshold, keeping the thick door open—and in the exposed doorframe they could see a tall, narrow slot of darkness.

Islif swung her lantern. It was a niche, running back into the wall, with something dark in it that looked like wood. Pennae pounced.

"Watch for foes!" she snapped, waving at the distant entry doors. Florin spun around obediently, but Islif watched as Pennae, on her knees, held her dagger ready in one hand and with the other drew forth . . . a flat wooden box, dark with damp.

The thief's arm started to spasm and shudder. She looked up at Islif, a tense frown on her face.

"There's a spell on this," she breathed. "I can feel the tingling clear up my arm! Let's take it yonder. Get Agannor back so we can close the door."

Islif and Florin sprang to do so, dragging the white-faced Agannor a little way into the slant passage. He was gasping blood and moaning when they started—but he'd fainted by the time they'd finished.

"Stand guard over him and the door," Pennae ordered. "Throw his sword and dagger at anyone who opens it, whether they have a crossbow or not."

Then she clutched the box to her breast and ran down the slant passage, past the silent, huddled heap that was Bey, to the clustered lanterns of the rest of the Swords.

Their weapons were drawn and their faces were grim—and Doust lay in their midst, pillowed on Semoor's leather jack, looking weak and pale. On the floor behind them was a dark and sticky lake that hadn't been there before: Doust's blood, the crossbow bolt Semoor had drawn forth lying at its heart.

"Martess! Jhessail!" Pennae hissed. "There's magic on this. Strong magic."

Jhessail spread her hands helplessly, but she and Martess knelt on the other side of the box from Pennae as the thief carefully set it on the floor.

Drawing in a deep breath, Pennae looked up into the intent gazes of the rest of the Swords, then down again at the box. Its lid was a slab of wood that slid along two grooves carved into the inside of its side walls, with a thumb-dimple handle. Pennae used the point of her dagger rather than her thumb to gingerly slide it open.

And nothing happened.

Everyone waited, barely breathing, but still nothing happened. Quietly, Martess laid her fingers on the box, flinched, and then asked, "Preservative spell, or some sort of message magic? We're feeling it because it's collapsing, perhaps?"

" 'Perhaps' just about anything is happening," Pennae agreed wryly. "But this is good to see." She pointed down at what the box held: a row of nine metal vials.

"Fine steel, completely free of rust, cork-stoppered and wax sealed . . . and all of them bear this same symbol."

She pointed at the nearest mark, a tiny red-painted character that looked more or less like a human right hand.

Atop the vials lay a scrap of parchment bearing the words: "Rivior, these are the last. With these, my debt is discharged. Look to see me no more." The message was signed with an elaborate rune.

"Never seen it before," Jhessail said, "but it takes no learning to know 'tis a wizard's sigil." Martess nodded.

"So these are—or were—potions," Pennae said. "Magic quaffs."

"But drinking them does what?" Martess asked.

"And are they all the same," Jhessail put in, "or is that mark the mage who made them?"

"Or the smith who made the vials," Pennae pointed out.

The three women stared at each other. There were shrugs ere they turned with one accord to look at Doust.

"He's dying," Semoor said bleakly, on his knees beside his wounded friend, "so pour one of those down his throat. You can't hurt him more."

Pennae took up a vial, sliced the wax with her dagger, teased forth the cork stopper, and sniffed the open top. Then she cradled Doust's head and put the vial to his lips, her thumb ready to become a stopper if he choked or spat.

Doust swallowed it down and his eyes flickered. Then he looked up at them, brightening visibly. "Pain going," he gasped. "Just like that."

Pennae nodded. "Clear, colorless, and no stink to it that I could smell. Sparkled, going into him." Doust was looking stronger, and his face was less pale. "Taste?" she asked him.

"Don't mind if I do," he jested feebly. "Cool, tingling . . . hard to find words . . . like swallowing a cool breeze."

"Good," Pennae said, letting his head fall back onto the jack. She looked at Semoor. "Watch him. If anything goes bad—he starts to turn to stone or grow scales or something—shout out quick!"

Sliding the case shut, she took it up and hurried back down the passage to Bey, Jhessail and Martess right behind her.

The warrior looked dead, but his mouth was open. She sat on his stomach and poured the potion down his throat, slapping her hand over his face to keep the potion inside him if he coughed—and he did—then pulled the crossbow bolt out of his innards.

He bucked and tried to roar, under her, but Pennae rode him firmly back to sprawled ease, then left him to race on to the last fallen Sword.

Agannor's slow, feeble spasms became a convulsive heave upward when the potion slid down his throat—then his twisted face smoothed out and he looked at her.

"Healing quaff," he said happily. "You never forget the taste. A priest of Tempus fed me one, once; cost me all the coins I had." He relaxed with a gusty sigh. "My thanks!"

"Six left," Pennae said, rising. She thrust the case into Jhessail's arms. "These'd cost us hundreds of lions each at a temple. So *don't* drop it."

The flame-haired mageling looked down at Agannor. "So they're all going to be . . . all right again?"

Pennae spread her hands. "If the gods will."

"Ah," Semoor muttered, helping Doust to sit up, "but what if the gods won't?"

Halfway down the passage, Bey was already reeling to his feet, leaning on the wall and managing a smile.

Florin said, "I think we've done enough strolling around the Halls this day."

Bey gave him a twisted grin. "I've certainly lost the *stomach* for it!"

"You," Pennae said severely, "can be wounded again, know you!"

"Indeed," Islif agreed, then said to Florin, "We all want to get outside again, but not to swallow crossbow bolts doing it." She looked at the mages. "Remind me what spells you have."

"A magic missile and something that helps me strike true," Martess replied.

"Batt—ah, a magic missile," Jhessail added.

"So you can do harm to quite a few crossbowmen, but you have to be able to see them—and they'll take one look at either of you, waving your hands and chanting, and know just where to send their bolts."

There were nods all around as Florin started to usher them back down the passage, to bring them all together. Doust was on his feet again, walking almost normally, and the Swords grinned at each other. Through the open doorway, unheeded, green slime dripped dismally.

"We need shields. Shields that can stop crossbow bolts at close range," Islif said. "Those strongchests, back in the bunkroom?"

Pennae shook her head. "Far too rotten. Those bolts can go right through good armor—" She waved at Bey, who gave her a rueful grin "—so wood that crumbles when I touch it isn't going to stop them much more than a tightframe of stretched silk would."

"Well, that's cheerful to hear," Semoor said. "So are we going to crawl out on our bellies after dark and hope they can't hit what they can't see?"

Islif gave him a thoughtful look. "Chancy—but our best chance, I think. Sometimes, Stoop, you *do* seem to have wits. For a few moments, once or twice a tenday."

"They're out there, somewhere, braving danger—tasting adventure! While I—whom the king—*the king!*—wanted to accompany them—sit here, chafing in idleness!"

Narantha slammed down her tallglass with such force that the stem burst right up through the bowl, leaving her holding only shards amid a flood of fine wine.

Tessaril Winter set down her own glass and made a swift gesture—and the shards were gone from Narantha's bloodied fingertips, whisked away through the air trailed by droplets of blood and wine. " 'Tis a good thing I put out the second best glasses, I see."

Narantha Crownsilver glared at her. "You're enjoying this! You're chuckling up your sleeve, like all the other wizards in this realm! Delighted to deny nobles their rights, hiding behind royal orders you refuse to share with us—orders that in this instance I *know* are false! I heard the Dragon's reply to me! I know what was in his eyes, his voice! He'll not be pleased when I tell him of this—that his own Lady Lord of Eveningstar defies his royal will to play Vangerdahast's little games, one more time! I am a Crownsilver, and far from the least regarded of those who bear that proud name—"

"True," Tessaril agreed, her face unreadable.

Narantha seethed, raising her hands into claws, but swept on. "And as such have every right to ride where I will, do as I will, and consort with whomever I will, so long as I do no treason and break not the decrees of the king! *Not* of Vangerdahast, not of you or any other jumped-up courtier! You have no right to hold me, you have no right to arrest me if I march right out of here now—as I've done no treason and intend none, and His Majesty knows it—and—and—"

"I'm afraid I do have that right," Tessaril replied, "and that duty. Please calm yourself and hear me, Narantha—"

"Calm myself? *Calm myself?* Why should I? How can I calm myself when my freedom is snatched from me unlawfully, my rights of birth are denied and dismissed, my—"

"Good manners quite desert you." Tessaril rose, in a shifting of skirts—and this was the first time Narantha had seen her in anything but breeches and boots topped by more mens' garb—and crossed the room in two smooth strides.

Face paling with rage, Narantha darted her hand to the tiny dagger at her belt, but Tessaril deftly captured her wrists and stood over her, saying as gently as before, "Lass, lass, don't you see how much I want to give in to you? I, too, have known love—"

"Love? Think you I'm in *love* with that forester? That my heart and loins rule me? Wench, you try me sorely!" Narantha spat. " 'Tis of *my* needs I speak! My hunger for adventure, my first chance to do anything in my life that strays in the slightest from my father's firm hand and my mother's constant spiteful spying! My—my—"

Words failed her, and she burst into tears of rage, struggling against Tessaril's strength with snarls and sobs and finally wild tugs and kicks.

Tessaril avoided her sallies with deft ease, saying flatly, "Don't make me spell-sleep you, Narantha. I will if I must. Yet know this: I *will not* budge. Save your curses and kicks for a time when they'll achieve something—if ever you find such a time, in all your hopefully long life. I cannot give in to my whims, for I long ago swore an oath to the Dragon, and I *will* keep it, or my life is nothing. I have specific orders regarding you, from the king's own lips."

"More lies," Narantha hissed furiously at her, between sobbing breaths. "You've had no time to speak with the king! I've watched you, every instant since my rising—just as you have watched me! I doubt *very much* that the Dragon crystal-chats with his lordlings in the heart of the night; I should think the queen would have something to say about that!"

Still holding her wrists, Tessaril said, "Your doubts, I fear, are unfounded. The king himself was here last night."

"Oh, I suppose he just stepped out of the heart of a spell, sat on the side of your bed, and discussed affairs of state, yes?"

"I don't recall him sitting," Tessaril replied, "but we talked, yes. About you, among many, many other things. His Majesty anticipated your displeasure."

She let go of Narantha, stepped back, and drew something out of her bodice, proffering it between two fingers: a finger of much-folded parchment.

Narantha stared up at the Lady Lord of Eveningstar, then at the parchment—and snatched it, unfolding it with hands that trembled in haste.

> *Dearest Narantha, Lady Crownsilver:*
> *Life is a series of hardships and hard choices for us all. This is one of yours. Every Cormyrean, noble or common-born, owes absolute loyalty to the Dragon Throne. You are to obey Lord Tessaril Winter as if she were me. Your spirit does you credit, but every noble must learn that obedience is worth far more to the realm and to its people, as well as to its sovereign. I pray you make me proud.*

It was signed "Azoun, Fourth of that Name."

Narantha bit her lip.

"You know what it says?"

Tessaril nodded. "I watched him write it."

Narantha read it again, holding it almost tenderly in one hand while her other balled into a trembling fist. Then she smote the arm of her chair, again and again, weeping.

This time, when Tessaril's arms went around her, she buried herself in that warm, soft comfort, and clung to it.

"Not much longer now," Florin said.

"Good," Jhessail sighed. "I'm tired, and I'm cold, and sitting here in the dark watching lightning bolts that snap just often enough to keep me from dozing off doesn't strike me as glorious adventure."

"You're not sitting in the dark," Pennae said. "One lantern's enough. The gods don't pour lamp oil down out of the skies, know you."

"Hrast! There goes my seventeenth scheme for riches," Semoor said. "Seen any ghosts yet, anyone? They call it 'the Haunted Halls,' look you!"

"Cleric-to-be of Lathander," Martess said, "still your tongue. Or I'll do so for you."

"That should be fun."

"Oho," Islif told the ceiling, "Semoor Wolftooth is about to have an adventure. He just doesn't know it yet."

Narantha read the royal letter for the thirty-sixth time. This time, when she refolded it carefully, slipped it back into her bodice, and raised her eyes to the ever-watchful Tessaril, she found amusement in the Lady Lord of Eveningstar's gaze.

"There are no hidden words there, I fear," Tessaril said, "and no lurking spell. It won't change what it says, no matter how often you read it."

Narantha sighed, then shook her head as if she could wish away all lords, towers, wizards, and commanding kings. "I . . . I just want to ride free," she said mournfully. "To burst out of this kind confinement. To ride with the Swords, and see adventures—"

"From a safe distance?"

"I—yes, from a safe distance, though that's cowardly of me, I suppose, and unworthy. I—hrast it, Lady Lord Tessaril, I am weary up to *here* with sitting cooped up in a lord's tower, surrounded by an everpresent escort of Purple Dragons and war wizards!"

"Of course. Have some more of this superb cheese—and the zzar?—and look into the fire."

The flames of the hearthfire danced strangely, shaping themselves into a scene of armed and armored horsemen riding along a road, a purposeful line of men all garbed alike, who rode under banners that swirled and flapped just like the Crownsilver banners did, when her father rode out to—

"Those *are* your family banners," Tessaril said.

Narantha's head jerked up. "You're reading my *mind?*"

"I don't have to, when your face softens so, remembering. No, the cleverness of my spell is confined to shaping flames."

"So just how is it that you managed to show me my father riding somewhere, if you plucked it not from my mind?"

"I saw it in my scrying crystal, when you last sought yon garderobe," Tessaril replied. "Your father is a-riding with all his men-at-arms, right now."

"Riding under arms? Where?"

"Here. Straight up to Eveningstar—rather angrily, I fear—to bring you home. Though even if he rides right through the night, he won't be here until well after the sun rises again."

Narantha stared at the Lady Lord of Eveningstar, aghast—then launched herself out of her chair with a snarl, storming across the room with her hands out like claws.

Tessaril sat unmoved, only the slightest trace of a smile twitching the corner of her lips. She went on smiling as her magic caught her seething captive steps away from her, spanked Narantha Crownsilver soundly with unseen hands, and hurled the sobbingly furious young noblewoman off to bed.

The Lady Lord of Eveningstar went on sitting in her chair, listening to the crashes of things being broken on the far side of that closed and spellbound door, and her smile turned sad.

"Gods above, child," she murmured. "You are so much as I was, when your age, that I almost want to defy Azoun. Almost."

As they squeezed through the rusty bars, there was a fair amount of crowding, and Semoor's boot brushed one edge of the heaped weapons.

Whereupon a mouth appeared on the battered and bare metal shield atop the pile, and said in a flat, deep voice like a Purple Dragon giving stern orders: "Beware! These were carried in by those who will never carry them out again!"

Standing tense in the silence that followed those ringing words, the Swords watched the mouth fade away again. And waited.

And waited.

Nothing else happened, as their held breaths stretched. It was Semoor who first grinned, shrugged, and asked, "So, can I take yon shield now? And go through the weapons for whatever I like the look of?"

"No," Pennae snapped. "You don't really need them, and you could be spreading some fell curse or other. If Agannor or Bey—they've the best armor—wants to use the shield as we go out, to stand like a wall while the rest of us go past in a crouch, fine, but I'd throw it right back in here after, if 'twere me. I trust none of it."

The Swords of Eveningstar were giving each other grim looks.

"I might have laughed at that warning, when we came in here," Agannor said, "but not now."

They moved on, Pennae tarrying to sprinkle a fingerwidth line of sand across the passage, from the third of four identical sacks tied to her belt.

"I saw you doing that earlier," Doust said with a frown. "Why?"

The thief finished her pouring. "To show us, on our next visit, if anything has come slithering around these passages since we left. To check on our intrusions, say."

Doust made a face. "Ah."

Blowing out the lone lantern, the Swords went out into Starwater Gorge, low and fast and as quietly as possible.

Truly, the gods were smiling this night.

No crossbow bolts greeted them.

There was a time when Alura Durshavin had helped her mother sprinkle precise, slender lines of decorative powders atop cakes, and her hand had grown steadier and more confident since then.

As a result, her thin lines of sand were as straight as a sword blade, every one of them.

Until something large and serpentine, that moved with velvet silence for all its bulk, slithered across one after another of them, as it quested after the intruders who smelled so intriguing. And edible.

Chapter 16

SOME ABRUPT ARRIVALS, SOME SUDDEN DEPARTURES

This court is like a slaughterhouse when royal tax collectors are seen approaching town: all abrupt arrivals, sudden departures, and a lot of sweating haste and spilled blood.

Arl Thandaster, Sage of Aglarond
Aglarond: A Wiser View
published in the Year of the Shrike

The war wizard spying ended as abruptly as if sliced off by a sharp knife.

Hissing in satisfaction, Horaundoon moved faster than darkness is banished by bright light, teleporting away from his inn room to—

A cavern he'd used a time or two before, spell-sealed and long forgotten in the Storm Horns. Some dead wizard's lair that now served Horaundoon of the Zhentarim as a hide-hold and cache of magic.

He stepped forward blindly but confidently in the silent, dank darkness.

Two measured paces. He reached out.

His fingers found the stone coffer just where he'd left it, on the ledge. The glowstones still waited inside it, and as their cold light kindled in his hands, Horaundoon strode along the stone wall to place them on either side of the mirror he'd hung there six—no, seven, now—seasons ago.

Gazing at himself in the mirror, cold-eyed and confident, he opened another box on the ledge and drew out one of the dreamstones, that held images spell-stored in them.

Calling forth a particular image from it, Horaundoon set about shaping the hargaunt covering his face into a likeness he'd never assumed before.

It was the likeness he'd called out of the dreamstone to float in the air, life-sized and frozen.

The head of a man Horaundoon had slain with his own hands—and much satisfaction—years ago.

The real head was now shattered, decaying bone somewhere in the woods of Daggerdale, but when his magic had captured its appearance, it had been very much alive, and belonged to a noble of Cormyr, one Lorneth Crownsilver.

Ah, yes, Lorneth: uncle to Narantha Crownsilver, and ne'er-do-well rake.

"A gambler and a fool, who made himself a fool all over again when he dared to try to swindle *this* wizard of the Zhentarim," Horaundoon murmured aloud. The hargaunt wriggled around his mouth to make his own lips more closely resemble the noble's wider, thinner, perpetually smiling ones.

"Yes, that's it," he said, turning his head this way and that. "Lorneth Crownsilver, as ever was." He gave the mirror a fiendish grin, then said softly to the hargaunt: "Worm time."

There was a single bell-like tone of acknowledgment—and that part of the hargaunt that was masquerading as the back of his neck started to ripple and darken. He watched in the mirror as it opened a mouth to let something dark and glistening slide out into his raised and waiting hand.

"Yes," Horaundoon breathed, gazing at the first of his mindworms. It was time, indeed.

He strode across the cavern to its rubble-strewn end and lifted a certain stone among the heaps of rock to reveal a stone bowl holding a spellbook he'd not consulted for years. It pages held a few vital words to add to his teleport incant, to bring him tracelessly through Tessaril's wards without alerting her or any war wizard—or being tugged astray by the nearby chaos of her Hidden House.

He smiled as he cast the spell that would take him thither.

There were times when war wizard traitors were *very* useful things.

It was pursuing her, dark, wet, and terrible, wriggling and slithering down the bright white marble passages.

Closer and closer, no matter how fast she fled or how recklessly she hurled herself down staircases and across the dark, bottomless chasms between balconies. It was going to catch her, going to . . .

She felt icy fear as she fell to her knees, midway down another marble hall. Must get up before it—

Warm and wet, welling up inside her, red-black and triumphant, choking her . . .

"No!" Narantha shrieked, falling into ruby-edged darkness, falling . . .

"Nooooo!"

She was gasping, panting wide-eyed into the moonlit night, hearing the echo of her own scream rebound again and again in her head, blinking at what she could see of the unfamiliar bedchamber in the reaching fingers of moonlight. Where *was*—oh. Oh yes: Tessaril's Tower, in Eveningstar, as an unwilling "guest."

Then something moved, in the darkness beyond the moonlight, and came forward. Smiling.

The mindworm going into her had driven her into nightmare, of course, and an abrupt awakening—but she hadn't screamed, making his carefully cast cloak of silence unnecessary. Thus far.

Horaundoon smiled and started his walk to the bed, keeping his strides slow, soft, and confident.

And now, we shall see.

Well-regarded mages of the Zhentarim necessarily spent more time working magic than acting.

Yet it was dark, the lass was young and used to paying attention only to herself, and a wayward Crownsilver could be expected to change a bit, over the years.

Putting on his best wry noble's smile, Horaundoon stopped at the foot of the bed.

It was a smile she knew.

Narantha felt her jaw drop. Could it be? Truly? After all these years?

"Uncle Lorneth?"

His eyebrows rose. "You're expecting someone? I can depart."

"No! I—Uncle, where have you *been*? We've not heard from you in *years!*"

"I've been rather busy. 'Twas a distinct pleasure for me to discover my business turning at last to kin, and someone I was fond of, at that. Someone young, beautiful, and brimming with promise. Well met, Lady Narantha Crownsilver."

"Uncle! Call me Nantha, as you always did!"

"Not grown too proud for the names of your youth? Good! Nantha, how would you like to be free of these confinements—and at the same time taste your own adventures *and* serve the Crown of Cormyr?"

Narantha stared at him. "Yes! *Yes!*"

"Then get out of that bed, put on good boots—and useful garb above them, trews or better leather breeches and a tunic, none of these silken gowns—and come with me. *Quietly.*"

Her uncle turned his back and strolled away from the bed, making a deft, intricate gesture as he did so.

Narantha froze, her bare feet just about to touch the floor. "You work *magic?* Uncle, you never said . . ."

"You never asked. Certain family members are so deathly concerned about the respectability of the Crownsilvers that I kept my increasing mastery hidden. Which is the very thing that made me useful to the king. Don't sit there all night, lass! Get some proper clothes on!"

Narantha moved hastily. "I—ah—sorry, Uncle. I—you serve the king?"

"Uncle Lorneth can still surprise, hey?"

Narantha was dressing in feverish haste, hopping awkwardly in the moonlight as she shrugged her most rugged tunic over her head and sought to put on breeches at the same time. "Tessaril will be furious! Won't she come after us?"

"Tessaril is the king's plaything no more. Even to squawk about your disappearance would harm her standing. I think you'll find she tries to pretend you were never here at all, and concocts some story about the Swords murdering you on the road to get your jewels, and dressing up some lowcoin lass in your gowns before they got here—only to help her escape, to keep the imposture from being discovered, when she got news that your father was on the way here."

"So he truly is coming hither," Narantha breathed, buckling her belt. Her mouth tightened. "Tluining bitch."

"Ready?" her uncle asked, turning to face her. Narantha tapped her dagger hilts to make sure they were in their sheaths where they should be, and nodded.

Lorneth smiled again, raised a hand—and blue-green fire blossomed in the air, a flickering line that curved purposefully into an upright whorl. With his other hand, in the grandly courteous manner employed by obsequious innkeepers, he waved for her to step into it.

Narantha didn't hesitate for a moment.

The bed curtains parted, and her Azoun was there.

The Dragon Queen smiled sleepily up at him. "I was beginning to think you'd quite forsaken me." She threw back the shimmerweave bedcloaks to reach up for him with long and shapely arms.

Azoun smiled. Shrugging his open nightrobe off his shoulders, he let her draw him down to her waiting warmth.

"Ah, Fee . . . Fee . . ." he murmured, settling into her familiar curves. "Never will I forget my queen. Passing time, I fear, does slip away from me unnoticed, when Vangerdahast—and Alaphondar, and a dozen scribes after him—come to talk to me, the scribes crowding in urgently when Vangey's finally done, with their 'sign this' and 'decree that—oh, but not in *those* words, Your Majesty, lest thus and so, *far* better to use these words I just happen to have penned for you.'"

"And talk to you," Filfaeril murmured, stretching restlessly under him. "Talk . . . talk . . . and more talk."

"Exactly," Azoun said, before his mouth claimed hers.

When he surfaced for breath, a long time later, it was to add in satisfaction, "You *do* understand."

"Always, my Azoun," his queen said. "I understand you always."

A gentle, steady breeze was sweeping down Starwater Gorge out of the Stonelands. In the moonlight, those perilous lands looked like so many frozen rolling waves breaking over jagged giants' teeth.

Or so Florin fancied as he sat on the grassy height above the rock overhang, high up on the east side of the gorge, where his fellow exhausted Swords were sleeping. Someone had to keep watch, and the cold metal of the sword across his knees at least kept him from falling asleep.

He looked north again. Whoever had attacked them in the Haunted Halls was out here somewhere, and everyone knew outlaws—and crawling beasts, from trolls to dragons that could tear apart castle keeps with their talons—lurked in yon Stonelands. Such fabled perils were why the king had sent them all here: to hack and harry and be seen, to curb boldness and make fell things think Cormyr was alert and well defended against their creepings.

Not that the Swords of Eveningstar had made a glorious start of it.

And Florin Falconhand, the valiant hero of the Battle of Hunter's Hollow? Even less.

Three of his companions had almost died, and Florin had done nothing to save them—and even less to keep them from blundering into danger in the first place.

He was no brave battle leader. He didn't know *how*.

Oh, he could be fearless enough, but fearlessness gets folk killed. He could be decisive and forceful, too—when leading only himself.

Yet in yon Halls, dark and unfamiliar places where scores of men had died, he'd hemmed and hawed, tramping those rooms and passages unsure of where to go and even how best to array the Swords for battle. If it hadn't been for Pennae—and how was it that she came to know all she did, about delving into dungeons and being ready for monster attacks and all? He must—

Florin stiffened. What was that?

Something moved in the night behind him. Something dark and wary, seeking to keep silent. Something creeping—

He sprang to his feet, took two swift steps to his right where the rock was, and in its lee spun around, sword flashing up, then lunged back around the rock, thrusting—

There was a little gasp, almost a shriek, and whoever it was fell back, whispering, "Florin?"

He sprang to see, blade held high and aside. A stride ahead, the land fell away into a little dell full of tall grass and bright moonlight, and a woman was lying in it, her boots right in front of him.

A moment later, he was crouched above her, beset with recognition —and astonishment.

"Narantha!"

The Lady Narantha Crownsilver gave him a crooked smile. "My hero," she whispered, staring up at him with eyes that outshone the moonlight. "You *are* a great adventurer."

Florin winced. "Nay, I'm very far from that. I'm—"

"Florin," Narantha whispered. "Kiss me. Please."

Florin looked down at her, then back over his shoulder to where the Swords slept unseen—but not unheard, thanks to the breeze that was now carrying faint snores to him. Then he sighed, carefully sheathed his sword, and leaned close to murmur, "Lady, I'm standing *watch*. I can't be—"

Narantha smiled catlike, and suddenly thrust her arms wide, taking Florin's hard-planted arm out from under him.

His face crashed down into rounded softness, smelling faintly of exquisite perfume, and he felt more than heard Narantha's warm murmur: "Oh, yes, you can, lord of my love."

Then he felt her hands, stroking his cheek and throat. "Lord

Florin," she whispered, "must I beg you? Please!" Her hands were at his buckles, now, tugging and—

Florin bent his head and tried to pray to Mielikki. He was still struggling to think of the right words when warm, hungry lips found his. And conquered him.

The man who was not Lorneth Crownsilver sat as still as stone in the shadowed lee of a moonlit pinnacle not all that far up Starwater Gorge from the tender tryst he was spell-seeing. He smiled much as the real Lorneth would have done.

Little Narantha was a natural, not that the ranger lad was all that unwilling—and so smitten with the moment was he, just now, that the second mindworm had flowed off the end of her tongue and into him without him noticing at all.

Horaundoon smiled up at the moon in quiet triumph. Deftly done, and a good night's work. The first of many such nights to come, as she obeyed his bidding through the first mindworm coiled within her head, and so slipped more and more under his command.

Ah, with the right spells in his hands, a patient man could rule the world . . . one seduction at a time.

"Right, King Azoun?" he asked the unhearing moon gleefully.

Dawn had been bright, and the morning moreso. Now, within sight of highsun, the sun beat down as mercilessly as a moneylender's smile.

Yet it seemed gentle indeed compared to the icily sneering grimace of a grin Lord Maniol Crownsilver gave to the guards he was spattering mud all over as he reined in his mount in front of Tessaril's Tower.

"Where's Tessaril?" he barked at them, throwing his reins in the face of the man who stepped to the head of his mount.

"Crave you an audience?" came a level question in answer. Lord Crownsilver swung himself down with a grunt, not deigning to reply.

He had swords enough in livery with him to deal with a few tower guards—and if his men had remembered his orders, several hand dartbows would be aimed at each of these helmheads right now.

Lurching from the stiffness of more time spent in the saddle than he was used to these days, he mounted the porch steps. Two Purple Dragons and two knights of the realm barred his way, but he neither slowed nor hesitated—and they drew smoothly aside moments before his striding would have brought him crashing into them.

"You are expected, Lord Crownsilver. Go right up," one said, as the doors magically opened themselves, taking Maniol's wordless grunt of reply with him as he stamped to the stairs.

Behind him, he heard his senior guards coldly insisting that they accompanied him everywhere—and gasps as something was revealed that stopped their blustering in mid-word. Not caring whether they slaughtered the tower guards in the street or were all turned to frogs by some war wizard spell or other, he ascended, finding the landing populated with highknights.

"Where's Tessaril?" he growled at them. They gave him identical looks of disdain and silently lifted their hands to indicate the bower at the far end of the floor.

Maniol passed them without another word or glance, fixing his eyes on the lone woman in high-booted black leathers who sat awaiting him.

"Where's my daughter?" he barked at her.

"Gone." Her voice was calm.

"*What?* Woman, if you're lying to me—"

"I can well believe women would oft have cause to lie to you, Lord Crownsilver," Tessaril Winter said, "if your courtesies are customarily so lacking. The Lady Narantha Crownsilver is no longer within these walls—but the Crown has neither jailed nor hidden her."

She lifted a hand to point. "She slipped out of a locked and guarded bedchamber—that second door behind you, as it happens—last night. And fled, I know not where. By her own designs."

"And you let her go? With all your spells and guards and—and—"

"Lord, I am the Lady Lord of Eveningstar, not a jailer. Nor yet a

Wizard of War, empowered to use magic at will on a loyal subject of the realm who stands accused of no crime, and is not only noble but enjoys royal favor—"

"*Yes!* That's it! Azoun wants to bed her! You've spirited her away—"

"Maniol, guard your tongue. Ranting and raging are one thing; speaking treason quite another."

"You *dare*—?" Maniol strode forward, fists clenched, to loom over Tessaril. "You dare accuse me of treason, and school me what to say and not to say? D'you *know* who I am, wench?"

Blazing eyes glared down into calm and steady ones.

"Yes, Lord Crownsilver, I do: an unpleasant boor of a man who is at this moment understandably lost in rage—but now demonstrating his lack of nobility. Nobles control themselves, Maniol. Nobles make masks of their faces, and guard their tongues with great care, and do the right thing. For the good of the realm."

"You jumped-up commoner! You trollop! Preening over an empty title won by letting the man who calls himself 'king' plow you thrice a tenday! How *dare* you lecture me, a Crownsilver born, on what it is, and what it is not, to be 'noble'! Before all the gods, this bursts all bounds! I—"

"—go on bursting them, Maniol Crownsilver, with every word you spit. Your phrase 'man who calls himself king' is clear treason, and I'll not hear more words like it! Belittle me if it pleases you, berate my guardianship—for you do so justly, and I am ashamed and will answer to the king for it—but spare us all unguarded words that can yet cost you your head!"

She rose to face him, nose to nose, and hissed, "I'm trying to keep you from going too far, idiot! Speak no more treason!"

Maniol sneered, his angry breath hot on her face. "Or you'll—what?"

"Or I'll tear off your codpiece with all that's in it, and jam it into your yapping mouth," Tessaril told him, letting him see the utter lack of fear in her eyes, "before breaking all of your fingers, dressing you in women's weeds, and sending you back home to your wife tied to a succession of peddlers' mules, with a banner knotted to you that tells the world: 'This fool spoke treason in the hearing of Tessaril Winter.' "

She shrugged. "Or I could just let slip my leash on yon high-knights and let them cut out your tongue, flog you from here clear across the realm to your keep, and behead you there before all your household, as the good old law still holds that nobles deemed traitors be treated."

His eyes burned into hers. He was breathing heavily, eyes bright with rage and desperation: the dawning fear that he had said too much and would soon face such fates.

"Or I could regard you as an angry father, driven to imprudent speech by love and care for his daughter, who has served the realm well for years, and just needs rest, a good feast, and time to find some calm," Tessaril added. "So as to consider what we can best do for Lady Narantha Crownsilver. Wherever she may be."

Maniol Crownsilver's gusty sigh became a growl, his eyes glittering. "It's those cursed Swords, blast and hrast them!" he burst out.

Tessaril shook her head. "No. We're keeping them under *quite* close watch."

" 'We'?"

Tessaril pointed, and Lord Crownsilver swung around. No less a war wizard than Laspeera Naerinth stood behind him, in a corner he was certain had been empty a few moments before. She gave him an expressionless nod—over the two wands in her hands that were aimed right at him.

"We," Tessaril repeated. "Both of us were concerned that Lord Maniol Crownsilver, so valuable and respected a lord of the realm, might in a moment of raging do something foolish, like speak treason or attack a king's lord."

Maniol felt her hand—cool and smooth—clasp his. He turned back to her, tugging free of her grasp. She was standing just as close to him as before, their chests almost touching.

"Hear me now, Lord Crownsilver," Tessaril said. "Narantha's not with those adventurers—for which you should be *very* thankful—and they've made no attempt to contact her or come here."

"*I'll* contact *them!* Where are they?"

"No, Lord Crownsilver," Tessaril told him, "you'll not. You'll take your house blades—*all* of them, leaving not a one behind 'by mistake'—and turn around and go home. If your daughter's not found by highsun on the morrow, the war wizards will start searching for her, all across the realm. I'll *not* have armed bands roving Eveningstar, looking for trouble."

"I'll not be looking for trouble," Maniol Crownsilver snarled, "I'll be looking for adventurers!"

She gave him a bright smile. "Oh? Are they not the same thing?"

His eyes changed, and his dark face of fury slipped. It twisted momentarily into a grudging grin, ere he whirled, spitting oaths, and stormed out.

Chapter 17
WHISPERINGS AND PONDERINGS

There's not a scheme that's been schemed that won't afford some entertainment to its conspirators, when they gather to whisper and ponder strategies and second guesses. However, when the scheme nears its end, for good or for ill—ah, that's when the real entertainment begins.

Ortharryn Khantlow, Scribe Royal
Thirty Years Behind The Dragon Throne
published in the Year of the Stag

It was hot and airless under the trees along the sides of Starwater Gorge, after highsun on the fifth day since the Swords had first set boot in the Haunted Halls.

The morning had been spent trading many of their fast-dwindling handfuls of coins to Evenor shopkeepers and farmers for food and lamp oil. Prayers added to such chores took Doust and Semoor longer than some of their fellows, so they were the last to arrive at the moot.

And knew it. They were sweating hard by the time they dumped their heavy packs under the broad leaves of a clump of starrach larger than some cottages in Eveningstar, and hastened through the thicket beyond.

Praise Tymora and Lathander, the path was right where they'd expected it to be, and they swiftly—if precariously—ascended the side of the gorge to the huge, lichen-speckled jutting rock they'd dubbed "the Snout."

Islif Lurelake was standing sentinel atop it, in her homemade armor, looking as alert as ever.

Semoor squinted up at her. "Anyone watching? Following?"

She shook her head, murmuring unnecessarily, "And you're the last."

The two friends nodded and ducked down into a small, dark hole under the Snout. Overhead, they knew, Islif would be taking a few steps back to stand over the crack that would carry their voices up to her, so she could listen in without leaving off her scrutiny of the gorge. Those mysterious bowmen—and, folk in Eveningstar insisted, outlaws by the score, trolls beyond numbering, and modest armies of orcs and goblins, to say nothing of fell hooded wizards, wyverns, and worse beasties—were still out here, somewhere. Somewhere near.

The crawl hole opened out into a dank little bowl of a cave that had been choked with windblown leaves, old dung, and older bones when the Swords had first found it. Now it held only them, standing all crowded together around a rough table of four felled saplings lashed together like a raft, wedged across the cave, and anointed with a lit lantern.

Its flickering glow fell on no less than six crudely drawn maps of the Haunted Halls. Semoor's faith let him buy parchment from the House of the Morning at a few copper thumbs less than the ruinous prices they charged everyone else, and he'd made good use of that favor.

"We got it all," Pennae was reassuring the other Swords. "At least, all the green slime in that room, and there was none in the privy here or the passage *here* that has the ambush elbow. Its smoke cleared fast enough that we know plenty of air gets down into the western halls somewhere—probably several somewheres—from above. This must be so, because with the front doors as open as they are now, everything blows out into the gorge."

"I care not a whit where the breezes blow," Agannor grunted, "so long as some gold coins flow into my hands from somewhere. Soon."

"All the tales say the Haunted Halls stretch on for room after room after passage—dozens at least, with feast halls and big chambers with pillars, too. I don't think we've found a twentieth of it, yet," Martess said firmly. "There *must* be some hidden ways on that we've missed thus far. Look you at this doubling-back hall, here: surely there's a room in this angle that we can't get to yet. Unless we break through the wall."

Bey gave her a look. "You want us to start digging in there? Mining?

Lass, have you ever tried to break apart stones? We'd be dead-dragon-tired in a trice, and making noise and shudderings enough to draw every monster that's anywhere in the place! So there we'd be, choking on rock dust and knee-deep in stumble-making rubble, too weary to lift weapons—and finding ourselves facing down a slug the size of two warhorses, or something that's all tentacles with fangs on the ends of them! Can your spells save us then? Hey?"

Martess reddened, her lips going thin.

Florin hastened to draw the converse elsewhere. "I think Martess is right about that room—there might well be one just *here*, too—but I don't think we've come to digging, yet. After all, we have this grand way on, that has doors as tall as two of us, and two statues pointing it out to us!"

"Aye, and it also features a death trap, unless you know some way to outrun lightning!" Agannor was frowning. "Or do our spell-hurling lasses know a way to undo that magic?"

Jhessail and Martess both shook their heads.

Agannor looked at Doust and Semoor. "Holy men? Anyone?"

More heads were shaken. Agannor sighed and sat back, growling, "Well, someone had better think of *some*thing, or 'tis going to be a long and hungry winter for us, and off to Sembia in spring to sell our charter, split up, and look for drudge-toil under the tongues of grasping merchants, for all of us."

Pennae sighed. "Such bright cheer you proffer, Agannor. Myself, I think there's much treasure to be found in the Haunted Halls—*if* we don't run afoul of whoever set up this guardroom, here."

" 'Twas empty when we came along," Bey growled. "Why worry you?"

"The new strike-gong on the wall, and the just-as-new wire running from behind it through a hole in the north wall to we-know-not-where. I'll wager all the gold in Sembia that wire runs to another gong, so striking one causes the other to echo. Who dwells where that other gong is? And when will they notice us? The place doesn't *feel* deserted, nor yet abandoned and roamed by beasts: it feels like someone lives there."

Agannor and Florin both nodded, and Jhessail murmured, "I have that feeling, too."

"I begin to see," Doust said, "why so many folk fell in yon Halls—and the rest fled to spread tales of it."

"Agannor's right," Semoor said sourly. "We'd better find something worth good coin to sell soon. We two holynoses resold that peddler's horse just now, to the next caravan through Eveningstar—"

Pennae looked up. "A caravan came through Eveningstar? And we missed it? I can scarce begin to believe—"

"Oh, *all* right: a merchant with five wagons, look you? Anyhail, he bought the pack-nag, and we made—hear this—all of three thumbs on the deal. *That's* not going to see us through winter, unless . . ."

Semoor looked meaningfully at Pennae, who gave him a flat stare and the flatter reply: "This is *far* too small a place to steal things, Wolftooth. You expect our necks to last long if I vanish one man's best shovel and try to sell it to his neighbor?"

Semoor nodded, shrugged, smiled, and turned his knowing look on Martess, who leaned past the lantern and said icily, "Not-so-holy-man, hear this well: I'm *not* going to dance in taverns or suffer the gropings of a lot of hard-breathing, gnarly handed farmers again . . . nor train Jhess here to do so, either!"

" 'Tis not such a bad fate as all that," Pennae told her map, as Semoor rolled his eyes up to regard the ceiling with an air of holy innocence.

"Semoor," Florin said, "such suggestions are more harmful than useful—and unworthy of a man of Lathander, to my way of thinking. Where's the bright new beginning in asking fellow Swords to fall back on shady work they've done before?"

"I was but trying to be helpful," Semoor replied, with an edge to his voice none of them had heard before. "If we're talking about coins enough to live, we should talk freely, raising all matters, yes?"

"Yes," Bey agreed, at the same time as Martess and Jhessail both said, "No."

A moment of uncomfortable silence followed, until Doust said,

"Well, then, we'd best manage a right swift success of this getting rich, hey?"

Pennae waved her hands as if to banish all discord, then put a finger on a certain chamber drawn on the most extensive and detailed of the maps; her own. " 'Tis my belief," she said, "there's another level of rooms hidden below this, here, that we've already scoured . . . probably *here*, beneath the undercrypt, and heading back this way . . ."

Semoor waved his hand. "So we go looking there next. Yes?"

He lifted his gaze to look at the lamplit faces all around. They were nodding.

Florin reached out to touch another place on the map. "And if we find no way down, let's try here. I've a hunch there are more rooms this way. The rock is softer, for one thing." More nods.

"Then let's go," Agannor said briskly. "Holy men, lead us out of this hole, into a brighter future."

"Do this, and I'll be well pleased with you," Lorneth Crownsilver said with a smile, turning back to his eager niece with a small, rather plain coffer in his hands. "This service to the Crown can only bring you the high regard of the king."

"Rellond Blacksilver is expecting me?"

Her uncle nodded. "For the usual reasons." He laid the coffer in Narantha's hands. "Put this in your chatelaine, and let no one take it from you until you are alone with the young gallant. Put it—or what it holds—directly into his bare hands."

Once she'd slipped the coffer into her girdle-purse, he clasped her shoulders.

Narantha had seen noble fathers hold their sons thus, when pleased and uttering orders that could only bring glory upon their houses.

"Don't drop the coffer," her uncle told her, "and don't open it until you're alone with him. Alone, mind: no trusted servants, no war wizards. Act like you want to flirt with him, and get him to send them all away."

Narantha's lip curled. "Dally with Rellond the *Roughshod?*"

"Come, now. You've feigned much you did not feel, and put on many a false face, down the years; 'tis what we nobles *do*. Shame all bards with your subtle, artfully done hints and sidelong glances. I called Rellond a 'gallant' now so sneeringly because in his case it means 'handsome, arrogant lady-chaser.' Think of this as a first step in teaching Rellond Blacksilver a lesson he should have learned long ago."

Narantha smiled, nodding slowly. "Put that way, Uncle, 'twill be a pleasure. In this Year of the Spur, Cormyr holds far too many nobles who are very far indeed from being truly 'noble.' I fear that I was very recently one of them. But now . . ."

She lifted her hands to clasp his, still at her shoulders, and gave them a firm squeeze. Then Narantha bowed her head to him as if she were his respectful son leaving for battle, stepped back and away, and hurried from the room.

Behind the hargaunt mask that gave him the likeness of Lorneth Crownsilver, Horaundoon of the Zhentarim smiled as he watched her go.

Afire with enthusiasm, that one. If ever she balked or disobeyed, he could of course use the mindworm within her to compel her—but right now, at least, such ruthlessnesses were very far from being necessary.

Narantha believed in him, and had been happily spreading mind-worms to nobles of his choosing far faster than Horaundoon could ever have ah, *wormed* his way into their towers, mansions, and the shapes of their most trusted servants or mistresses.

Creth, Huntinghorn, Ammaeth, and now Blacksilver—this was almost too easy.

+ + ✦ + +

The stink of rotting fish was sickening.

Lord Crownsilver thrust the lantern forward to almost touch the worn, much-pitted stone. The paint was both faint and flaking, but in the lanternlight they could clearly see the curl-tailed hippogriff sigil.

"This is the place," he grunted. Passing the lantern to the cloaked and hooded figure who stood in the midst of their three hulking bodyguards, he nodded curtly to the nearest boldblade.

That brute was a bald and much-scarred warrior whose name Maniol had forgotten for the moment. A head taller than his lord and master, he strode silently forward, his plain black war-harness bristling with blades, spikes, and skull-shatter knobs, and thrust the closed door open.

His two fellows had already stepped swiftly in front of their noble charges, but nothing erupted out of the revealed darkness beyond the door, or fell or fired at the boldblade who'd opened it.

Lord and Lady Crownsilver would have chosen safer and more pleasant surroundings than the Scaletail Door—if they'd had any say in the choosing. Swallowing, Maniol Crownsilver reclaimed the lantern and trudged reluctantly forward, seeing stone walls slick with wet slime ahead. The way was narrow, and after a few paces ended in worn steps descending into dripping, noisome darkness with crude handholds scooped out of the rock.

"You will wait for us," Lady Crownsilver reminded the boldblades icily, "until dawn. Then one of you will remain to watch this door, and the other two bring back all of our house blades to forthwith go down yon stair and find us, slaying everyone who stands in your way. *Everyone.*"

She glared at them until she'd collected slow nods from all three, and only then stepped forward into the passage, unhooding as she went.

"I am less than pleased with this, Maniol," she hissed.

Her lord stood waiting at the head of the stairs, hand on sword hilt. "The slayer's of your choosing," he muttered. "Blame me not for this place of *his* choosing."

"Take your hand off your sword," Jalassa Crownsilver snapped, the bite in her voice warning him to say no more about choices of her making. " 'Tis useless in so close-confined a way. Draw your dagger."

Her husband obeyed with an angry flourish and set off cautiously down the stair. "Take care, wife," he commented. Maniol only dared address her thus when he was too angry—or afraid—to care about consequences. "The way is wet."

Seething in silence, Lady Crownsilver followed her lord, down into unknown cellars, somewhere in Marsember. With every step the air grew colder and the smell of dead fish faded, being replaced by a strange seaweed smell: a smell of living weed rather than the rotting shore-tang she was familiar with. With every reluctant step, Jalassa liked her decision less and less.

Indar Crauldreth might be the best assassin in Marsember, and might have lived to acquire that reputation by such one-sided precautions, but she hated to be groping in the unknown, bodyguards and magic left behind her. Crauldreth insisted on much. Why could he not deal with a Crownsilver agent? After all, lawful or not, this was still business . . .

The narrow stair ended in a much larger, many-pillared place, everything black-green and glistening. An old storage cellar, that flooded too often for anyone sensible to use it for storage.

The rusty ends of many ladders protruded down into it, here and there, descending through narrow chutes from unseen buildings above. There were ends of pipes, too, dozens of them, gaping ovals like so many hungry maws of eels.

Lord Crownsilver came to an uneasy halt. "I see no red shield."

"The floor, Maniol, shine the lantern on the *floor*. D'you expect it to be hanging from a pillar in front of your nose?"

Her husband let out an angry hiss and took a few reluctant steps off to his right, then returned to head left about the same distance. Then, with a shrug that set the lantern swinging crazily, he forged on ahead another dozen paces or so and repeated his side forays. This time, they ended in a bark of: "Aha!"

Lady Crownsilver hurried to stand with him, and gazed down at a red shield, about the size of her smallest personal carriage, painted on the floor. Someone had washed the slime and mold away from it, to leave its worn paint standing forth clearly from the surrounding—

"Put the lantern on the floor," a cold voice came to them, sounding as if it came from right at their elbows; both Crownsilvers jumped. "And put your dagger away, Maniol Crownsilver. I don't want you to cut yourself and bleed to death before you can pay my fee."

Lord Crownsilver fumbled to obey, almost dropping the lantern. His lady went cold as she realized that if darkness descended, she had no way of finding the steps back up. She whirled around, found them, and planted herself facing them, hissing, "Get *well* back from the lantern, Maniol."

"I'm a busy man," the voice told them. "So who am I to kill for you?"

It could be coming down any of these pipes—which weren't for water or pouring grain at all, Lady Crownsilver realized: they were speaking tubes that had once carried orders from the buildings above down into this place, where cargo was stored.

"One Florin Falconhand, of the Swords of Eveningstar chartered company." Lord Crownsilver, to his lady's disgust, was unable to keep a quaver of fear out of his voice.

"An adventurer," the unseen assassin said. "This will be expensive."

"How much, Crauldreth?" Lady Crownsilver snapped.

"About three times as much as I'd accept for killing either of *you*," came the cold reply.

Lord Maniol Crownsilver went pale and started to shake.

Lady Jalassa caught sight of his movements as he started to peer this way and that, darting swift and futile glances into the gloom all around.

Without turning her head to look at her husband, Lady Jalassa slapped him and snapped crisply, "Stop that."

Then she lifted her head and asked the unseen Crauldreth, "How much?"

Sarhthor of the Zhentarim hadn't lived this long by being stupid. He often walked the Stonelands north of Starwater Gorge to choose spots to teleport to in future—and he brought himself to one of those locales now, rather than to the chamber where the most successful of his underlings should be waiting for him.

Whisper was becoming just a bit too ambitious to be trusted. In the slightest.

Standing on the flat rock he'd remembered, surrounded on three sides by a natural rampart of taller boulders, Sarhthor gazed south into Cormyr.

Not far away, under the sharp-edged rock ridges in front of him, lay the ancient and undead-haunted burial catacombs long known as Whisper's Crypt; the wizard Whisper had taken his Zhentarim name from them, rather than what was now his lair being named after him.

Whisper was an energetic sort. He'd done far more than taming a part of the perilous crypt to be his abode. He'd found some of the ancient automatons, constructs, and colossi in those tombs and other Netherese crypts of the Stonelands, and awakened them to walk, fly, and slay at his bidding.

Yes, Whisper was becoming formidable, with schemes of his own and an increasing ability to enact them.

Sarhthor took the time to cast not one but two snatch-fetch spells to shimmer and spin about himself before teleporting himself into the crypt. Any metal seeking to pierce or fall through those fields would be vaporized, and almost any spell striking it would be twisted into making the fields stronger. Moreover, either snatch-fetch could be commanded to snatch Sarhthor back from the crypt to this rock.

Sarhthor carefully wedged a vial between two of the great rampart rocks, covering it with a small stone shard. If he should need healing in a hurry . . .

He cast the teleport, knew the usual eerie moment of falling through endless vivid blue mists, and found himself standing in the spot he'd chosen last time: at the head of three shallow steps, in the passage Whisper liked to use to descend into his spellcasting chamber.

Whisper's back was just ahead of him, and Sarhthor permitted himself a tight smile as he padded down the passage in his underling's wake. He let Whisper take one stride out into the spell-casting chamber and look toward the cleared area where Sarhthor of the Zhentarim was supposed to appear—an area, he noted, where Whisper seemed to have set up a lingering, almost invisible spell of some sort—then said curtly, *"Report, Whisper."*

Whisper did not—quite—jump three feet into the air. He did, however, flinch violently and stiffen into immobility, perhaps fearing the worst.

Sarhthor didn't intend to give it to him. Yet. However, there was no need to begin by reassuring Whisper on that matter.

"I'm waiting," he said. "I see I must inform you that extremely busy senior mages of the Zhentarim dislike being kept waiting."

Whisper controlled himself rigidly. His turn to face Sarhthor was slow and almost casual.

"Honored superior," he said, wearing a tight smile, "I have little to tell. Matters in the vicinity of Eveningstar have been very quiet. I continue to work slowly and subtly to increase our influence without the local crop-muckers hearing the name 'Zhentarim' overmuch. At the same time, using spells to assume a variety of guises so no war wizard can trace things here or to me, I'm recruiting suitable knaves as agents."

" 'Knaves'? Just men?"

"No. Aging women, past their years of looking good and enjoying the good regard of fellow Evenor, are my best eyes and ears. Capable and vengeful—and already experienced at peering and gossiping, and known in the village for doing so, hence unsuspicious."

"What are the local war wizards up to during this oh-so-quiet time?"

"Scrying Arabel, seeking petty lawbreakers among the merchants there."

"Come now! Whilst the war wizards of Arabel do what?"

"The same task. It seems they've one of those pushes to cleanse Arabel; they start one every five or six summers."

Sarhthor shook his head in disbelief. "Cleansing Arabel I can well believe. Leaving Eveningstar unwatched, I cannot. Watch sharp, or you'll be caught. This 'attentiveness elsewhere' of the war wizards known to you means some of Vangey's *other* spell-vultures are scrying Eveningstar—rotation of duties to lull you, catch you unguarded, and train fresh eyes in the detection of Eveningstar's little troubles. Such as you."

"No one can scry me unnoticed," Whisper said, "and I've found no hint of anyone trying. Vangey's skulkers are busy elsewhere, I tell you. Most of them in and around Arabel, and others gathering at High Horn—I know not what for, but I'm trying to find out."

"Huh. Next you'll be telling me the Purple Dragon has returned, or someone with spellfire's been found striding around the Dales. Be careful, Whisper, or your blind overconfidence may soon be the death of you."

"Thank you, honored superior," Whisper replied tonelessly.

"Dismiss my advice *not*, mageling—to do so brings you near to death from two directions, and I doubt you're a good enough dancer to dodge both the war wizards *and* the Zhentarim. So take my warning to heart. In the meantime, keep in mind two things: that 'caravans quietly through' remains our policy, and that there's much infighting going on at Zhentil Keep right now; we must all be very careful to obey orders diligently and in every detail."

Whisper nodded with enthusiasm. "Yes, Sarhthor. I hear and will obey. You may count on me."

As he spoke, a ruby-red radiance flared into being far down the room. Part of a map graven into the top of a massive stone table was glowing balefully.

Sarhthor's eyes narrowed. "What intrusion does yon spell warn of?"

"Several persons wearing garments marked by my agents have entered a part of the subterranean stronghold known as the Haunted Halls. Specifically, a part where I may well be able to slay them with relative ease, given the traps I've crafted there and the layout of the rooms and passages."

"And your agents marked these 'several persons' because?"

"Because I was suspicious of them. These individuals are the

Swords of Eveningstar, members of a newly chartered adventuring band, just arrived in Eveningstar. Mere restless younglings out of Espar, who saved the life of the king of Cormyr and claimed a charter as their reward—but bumbling and soon-slain as adventurers may be, they can still draw unwanted attention and unwittingly harm many schemes and proceedings in their blunderings."

Sarhthor nodded. "Agreed. Deal with them." And with those blunt words still hanging in the air, he was gone, leaving Whisper gazing across his empty spellcasting chamber at that distant ruby glow.

"Deal with them, indeed," he murmured, and waved a hand to awaken a nearby scrying crystal.

It floated obediently nearer, quickening into brightness: the glows of no less than four bobbing, approaching lanterns. The Swords of Eveningstar, shining-eyed with the excitement of having found no less than *two* secret doors, and through them a huge labyrinth of rooms and corridors running in seemingly all directions, were coming along a passage into what had once been a throne room—and was now home to one of Whisper's most cunning traps.

Whisper smiled as he strode forward to peer closely into the Haunted Halls—or at least, what little could be seen of them in the depths of the crystal. 'Twas enough, though. 'Twas enough. This should be *good*.

"I mislike the look of this," Martess hissed. "There's magic *everywhere* in the room ahead of us."

Agannor and Bey were almost leaning through the open doorway, holding their lamps high. A heap of splintered, gilded ruin lay right in front of their boots: the remnants of fallen, once-grand double doors that had echoed in wood the size and grandeur of the bronze doors guarded by the lightning-spitting statues, somewhere back behind the Swords.

Only, these doors had been adorned with magnificent relief carvings of knights riding leaping war-horses, and from their saddles hewing down orcs, sinister helmed men whose arms seemed to be long tentacles, and what looked like wyverns and wingless dragons. It was hard to tell what all of the monstrous foes were, because the blows of a hard-driven axe had long ago cleft and marred many of the carvings, and time and the damp had caused the edges of those wounds to crumble.

"Looks like a throne room," Agannor grunted. "A fair place to look for treasure, wouldn't you say?"

"I say again," Martess murmured, still on her knees. "Magic— some of it very strong—is everywhere in yon chamber."

"Hah! Couldn't some of the treasure we seek be magical? Hey? Like the healing flasks Pennae found?"

"Agannor," Pennae told him, "we are *not* alone in these halls. If someone—or some*thing*—that speaks Common and understands us is lurking in the darkness anywhere near, you're loudly telling them everything we're doing and so telling them exactly when and how to best harm us. So still your tongue. Please."

Agannor bared his teeth in anger at the slender thief—who shrugged, smiled, and murmured to Martess, "Take all the time you need to be sure, Tess. I want to know exactly where the magic is before I put one toe into the room. And so help me, Agannor, if you lose patience with our caution and go striding in there: I've got some concoctions that can make the bites of my knives *very* interesting—and you'll feel those bites, if you go on endangering the rest of us by playing the reckless fool here and in any more rooms."

"Sabruin," Agannor spat at her. "Just *sabruin!*"

"After you do, dearest," Pennae replied lightly. "After you!"

He growled and waved disgusted dismissal at her—but stayed out of the throne chamber. It was Bey who gave Pennae a hard look and asked, "So, Sharptongue, where would you head from here? What would you do, that's so much better than just walking into yon room? Hey?"

"Well," Pennae said, "the first thing I'd explore, before I moved on into that throne room and so left the thing behind me—and between me and the sunlight!—is this niche here in the wall. Small, but placed just where a hand can easily reach into it, and graven with these two symbols. Anyone seen them before? Anyone know what they mean?"

The Swords took turns shuffling forward to peer, and one after another shook their heads in open, obviously sincere denial.

"Well," Pennae said, when they were done, "I can see something at the back there that I want to probe with my dagger. See the carving of the castle rampart? I wonder why—"

Something cold and blue flashed around her extended dagger— and the passage in front of the throne room was suddenly empty of all trace of Alura Durshavin.

Chapter 18
JUST ANOTHER NIGHT IN ARABEL

Daggers are drawn
Look, one man is down
fading his eyes
fallen his crown
Wizards rush in
Wizards rush forth
Dragons swoop down
To eat towers out
Priests run screaming
Temple domes fall
Orc hordes are coming
And plague will take all
But one thing I know,
And I know it full well
'Tis just another night in Arabel

Thumbard Voakriss,
Minstrel Mighty, from the ballad
Another Night In Arabel
published (as a broadsheet)
in the Year of the Spur

As full night fell over Filfaeril's private garden, the servants lit the last of the lamps to keep its darkness softly at bay and fled in soft-skirted haste, unspeaking. All in the palace knew how much the queen loved her privacy.

In twilight and the early night, when affairs of state permitted such leisure, the Dragon Queen liked to walk alone, or sit quietly in a bower seat and think. Save for the rare occasions when she shared this time with her husband the king or the even rarer occasions when she was accompanied by someone else, she preferred tranquility and solitude, free from all prying. She had famously insisted on this in discussions with the royal magician, disputations that culminated in an argument Filfaeril had ended with a punch to Vangerdahast's jaw.

Whereupon (once the reeling wizard had fallen, regained his feet, and collected his stammering wits) she had won matters her way, and now walked her gardens very much alone. Powerful wards prevented anyone from stealing up on her through the thick forests and rolling lawns of the royal park, and trios of war wizards and highknights guarded all access between the palace and her small, exquisite garden, their attention carefully turned away from the queen, toward the palace itself.

This still and surprisingly cool evening, Filfaeril lingered not as long among the opening, faintly glowing night-blossoms as she usually did. Instead she strode soft-slippered, in plain skirts and with a half-cloak about her shoulders against the chill, to the darkest back corner of her nine linked bowers, under the tree-shade where the moonlight would take some time yet to reach.

Hooking her fingers through the wide belt she wore around her slender hips, Filfaeril on a whim broke into a few dance steps and kicks, then spun around to stare back at the palace.

Only one balcony overlooked her here, and it was empty. The battlements high above it bore no trace of staring Purple Dragon heads. The garrison was up there, she knew, but had their orders not to look down into the garden and, she knew from covertly testing them in the past, were diligently obedient in this regard.

Stretching as luxuriously as any idly purring cat, the Queen of Cormyr went to her favorite bower seat, settled herself gracefully, and idly sang a snatch of a well-known ballad: "Are you there listening, pretty nightbird? Pretty nightbird?"

"Yes," came the soft whisper beside her ear, "but so is a highknight spy, behind yonder statue. Send him away."

Filfaeril did not have to feign her anger. Springing to her feet, she marched across the velvety sward to the whitestone statue of Azoun Triumphant—the only statue in her garden—and snapped, "Come out, man!"

The only reply was silence. Mouth tightening, the Dragon Queen sprang up two artfully placed stones among the plantings and embraced the statue, swinging around it to confront—a black-garbed man crouching behind it.

"Highknight," she snarled, "who ordered you to this duty? Tell me!"

"I—Your Highness, I—"

"I've given you a royal command," Filfaeril said, striding forward until her great belt buckle was almost touching the man's nose.

He could feel what she could hear: the crackle of the spell-shield emanating from it. If he bore any steel about his person, he must also be feeling the pain of its ironguard warding.

The highknight rose and stepped back from Filfaeril in one

smooth motion, to kneel to her then rise, saying, "The wizard Vangerdahast, my queen. I am to report any speech you may have with other persons whom you meet with here, and identify such persons."

He hesitated, eyes meeting the queen's simmering gaze, and added, "I should tell you that it is my belief that Wizards of War assigned by him indirectly scry you, even now, by scrying me. I submit myself to any punishment you may decree."

Filfaeril threw back her head, drew in a deep breath as she looked at the stars, and then told the man tightly, "Loyal Highknight, go you and tell the Royal Magician Vangerdahast I would speak with him. Immediately. Seek not to compel him, but deliver this my message and depart from him, saying other orders of mine ride you. Answer not any queries as to those orders, but absent yourself from duty until the coming highsun. Go to a tavern, a festhall, or a club, and take your ease this night through—but go *now*."

The highknight bowed. "I hear and will obey. Your Highness is merciful."

"With some," Filfaeril hissed at him. "With some."

He descended onto the sward so she could clearly see his departure. The Dragon Queen swung down from her statue to stand and watch him go, the length of all her bowers, ere returning to her seat.

"Well, *that* was fun," she remarked, her breathing still faster than normal. "How goes your harping?"

"I can still break strings," came the low-pitched reply, "and have eyes that yet work well enough to notice your signal. How d'you keep your maids from tidying that coverlet right back off the balcony rail?"

"Promise to flay them alive," Filfaeril said sweetly. "I had to start in on one of them once, but from the moment I cracked the whip and ordered her to bare herself, and they all stared at me and got a good look at my face, they . . . found obedience."

The woman lying at ease under the bushes chuckled. "You should try the same tactic on Azoun."

"Dove," Filfaeril said, "*don't* tempt me. He'd probably enjoy it, which is about all I want to say on the matter—given that Vangey just might decide that teleporting himself into my lap and storming at me, any moment now, is *his* best tactic. 'Tis more likely he'll make sure he can't be found by anyone this night, and in fact has been at some remote border locale of the realm all along, but . . ."

Dove chuckled again. "Wise words. So, what would you learn from the Harpers, and what will you trade in return? Bearing in mind that if Vangey is still eavesdropping, you may be handing him the chance to rant to the king that high treason flourishes in the bosom of Cormyr's queen."

"Let him try," Filfaeril snapped. "Just let him try."

Her fists were clenched, Dove saw—and so leaned out under the foliage to gently knead Filfaeril's tense shoulders.

The queen stiffened at first, but slowly relaxed under the Harper's skilled fingers, going so far as to groan briefly, three or four breaths later.

Then, without preamble, she said, "Bhereu's pryings are aimed at uncovering what he believes to be men under his command making covert investments in Sembia via Sembian factors who've come to court several times, now, with trade proposals. The investments are probably nothing sinister in themselves, but he's concerned that the Sembians are buying influence over his officers. The two most energetic factors go by the names Rrastran Ravalandro and Atuemor Ghallowgard. I believe that was one matter you Harpers were curious about."

"You believe correctly," Dove replied, her massaging fingers digging deeply into Filfaeril's hitherto rigid neck and shoulders. "Anything else?"

"No. Court is quiet at the moment, so those who scheme and intrigue most vigorously—Vangerdahast and those my husband directs in their whisperings included—confine their hissings and soft threats to private moots well away from here. When they see the queen approaching, they recall an urgent need to be elsewhere."

Dove chuckled again. "So, you've given me no state secrets but mere gossip; what would you know?"

"To match my paltry offering, a minor matter, to whit: this new band of adventurers my Azoun took such glee in anointing. He came back from Espar bubbling like a young lad at play, Dove! These Swords of Eveningstar: who are they, and what are they up to?"

"A handsome young forester of Espar who saved your Azoun's life when he was attacked in Hunter's Hollow by Sembian hireswords in the employ of certain nobles of this fair realm—just who, we Harpers know not, but we *do* know Vangerdahast has personally mind-reamed the lone hiresword Florin spared, when Azoun ordered him to do so—and the forester's friends, and a few seekers-of-adventure they picked up in Waymoot. Ah, sorry: that 'Florin' is the young forester; Florin Falconhand."

"That name I *have* heard," Filfaeril murmured. "Are they young, eyes shining with thoughts of treasure, or—?"

Dove nodded. "Young and filled with hope, indeed. Your Azoun sent them to scour out the Haunted Halls—"

"As he does all adventurers who lack noble parents to protest them being sent to their deaths," Filfaeril murmured. "They are, then, not deemed sinister, but merely untested in their loyalty and heroism?"

"Indeed. They may yet fall, of course, but already their naive explorations are doing more to discomfit the Zhentarim in northern Cormyr than anything you—or we—have managed thus far. Zhentil Keep still has its spies, drug-sellers, and smugglers everywhere, but stolen goods and Cormyreans drugged to be sent into slavery are no longer casually added to every third caravan passing through Arabel or Eveningstar. The Zhents are being forced into the longer and more dangerous Stonelands routes—and I've even heard tell of their trying again to run large caravans through Anauroch."

The queen turned her head, eyes widening. "You tell me true? One band of adventurers has managed all this? Unwittingly?"

Dove nodded. "And if unwitting adventurers can do this much damage, just think of what a handful of your worst idiot courtiers can wreak. Unwittingly."

"Pennae! *Pennae!*" Florin rushed forward, his drawn sword flashing.

"Agannor!" Florin snapped, standing where Pennae had been, moments before. "Your lantern! *Here! Now!*"

Blinking in astonishment, Agannor obeyed, thrusting his lantern forward, low, where Florin was waving frantically at the floor.

There was nothing. No scorch mark, no ashes, no tiny, thumb-tall Pennae squeaking up at them and waving insect-sized arms. She was simply—gone.

Florin pointed furiously up at the niche Pennae had been probing, and Agannor brought the light up to show everyone . . . a carving at the back of the niche that looked like a castle wall, crenelated and with a tiny hinged door that looked like it actually swung back and forth, if touched.

Eyes hard and breathing heavily, Florin looked around wildly at the rest of the Swords—then thrust the point of his sword into the niche.

There came the briefest of blue flashes—again—and the passage was suddenly empty of all trace of Florin Falconhand.

"Oh, ye gods most marvelous," Jhessail cursed. *"Now* what?"

Islif shrugged. "None of us live forever," she said, striding forward with her sword ready. "Adventure, remember?" She slid her sword deftly into the niche, and vanished in an instant.

Doust shrugged, fumbled forth his belt knife, and followed suit. Then Martess and Bey, who laconically handed his lantern to Jhessail.

With various shrugs, in their own manners, every one of the Swords followed, leaving the passage in the Haunted Halls dark and empty again.

Jhessail wrinkled her nose and blinked into many wet reflections of lamplight. "It *stinks,*" she murmured, looking around her at her fellow Swords, who were crowded together in an alleyway, peering in all directions and looking just as lost as she was. "Where are we?"

The alley reeked of rotting refuse and chamberpots. The lamp-light was coming from a cobbled street the alley opened out into, a street walled in by tall, narrow stone buildings on all sides, where wagons were rumbling through the night.

Folk were trudging purposefully everywhere, close-cloaked against the light rain, and Pennae was flattened against the alley wall, beside its mouth, gesturing frantically to her fellow Swords to get over to the wall beside her and *quiet down*.

Looking right down the alley and across the street beyond, Jhessail found herself gazing into the hard stares of a trio of Purple Dragons, who were nodding together as they watched the Swords, suspicion written large on their tight lips, narrowed eyes, and set jaws.

As she watched, they seemed to reach some sort of agreement. One hurried off, his boots splashing through puddles. The other two stayed right where they were, glaring at the Swords.

Doust stepped away from the wall, Semoor inevitably trailing by his elbow, and strode right out of the alley, ignoring Pennae's hissed warnings.

The Swords all watched, Agannor starting to grin openly, as the two priestlings marched right across the street to the two Purple Dragons.

Giving those still in the alley a stern 'stay here' hand signal, Islif started after Doust and Semoor, sheathing her blade. Then she changed her mind and spun around to stop her fellow Swords from spilling across the street. Pennae ducked past her, but the rest crowded forward, leaning over Islif's outstretched arms to best hear what befell, but making no move to win past her.

They found the street busy in both directions with stopped wagons involved in the busy loading and unloading of crates, coffers, and kegs to and from various shops.

Across that cobbled way, the holiest of the Swords reached the unsmiling soldiers.

"Well met, this fair even," Doust said with a bright smile. "We've just been brought here by the favor of the goddess Tymora—"

"Ahem," Semoor interrupted, "*and* the magical might of the bright Morninglord Lathander."

"—and though we know full well by your very presence, stalwarts, that we stand yet in Cormyr, we are sadly unaware of what city this is. Ah, around us. Here."

The flat stares of the Purple Dragons had been burning holes in the smiling priestlings during their approach, and went right on doing so in the silence Doust gave them, in which to reply. Neither Dragon said a word.

Smile wavering, Doust tried again. "We all of us find our surroundings unfamiliar, and would very much like to know where we are. So, could you tell us? Please?"

"You're drunk, that's what you are," the tall Purple Dragon growled.

"Or playing us for fools," the other said. "Get gone with you!"

"I . . . could you at least tell me where the local temple of Tymora is?"

"If you're truly favored of Tymora, just start walking," the first Dragon sneered, "an' you'll be sure to find it, hey?"

"This," Semoor said, "is less than good." He put a hand on Doust's arm. "Fellow priest, we should tarry no more talking with these impostors. We can tell Azoun of them, and he'll see that they're rooted out. Or rather, Vangey's pet war wizards will."

The Dragons blinked at him. Then their eyes narrowed.

"Impostors?" the tall one snarled.

"Speaking slightingly of the king?" the shorter, stouter one growled. Their hands went to their sword hilts in unison, and they seemed to *loom* forward over the two Swords.

"Just why," the tall Dragon asked Semoor, jaw jutting angrily, "d'you call us 'impostors'? Hey?"

Semoor spread his hands, looking earnest and eagerly helpful. "Look you, sir, no *true* Purple Dragon would answer a citizen of Cormyr so—and even less, a priest of Lathander. Still less, *two* priests, both of whom personally stand in the high regard of the king."

He shrugged, almost mournfully. "Wherefore I can only conclude that you're impostors. Or, just perhaps, high-ranking, veteran Dragons, playing a game of words to flush out enemies of the state, who have merely mistaken us for such."

The two Dragons looked at each other, their faces sagging a bit.

"Oh, *great,*" the stout Dragon said sourly.

The tall Dragon looked at Doust, then at Semoor, before he asked the priest of Lathander reluctantly, "So you're friends of the king? Is that it?"

"The king himself poured me wine—at his table—less than a tenday ago," Semoor replied truthfully.

"Naed," The tall Dragon muttered. "Pray accept our apologies, holy lords. When we saw you come through yon way, we were sure you must be Zhents, an' were treating you accordingly."

"Zhents? The dark wizards of Zhentil Keep?" Doust managed to look shocked. "They use, uh, 'yon way' often enough that you keep watch over it?"

"Lord, they do. That's why we're standing here, in the rain an' all: to keep watch down that alley. Where all your friends are." The tall Dragon squinted. "Any wizards among 'em, anyhail?"

"Yes," Doust said reluctantly—at the same moment as Semoor said, *"No."*

The Dragons frowned in unison, patting their sword hilts, before the stout Dragon said with heavy sarcasm, "So, now, which is it? Have you mages among you—or not?"

Doust put his foot down hard on Semoor's instep, and said firmly, "We have two young lasses among us who have *just* learned to cast their first spells. To me, that makes them mages. Obviously, to my fellow servant of the divine here, it does not. Look you at the one with flame-orange hair? And the dark-haired one standing beside her? Those are the two we're speaking of. Look they like sinister Zhent wizards to you?"

The stout Dragon's smile, as he shook his head, was almost a leer.

The tall Dragon, however, was frowning. "I'm more concerned

with the one in black," he said—then blinked. "Hoy! Where'd she go?"

Semoor leaned close. "Shush! She's a highknight, and doesn't take it kindly if any of us so much as looks at her sidewise. If you go hollering after her, there's no telling what she'll do!"

"And if you lay a hand on her," Doust added, "there's no telling what the king will do. Seeing as how *he* likes to be the only one who—ahem—lays hands on her."

"Arntarmar!" The tall Dragon hissed feelingly.

Wincing, the stout Dragon nodded, growling, "Talandor!"

Oaths of Tempus. As might be expected of Purple Dragons.

"So, men of the Wargod and of the Great Dragon who rules this land so gloriously," Semoor asked, his face and voice perfectly serious, "what city is this?"

Both men blinked at him. "Arabel," Tall Dragon said. "Of course."

"*Thank you,*" Semoor could not resist saying, pique clear in his voice.

The stout Dragon's face started to darken, and Doust hastily spoke up. "You've been most helpful to us, stalwarts of the king, and we shall remember you in our prayers this night, to Tymora—"

"And Lathander!" Semoor put in.

"—after we report to the Lady Lord of Arabel, as Az—as the king asked us to," Doust concluded grandly. He turned back to face the alley and pointed at what was just visible over the roofs of the buildings there, flickering in the rain-filled night as sodden banners flapped half-heartedly: storm lanterns atop the battlements of tall, frowning fortress towers. "Yonder is the citadel, yes?"

The Dragons both nodded, and the tall Dragon pointed and spoke: "An' the palace where you'll find her stands just in front of it. The temple you seek, the Lady's House, is the second building north of the citadel, going along the west wall. Looks like a grand house, all cone-shingled turrets, five balconies high."

"Well met and better parted," Doust said, bowing his head to them with folded hands. "The Luck of the Lady be upon you, and shine back from you to please the Lord of Battles himself."

"And the rosy glow of Lathander also, that Holy Tempus be most richly pleased," Semoor added glibly, turning away before the two Dragons could see him rolling his eyes.

Dodging rumbling carts, they returned to the alley, where Islif greeted them grimly, "Swagger not *too* proudly, you two. Remember that Dragon we saw hurrying off? He went to report to someone—probably his duty commander. And who stands beside every duty commander?"

"A war wizard to mind him," Florin said. "So we're being watched—unless we can 'disappear' very quickly."

"So let's move!" Agannor growled.

"Wait!" Florin snapped. "Where's Pennae?"

"Here," came her voice, from the shadows down the alley. "I like to see where alleys lead to—in case I have to hurry that way. This one takes us past a *very* well guarded warehouse, into the heart of this block and then out its far side, onto a street that in *that* direction leads to the local temple of Tymora. Oh, yes: this is Arabel."

"We know," Semoor said grandly. "Yon Purple Dragons told us."

"Well," Pennae observed in dry tones, "they do have orders to assist simpletons."

"The Lady's House," Florin said. "Let's get to it! I don't want to be standing here a few breaths from now trying to bluff my way past a few sternly disapproving war wizards. They may well take the view that we've disobeyed the king's commands just by coming here."

"Well said," Bey growled, shoving Semoor forward. "Hasten, hrast it!"

In a few breaths they were all trotting along the alley, heading away from the busy street and the two watching Purple Dragons. The warehouse was a gigantic, very new stone building bristling with hard-eyed armored men with loaded crossbows in their hands—Agannor shuddered involuntarily—and the Swords hurried past it, out onto a street of rich-looking shops. Under ornate awnings, all faced Arabel through fine glass windows, through which could be seen ornate lanterns, glittering wares, and smartly uniformed nightguards standing watchfully within.

Pennae led the Swords north, past shops selling fine silk gowns, masks, and gem-adorned boots, and several dazzling shops that contained only several guards each, standing amid all manner of gemstones that flashed and glimmered back reflections from the rain-soaked streets. The street soon ended in a moot with a wider, busier way, down which could be seen three grand, towering buildings.

The most distant, central one matched the Dragon's description of the temple to Tymora—and reeling out of its tall, ornate double doors, as the Swords strode purposefully toward it, came a large man in robes and a weathercloak of rich blue: a priest of the luck goddess.

They could tell what he was by what bounced on his ample chest and belly at the end of a heavy neckchain: the largest silver coin they'd ever seen, as wide across as both of Florin's hands, bearing the face of a smiling yet dignified Tymora, rendered in the old fashion.

The priest wearing it was somewhat younger. He looked to be an energetic forty summers old or so. Beneath unruly brown hair, his nose, jaws, and ears were all as overlarge as the coin; it looked as if the head of a giant rode human-sized shoulders. He also looked (flushed scarlet and drooling slightly), sounded (by his incoherently slurred bellows), and *smelled* (Jhessail winced at the reek of strong spiced wine, laced around the edges with spew) very drunk.

As tall as Florin, and long-limbed, he covered much of the cobbles as he came staggering, growling half-audible oaths and complaints through his scraggly mustache.

"Wors' novice ever? Worst novice *ever?* I doan' *think* so! Rabra—Rabbraha—Radrabryn was a *killer* an' a thief, an' I . . . I never killed anyone yet, a-purpose, at leas' . . ."

He caught sight of Doust's homemade Ladycoin and drew himself up to fix the Swords with piercing brown eyes. "Pilgrims, be ye? Hey?"

"Well," Doust began, "not exactly . . ."

"*Doan'* go in there! Fellow Ladysworn, stay away from the House this night! They've all gone crazed—crazed, I tell thee!"

"Crazed?"

"Crazed, or my name's not R-Rathan Thentraver." He hiccuped. "Which 'tis. So, they are. Y'see?"

"Ahh," Semoor ventured, "you're saying this isn't the best time for us to visit the temple?"

"S'right. Not." Rathan waggled a finger. "Go 'way. Come back 'morrow. Better then. Trus' me." Drawing his cloak around him, he lurched away.

Semoor smirked at Doust. "Well, if they all drink like that, you chose the right faith, of us two."

Doust reddened. "I did not 'choose' the Lady," he said. "She chose me. Appearing to me in my dreams, so strongly that . . . well . . ."

He waved his hand, as if to hurl away Semoor's suggestion, and stared after the reeling priest. Beyond Rathan, he saw a Purple Dragon patrol approaching briskly out of the night, a robed and hooded man marching grimly in their midst. *"Look* you," he said warningly.

"Another patrol yonder," Pennae added, nodding down a different street. She peered in all directions, then pointed. "An inn! *Hurry!"*

" 'The Weary Knight'?" Agannor read aloud. "Lass, 'tis right across the street from the citadel—which is also the city *jail!* Are you trying to save the Dragons trouble?"

"In the back door, fast," she snapped, "and straight through, out the front. The moment I open that door and start talking to guards, no one act anxious or in a hurry. I'll be haughty, and will likely tell some very large lies, hear you?"

Semoor rolled his eyes. "Now why does that not surprise me?"

"Purple Dragons everywhere," Jhessail murmured as they ran. "Doesn't this city have a watch?"

Bey laughed. "Lass, Arabel's rebelled so often that the Dragons *are* the watch, these days! Just as the Blue Dragons serve in Marsember, the *other* city that's none too happy to be ruled by the Dragon Throne!"

Then they were at the inn's back door. Pennae whirled, snatched Florin's sword out of its sheath, and held it up solemnly before her, blade vertical. Assuming a stern look, she opened the door.

Two startled nightguards shoved themselves away from where they'd been lounging against the walls, grabbing for their weapons.

Pennae ignored them, both hands holding the sword out before her as she strode between them with slow, stately tread.

"Hoy!" one guard told her, skipping sideways to get in front of her so he could bar her way with his arm. *"Hold!"*

"Hold what?" Semoor inquired innocently.

"Sirrah, make way," Pennae told the man. "We are pilgrims of Tempus, the Drawn Sword."

"You're *what?*" the other guard asked. "Well, you can't all just come charging in here, after dark! This is—"

"One of Arabel's best inns, I've heard," Pennae said, "which is why we chose it. Make way, lest holy displeasure fall upon the Weary Knight! Make *way!*"

Uncertainly, the two guards did so. "Uh, the steward of the house can be found straight down this hall, in the front—"

"Thank you," Pennae called back in firm dismissal, pacing on in a stately manner, her sword held high.

Florin matched her gait, and so did Islif; the other Swords saw and did likewise.

Behind them all, the two nightguards traded looks, shrugged, and rolled their eyes. Truly, the strange-in-the-head guests came thick and fast, this time of year . . .

At the sound of the chime, Narantha Crownsilver put down her goblet of warmed zzar, rose, retied the sash of her gown, and went to the door.

It opened onto a smiling face.

"Uncle Lorneth," she said in genuine pleasure, stepping back to let him in. "Zzar?"

"My thanks for your thoughtfulness, Ladylass, but I fear not. I've much clear-headed work still ahead of me this night."

"Work I can help with?" Narantha asked wistfully.

Her uncle hugged her. "Ahh, would that Cormyr had a dozen like you! You're doing the Crown great service!"

Narantha grinned at him. "If I go on doing it well enough, will there come a time when I'll truly be told what I'm doing? How it fits in with greater plans to confound the foes of Cormyr? Learn some deep secrets?"

Uncle Lorneth's face grew solemn, and he laid a warning finger across her lips. "Little one," he murmured, "you already know several deep secrets. That I'm alive, for one thing."

"Wha—do Mother and Father not *know?*"

"No, and they must not, yet, for fear they'll tell 'just a few close friends,' and so warn certain folk who should not yet be warned. As for secrets, your mother and father have never known what you already know: that I'm among the most secret and highly placed agents of the Purple Dragon himself."

Narantha smiled. "In a handful of days I've learned my own worth, found something useful to do—and drunk deep of *adventure!*" She raised her goblet in salute.

"Actually," Lorneth Crownsilver said brightly, "I think you'll find that's zzar . . ."

Then he turned his back in a flash, in case her snort of laughter heralded the goblet being flung at him.

It did not. When he turned around again, the glass was empty and Narantha was poised over it, chin on hands, regarding him with bright and eager eyes. "So, my highly secret uncle, what's my next task?"

"There are *always* guards at the citadel gates, and around the palace," Pennae snapped. "Just match my pace, keep walking, and don't look guilty. Ignore the Dragons; to you, they're . . . furniture."

"Really?" Semoor murmured. "Remind me not to sit down on anything in your home."

"If I *had* a home, Holy Wolftooth, you'd be the sort of man I'd turn away from my door," Pennae hissed. "Now stop playing the fool! There are Dragons and war wizards all around us!"

"Strangely enough, I'd noticed as much," he muttered as the Swords passed between the palace and the gaudy windows of Dulbiir's Finery and Finer Promises, still bright at this late hour. The rain was no more than a light, clinging mist now, but the Swords were growing more worried about the clinging tendencies of the lawkeepers of Cormyr, patiently closing in around them.

"Pennae," Florin murmured, "I hope you know where you're—"

"I'm looking for an inn I know only by name," she muttered over her shoulder. "It should be right along here . . . and if we've coins enough, or give good weapons in lieu, they'll both give us rooms and help hide us."

They walked in slow, steady procession the length of a long block ere Pennae relaxed with a sigh, and turned in at the door of the nearest corner building of the next block.

"The Falcon's Rest," Islif and Agannor murmured in rough unison, looking up to read the sign.

Pennae tapped at a small sliding panel in the door. When it slid aside, revealing only darkness, she announced, "We must go to ground, for the Dragons hunt."

The door clicked open and a dry, elderly male voice said, "Then hurry in, turn to the right, and walk far enough to let all your fellows in behind you. Be welcome in the Rest."

The Swords hastened inside, the door was closed, bolted, and barred, and lamps were unhooded to reveal a common room with a huge oaken stair rising up to unseen levels above. As they blinked at the staff of the Rest, who nodded welcome to them over loaded and ready handbows, the owner of a rather sly smile stepped back from a lofty landing on the stair, nodded, and stole away into deeper darkness.

The Swords of Eveningstar were in Arabel, and in the Rest. Which meant a certain someone, whose orders had been explicit and force-ful, must be informed without delay.

Green adventurers are so easily baited and blamed. This was going to be *fun*.

Chapter 19
DARKSOME CESSPITS, AND MORE

Married thrice, and a lover of many men more, I have seen into the minds of many men with my spells. 'Tis astonishing, even after all this time, what darksome cesspits most men's minds are.

Murathauna Darmeir
Forty Years Loose-Gowned:
Memoirs of a Noble Lowcoin Lass
published in the Year of the Wanderer

Narantha knew by now what she carried. The small coffer in her chatelaine held something Uncle Lorneth had told her to describe to the disloyal young lordlings as "my gift to you: a thing of pleasure magic deemed suitable only for those of noble blood by its makers, a priestess of Sharess and her lover, a priest of Siamorphe."

Like all of her earlier offerings, it was a gem enspelled to display softly shifting scenes of beautiful unclad women in its depths, that she could handle safely but that would magically sink into the skin of the men she met with, and melt away.

Uncle Lorneth claimed not to know the precise details of what it did to those lordlings, but Narantha suspected it laid a magic upon them that allowed the war wizards to eavesdrop on their thoughts for signs of treason—and perhaps even trace their whereabouts.

She was well content to broaden the reach of the Crown against those who plotted against it, though she found most of the young, perfumed, arrogant lordlings she encountered even more stomach-turning than she'd thought them before coming to know Florin Falconhand.

Now there was a *man* . . .

Narantha purred at the memories that rose at the very thought of him, and almost bit her lip as she smiled. Then she remembered she was alighting from her carriage at the very gates of Erdusking House, and hastily schooled her face and mind to cool attention to the task at hand.

So far as the finer folk of the Forest Kingdom knew, the Lady Narantha Crownsilver was seeking suitable mates among the eligible male nobility of Cormyr. Her quest had commenced with this tour of brief courtesy visits, that favored no particular young lord, but allowed her to meet them all—alone and face to face—without the many distractions of revels and court balls.

Her gown was demure yet spectacular in its elegantly shaped and luxurious way, the spires of its high collar rising on either side of her elegantly piled and styled hair. Her earrings dangled a-sparkle with gems of the most exquisite gaudiness, and her eyes glowed as large and mysteriously dark as her maids could make them.

One of the Erdusking gateguards swallowed visibly as he handed her down; the other, kneeling before Narantha with his greeting-cloak flourished just so for her to tread upon, was devouring her hungrily with his eyes.

She gave him the briefest of winks, and made sure to advance her left foot first so her slit gown swirled to show him a daringly high glimpse of her upper thigh, but kept her face expressionless.

Having a servant in charge of a gate smitten with you might well come in useful in time to come.

Narantha carefully kept her face blank as she passed through the gate and felt the strange fluttering in her mind that meant a wizard's probe was biting deep, battering against whatever it was that Uncle Lorneth had put in there to defend her.

She was annoyed at the invasion—but, uncomfortably, something inside her head was even more angry than she was.

"I'm beginning to truly like the lass," Horaundoon said, in answer to the hargaunt's inquisitive chime. " 'Tis almost a pity she'll be dead soon."

The hargaunt gave forth a melodious rising burst of chimes.

"No," the Zhentarim told it, "they're not really gems at all. They look and feel like gems when my spells are complete, yes. That's to stop anyone from destroying a mindworm before it goes into them."

Horaundoon strode across the chamber to the articulated claws set atop a spell-scorched pedestal, and the faintly glowing not-gem in their grasp. He plucked it forth and turned it in his hand, watching tiny sparkling motes of unbound magic play along its facets.

"A beautiful stone, or so it appears, with a sequence of spell-images in its depths, of languid unclad maids that fade in and out of view in an endless cycle. They make the males Narantha's subverting for us pick up the stone, to gaze in at the beauties more closely."

The hargaunt chimed again. Horaundoon put the stone back into the claws, and smiled a slow wolf's smile. "The moment they touch this mindworm of mine, a spell floods into them, imparting such intense pleasure—the greatest rapture most of them will ever know—that they clutch and hold it, enthralled by the sensations, as it melts into them. Conquering another mind in this ripe-for-plucking kingdom."

The Erduskings were a suspicious house, it seemed. Two hulking guards—in full plate armor, all black enameled and teased into spike points in many impractical places, and worn with skirling, clashing scabbard chains—met her at the grand entry doors with their visors down and pointed the way she was to proceed with the spikes on the heads of their battle-axes. Then they escorted her, their boots making ominous thunder on the thick owlbear rugs.

Up a grand and seemingly endless stair with steps broad enough to be landings, then down a passage past the stuffed and mounted heads of many beasts who looked quite annoyed to have been slain by an Erdusking, to the double doors that led to an audience room furnished in old Erdusking armor and yellowing marble heads of Erdusking ancestors.

Narantha's quarry stood alone in the center of the room, smiling ever so slightly. The eldest son and heir of House Erdusking had to dismiss the guards no less than three times before they reluctantly stepped out of the room, closed its doors—and undoubtedly took up swords-drawn positions on the other side of them.

The treasure they were guarding seemed hardly worth the trouble.

Malasko Erdusking was tall, hook-nosed, and cruel of face and manner, supercilious when he wasn't being openly lustful. The reek of his oiled, dyed, jet-black hair made her nostrils flare and her throat tighten, and Narantha had to fight for the control of her face and eyes she'd need to fulfill her latest delivery for Uncle Lorneth.

Thankfully, like many nobles, Malasko saw what he wanted to see.

"You shudder for me, I cannot help but notice," he purred archly, shifting his long limbs to strike yet another pose. The man seemed to live in a series of indolent poses, impressive in his skin-tight black hose and tunic.

Malasko saw where her gaze rested and smiled a velvet-soft smile. "We seem very well suited for each other. Don't you agree?"

Narantha ducked her head a little, letting him think her smile was one of shy desire. "My lord," she murmured, "I *need* . . ."

She let her words hang, to see how he filled the silence.

His smile broadened. "A lord and master worthy of your beauty," he breathed. "Little Crownsilver lass, I am the answer to your *every* need."

Afraid she might giggle, Narantha bit her lip, cast her eyes down to the eternally snarling head of the dire bear rug at her feet, and murmured, "I begin to believe so, Lord Erdusking. Yet, as you must have heard, I am, above all, obedient. To you, if we are wed, but until then to my parents—and 'tis their will that I see all unmarried noblemen of suitable age in the realm who will receive me, ere I make a far narrower choice. I have other mansions and men to visit yet, I fear."

"Ah, but surely none can even *begin* to—"

"Lord Erdusking, this may well be so, but I follow my father's will in this." She raised her eyes to him, and said almost pleadingly, "And while it would take a man of Cormyr-shaking bravery to defy Lord Maniol Crownsilver, any man who would think to defy the Lady Jalassa Crownsilver must be several different kinds of babbling fool. A description that obviously can never fit you, Lord."

Malasko was momentarily—for the first time in more than a season—at a loss for words. Laughing uneasily—had he just been insulted, or had he not?—he said soothingly, "Of *course* not, Lady Narantha."

"Yet so that hope fades not entirely from your eyes," his shapely visitor said huskily, taking a small, glossy coffer from her chatelaine, "I deeply desire that you accept this small token from me, to remind you of *my* desires, that burn always, close beneath the smiles and manners I present to the watching world."

She held out the coffer, opening it with deft elegance.

Malasko Erdusking was chuckling, "Ah, Lady, such a gift is hardly necessary, between such as we two . . ."

His voice trailed away as he caught sight of the gem—impressively large even to the wealthiest of nobles, which the Erduskings were not—and his eyes grew larger.

Then he peered closer, and his eyes grew larger still.

Plucking the gem from the coffer, Malasko held it under his nose for a searching examination of its depths, his gaze filling with wonder.

He stared for a long time, swallowing once, ere he lifted his eyes from the gem in his hand to look at her with a gaze that smoldered with promise.

The Lady Narantha Crownsilver met that gaze with a look that sizzled. Parting her lips, she licked them very slowly, as one of her hands strayed to her own throat, and caressed it languidly.

She was lifting that hand to her mouth when the gem sank entirely from view into Malasko's fingers, and his look of naked lust slid into blank-eyed happiness.

Suspicious eyes peered through an ornate oval window, watching every moment of Narantha Crownsilver's disappearance back inside her waiting carriage. As that conveyance rumbled away over the cobbles, the watcher sighed, turned from the window, went to a room hung with tapestries and lit by a lone lantern, and carefully cast a spell.

The palm of his left hand tingled and glowed—then he seemed to be holding the moving, talking face of a woman in it.

"Yes, Nardryn? What befalls?"

Nardryn Tamlast was a careful, conservative man. To last more than a month, any house wizard of the Erduskings would have to be.

"Laspeera, some misgivings have arisen here."

"Yours alone? Or are the Erduskings party to them?"

"Mine." Tamlast was a middle-aged man with a forgettable face, who had never had much coin to call his own. He was as sparing with words as with the spending of his wealth. "You're aware of Lady Narantha Crownsilver's tour of suitable nobles, I'm sure. She's just departed here. I do not believe she found the younger Lord Erdusking to her liking—but I also fail to believe she is truly seeking a mate. She's not quite the skilled actress she thinks she is."

"She'd not have to be, to cozen young Malasko—or most of his ilk, for that matter. Yet I agree with you. Her public reason for visiting all of these young noblemen is so much piffle. Did you observe anything of their meeting?"

"No, Lady. Such things are not done in *this* house." Something that might have been the long-dead ghost of a smile rose briefly to the vicinity of Tamlast's lips, ere vanishing without a trace. "Not with all the spell-shields and trap-magics the Erduskings collect so enthusiastically and apply so lavishly. They think themselves of vital importance to the realm—and important folk deal in many secrets."

"Of course," Laspeera agreed dryly. "So you believe we war wizards should—"

"Lady, *please*. I'd not waste your time just to send needless advice. I uncovered something specific that should be of great interest to you."

"I'm sorry, Nardryn. What is it?"

"I made so bold as to probe at Lady Crownsilver's mind, upon her arrival. She's protected, of course, by something that seemed to respond to my spells as if it could think—though the lady cast no spells of her own, that I observed. Yet before it walled me out, I learned this much: the lady believes she's carrying out some sort of secret mission for the king."

The face in Tamlast's palm cursed, uttering the most fearsome words in a whisper.

Tamlast quirked an eyebrow. "Is this reaction due to a fear you've uncovered treason? Or some private stratagem of the king's? Or the hand of the royal magician at work?"

"Yes," Laspeera replied, in an even drier voice—and winked into nothingess, leaving the house wizard staring thoughtfully at his empty palm.

In all the years they'd worked together, the motherly second-in-command of the war wizards had never abruptly broken off a spell-link before.

Horaundoon grinned. The hargaunt's chimes sounded strange when it was plastered over his face.

"That makes eleven she's wormed for me, now," he told it with solid satisfaction. "And the beauty of it is that the war wizards can't find me. All the mindworms are linked to the first one: *Narantha's* worm. Not to me directly. If they move against her, I can just withdraw and be 'not there.' In fact, never there for them to find."

The hargaunt's chiming was almost a trill this time. Even it was getting excited.

Horaundoon put his fingertips together and smiled at nothing over them. If this scheme worked, it would be his most brilliant achievement, and should win him the favor of Manshoon and much awe among all Zhentarim—and make his planned "disappearance" urgently necessary.

The hargaunt chimed again, insistently, and Horaundoon hastened to answer. "Through the worms I can make those young nobles speak and act as I desire. If one fights me, I can prevail only for a short time—yet it will be more than enough to mislead war wizards, Purple Dragons, and others as to his loyalty and plans."

Horaundoon strolled across the room toward his decanters for a spot of Berduskan Dark.

"This," he added, before the hargaunt could tell him again that it was tiring of half-answers, "should result in these nobles being discredited and killed while resisting arrest—for unless they've minds stronger than most archmages, they'll remember nothing coherent of my compelling them, and so will be bewildered at the treatment they get from the authorities. If they submit, they may well get executed for treason—and surrender, die fighting, or flee into exile, whichever they choose. Their families may well end up dispossessed and exiled."

He unstoppered the decanter he was seeking, spun around on his heels triumphantly in search of the right tallglass, and continued, "The Obarskyrs acting against these nobles will of course spread fear and hatred of the royals among the rest of the nobles, about the Obarskyrs mayhap turning on *them* next. Which will make"—he poured, sipped, sighed appreciatively, and filled the tallglass—"said nobles much more receptive than they've traditionally been to sly, secret offers of coin, alliances, trade assistance and ties, and suchlike, from handy, smiling, local Zhent agents."

Horaundoon set down his glass and murmured, "Speaking of which . . ."

He settled himself in the nearest chair and thought of Florin. When the mindworm in the forester's head stirred, he reached through it very gently, not wanting to have the young man feel his presence, get alarmed, and fight him.

Ah. Our Florin was upset and angry with someone—a friend—and striding to a confrontation with her. Good. He'd not notice a light delving to capture the way he spoke, the phrases he liked to use . . .

The knowledge settled into Horaundoon's busy mind like a cold, heavy weight, and he winced, wiping sudden sweat from his face. Forcing a mind to reveal something or say something was swift, simple work; this was more like trudging, on a slippery hillside, under a heavy load that kept shifting . . .

Steadying himself under the cold heaviness, he thought of Narantha Crownsilver—and in a trice *felt* her stiffen at his touch in her mind. He made himself feel like Florin, so he'd sound like Florin when mind-talking.

Narantha? Lady? Hear you me? A kindly war wizard has cast a spell to let me mindspeak you.

Florin! Lord of my love, how fare you? I miss you!

And I you. I fare very well, but cannot speak long, and of course have no privacy for our speaking. So I'd just like to say this: I've just spoken with someone special to all Cormyreans, and learned about your superb service to the king. Nantha, I'm so proud of you. All the realm should be thanking you, and yet can never know what you're doing, but I must thank you. And pray you keep safe. And thank you again!

Oh, Florin.

Narantha's flood of affection was like a warm rush, so strong that it left Horaundoon's mouth dry. He blinked; Bane and Mystra, he was squirming in his chair!

His influence over Narantha via the mindworm in her head was well-nigh perfect! He felt delight to match Narantha's own, now surging through him . . .

Gods, this was hard work. Pleasant, thanks to this wench's emotions, but—best ended now.

Narantha, the wizard wilts. I must go. I love you.

And I you, Florin. And I, you!

Horaundoon broke the link and found himself drenched with sweat, the hargaunt rippling and quivering across his face. He smiled and reached for his glass.

The success of his deception and the efficacy of his control were both worth toasting.

"And," he told the hargaunt triumphantly, "while we're gloating anyhail, it will soon be time to send the oh-so-handsome Florin to the noble bedchambers of Arabel, and start subverting some noble *ladies*, too!"

Rhalseer's was a much cheaper place to live than any inn, but it was a lowcoin Arabellan rooming house.

Which meant it was rather bare, none too clean, as cold inside as the wind was outside, and had been down-at-heels to start with. Shutters covered windows that had never known glass, and boards creaked underfoot.

They were creaking now, as Florin marched across the sagging upper floor and angrily flung open the door of the chamber shared by the female Swords.

Pennae, barefoot and wearing breeches and dethma, was sitting cross-legged by the lone open window, where the light was strongest, sewing up a long tear in the sleeve of her leather jerkin. She looked up at Florin, saw his expression, and sighed.

"Close the door, Florin. If you've come to shout at me, we'd probably prefer the rest of Rhalseer's lodgers not to hear every last word."

Florin reached out and closed the door. Then he strode across the room, sat down beside Pennae, and said to the wall, "I'll try not to shout. D'you know how *foolish* you're being?"

Pennae gave him a lifted eyebrow. "By indulging in a little merry thieving?"

"Yes," Florin snarled, "just that. By indulging in a little merry thieving."

"Lad," Pennae asked, "how heavy is your purse?"

"That's not the point—"

"Ah, but it *is*. We'll starve and freeze come winter, if we haven't amassed enough coin for a fire in the grates of both these rooms, and Rhalseer's rent, and food to fill our bellies. The king gave us a charter, but no coins to live on—and thus far, our grand adventures haven't won us much more than a handful."

"Arabel's expensive," Florin said, "but we shouldn't be here at all."

Pennae laid aside her sewing and put a hand on the forester's arm. "We're *not* going back to Eveningstar," she told him. "Not now. Not with Tessaril watching us with the help of every war wizard she wants to call on—and a number of men with crossbows all too eager to shoot holes through us all; men we don't even know the names and faces of, to strike at before they take us down. Oh, no. In Arabel we're safely away from making trouble in the heart of Cormyr, and besmirching the reputation of a certain young Lady Crownsilver— don't blush, Florin; I know you were forbearing nobility itself toward her, but you must admit *she* was smitten with you—so the king can safely forget about us."

"But I—"

"You're smitten with guilt that we're not dying in the Haunted Halls, to please the king. You're also—forgive me, lad, but we can all see it—as restless as a boar come rutting season, stuck here in this city without trees, thornvines, and small furry things everywhere underfoot, scurrying to and fro. If you want to return to Eveningstar, tell me this: how? Are we to walk, with no coin for food, drink, or shelter, and our horses back in Eveningstar? We haven't enough to pay a carter to share an open cart with his turnips, by all the helpful gods!"

Florin stared into her eyes, anger still alive in his own—then shook his head, looked away, and said, "You have the right of it, as always. 'Tis just . . . this is *not* what I dreamed of, when wanting to be an adventurer!"

"Oh?" Pennae asked, casually flipping up her dethma to reveal a rope of coins bound around her ribs. She tapped a tricrown, amid a long row of golden lions. Florin, who was trying to look away and failing, leaned forward to peer at it in spite of himself.

"Aye," Pennae said dryly, "a tricrown. Never seen one before?"

Florin flushed and quickly looked away. "No," he said shortly. "Never. But those coins right there are enough to get us back to Eve—"

"No," the thief told him. "Unless," she added slyly, "you think you can seize them from me."

Florin looked back at her, scarlet to the tips of his ears, and mumbled, "You know I'll not try any such thing. I—"

Pennae put her thumbs under the coin-rope, and thrust it toward him. "Take a good look, lad, before you start flapping your jaws abou—"

The door opened, to reveal Doust and Semoor. Their faces lit up.

"Well, now, valiant hero of the Battle of Hunter's Hollow," Semoor said, "it seems we arrived just in time to share in whatever Ladylass Durshavin's offering! Share now, there's a good lad!"

Still proffering her treasures in her cupped hands, Pennae smiled at Florin. "And then, of course, there's the pleasant prospect of traveling all the way back to Eveningstar with Master Cleverjaws, Bright Servant of Lathander, here."

She put her dethma back in place, took up her sewing again, and left Florin staring at her . . . then at the two priestlings . . . then back at her.

Doust took pity on him. "We're here," he explained, "to tell Pennae we loaned Vaerivval the gold, just as you suggested. He tried to offer us a coach as surety, rather th—"

"You didn't take it?" Pennae asked.

"Nay, nay, sit easy, lass," Semoor told her. "We have the deed to his share of the Touch, right here, to be surrendered only upon payment of our gold and another gold piece every tenday, or, ahem, 'remaining part thereof.' See? I can follow directions surprisingly well for a holy man."

"Good dog," Pennae said. "Be sure to give the deed to Islif, to put in her codpiece, the moment she's back."

"Her—? Give it to Islif *why*, exactly? 'Twas *my* gold, for the greatest part, and—"

"Oh, stop blustering, Semoor. Vaerivval saw you take the deed into your hand and put it into your pouch, did he not?"

"Uh, yes . . ."

"So he knows where to have the young snatchfingers he'll undoubtedly hire retrieve it from. Wherefore 'tis time for you to carry this in your pouch instead. Only this, mind; give your coins to Doust to carry."

"This" proved to be a folded scrap of rather dirty parchment with a snatch of someone's woodcutting accounts on one side, and a sentence in Pennae's hand on the other: "Don't expect to keep our gold this way, Vaerivval."

Slowly, Semoor started to chuckle. Doust nodded and smiled—and so did Florin, when the note was shown to him.

"You're a witch," he said to Pennae almost fondly, watching her finish sewing and bite off the thread. "You have us all dancing to your tune."

She gave him a wink. "You mean to say I'm a minstrel, lad. Drinks are my treat at the Barrel tonight. Oh, and expect this minstrel's thefts to grow bolder. Mere shady investments with lone shopkeepers won't bring us enough coin—and we dare not deal with larger schemers."

"The Black Barrel, then, at dusk?" Semoor asked.

Pennae nodded. "Don't be sneaking out to the cheese shop, Master Wolftooth. You've got just time to get our forester here out the south gate and back in again before they close it."

"What? Why would we rush to do *that*?"

"To show him a tree, of course."

Chapter 20
THEIR FANGS WANT BLOOD

Guard yourselves well, all, for the vipers are out, and their fangs want blood.

The character Borstil Roaring,
in the first act of
Dooms of the Dragon
A play by Athalamdur Durstone
published in the Year of the Highmantle

"The Lady Jalassa Crownsilver," the aging steward announced with precise dignity, ushering the last of the three noble guests into the Turret Room.

Lady Amdranna Greenmantle inclined her head to him imperiously. "My thanks, Thaerond. You may now withdraw from the North Tower and wait in the entryhall until we ring for your presence. No one is to enter the tower—or the hall itself, for that matter, until I say otherwise."

"*Very* good, my lady," the steward replied, bowing low and backing out of the room. They heard him close the doors, and the doors of the passage in the distance beyond.

"Is he reliable?" Lady Muscalian asked.

"Completely." Lady Greenmantle handed her a decanter and a tallglass. "I let him pleasure me once, and he hungers to do so again. Fulfillments of *special* orders I reward with *special* favors."

"He looks about sevent—" Lady Yellander started to say, then blushed and went silent as Lady Muscalian gave her a glare as chill as the winter winds.

Imruae Muscalian had seen somewhat more than eighty winters, and had no hair left to call her own. Her long lustrous black mane outshone Rharaundra Yellander's own, but was said to owe more to the manes of certain palfreys than the scalps of servants. Most noble matrons of Waterdeep had a wig or two, if only to thrill their husbands on rare nights with memories of long ago moonlit adventures with other women, but "Old Shrew" Muscalian was the only person Jalassa Crownsilver knew who owned—and always wore—a wig-mask.

It was a thing crafted in Sembia by locksmiths and wizards, a metal band that screwed tightly to Imruae Muscalian's skull. That was unusual enough, but it did more than bore into the head of its wearer: its fore-edge was adorned with a row of little claws that pulled the wrinkled skin of her face tight before all the powder was dusted on by her three hard-working maids. Some said Imruae Muscalian's shrewishness was due to years of the barbed cut-and-thrust of Suzailan high society; others said it was rooted in the everpresent headache her wig-mask gave her. Whatever the cause, stooped, birdlike, sharp-boned Lady Muscalian seldom engaged in converse without making dry, nasty comments.

By contrast, Lady Rharaundra Yellander had seen perhaps forty winters, and was tall, jet-haired, statuesque, and briskly cutting-tongued when she wasn't being loftily urbane.

Their hostess, Lady Amdranna Greenmantle, seemed altogether more approachable. She was a shorter, plumper honey-blonde of lush charms, sleek wit, and warm, welcoming beauty.

All three women were looking to Jalassa for guidance.

She gave it to them, as briskly as was her wont.

"Your house wizard?"

Lady Greenmantle smiled. "Safely on the way to Marsember, riding alongside my husband. To ensure that House Greenmantle does nothing *too* stupid—or treasonous—in our dealings with fleet owners."

"You should have bought your own boats, long ago—" Lady Yellander began.

"Ships, dear. They're called *ships.*" Lady Muscalian was as peevish as ever. "And we can talk about them another time. Jalassa's here and by the look in her eye, 'tis time to thrust hard into the vitals of the Crown of Cormyr at *last!*"

"*Hush*, Imruae," Jalassa hissed. "Until you all put on these neck-laces, my warding protects only *me* from war wizard spying!"

"Oh, but Jalassa, we're *all* wearing ward-baubles—the best that coins can buy! Really, I—"

"Mine, I'm certain of. Yours could be anything, sold to you by any trickster—even Vangerdahast himself, in a spell-spun disguise! And even good wards can clash with each other, leaving gaps a war wizard can find from afar. Take yours off, throw them on yonder couch, and put these on!"

Three hands reached eagerly for the plain silvery chains she held forth. Jalassa watched a ring on her hand. When its changing glow showed her all of the wards were linked and working, she smiled, took up the decanter and tallglass Amdranna had put in front of her, and leaned forward.

"Yes, ladies, the time has come at last!"

She let them cheer and wave their glasses, then added, "As you know, I have schemed against the Crown of Cormyr for years, seeking to free our fair realm from the decadent, lust-brained Obarskyrs and the sinister war wizards who have made the foolish Obarskyrs their toadies—mages who truly rule the land without having the *slightest* right to do so. Since I recruited you, those I've been working with have covertly tested all of you, several times—"

There were stiffenings of alarm and looks of dismay, which Jalassa smilingly waved away.

"Fear not, ladies; none of you have been found wanting. My superiors have gone so far as to promise me that I *and all of you* shall be given positions of importance in the governance of Cormyr after the Obarskyrs and the wizards who own them are gone. Provided, that is, that we carry out certain tasks."

"Tasks?"

Three faces were thrust forward, eyes blazing into hers.

Jalassa smiled thinly. "It is work of a certain . . . delicacy, that I know—for your tongues have told me so, repeatedly, in our gossip together—we are all suited for. And in doing it, we will do much to free Cormyr!"

"Yes?" Lady Greenmantle blurted out, unable to wait longer.

Jalassa examined her freshly painted nails, then addressed her remarks to them. "Most war wizards are men—and all men can be seduced, one way or another."

"Yes?" It was Lady Yellander's turn, this time, and the delight in her voice made it clear she'd guessed just what was coming.

Jalassa's smile broadened. "We shall each contrive to be alone with a certain senior war wizard. These men have been chosen because they are suitable, and because they are known to favor older women of sophistication and power. We shall bring about 'accidents' that befall them in private. Harming their heads is best. Topples down stairs or over battlements, being underneath falling statues . . . that sort of thing. To maim or preferably slay—but 'tis vital that no magic nor any overtly hostile acts on our part be involved, so if our unfortunate old war wizards happen to survive, they won't suspect we meant them any ill."

Jalassa knew her fellow conspirators. Bored, jaded, and spiteful, they erupted not with scandalized fury or misgivings, but with savagely eager glee.

Even Lady Muscalian had nothing sneering or belittling to say. What she did was lick her wrinkled lips and hiss, "Who and when?"

Even Jalassa knew not that the ward-necklaces were shields against all but one watching wizard.

To that smiling watcher, they were eyes and ears.

It was why he was smiling, despite the annoying singings clashing and ringing around him: the collective din of the strongest ward-spells he knew how to craft, which were now cloaking the meeting in the Turret Room of Greenmantle Hall far better than the necklaces alone could.

The noblewomen could not help but be caught, of course, and removed. That had become desirable. It was past time to be rid of them and their meddlings. He'd been careful that no link even the brightest mage might follow stretched from him to Jalassa Crown-silver. So he was safe.

The four would probably fail, in the main. Yet any harm they managed was helpful. Their targets were the very war wizards who by inclination or active investigation stood closest to uncovering *this* watching wizard, whether they knew it or not.

Ah, such spite, ladies. You are the perfect dupes.

As he toyed with his favorite ring, tracing the smooth curves of its unicorn head, the watching wizard's smile grew.

It shone even brighter a breath or two later, when Jalassa so precisely relayed the task he'd given her to her fellow lady traitors.

Precisely, that is, save for one small omission. Somehow Jalassa Crownsilver neglected to tell her eager audience that her mysterious superiors based in Westgate—for so Jalassa believed "them" to be, never knowing who she was truly dealing with—had promised her two thousand rubies, all of them larger than her thumb, if she successfully carried out all of the killings.

But then, perhaps Lady Crownsilver was smarter than he'd judged her to be. Perhaps she knew the rubies did not exist, or that neither she nor her three conspirators would live long enough to collect them.

Perhaps she even thought the paltry magic items she'd so carefully collected down the years would safely whisk her away to a far country, to dwell out her days under another name, safe from any vengeful spell that could reach out to her from Cormyr.

Now, *that* would be amusing.

There was nowhere in Rhalseer's to hide coins. Every second floorboard could be easily pulled up—they were riddled with dry rot—and every lodger knew it. The ceilings were hardly better, and trying to make holes in the walls was more likely to bring the place down on an energetic thief's head than craft a hiding place.

Now that it was full dark and Dragons on the battlements of the citadel and along the city wall couldn't notice her at a casual glance, Pennae was up on the crumbling slate-shingled roofs of Palaceside Arabel, seeking to lash her precious bundle in the right sort of angle between chimneys, and cover it with the bird dropping-infested remnants of old birds' nests she carried in the small sack at her belt.

She found just what she wanted on the roof of Hundar's Fine Carpets, Perfumes, and Lanterns, and was able to secure and disguise her riches in a few hard-breathing moments. The rumblings of four passing slate-carts even raised enough echoing racket to cloak any small noises she made.

Then she stretched, catlike—it had been a long day—and crept to the edge of the roof to peer down. Her friends should be strolling out of the Barrel about now . . . yes, there they were, Florin turning to say something to Islif as they spilled out into the street . . . probably something about having a thief among the Swords who left early to do dark-work . . .

Then Pennae saw something more.

Something that had her tense and alert in an instant.

A gently sloping half-roof ran along the front of Hundar's, a floor below her perch, and a man in smoky gray hostler's leathers was lying full-length on it, cradling something in his hand that few hostlers would have carried casually at their belts: a handbow. Four more of the little hand crossbows—all cocked and loaded—were laid ready on the roof, arranged in an arc in front of the man's hands. The man looked vaguely familiar . . . Ah: because he'd come into the Barrel earlier, for a lone drink at the bar, and had looked across the taproom at the Swords.

An assassin. Who was even now raising his bow, steadying the arm that held it with his other hand, taking aim—

Pennae had the knife that lived in her sleeve in her hand and was dropping heels-first over the edge of her roof, body angling back so she'd slump against Hundar's uppermost windows and shove the hired slayer out toward a fall over the edge, rather than taking that tumble herself.

He'd have a backup—must look—find—

Indar Crauldreth heard something, twisted his head to look up, holding fire—and Florin Falconhand lived a little longer without a crossbow bolt buried fletchings-deep in his face. Indar's neck was twisted when both of Pennae's boots, with all her weight behind them, came crashing down on it.

The assassin bounced, writhing spasmodically and sending a crossbow bolt cracking away into the night, in the general direction of the rear of Ongluth's Ropeworks. As Indar, his neck and throat crushed, made a sort of wet spewing sound, Pennae landed hard on her behind, grunting at the pain. The last despairing, unthinking thing Indar did was to try to get away, to spring . . .

Into oblivion. Over the edge, plummeting to the cobbles below. With Pennae's left boot caught somewhere in his clothing, dragging her—

Pennae made a desperate, twisting lunge, and managed to pluck one of the handbows into her grasp as she went over the edge.

They crashed to the cobbles together, right in front of the astonished Swords, and Pennae, feeling bones break under her, slit the man's throat out of sheer habit ere she rolled to her feet, looking wildly around at the rooftops.

"Scatter!" she spat at her fellow adventurers. "There's sure to be—"

Even as the words left her lips, she caught sight of what she was seeking: a small man in the shadows behind the Barrel, balancing a full-sized crossbow on some crates, aiming—

Pennae shouted wordless alarm as she raised her handbow and fired.

Fired nothing. The string hummed and writhed uselessly; the bolt had fallen out during her tumble.

The second slayer's crossbow cracked, deep and loud, and a war-quarrel capable of tearing a hole through a man came humming hungrily at the Swords.

Pennae was already sprinting at the man, knowing she was too late, and hoping—

There was only one Sword anywhere near the path of the quarrel, and he was a tired forester who'd recently downed two large drinks. A forester who seldom hesitated in battle, and thought nothing of hurling himself face-first at hard, dirty cobbles.

Florin dived and rolled. The quarrel passed harmlessly through where he'd been, streaking across the street to smack deep into one of the ornate window frames adorning the turreted mansion of the wealthy local landlord and sundries merchant Kraliqh.

Whose servants heard nothing—or affected not to—as Swords shouted, weapons singing out of their sheaths and scabbards and into their hands, and a hard-running Pennae saw the hired slayer let the bow fall as he turned to flee.

Bey's hurled dagger flashed past her to bite deep into the back of the man's neck. He fell, as heavily as a full, wet grainsack, groaned once, and lay still.

When they turned him over, his eyes were staring at nothing, and the dagger was protruding bloodily from his throat.

"Let's get gone," Bey snarled, jerking his blade free. "I don't want to spend all night explaining to suspicious Dragons why we butchered two fine upstanding citizens of Arabel in the street."

Pennae whirled and called, *"Move!* To our rooms, like the very wind!"

The Swords moved.

The war wizard came up the trail stealthily, wand ready in one hand and dagger in the other—and at his every move tiny motes of light winked, sparkled, and faded.

Maglor's lip curled. A shielding spell of some sort, to keep the mage oh-so-safe against spells, arrows—and swords, too, no doubt.

Brave men, wizards were, these days.

The cleft between the two rocks gave the apothecary a limited view, but he could see his trap well enough. Three of his mixing bowls, the cups that had held the two powders and the third he'd combined them in . . . and the glowing symbol he'd made, once the mixed powders had begun their glow.

Wizards can never resist magical-looking symbols.

This one came cautiously to the edge of the old campsite and peered warily around into the deepening night-gloom. The symbol—a thing of circles, arcs, squiggles that looked like writing, and similar nonsense, a mere fancy Maglor had gone on drawing until the powder had run out—glowed at the mage's feet, bright and impressive.

Scarcely daring to breathe, Maglor crouched, watching.

The wizard looked around, long and hard—and his eyes fixed on the trap itself: a rock, six or so paces from the symbol, lying on the ground. It was covered in glowing fingerprints, where Maglor had picked it up with the glow-powder still thick on his hands, and set it down again. Atop a piece of parchment.

Wizards can never resist pieces of parchment.

The war wizard stalked forward, carefully keeping to the edge of the trees, looking around often for signs of movement, and peering the rest of the time at the ground in front of his boots.

The night was almost still, and Maglor kept his breathing as shallow and quiet as possible, the six large, sharp stones arrayed in front of him for throwing. He hoped he'd not have to face this hound's spells.

The war wizard had been snooping around Eveningstar for days now, obviously under orders to seek out lawbreakers and conspirators. Zhentarim, for instance. And suspicious local apothecaries, who might well concoct poisons. Malbrand—that was his name—had spent the better part of a day poking into simmering concoctions and peering at the fading labels on Maglor's vials, asking oh-so-casual questions about the uses of this and who'd ordered that.

He'd hinted heavily that Vangerdahast and every mage who worked with him knew all about Maglor's Zhent loyalties, and were just waiting for some Brotherhood mage of importance to visit before swooping down to capture, torture, maim, and slay the apothecary of Eveningstar and his guest. For why butcher one, when two could be had by using the one as bait?

Why, indeed? But let us see, now, what bait tastes best . . .

Maglor held his breath. The wizard was much nearer, only a few paces from the rocks where Maglor was hiding. And he was stopping just above the rock pinning down the parchment.

Stopping, and squatting down over it, he peered all around, listening long and hard.

Silence. Stars glimmered, no breeze stirred . . . here on the edge of the high pasture overlooking the mouth of Starwater Gorge, high above Eveningstar, the night continued to pass, uncaring.

Abruptly Malbrand turned back to the rock, pushed it aside with his dagger, and sprang away to avoid any eruption, striking snake, or—

The stone rolled over, revealing more glowing writing: also nonsense, but small and close-packed, intricate nonsense. The war wizard peered at it, then picked it up to look at it more closely.

Still holding his breath, Maglor smiled in relief and satisfaction. The man had doomed himself.

Malbrand took up the parchment in his other hand and turned it over.

Which meant he was now, in the glow of the rock still in his other hand, reading the words Maglor had written there:

Die at the hands of one who has outwitted you all along, War Wizard fool. Maglor murders you.

The war wizard's head came up sharply. Then he got to his feet—or tried to. Halfway up his limbs started to tremble and failed him, leaving Marbrand to topple helplessly onto his face in the trodden earth and old ashes.

The same poison was thick on the rock and on the parchment, and to someone who hadn't imbibed the antidote, touching either meant death.

There was enough hardiclaw on either to slay a dozen war wizards.

The paralysis would have reached Malbrand's lungs already, slowly suffocating him—but Maglor had gathered the stones to hurl, and he wanted to use them.

They thudded into the helpless mage's head and shoulders with satisfying force; when he was done, the back of Malbrand's head was far less shapely than before.

Chuckling, Maglor bent to pick up his satchel and the largest basin he owned.

It would take a lot of the concoction he'd have to mix now to dissolve the wizard's body, and he might as well get started.

Just as soon as he'd harvested the eyes, tongue, brain, and heart, of course.

The door banged shut behind Doust, and Pennae reached out of the gloom by the wall to hand him the door-bar. He helped her to settle it into its cradles, puffing from the haste of his run, and look up at her to gasp, "What I . . . want to know . . . is how you knew to look for a second killer."

"Good hired slayers work in pairs," Pennae gasped in reply as they clung to the railings in Rhalseer's unlit back stairwell together, trying to catch their breath.

"Oh?" Semoor looked shaken. "And how is it you know that?"

Pennae, still panting hard, stared at him without saying a word.

All around her, hard-breathing Swords waited.

For a reply that never came.

When it became clear she would say no more, Florin observed, from beside her, "I don't believe you've ever told us anything specific about what you've done in your life, up until we met in Waymoot."

She gave him a level look and said flatly, "No. I don't believe I have."

"It's been a full tenday since Indar Crauldreth tried for them and failed. Are these Swords still looking for hired slayers around every corner and inside every shadow?"

"No," the best of Varandrar's spies replied. "They did for five or six nights, yes, but they're young, and still think themselves nigh-invincible. Even the gravest of warnings fades fast at that age."

"I remember," Varandrar said. "My youth wasn't all *that* many years ago, whitebeard!"

"Your words are heard and heeded, Lord," Drathar replied.

Varandrar almost chuckled. Most Brotherhood mages he'd met

were cruel, humorless men, only too eager to slay or maim underlings who so much as looked at them askance. They'd not have been able to coax a tenth of the loyalty out of any band of spies that Varandrar had managed to foster in his men.

For that reason, Varandrar, lacking the slightest ability to craft spells or even feel most magic, made money fist-over-gauntlet for the Zhentarim in Arabel, where wizards of higher rank and much higher opinions of themselves had met with swift disaster.

"Does anyone know who hired Crauldeth, anyhail?"

"No, Lord. Or rather, there are the usual twoscore wild rumors, none of them backed by much of anything."

"And have the Swords crossed any of our men or doings?"

"No, Lord. The one called Florin—with the aid of the woman Islif Lurelake and the novice of Tymora, Doust Sulwood—is keeping them well-behaved and seeking work. Not that they've found any, yet. A few merchants need warehouses or their own bodies guarded, but they haven't happened to meet with these adventurers yet. The Dragons are suspicious of them, of course, and the regular patrols are watching them, but the stalwarts have put only a few coin-hire lads to tailing the Swords thus far, rather than raising an alarm. They're mindful of the fresh ink on the royal charter, I'd say; no one wants to be too quick to show the king he's been a fool."

Varandrar did chuckle, this time. "You say this Florin is keeping his fellow Swords in line; what then of the overbold thieving that drew your eye in the first place? Are these Swords learning caution, or—?"

"Ah. Aye. The lone exception to their good behavior is a lass hight Alura Durshavin, whom they call 'Pennae.' A thief of some daring, who's thus far confined herself to emptying merchants' bedchamber coffers and snatching the occasional haunch of roast boar, but seems to have an eye for larger and larger prizes as the days pass. So circumspect are the Swords that the Dragons haven't yet connected them with the thefts—but if she goes on snatching like this, half Arabel is going to be looking for her, and when uproars start, outlanders tend to get blamed."

"True. Well enough. It seems you have this well in hand, an—"

Varandrar stiffened, and as his speech faltered, his eyes momentarily rolled up in his head.

Drathar drew back in alarm, making the swift 'Mask be with me' gesture to ward off fell magic or peril—but by the time he'd done it, Varandrar had reeled and relaxed again, his eyes his own and his voice as steady as before.

"—and I'd caution you in only one matter: pay no attention to the Swords Agannor Wildsilver or Bey Freemantle. You are to watch only the others."

In the bright depths of the scrying orb, the last of the spies could be seen filing out. Varandrar waved a friendly farewell to Drathar, who closed the door.

Leaving Varandrar alone again.

Horaundoon smiled and ended his spell.

The orb showed the Zhentarim trading lord reeling again, and looking bewildered.

Hmm. Not a mage at all, yet the man had a more sensitive mind than most. Merely withdrawing from it left him like that, hey?

Perhaps Horaundoon of the Zhentarim needed to recruit a dozen Varandrars of his own.

The figure came out of the night like a flitting shadow, landing on the moonlit roof of Rhalseer's rooming house with the softest of footfalls.

Florin let her gain her balance and draw in a calming breath or two before he uncoiled himself from the shadow of the tumbledown wreck of Rhalseer's cluster of aging chimneys.

Her knife came out in less time than it took her to hiss and back into a crouch, ready for battle.

"Pennae," he said, " 'tis me. Put the blade away; I mean no harm. I only want to talk."

"You waited up here for me?"

"It seems so."

"Why?"

"I very much need to know some things. Before 'tis too late, and the questions I'll ask gently will be roared at you—at us all—by many furious Purple Dragons, as we hang in chains in the darkest cell they have."

Pennae sighed. "You want to know all about my lurid past."

"Just the jailings, and the crimes you're still sought for. If any, of course. Oh, and what folk say about you. And where they say it: the realms, the cities . . ."

"Of my notoriety?" Pennae sounded amused. Sheathing her blade, she went to the three-board-wide walkway that crowned the peak of the roof, hard by the chimneys, and sat down, beckoning Florin to sit beside her.

He did, and they stared at each other in the moonlight for a breath or two, arms clasped around knees, elbows touching.

"I was born here," Pennae said. "In Arabel, not all that many years ago." She stretched then let her knees fall and stretched out on her back, bowed over the roofpeak with her hips closest to the stars. Florin turned onto his side so he could hear what she murmured next.

"My father I never knew. I gather he was here for but a season. A Purple Dragon of the garrison, who caught the eye of my mother: Maerthra Durshavin, not a bad pastry cook, but hard of hand, voice, and manner. She had few friends, drank much, and beat my bones raw until I fled. She's dead these three winters, now."

Pennae fell silent, stretching her lithe arms again, arching her shoulders—and wincing.

"Bruise there, that I knew not I had . . . anyhail, I made my own life. Ate what I could get, took all I could, hadn't much to conquer Faerûn with but my wits, my scampering, and my good balance and leaping about. Alone, always alone. Whenever I trusted someone else, they made me rue it soon enough."

She let silence fall again.

"Ah, Pennae?" Florin's voice was uncertain. "Have we Swords made you . . . rue trusting us?"

She sat up, managing to keep a flaring flame of amused satisfaction out of her eyes. Men were *so* predictable; so easily led by reins they didn't even know they wore.

Nose to nose, she said huskily, "Not yet. I pray me: never."

She let her voice become a desperate whisper. "Oh, Florin I am so *tired* of being alone." She shaped the last words into a sob and opened her arms to him. When his lips timidly found hers, Pennae devoured them hungrily, rolling against him.

Yes, men were so predictable.

Her tongue entwined with Florin's, Pennae glanced up at the stars overhead with eyes that smiled, and allowed herself one more prediction: there would be no more questions about her past *this* night.

Chapter 21
THINGS CHANGE

That's the hard thing about life: things change. We hate it. We all hate it. Loved ones die. Friends drift away. Remember this: You can cling to nothing without harming it.

Blors 'Brokenblade' Ghontal
One Warrior's Way
published in the Year of the Storms

"Ah, I'm afraid you've been sadly misled, Lady Greenmantle," the elderly war wizard said. "These aren't spell scrolls at all."

He looked up from them, genuine sorrow in his eyes. Bleys Delaeyn was a kindly man, and it distressed him to think that someone had caused any upset to one of the kindest and most beautiful noblewomen he'd ever met. Still more that she'd been duped out of coins, and might well be angry with him for telling her so.

She'll think I'll rush back to my fellow Wizards of War to have a good laugh about her.

Lady Greenmantle was, indeed, looking upset. Her lower lip trembled, and what looked alarmingly like tears glimmered in her large emerald eyes.

"Lady," Delaeyn said, "rest assured that this shall remain a secret between us, not shared with *anyone* else—even Lord Vangerdahast himself. I'm afraid you've been duped by a clever charlatan. If you'd like me to try to recover your coins by hunting him down with some of the best Crown agents Cormyr can muster, I'll be happy to do so, but if my silence is what you prefer, I—"

Lady Greenmantle had somehow found her way around to his side of the table, and was plucking the offending sheets of parchment from his hand. As he stared at her, open-mouthed, she flung them over her shoulder, heedless of where they might fall, and faced him, their knees touching.

"Lord Wizard Delaeyn," she whispered, "I care not a whit about spell scrolls or false scrolls, so long as you call me Amdranna, and bide here with me for a time. There *is* something I very much need you to do."

Bleys Delaeyn blinked at her. "Uh, Lady, uh—"

"Amdranna," she whispered, leaning forward to say the word almost into his mouth. Her bosom brushed against him, and Delaeyn was suddenly very much aware of her nearness, the spiced scent of her perfume, her softness, gliding against him . . .

"Uh, La—*Amdranna,*" he almost wailed, leaning back from her, "what . . . what're you *doing?*"

"Seducing you," she murmured, licking his throat and the edge of his jaw and leaving Delaeyn trembling with unaccustomed excitement—and the realization that his aging back wouldn't bow away from her any farther. "If you'll let me. For years I've admired you, Lord Delaeyn—"

"Uh, ah, I'm not actually a 'lord' of any s-sort, Lady—"

"Amdranna," she told him sternly, crawling up him like an affectionate tressym until he was on his back, draped over the flaring arm of the bench, with her avid face poised above his. She reached up, nostrils flaring, and tore her gown with sudden ferocity.

"Amdranna, I—this is so *sudden!* I—"

"Don't you want me?" she asked, sudden tears on her cheeks. "After I've dreamed of you so long?"

She ground herself against him, and a shuddering Bleys Delaeyn knew that he wanted her very much, and—and—

Her hands were at his belt and the lacings of his breeches, and he moaned a wordless protest and tried to throw her off, thrusting upward with his hips.

With a smile that was pure tressym she caught hold of his belt buckle and sat back up, pulling him with her. The buckle proved unequal to the strain, and came open—and in a trice Bleys Delaeyn found himself being towed across the room to a low couch right at the edge of the open stair that descended to the entryhall.

"Lady!" he hissed. "What if one of your servants sees—"

"Hush," she said, and covered his mouth with hers as she dragged him down.

He shouldn't be doing this, Delaeyn told himself, he was a long way from nineteen winters old, and an even longer way from—

Memories that faded like morning mist before her warm yielding, her hot kisses, her—

She was under him no longer, but above him, hair a wild tangle about her bare shoulders, eyes afire, bending down to him, falling sideways—

Oh, no, they were—

Amdranna Greenmantle rolled, tucking herself down tight beside the couch, shoulders slamming hard onto the stone floor. Her hands held the old mage's sagging, hairy chest like claws, her knee came up into his crotch as she let go of him, and she twisted—

And with a startled, despairing cry, Wizard of War Bleys Delaeyn was hurled over the unguarded edge of the old stone stair.

The steps were of old, smooth-worn stone, some sixty feet down, and he greeted them headfirst. Lady Greenmantle listened to bone shatter and teeth spray, and then calmly rose and went to hide her torn gown—it was best kept, rather than tossed down a garderobe, in case she needed it to prove her claim of the old wizard going mad with lust and trying to force himself on her—and wash and redo her hair.

It had been so long since she'd seen to her tresses without the maids—like all the other servants, banished for the day—that she'd almost forgotten how. Almost.

The precious cigar was almost done. Taltar Dahauntul tasted its smoke and leaned back in his chair, in the heart of the aromatic blue cloud, with a contented sigh.

Narooran's Finest were halfling-crafted, somewhere in Sembia—seemingly *everything* was crafted somewhere in Sembia—and all too rare. He hoarded his dwindling supply like the precious things they were. Even on an ornrion's coins, they were dear, and the extra lions now falling into his lap for being Acting Captain of His Majesty's Loyal Watch of Arabel wouldn't last forever. Nothing did.

Aye, if there was one lesson long service as a Purple Dragon taught, to those who cared to learn, it was that nothing lasted. Things change.

Perhaps, one day, things would change for the better. Perhaps, though it was so hrastingly easy to put a foot wrong these days. Yet even those who disliked him respected him for being capable. The men called him "Dauntless," and that was far better than "Old Ironbreeches" or "Idiot Screechtongue" or "Lord Stonehead the Sixth," which is what they referred to his three immediate superiors as, among themselves.

"Lord Dauntless"? Nay, not for him. Lords were arrogant, fat-bellied idiots with monocles, foolish notions, and casual rudenesses, who deserved all the contempt they were held in.

Sir Dauntless, now . . . a man had to earn a knighthood. He stared at the shield in his lap through the last of the thinning smoke. Its blazon was an unfinished chaos of chalk, because Dauntless wasn't much of a limner and because he hadn't quite settled on what he wanted—wings and a lion, yes, yet a lion with wings was a manticore: a stupid, evil, nuisance beast—but he could copy out ornamented characters with the best of them. His motto, framed by a flowing scroll, blazed forth from the shield proudly: "Bold to face the foe."

Well, so he was. Someday, perhaps, Cormyr would say so.

Reluctantly stubbing out the butt before it burned his knuckles, Dauntless slid the shield safely back into its hiding place in the lid of his locker, between the real top and the false top he'd constructed so long ago, folded down the edge-flap over the slot between them, and carefully adjusted the pins that secured it, sprinkling a pinch of pepper over them to look like dust. If the wrong person found this, it would mean utter disaster.

The distant bell tolled, right on time. Sighing, Dauntless stood, put the cigar butt on the usual tray on its high shelf, jammed his helm onto his head, and strode out of his quarters, every inch a stern, erect, on-duty ornrion.

It was time for this particular gruff, cigar-smoking veteran of burly build, shrewd sense, and a huge mustache to flog Purple Dragons into shape once more.

And by Helm and Torm both, they took a lot of flogging.

"We—that is, all house wizards—are under orders to investigate any accidental death of any noble, knight, mage, or priest, Lady," Treth Ohmalghar said. "Moreover, both your lord husband and myself find your orders to all Greenmantle servants to depart the hall for the day . . . interesting."

Lady Greenmantle's face was white with anger. "You *dare*—?"

"Lady," Ohmalghar said gently, "I do, and must. Please bear in mind that Lord Greenmantle and myself have taken care that I speak with you in private, to spare you even the slightest stain to your reputation. Just as you consulted with Bleys Delaeyn in private."

"Very well," the noblewoman said, still obviously furious. "Ask your questions."

The Greenmantle house wizard inclined his head to her politely, spread his hands, and murmured an incantation too quiet for Lady Greenmantle to hear.

"Mage, what are you *doing?*"

"To save us both much time and ill-feeling, I'm seeking answers in your mind," Ohmalghar explained. "Innocent folk have nothing to fear from such a proced—" He stiffened, his eyes going sharp.

Lady Greenmantle gave a little cry, like a dismayed bird, one hand going to her mouth. Her eyes darted to the bell that would bring servants on the run, then to the two doors out of the room . . . and all her rage seemed to drain away from her, leaving only fear, when she realized the house wizard—who suddenly seemed an above-himself servant no longer, but something far more menacing—had deftly placed her so that he stood between her and both the bell and the doors.

There was a wand in his hand, and it was pointed at her.

"Lady Greenmantle," he said, the snap of command in his voice, "sit down. In the chair just behind you. *Now.*"

Amdranna Greenmantle sat.

Eyes never leaving hers, Ohmalghar cast another spell and spoke softly to the empty air. "Treth Ohmalghar for Ghoruld Applethorn. Urgent."

The noblewoman sat staring at him, trembling, her white face gone almost yellow.

"Yes, Treth?" The voice spoke from nothingness.

"Greenmantle Hall, Twohelm Chamber. I'm with Lady Amdranna Greenmantle, and from her mind have just learned that she murdered Wizard of War Bleys Delaeyn. As her part in a plot to murder senior war wizards, unfolded to her by the Lady Jalassa Crownsilver, and also involving the noble ladies Muscalian and Yellander! We must inform Lord Vangerdahast at once!"

"Indeed. Knows she any other intended victims?"

"I . . . think not. I lack the spells to *truly* probe."

"I'm coming through."

Lady Greenmantle whimpered, the air between her and the house wizard shimmered, and then there was a tall, impressive-looking man in rich robes standing on her dapple-dyed ghost-rothé rug.

Wizard of War Ghoruld Applethorn's hair was white at the temples and he had a face as handsome as it was commanding. There were rings on his hands—one of them adorned with a large, strikingly carved unicorn head finer than anything in her own coffers. He gave her a hard look, turned slowly on his heel to look all around the room, nodding to Ohmalghar, and ended up with his back to the house wizard. Amdranna Greenmantle saw him cup one hand against his chest as if holding an invisible bowl, murmur something into it, then turn. Smiling at the house wizard, he stepped forward—and slapped that hand against Ohmalghar's face.

The house wizard staggered, gasping, and fell to the rug, tiny wisps of smoke streaming from his eyes.

"Dedication, Ohmalghar," Applethorn said almost jovially, "gets you only one thing: killed. Who'd have known Delaeyn was such a devious traitor that he'd cast a backlash on Lady Greenmantle to mindblast anyone probing her, burning out his brain and leaving him forever a drooling idiot?"

Giving Amdranna Greenmantle a soft smile, Applethorn cast another spell.

The air shimmered again, and a creature that Lady Greenmantle had only seen depicted in one of her husband's hidden books appeared beside the war wizard. It was a gray-skinned, gaunt echo of a man, with huge eyes set in a larger head, and had long, spidery talon-fingers but no nose, mouth, nor privates.

"Your time has come at last," Applethorn told the doppelganger—and pointed at Lady Greenmantle.

"Much thanksss," it hissed, with lips that swam into being and gained shape even as it spoke. It was looking straight at her . . . and becoming shapely and feminine, its eyes going emerald green, an ample bosom form—

Great Gods Above! 'Twas becoming *her!* Herself, the Lady Greenmantle she gazed at in her dressing-glass of mornings!

As Amdranna Greenmantle stared at it in horror, her own voice issued from its lips: "Applethorn, *try* not to destroy the garments this time. I'd rather not stalk naked around this house trying to find the right wardrobes and upsetting the maids."

As the wizard nodded and started to murmur a spell, the—the *thing* wearing her shape started purposefully toward her.

Amdranna Greenmantle opened her mouth to scream, rising to flee she knew not where, dashing wildly across the room.

Calmly, Ghoruld Applethorn blasted her down.

Dauntless swung open the battered door of the ready room—and stiffened, frowning.

Lionar Almarr Toliphur was sitting in his chair. A *lionar* sitting in his chair!

"What's this?" he barked.

Rather than leaping upright and stammering excuses and apologies, Toliphur favored his superior with an easy grin, and held out the duty scroll. "I have to sit here and growl at the stalwarts as if I were you, because *you* have to report in to the She-Dragon herself."

Dauntless sighed, smote his forehead, and growled, "I clean forgot. These 'Swords of Eveningstar,' right?"

"Right," the lionar confirmed happily.

Dauntless plucked the scroll from Toliphur's grasp, turned on his heel, and marched out. The scroll rattled in his hand as it trailed behind him in the wind of his haste.

He rolled it up without slowing, striding hard and fast toward the She-Dragon's lair.

The Lady Lord of Arabel knew very well what the watch called her, just as well as the folk of Arabel knew it.

And just as Arabellans chose to overlook the slight on their loyalty represented by the Crown making every officer of the watch a Purple Dragon of experience and standing, Myrmeen Lhal chose to ignore the fact that those men—and most of the city, echoing them—called her "the She-Dragon."

She'd even been heard, when someone bellowed it at her in an unfriendly fashion across a busy street, to remark that it was a rather more catchy name than "King's Lady Lord of Arabel."

Yet Myrmeen was called the She-Dragon for good reason. She slept less, worked longer, ran harder, fenced better, and thought faster than almost all who served under her. She was the only woman in all Arabel that Dauntless feared.

That was why his "Acting Captain Dahauntul, to see the Lady Lord of Arabel on official duty" was respectful as well as gruff, and the first two gateguards stepped aside with alacrity.

The second pair demanded the password. Dauntless, who'd chosen it and given it to them himself, along with their orders, just after dawn, said it to them now rather coldly. They kept their faces expressionless as they handed him on to the third set of guards—four, this time, bolstered by a war wizard young in years and Art, who watched him stop and stand on the glyph that would show them his true shape and likeness, then the glyph that would cause any magic at work on him to blaze forth like pink fire.

Neither showed them anything suspicious, of course, and they escorted him into a room where a woman in worn and plain battle-leathers, with a sword scabbarded at her hip, was leaning on her long arms over a table spread with maps, conferring with several scared-looking city courtiers.

"I haven't forgotten giving orders that these sewers were to be checked by a patrol every sixth day, Bluthskas—why have you?" she was saying sharply, tapping two many-branched lines on the largest map.

"Lady, I—"

"Lady *Lord*, I—" Another courtier corrected, before Myrmeen could.

She nodded, let them both see her rolling eyes, and said, "Get out of here, both of you, to think up whatever excuse you want to offer me. Make it good; I'm in need of entertainment." She turned her head. "Dauntless! Good to see you. More cheery news?"

Ornrion Dahauntul saluted. "Lady Lord, I've not judged its cheeriness, one way or another. It has one virtue I have noted: 'tis short."

Myrmeen gave him both a nod and a snort of appreciation, and gestured for him to deliver his report.

Dauntless plunged right in. "Two tendays ago, or a few days less, a band of adventurers arrived in the city. Interestingly, they do not appear in any of the gateguard reports. They took rooms at the Falcon's Rest, but moved on to Rhalseer's rooming house after only two nights. They have been guests of Rhalseer's ever since, and do most of their drinking at the Black Barrel. Despite staying at one of the lesser rooming houses of the city, they seem to have plenty of coin to invest, and some shrewd idea of where to place it. They have avoided weapons-outs and brawls, but are suspected of having been involved in a double slaying: that of the professional slayer Indar Crauldreth, late of Marsember, and an accomplice."

Myrmeen's eyebrows lofted. "They must have *really* upset

someone—or upset someone truly wealthy. And they took him down, too! What else have they been up to?"

Dauntless shrugged. "Much thievery, we suspect, but can prove nothing. None of their victims have seen fit to talk to us." He and Myrmeen shared wry knowing grins.

"There are two holy men amongst these adventurers, and probably two minor wizards. They show no signs of preparing for travel to elsewhere."

"Are they chartered?" the Lady Lord of Arabel asked.

Dauntless spread his hands. "I know not, Lady Lord."

Myrmeen's lips thinned. "Bring their leader, if they have one, here to me," she commanded, "and we'll put a little scare into them."

Azimander Godal was very tall. His beard was long, thin, pointed, and gray-white with age, and his brown-mottled head was bald for the same reason. Yet his eyes were bright with alert wisdom, his manner impeccably dignified, and his robes splendid and cut to echo the latest fashion.

Just now, he was giving the Lady Rharaundra Yellander a very direct look. "Forgive me, Lady Yell—"

"Rhar," she purred, reaching out one long-nailed hand to stroke his cheek. "Call me Rhar. Please."

"Very well, Lady Rhar. I cannot help but observe—and I pray you forgive the bluntness of this—that you have hithero spoken to me as if I were a barely tolerated annoyance, and called me to my face a lowborn simpleton unfit to share air with you, at that."

He had to admit that the Lady Rharaundra Yellander looked sleekly elegant at all times, and breathtakingly beautiful, to boot—and just now, with her long jet hair loosed to tumble around her shoulders, and her strikingly cut shimmerweave gown, she looked stunning.

She'd have looked stunning even if she weren't thrusting herself at him, lips parted and tongue licking them hungrily, eyes fixed on his with longing.

"I said much to goad you to anger," she whispered, "so you'd remember me and think of me. And I would have good reason to apologize to you and . . . submit to you. I—I need to be humbled, by a man who awes me—as you do, more than any other I've met."

"Me, Lady?"

"Rhar, *please*, Azimander. I desire not to be a 'lady' with you, but . . . a woman who deserves to be called something considerably more wanton."

The elderly war wizard blinked at her. "You must admit this *is* sudden, Rhar."

"My husband and our everpresent spy, the house wizard, haven't both been apart from me for more than two *seasons*, Az. This is my chance." She crossed her wrists, one over the other, and held them out to him.

"I beg you, Azimander," she whispered. "Take me."

Wizard of War Azimander Godal got up from the bench unhurriedly, straightening to his full looming height. The Lady Rharaundra was a tall woman, but even if she'd gone up on tiptoes, she could not have matched his stature. He looked down at her, face expressionless.

Rharaundra looked back up at him, rolling over onto her back, wrists still held crossed, and wriggled forward onto the part of the bench where he'd just been sitting. Her movements dragged her gown down, baring skin.

Godal took two swift steps back from her, waved at her to stay where she was, and half-closed his eyes. She heard him muttering a spell and lifting one hand to make an intricate gesture and point at the air. He kept on pointing as he turned himself, slowly, all around—then let his hand fall, nodded, and said, "We are truly alone. I must admit I feared some treachery on your part, La—Rhar."

Rharaundra gave him a reproachful look as she crawled languidly off the bench. Standing, she shook out her hair with her fingers so he could see nothing was concealed in it, turned slowly around under his gaze, and murmured, "Treachery *how*, Az? This is all I have, and am. I would prefer to be more moonlit, mysterious, and teasing, but I am mindful of how careful war wizards must be. Behold this bench, yonder."

She went to it. "Bare. Simple. Nothing beneath or behind, here against the railing. Nothing on it but"—she gave him a wink and smile, and sat herself upon it provocatively—"me. Safe enough?"

Slowly—very slowly—Azimander Godal smiled. And nodded.

He walked forward unhurriedly, undoing his sash. It fell away and took his overrobe with it, revealing a belted underrobe with its open seam down one leg rather than centered as the overrobe had been.

"May I?" Rharaundra breathed, reaching for the underrobe. Godal shrugged and spread his hands wide in invitation.

She took it.

"Leave your boots on," she whispered, as the bench creaked under their weight.

It was some time later that she turned around, giggling and slapping, beneath him, and Godal found himself on his knees over her, his back to the railing—and it was then that she rose up under him, with a catlike growl of triumph, to drive him upright, chest to chest.

"Farewell, Az," she whispered, a flash of triumph in her eyes—and plucked something up from behind him even as she shoved hard on his stomach, pushing herself back onto the bench—

And hurling him the other way.

Over backward, the railing she'd just unspiked falling away as his back struck it, leaving him to plunge head first, down into the dark and shadowed great hall beneath the balcony they'd been dallying on.

Azimander Godal bit his lip in sadness as the ring on his finger winked into life, slowing his fall to the gentlest of downward driftings.

"Just for a moment," he said softly, "I believed you, Rharaundra. I let myself hope."

Then his boots touched the tiles, and he cast another spell.

Up above him, on the balcony, the softly cursing Lady Yellander started to scream in terror. "Wizard! What're you *doing?* Get *out of my mind!*"

"Az," he told her. "Call me 'Az.' And I'm not going to turn you into a bat or a frog or a mewling idiot: I'm just reading what I can of your thoughts and memories."

Rharaundra sprang from the bench and fled into the darkness, a door banging in her wake.

The elderly war wizard stood motionless, eyes half-closed, walking among the dark-with-rage murk of her thoughts.

Then he broke off his spell and cast another in haste, to snap, "Vangerdahast! Hear me!"

Godal saw as well as felt Vangerdahast stop in mid-word in a conference, and turn his head. Their eyes met, across miles of intervening Cormyr, and in flashing thoughts the two conversed—a few breaths of lightning-swift, silent speech that ended when Vangerdahast snarled, "Tsantress—find the Lady Jalassa Crownsilver! Mindshroud her and bring her here to me at once. 'Ware her magic; she's been collecting baubles! Luthdal! To Greenmantle Hall, to serve Lady Amdranna Greenmantle in the same way. Murtrym! Do the same to Lady Imruae Muscalian, who may have all sorts of tricks to welcome you with. All of you, take any Wizards of War you deem needful with you; none of you are to go alone. Accept no delay nor authority to delay or gainsay you. Have those women here as fast as you can do it. You, too, Azimander!"

The link was severed so abruptly it left the elderly Godal reeling. He smiled, shook his head, and started up the stair, spinning a swift spell to find Rharaundra's mind.

She hadn't gone far.

The door was locked, and had furniture heaped against it, and some sort of magic waiting to sting him beyond that, too—so Azimander walked several rooms away, found the panel he was looking for, slid it open, and stole through the secret passages Rharaundra thought she alone knew about.

When he emerged in her bedchamber behind her and spoke

her name, she whirled around, real fear in her face, and whispered, "What are you going to do to me?"

"Take you to Lord Vangerdahast. What he sees in your mind will determine your fate."

Rharaundra trembled, her fists clenched so tight that blood dripped down along her knuckles from her own nails piercing her flesh. "Kill me, Azimander," she pleaded. "Kill me now, that I need not face him."

"No," he said. "Come with me quietly, Rharaundra, and I'll plead for mercy for you."

She peered at him. "You? You'll plead for me? You mean that?"

He nodded.

"Why?"

Azimander Godal stretched out a hand and stroked her cheek, very gently. She flinched, but then deliberately moved her head to let him touch her more easily. Her teeth were chattering.

"You may have done what you did to bring about my death," he murmured, "but you did it. You could have just shoved me through the railing right away, but you gave me pleasure first."

He put his arms around Rharaundra Yellander and hugged her. "And no one has done that for a very long time."

Her sobs started even as the light around them changed, and they were standing in a room crowded with war wizards, Vangerdahast among them.

The royal magician regarded them, smiled, and said in a dry voice, "That's certainly one way to fetch a noble lady of the realm. Remind me to try it some time."

Chapter 22
AND I AM SENT TO TAKE THEE

With aid of minstrel and dancing lasses three,
I forth ride past many a rock and tree
My high lord calls for to speak to thy body
And I am sent to take thee.

Tanter Hallweather, Bard of Elturel
And I Am Sent To Take Thee
minstrels' ballad, first popular in
The Year of the Lost Helm

The Two-Headed Lion was the fourth tavern Dauntless had trudged into thus far in search of these suddenly elusive Swords, and he was in less than the best of tempers.

Therefore, he loomed up over the table of laughing, chattering drinkers, flung back the cloak that had hidden his uniform, swept his helm up from under his arm and onto his head as if it were a weapon, and roared, "*You!* Swords of Eveningstar! In the name of the king, I arrest you!"

Agannor and Bey were up out of their seats in an instant, swords grating out, and Dauntless barked, "Nel-*vorr!*"

A dozen Purple Dragons or more appeared out of doorways all around the taproom. In the sudden, tense silence Swordcaptain Nelvorr snapped, "Sir!"

The Swords were surrounded.

"Agannor! Bey! Sheathe weapons!" Florin commanded, his voice sounding far more calm than he was. He set down his tankard and looked up at the cold-eyed ornrion. "We happen to hold a charter, sir—in the name of the king. Given us by the king himself less than a month gone, now. The king I know and obey. You I do not know. So who are you, and why seek you to arrest us?"

"I am Dauntless of the watch, and have been ordered by the king's Lady Lord of Arabel to bring you into her presence, for reasons that are her own. Will you come with us now willingly—or are Swords of Eveningstar going outlaw, and getting themselves hurt in the process?"

"As to that," Agannor growled, "we won't be the only ones getting hurt. The watch is little loved in most taverns, and here in Arabel even less. Were I you, ornrion, I'd go back to my barracks and think on a politer, safer way to get law-abiding adventurers to visit the palace. A written invitation, perhaps?"

Ornrion Dauntless let his lip curl, and Agannor's face darkened.

"Well?" he asked, looking at the silent tables all around. "What say, folk of Arabel? Do we let watch jacks swagger in and just take away this man or that, on what might be their personal whim? Or do we show them what broken pates feel like, and send them packing?"

A scar-faced man sitting not far away looked at him sourly, and said, "Man, I know not where ye come from, but in *this* city the watch is to be obeyed."

"Aye," a burly carter said, turning to face Agannor. "For the good of all."

"Obedience, not defiance," a gray-haired, worn-faced woman agreed. "The law and its fair keeping is all we have to keep all here from boiling up into swordfeuds—so we all help to keep it. Draw steel, you Swords, and we'll aid the watch against you, not raise hand against them. The Dragons are the hard hands we know; you could be anything."

"Well," Doust said, "that's clear enough. We obey these officers, quietly and without giving them trouble. Unless they're foolish enough to hamper the holy devotions of Semoor or myself—and I believe no Purple Dragon truly loyal to the Crown would do that."

"You believe rightly," Dauntless said, and pointed—once, twice, and thrice. "You," he said to Florin, "seem to lead, or at least give commands to some of your fellows. You will come with me." He turned his head to Pennae. "You, we've had reports of, so you'll come with me and *not* slip away, or your companions will pay for it." He looked to Jhessail. "And you've been reported to cast spells, wherefore the war wizards desire to speak with you—or should do. You also will come with us, and work no magic on the way or in the presence of the lady lord."

"Our charter—" Florin began, but Dauntless raised a quelling hand.

"I know what Crown charters usually say," he growled. "You were about to say that no such restrictions are placed on this lady mage?" When Florin nodded, Dauntless added, "I'm asking her to agree to this behavior, here and now. If she refuses, she'll be brought into the presence of the lady lord bound, gagged, hobbled, and blindfolded."

Semoor stirred, growing a smile—but Martess lifted her boot deftly under the table, and in sudden, gasping agony the novice of Lathander bent his head and said nothing.

"I agree to this," Florin said, "but can speak only for myself. Pennae? Jhessail?"

"I agree to this," both women echoed, finished their drinks, and rose. Around them, chatter started up again, and the air of confrontation faded away with the silence that had heralded it.

The Purple Dragons converged warily on Florin, Pennae, and Jhessail as the three walked with Dauntless to the door. Florin nodded to the tavernmaster as if he were royalty rather than under arrest, plucked a gold coin from his purse, and tossed it to the man.

At his next stride, his gaze happened to fall on a table along the wall beside the door, where a weary-looking woman—a shopkeeper, by her garb—was drinking alone. Their eyes met, and Florin blinked.

He'd have sworn he'd never laid eyes on this woman before, yet her face looked somehow familiar.

No, not her face—her *eyes*. Dark blue, wise, knowing. Yes, he'd looked into those eyes before! Recently, of course . . . in a tavern?

Dark blue depths . . . that flared silver, just for an instant—

An instant that left Florin remembering nothing of them at all, and trudging out of the Lion with Dragons before him and behind him.

"We can't find Greenmantle," a young war wizard snapped, striding past. "She seems to have disappeared completely."

Laspeera sighed, took Godal by the shoulder, and steered him through a door into a robing room. "Put something on, and let's talk."

The tall, aging war wizard nodded and went to the row of wardrobes. Laspeera brewed thornapple tea, and had a steaming goblet of it waiting for him when he sat down with her, smiled, and waved at her to begin.

Laspeera hesitated not a moment. "Why didn't you go into Lady Yellander's mind when she first made her advances? 'Twasn't as if she usually treated you so familiarly. You must have been suspicious."

"Lady," Godal said, inhaling the scent of the too-hot tea, "*I* have scruples."

"Fiddlebats, Az! You went into her head fast enough, later!"

Godal cupped his hands around his goblet, looked into its depths, and said, "I didn't *want* to know if she had . . . dark motives. After all these years, just once, I wanted it to be real."

"Oh, Azimander," Laspeera said softly, leaning across the table to put her arms around him.

Godal set his tea down with a trembling hand and hugged her tightly. After a breath or two, he started to cry.

"By the blood of Alathan," Semoor cursed, giving Martess a dark look for her kick to his cods, "*now* what?"

"I'd like to feed that ornrion his own sw—"

"Agannor," Islif said in a low voice that rang with hard steel to match the glare she gave him, "still thy tongue. Right now. There could be watch spies sitting at every table around us. Just belt up—and listen."

"We're listening," Bey said, elbowing his friend.

Agannor scowled but nodded, as Islif leaned forward over the table and said, "I'd like the two of you to remain here in the Lion to meet Florin, Pennae, and Jhessail when they return. Depart for our rooms at Rhalseer's if they don't appear by closing time, or if any sort of brawl erupts or anyone tries to make trouble for you—and for the love of all the watching gods, *don't* get drunk and don't pick any fights yourselves!"

Bey nodded, and Islif reached across the table to take Agannor's hand and mutter, eyes fixed on his, "Agannor, you have a temper. Conquer it, and ride it well, for all our sakes. Our healing quaffs are back at Rhalseer's, remember?"

With a sigh, she added, "Martess, I hate to ask this of you, but I need one of us, right now, to get out there and trail the watch to see where they take Florin, Pennae, and Jhessail, and you're the least noticeable of us all—"

"You needn't ask," Martess said, springing to her feet, "for I'm glad to do so. I'm gone!"

And she was, ducking and darting among the tables. "All of you," Islif said, "watch to see if anyone follows her out of here. Doust and Semoor, come with me. Our first task will be to stop anyone who follows Martess, and our second to find new lodgings. I think our time at Rhalseer's is just about over."

"I think you're right about that," Doust agreed.

"And I," Agannor said darkly, "am *afraid* you're right about that."

Horaundoon smiled down at his scrying orb.

"Well, now," he said, setting down what little was left of his haunch of roast boar, "Islif certainly seems like a proper war commander. I wonder if she's been the real leader—her and bright little Pennae—all along?"

The hargaunt's trill told him *it* certainly thought so.

He wondered briefly how much hargaunts learned of humans, then shrugged, gnawed one last time on his boar, washed his hands in the bowl of petal-water, and hurried from his spellchamber.

A floor down, he rapped on the door of the rooms shared by two busy and popular lowcoin lasses. Kestra and Taeriana were rather slow to open their door, for neither of them was alone, and a hurried customer is a poorly paying customer—but when they did open to him, the men they'd been entertaining departing by the door that opened out onto the end stairs, he smiled into their eyes, mastered their minds easily with the magic he had ready—and sent them into a whirlwind of donning cloaks and boots over their daring silks, and hurrying out to the Lion.

The robing room door opened. Arms still around Godal, Laspeera looked up to see who was there. Just for a moment, she looked astonished.

Then she glared.

Lady Rharaundra Yellander, an ill-fitting war wizard robe draped around her shoulders, was closing the door behind her.

Laspeera said not a word, letting her silent glare speak for her.

The noblewoman stared back at her, looking miserable, and said quaveringly, "Vangerdahast is going to do something to my mind."

"And so?"

"And so," Lady Yellander whispered fiercely, stepping forward, "before I forget everything of who I am and what I've done, there's something I find I want to do, first. Vangerdahast has given me permission—if Azimander will."

She reached out her hand almost beseechingly to Azimander Godal.

Slowly uncurling from where he was huddled against Laspeera, the old war wizard looked up at her. Then, slowly, he reached out and took the noblewoman's hand.

She drew him to his feet and into her embrace, asking Laspeera, "Do you have a bed anywhere around here? Or a table someone's not using?"

Lord Maniol Crownsilver stared, blinked, and stared again.

However, the purposefully striding dark-robed figures didn't go away. In fact, they came swiftly closer, hurrying down his grandest passage straight at him.

"What by all the *Nine Hells*—?" he snarled, reaching for the intricate hilt of his ornamented sword.

There came no reply, though the somber gaze of the good-looking woman who walked at their fore measured him. Coolly.

"Just who by the Dungfaced Dragon do you think *you* are," he addressed her, "bursting into my home like this?"

The intruders slowed not a whit, and an infuriated Lord Crownsilver spread his hands and awakened all the rings, bracers, and wristlets on them to glowing, menacing life. "Come one step nearer—!"

The woman gestured, and the air around Maniol Crownsilver seemed to freeze—an icy grip that settled around his heart and throat and left him gasping.

"If by 'Dungfaced Dragon' you mean the king," she said coldly, "you can unsay those words right now, Lord Crownsilver. We are Wizards of War, here on Crown business. If your wife hadn't spell-guarded her chambers—and when did she master such Art without a word to anyone, Lord?—we'd have teleported there and you'd never even have seen us. I am Tsantress of the Wizards of War, 'bursting into' here, as you put it, on the explicit orders of the Lord Vangerdahast, to apprehend a traitor to the realm."

"A trait—*Jalassa?*" Maniol Crownsilver was incredulous, and looked it.

In that moment, Tsantress believed he knew nothing at all about his wife's dark doings, but allowed herself no shred of pity. He was noble, and the head of one of the oldest, proudest houses of Cormyr to boot; he would bluster—

He did. "And you think you can just march in here, like the rutting king himself, and—"

"Treason, Lord Crownsilver," Tsantress said sweetly, making a gesture that turned the icy force holding Maniol Crownsilver so cold he couldn't breathe. "That's what those words you've just uttered are: clear treason. Spoken before many witnesses, too. And the penalty for treason is . . ."

She waved her hand, and her magic was gone, dropping Lord Crownsilver with a crash onto his face, breathless and barely able to moan. *Death.*

The war wizards hurried past him, and up the grand stair.

He was vaguely aware of one war wizard calling, "It's this one, here!" and another saying, "Stand ye back, all!"

Then there came a loud crackling, laced with cries of alarm—and something that looked like a leisurely, many-forked bolt of lightning spat out from the floor above, writhing and spitting across the empty air high above him almost hesitantly.

Maniol Crownsilver was on his feet before it faded, staggering up the stairs on suddenly weak legs, hauling on the rails with his hands to drag himself up the long flight as more bolts erupted from the floor above.

" 'Tis spellguarded, all right!" a war wizard shouted, reeling back against the balustrade beside the stairs.

"Enough attempts to grandly impress," the voice of Tsantress rose, firm and calm. "Cast together, at my command, thus . . ."

As Lord Crownsilver reached the top of the stair, white light flared blinding-bright, war wizards cried out in dismay—and the radiance faded and the door of his wife's retiring room sighed open, tiny cracklings and glows playing about its edges.

The room beyond was as femininely opulent as he remembered—save for the blackened area at its heart, where forlorn, still-smoldering ashes outlined the shape of a sprawled, spreadeagled human body.

A stocky young war wizard cast a swift spell, waited with arms spread and eyes closed, then reported, "No one. No one alive."

Silently the other war wizards stepped into the room, spreading out to either side of it to form an arc along the wall, rather than advancing. At its center, Tsantress turned to the unmoving mage. "Lorbryn?"

He shook his head, hands still splayed out into the air. "No one

on this level, clear out to . . . there's a turret, that way, that's shielded
against me."

"End it," was the curt response.

"What're you saying?" Lord Crownsilver demanded, as the man
opened his eyes and brought his arms down. "Jalassa? Where's my
Jalassa?"

Tsantress turned to face him, face unreadable. "Stay here," she
said. "Come no closer to yon chamber." She looked meaningfully at
Lorbryn, who stepped in front of Crownsilver, blocking his way on.

Over Lorbryn's shoulder, the lord saw Tsantress turn back into the
room and murmur orders. Arms lifted in castings, the air glowed an
eerie blue-white, and then . . . something ruby, orange, and sudden
roared up from the ashes, whirling around the room in a shrieking,
scouring cloud that left war wizards staggering or on their knees,
clutching their eyes or covering their noses and mouths with desperate
hands.

Then, quite suddenly, the roaring and roiling were gone, and
Maniol Crownsilver was peering into a room that seemed to be full of
dust—and dust-caked, coughing and choking war wizards, moving
dazedly through the drifting clouds.

"Tsantress?" Lorbryn called urgently, over his shoulder. "Art
well?"

"I've been better," came the glum reply, from a soot-faced, barely
recognizable apparition that came out of the dust to stand with him.
"That was a trap-spell left on her ashes, to mix them with our own
sweat and hairs, and make necromantic interrogation impossible."

Maniol gaped at her. "Necro . . . ? My Jalassa—is she—?"

Tsantress nodded.

"Nooo! No, she *can't be!* My—my—not my Jalassa!"

Tsantress thrust Lorbryn gently aside and stepped forward, a
soot-caked scarecrow, to put comforting arms around the sagging,
weeping lord.

"Lord Crownsilver," she said, "I'm afraid Lady Crownsilver is no
more."

"Jalassa! *Jalassa!"* the man in her arms sobbed, clawing at her, trying to get past her. War wizards coming out of the room stared at him grimly.

"Bring her back!" Lord Crownsilver howled at them. "You've magic, you can do that! *Bring her back to me!*"

Tsantress shook her head sadly, her blackened face almost touching his.

"Please," he sobbed, shaking her. *"Please!"*

"Lord Crownsilver, your wife was working with an enemy of the Crown of Cormyr. That traitor is unknown to us, thus far—but that traitor murdered Lady Crownsilver to keep us or anyone else learning of them from her. Murdered her, spellguarded the room her ashes were in against scrying and translocations, spell-sealed its doors, and left trap magics waiting for anyone who came to investigate. Take whatever comfort you can from knowing the Wizards of War will leave no hint or trail unfollowed until that traitor is found—and destroyed."

Maniol Crownsilver threw back his head to gulp in air, still crying, and after a few shuddering breaths managed to gasp, "No comfort at all!"

Tsantress kept firm arms around him. "Would you like to accompany us to the palace? Or have some of us remain here with you? You should not be alone—"

"No," Crownsilver sobbed, "I don't want war wizards standing around me speaking empty soothings. I want them at my side, casting every spell they have, to find me my daughter!"

"Your daughter?"

"My Narantha! I *must* find her. She's all I have left of my beautiful Jalassa, now."

Each group of guards searched the three with stony disregard for modesty or gender, removing all the weapons they could find. It took a long time to reach the innermost chamber.

"State your name, each of you," Dauntless growled then. After Florin, Jhessail, and Pennae had done that, he nodded, raised his hand to indicate the unsmiling woman in worn, unadorned battle-leathers standing behind the map-strewn table, and said, "Swords of Eveningstar, this is Myrmeen Lhal, the Lady Lord of Arabel. In this city, her word is law—and you stand here at her pleasure."

Florin bowed low. "Lady, we are loyal to the king. What would you, with us?"

The lady lord said, "Produce your charter. Now."

Florin bowed again, stepped back, and turned his back. Dauntless was at his side in a moment, sword half-drawn, to watch suspiciously as Florin unbuckled his codpiece and flipped it up, to undo a lacing inside, and pluck forth—a much-folded, tiny square of parchment.

Jhessail covered her eyes in disgust, but Pennae, Dauntless, and the guards behind Dauntless were all grinning as Florin tucked his codpiece back into place, spun around, and triumphantly unfolded the royal charter.

Myrmeen Lhal's wry amusement gleamed in her eyes, but had completely failed to reach the rest of her face. She took the parchment from Florin almost reverently, read it, and handed it back.

"Your charter is in order," she announced, "wherefore 'tis my duty only to give you fair warning. Swords, your activities within Arabel's walls haven't gone unnoticed, and further thievery *will not* go unpunished. Pennae, you could very easily find yourself imprisoned for a long time, with some of your nimble fingers broken so they'll heal with rather less deftness than they've displayed thus far."

She started to stroll, hands clasped behind her back like a swordcaptain glowering at disobedient novices, and added sharply, "Cormyr needs gallant adventurers—but Arabel has no room for villainous rogues, miscreants brutish in words and deeds, and impudent, cheating, lying, thieving outlaws. Your charter gives you no right to take coins by force from others, nor swindle them to support lazy, sneaking, or disloyal lives within our walls."

Florin's eyelids flickered. He'd heard such words before, from . . . ah, yes. He smiled. Dauntless tensed.

"Many folk do little but cower and try to keep warm in winter, sewing or whittling or honing blades," Myrmeen added. "I will understand if you do little while the snows howl and deepen. I will understand far too well if you grow restless, and decide a little danger—lawless danger—is a good way to pass the cold days. It is my hope never to have cause to suspect you of anything, and to be able to smile when I hear of the Swords of Eveningstar, recalling heroism and gallantry. It would please me very much if you did not dash my hopes and disappoint me."

She stopped strolling. "Have you anything you wish to say to me?"

"Lady Lord," Pennae said, "you can depend on me, and us all." Jhessail nodded.

Florin raised a hand. "May I request a private audience with you, Lady Lord? Now?"

"You may. All save Falconhand, withdraw to the outermost guard-post. Return their weapons to them."

Dauntless and several other guards frowned, and the ornrion was bold enough to ask, "Lady Lord, is this wise? This man—"

"Heard the orders I gave as well as you did," Myrmeen Lhal said. "And probably expects you to obey them as much as I do."

Dauntless dropped his gaze to his boots, mumbled an apology, and turned and gruffly began to shoo everyone out.

"Horses of the Wargod," Agannor growled, "but I mislike the smell of this! What if they never come back? The lady lord could clap them all in irons in her deepest cell and just forget all about them! Leaving us . . ."

His voice trailed away as a slender, large-eyed, pretty lass whose skirts seemed slit right up to her armpits sat gently in his lap and murmured, "You were *so* brave, both of you! Standing up to the Dragons like that, without even drawing blade! I'm Taeriana."

"Uh, well met, Taer—"

"And I'm Kestra," a slightly shorter and plumper version of Taeriana said breathlessly to Bey, deftly depositing herself in his lap.

"Ladylasses," Bey said, "we must watch for our friends, and haven't coin to spare for—"

"We understand," Kestra said, licking his stubbled jaw. "We don't want coin—not this time, at least—"

"And feel you deserve a reward," Taeriana purred. "How about just a few moments together, behind yon curtain? Aviathus keeps yon for us, clean and safe; he'll come if your friends return." The wandering tip of her forefinger dipped inside Agannor's jerkin, heading for his left nipple, as she added, "Like us, he admires you for standing up to the Dragons. So peacefully . . . but, ohhh, so *sternly!*"

Agannor and Bey exchanged glances and shrugged.

"I like to look behind curtains," Agannor said, clapping a wary hand to sword hilt.

The hearty din of the Lion continued unabated as the four rose together—the tavernmaster bustling up with a nod and smile to cast his apron over the table to signify that it was still claimed—and made for the rear of the taproom.

The two Swords were almost surprised to discover no men waiting for them with knives or clubs, but a low-lanterned alcove with two well-padded cots.

Kestra and Taeriana were affectionate, eager, and had their tongues in the ears of Agannor and Bey within a breath of sitting down on the cots together.

A breath later, both Swords stiffened as cold and slimy mind-worms rode those warmly darting tongues into their heads.

Then, of course, Horaundoon's spell hit them.

+ + ✴ + +

Lord Maniol Crownsilver stared blearily at the ceiling for a long time before his mazed mind told him that it *was* a ceiling, and was in fact his own.

Faces were bending over him. Drawn and sour faces. Holy men.

"You're healed, Lord," one told him. "We'll leave you now."

The priests filed out, leaving Maniol blinking up from his bed at other, frowning men who'd been standing behind them: war wizards, dark and terrible still in his mind, their cold voices thrusting like sharp blades into his innermost secrets, his private reveries . . .

He turned his face away, knowing hatred and fear were all over it. After the lass who'd led them had departed, these mages had hurled their spells into his mind, uncaring of his grief, hounding him from misery into senselessness.

Misbegotten goat-whoring bastards.

"So just what was it you wanted to say to me, young forester?" Myrmeen Lhal gave Florin a smile, and indicated an empty chair at her table.

Florin remained standing, suddenly hesitant. What was he *doing* here? This woman was of the king's lords, a hardened, keen-witted veter—

Something warm *smiled* inside his head, and he let that smile take over his lips.

"Lady Lord," he heard himself saying, "until this day I'd never met a woman I could admire more than . . ."

Lorbryn looked down at the shattered nobleman and traded sighs with Jalander Mallowglar. Lord Crownsilver was guilty of nothing more than being an arrogant fool and boor—and he'd loved his wife far more than Cormyr had thought he did.

"Mages," the man said, rolling over to fix them with burning eyes that trailed tears down his unlovely face, "help me find my jewel—my Narantha! Please!"

Well, why not?

Lorbryn leaned forward. "We've been watching over her closely for some time, Lord. She's just arrived at the house of the Creths, in Arabel."

Crownsilver shook his head, bewildered. "Whatever's she doing *there?*"

Jalander gazed across the room at the Crownsilver arms, gaudily emblazoned on a tapestry, and told them, "We believe she's seeking a husband, Lord. She's been visiting many young noble lords, all across the realm."

"What?" Maniol sat up, slack-jawed in horror. "Doesn't she know *I'll* pick her husband? Uh—*hem*—myself and the lad's father, of course!"

"Of course," Lorbryn echoed, unable to entirely keep contempt out of his voice.

"Well," Lord Maniol snarled, not noticing, "at least she's over that foolishness of wedding Falconfoot, or whatever he is, of the Swords of Eveningstar breaknecks! Where are *they*, anyway?"

"In Arabel," Jalander said, with some satisfaction.

"*What?* I *must* get to her!" Lord Crownsilver's howl was comical. "And *you,*" he spat, scrambling up off the bed and wagging an imperious finger at the wizards, "must arrest those Swords at once!"

Wizard of War Tathanter Doarmond, who'd been listening from the doorway, announced grandly, "We'll send her to you, Lord Crownsilver. I trust you'll be pleased to learn the Swords are under arrest right now."

"Gods be thanked!" Maniol Crownsilver exulted, reaching his decanter-adorned sideboard and filling a goblet.

"To the watching gods!" he made offering, holding the goblet on high. Slamming the flaming fortified wine down on the sideboard, Crownsilver caught up its decanter again, grinned fiercely at the dark-robed wizards—and drained the entire vessel in one long quaff.

Reeling back to the bed, he sank down onto it, still clutching the empty decanter, called out, "Victory at last!"—and promptly sank back into insensibility.

The war wizards looked down at him.

"*Nobles,*" Jalander said in disgust. "And they think *we're* unfit to be anywhere near the service of Cormyr!"

Lorbryn nodded. "Some of us are. But at least we know it."

"*Out*, clumsy gallant," Myrmeen Lhal said with a smirk. "I'm not one of your husband-hunting Esparran lasses. Take your good looks and come-kiss-me smile elsewhere. *Lad.*"

Florin stared at her, his hopes of winning some favor and leeway for the Swords falling in shards around him. He felt—stunned.

What had gotten *into* him? Of *course* she thought of him as a boy who had nothing to offer her but smilingly insulting effrontery . . .

"I'm sorry," he whispered, staring at her in horror. "I'm so sorry. I've insulted you beyond all honor, and—gods, Lady Lord, I'm sorry." He sank to his knees, despairing. What had he—

Firm fingers took hold of his ear and pulled, hauling him painfully—and in great startlement—up to his feet, to stagger nose-to-nose with the Lady Lord of Arabel. Who was smiling almost fondly.

"Flog yourself not," she told him. "You were, at least, flattering and entertaining. Idiot." She kissed the tip of his nose, then turned him around by his ear. "Now, *out!*"

Chapter 23
SWORDS-OUT AND SHOUTING

Oh, so 'tis time for the old swords-out and shouting, hey? How many do I get to kill this time?

The character Veldin the Valiant,
the third act of Old King Dragon
A play by Thelva "the Maid" Dunstel
published in the Year of the Sword and Stars

Horaundoon scowled into his scrying orb. A tight-lipped, crestfallen Florin striding through the streets with the two loudest Sword wenches at his shoulders, heading back to the Lion. There—and there—and there, too—behind them, the watch spies, following. Last, the Martess lass, following the watch agents.

Enough to make this Zhentarim smirk, yon little parade. If he hadn't been so hrasted annoyed, that is. The lad had seemed to throw off much of the influence of the mindworm, even before Myrmeen Lhal had spurned him! But how?

Florin peered around the busy taproom, fire rising in his eyes. There was the table, right enough, with the tavernmaster's apron spread across it to—

"Tavernmaster!" he called, letting some of his anger show. "Where are my friends, who were here with us? Did the watch—?"

"Nay, lord," Aviathus assured him, bustling up to them. "The way of it is: they conferred, heads together—your friends, I mean—then the hard-faced woman—ah, forgive me . . ."

"Forgiven," Pennae said. "Out with it, man!"

"I, uh, yes, well, she led them out, all but the two war-swords, who sat right here for a time—long enough to empty a talljack of firewine between them, and eat a skewer of roast bustard each, too—ere they went behind yon curtains, and out, with Kestra and Taeriana."

"Who," Jhessail asked flatly, "are Kestra and Taeriana? As if I can't guess."

The tavernmaster's head bobbed eagerly. "Coinlasses, right enough, and the best and cleanest in the business, let me tell you! Six seasons a-working here, and never a—"

"Out *where?*" Pennae snapped.

"Ah. Well, 'tis my way of speech more than truly 'outside,' really," Aviathus said hastily, pointing at the ceiling. "Faster than saying 'up the back stairs.' "

Jhessail rolled her eyes, Florin growled, and Martess and Pennae both gave Florin "See? Someone else besides you" looks.

Pennae told Florin firmly, *"We'll* go and look for them. A woman looking gives less offense, but can deliver more scorn to shame them back down here, when they're found."

Horaundoon gasped, reeled, and shuddered, sweat streaming down his face and dripping off his chin. Four minds, now, two of them strong-willed and wayward . . .

Riches, he promised Agannor and Bey, showing them chests of gleaming coins and coffers a-glitter with gems. *Women*, splashing through their minds ivory curves, dark and mysterious eyes, alluring smiles, and languid beckonings. *Power*, and each of the two Swords saw himself striding, a great-cloak streaming from his shoulders, through palatial rooms, hurling open doors by which servants hastily knelt, and emerging into courtyards where white stallions in gold-plate-bedecked harness awaited, and riding forth through portcullis after arch after tunnel, out of a soaring castle, as folk thundered acclaim from balconies . . .

All theirs, the sweating Zhentarim mind-promised, if they but willingly served him.

More splendors he conjured, and thrust upon their minds, burying them in banners and glittering courts, impossibly beautiful

courtesans writhing in welcome on beds made of thousands of coins
. . . and he saw their mistrust, reluctance, and wary fears crumbling
and fading, loose black earth swept away before his cleansing flood,
an onslaught that laid bare eagerness, leaping up bright with desire,
daring hope—

Agannor, he mind-spoke. *Bey. Are you with me?*

Their roars of assent were like raging flame in his mind, searing
him even as his delight grew, sending the hargaunt into wild, clashing chimings of alarm and excitement.

Horaundoon shuddered in pain, slumped over a table with his
fingers trying to pierce its edge as if they were claws, and smiled.

*Then show me your loyalty. Step onto the great way to glory I've
shown you. Slay these two wenches—who are in truth foul witches seeking to enslave you!*

He spun an illusion of leering fanged fiend-faces, revealed dark
and gloating behind the slipping masks of Kestra's and Taeriana's
ardent smiles—and was still strengthening and improving that imag-
ining when Agannor snarled, snatched his dagger out of its sheath,
and drove it hilt-deep up under Taeriana's chin.

Pennae frowned. The bedchambers in the Lion stood dark
and empty, doors ajar, awaiting brief use by coinlasses and their
clients.

From the landing where she stood, the stair went on up to the roof,
and a narrow, gloomy hall stretched away from her a surprisingly long
way. Martess was already going from door to door on the left.

Pennae sighed, shrugged, and started down the doors on the
right.

In the other bed, Bey backhanded Kestra so viciously across her
face that her head boomed against the wall. Dazed, she had time
neither to draw breath nor scream before she was choking on her own
blood, slumped over the edge of the bed, dripping and dying . . .

The partition walls between the Lion's bedchambers were but a single panel thick, and Agannor's snarl had been unmistakable.

Pressed against the wall in one corner of the dark and vacant next room, Martess listened, shuddering.

Plink. Plosh. Plink. Life-blood, dripping. They'd just killed the two coinlasses.

Mother Mystra, preserve us all . . .

Agannor blinked at Bey. "The master—he's gone from my mind!"

"Mine too," Bey muttered, "but I can still feel his regard. He's watching us. Seeing if we stand strong, I think."

He rose from the bed, looking down at what he'd done. "Naed," he added, turning to the washstand and plunging his bloody dagger and hand into the full ewer of water. "We can't let the watch see *this*."

Agannor nodded and tugged forth his own fang, looking away as Taeriana's jaw fell open in its wake, sliced tongue dangling.

Wincing, he went to wash up, too, glancing at the closed but bolt-less door. "What'll we—?"

"The roof," Bey said. "That stair went on up. Bundle them into the bed-linens, get them up there for the carrion crows, and use the wash-water to get rid of the blood. We'll be long gone from Arabel before rats start gnawing off fingers and dropping them around for folks to find."

Agannor nodded. "The master should be pleased. Gods, such *power* he has! None of this fighting orcs for a few coppers, winter after winter, while Purple Dragons give us suspicious glares. We're going to be *lords!*" He grinned at Bey. "Any regrets?"

"Having to break from the Swords this swift and sharp. I'd sort of hoped to bed our own Flamehair, sooner or later."

"Gods, yes, little Jhessail—though in truth I'd want Pennae. Now, *there's* a wench!"

"Aye, if she was safely tied down so you'd live through it," Bey said wryly. "Perhaps the master . . ."

Agannor grinned. "If we plead prettily enough?"

Pressed against the cold, hard panel, Martess shuddered. Dared she stay still and silent, to keep safe? Or run like nightwind out of here, to warn Pennae before they came for her?

If they caught her, 'twould be *her* blood dripping onto the floor—and all her friends would be doomed. These two would blame the Swords for any killings they did, falsely reporting to the watch or arranging matters so folk would think the Swords of Eveningstar were guilty . . .

My head full of spells, yet I'm so helpless.

"There's another mind very close to them," Horaundoon muttered, frowning. Surely a mere coinlass can't be under magic to bring her back from a slaying?

Unless she's not a mere coinlass . . .

A Harper? One of Vangerdahast's spies?

Ignoring the hargaunt's curious queries—chiming so rapid and shrill it sounded like a tree-cat chittering—Horaundoon closed his eyes and felt for that errant mind with his spell, putting a hand on the scrying orb to call on its energies, to make his seeking more powerful . . .

There! In the chamber next door, a mind dark with fear and despair, the glows of feeble spells riding it—one of the Sword magelings!

Charging into her mind would burn his own; even those feeble spells would burst, blaze, and sear, wrecking her mind but doing him harm he neither wanted nor dared suffer.

Horaundoon snarled and thrust himself back at the two handy mindworms, bringing Agannor and Bey out of their room in a snarling rush. Sometimes a sharp sword is enough.

Martess heard the thunder of boots through the wall and thrust herself up and away from it, feeling sick. Against those two she was nothing, less than nothing. She must—

The door behind her burst open. She whirled, gasping in alarm—and managed the beginnings of a shriek before Agannor's sword, his teeth furiously bared behind it, burst into and through her, plunging like ice, driving her stumbling back.

Bey Freemantle, wearing the same wide and friendly grin on his face she'd seen so many times before, rushed in from the side.

His steel slid into her like fire, so hot against the cold of Agannor's blade that Martess couldn't breathe.

So the spell she might have lashed them with, that she not perish without at least dealing pain to her slayers, faded unleashed as Martess Ilmra sank down into soft and endless darkness, fire and ice fading around her.

Pennae knew what that sliced-off scream meant.

Martess was dead or dying—and if the gods willed it, she'd see that Agannor and Bey followed her!

She came out of the room she'd been peering into like a dark cloak hurled along in a gale, cursing herself for leaving her sleep-dosed daggers back at their rooms this night. Well, she'd just have to make this a little more *personal*.

She was still four doors away from the one Agannor and Bey were ducking out of, running hard with daggers raised to hurl, when something like a fog with fists descended on her mind.

Rolling and shaking Pennae like thunder, it struck her head from the inside, thrice and a dozen times and more, sending her stumbling.

Agannor grinned from ear to ear, a light like madness in his eyes, and raised his sword. "Yes, my beauty!" he hissed. "Come and play!"

His blade lashed out, flashing.

Fetching up bruisingly against the wall as the floor seemed to heave under her, Pennae clenched her teeth and fought for balance. Bey's sword was coming at her, too—

"Alura Durshavin, you're one *strong* little tigress," Horaundoon of the Zhentarim murmured, hurling his mind against hers again.

The scrying orb in front of him was flickering, enfeebled by his drainings. Yet even as it drifted lower, he could see in its darkening depths the thief fling herself into a blackflip, as supple as any eel he'd ever watched eluding the nets of eel-cooks back in the keep.

His two warriors thrust and hacked at her again—and both missed. Again.

Dazedly, Pennae got herself turned around and fled.

Horaundoon bore down hard. If she got to the taproom, or managed to shout an alarm down the stairwell, he'd likely soon lose both of his Sword minions. She was worth ten of them, but she was fighting him even now; taming her would take all his power and attention, day and night.

Hah! Horaundoon thrust into, shook, and tumbled Pennae's mind, watching her moan and stagger. Bey was right behind her, now, blade raised to—

In the orb he watched the thief thrust herself back and down, rolling into an erupting, kicking ball that had Bey toppling over her, and her spinning on one hip to scissor her legs around the ankles of the onrushing Agannor, sending him helplessly crashing down onto Bey, sword stabbing air and shouting in fear.

Pennae sprang over them, or tried to, but the battering, snarling weight of Horaundoon in her mind drove her aside into a wall. She fell hard atop the two tangled, vigorously cursing warriors, rolling and kicking.

Agannor grabbed at her, tearing her leathers, and she sliced and stabbed viciously, managing to catch his palm briefly with the point of her blade. He shrieked in pain and snatched his hand back and away—just as Bey's sword thrust across her stomach, slicing leather with swift ease.

Pennae twisted, heaved, and managed to win free, her sprint down the hall becoming a whimpering crawl that had her clawing her way to her feet, leaning hard on a wall to keep from falling. Staggering on, she slid along it, trailing smears of blood, as Horaundoon hammered in her head and Bey came pounding along the hall behind her, Agannor right behind him.

The stair had a rail, and Pennae caught hold of it just in time, swinging herself up and aside as a sword bit deep into the floorboards she'd just been standing on.

Bey hacked at her again, and again, hewing air hard enough to smash ribs and limbs if ever he hit leather-clad thief.

Pennae ducked, kicked his knee hard to send him staggering back into Agannor, and raced up the stairs, hoping the trapdoor at its top wasn't locked.

The gods were with her. A simple through-two-straps longbar kept anyone lifting it open from above. Pennae plucked out the metal bar and smashed aside Bey's seeking blade with it, leaving the sword ringing like a bell and him shouting at the eerie pain of a numbed sword hand.

And Pennae was across the roof, the slammed trapdoor bouncing in her wake, and running hard for the next roof along. 'Twas the first of seven in the block, if she remembered rightly, and at least two of those shops had wooden stairs descending from their rooftops to balconies.

She jumped, landed awry and bruisingly as the foe in her mind slammed into her wits, hard and sudden, just as she was launching herself, and staggered sidewise until she fetched up against a crumbling fieldstone chimney, brittle old birdnests crunching underfoot. Pennae winced; if these head-splitting, nigh-blinding attacks continued, she'd best get down to street level, where at least she couldn't die just from falling over!

Agannor shouted, behind her, and Pennae hissed a curse and ran on, heading for the next roof—and the next stab inside her head.

Horaundoon frowned. Out in the open, the wench would swiftly best his two lumbering minions. He ached to finish her, to burst her mind like a new-laid egg flung against a wall . . . but—whiteblood!—he'd been trying to do just that for how long now? And still she fought him.

No, 'twas time to leave off trying to fry her wits, and cast a spell that would send his orders thundering into the minds of a score of Zhent agents all over Arabel. Telling them it was high time to load their crossbows and go Pennae-hunting.

In the wake of the shrieks, shouts, and the ringing clang of swords, there came the thunder of boots on the stairs, and the booming thunder of something heavy falling, twice.

"I'm going up there!" Florin snarled, struggling in the grip of the four grim, plainly clad Purple Dragons who'd risen from a nearby table to drag him down when he'd first drawn sword.

"*No*, outlander," one of them snarled into his face, as they twisted and strained together in a sweating, grunting heap on the floor, "you'll *not*. Our orders—"

"Unhand Florin Falconhand, and *get back, all of you!*" Jhessail shouted, her high, usually gentle voice ringing out across the taproom of the Lion and bringing down a hush of tensely staring drinkers. There was a dagger in her hand, and bright flames raced up and down its blade. "Or I'll cast the strongest spell I know, and bring down this tavern on us all!"

The attacks—thank Mask!—had ceased, but her head still throbbed as if she'd taken a solid mace-blow. Worse than that, other men seemed to have joined the chase: men with swords and daggers and no hesitation in using them. So where were the lady lord's oh-so-efficient, thrice-accursed watch *now?*

Agannor was stumbling along well in her wake, obviously winded, and Bey was ever further back, but—*naed!*

This unwashed, stubble-faced man, stepping out of an alley right in front of Pennae, had a cocked and loaded crossbow in his hands. It cracked even as she flung herself aside and brought her daggers up.

A moment later, she was wringing a numbed and bleeding hand, the dagger that had been in it was gone, and she heard the crossbow bolt bouncing and splintering on cobbles far behind her left shoulder.

"Naed! Hrasting *bitch,*" the man cursed, staring at her over his fired crossbow. "How the *tluin* did you step aside from *that?*"

Pennae wasted no breath in a reply, but hurried toward him, hefting the dagger in her right hand. The man cursed again and flung the crossbow full in her face to buy himself time to drag out a rather rusty short sword.

Pennae launched herself up the wall, caught hold of a stone windowsill under a crudely boarded-over back window, and swung hard, boots first, catching the man in the throat at about the same time as he got his sword free.

He went over in a heap, arms twitching in spasms, and Pennae landed hard, heels first, on his ribs.

Just who was chasing her now was—

A crossbow bolt sang past her ear with the high, thrumming whine that meant it had only *just* missed her, and Pennae snarled and darted into the alley.

A moment later, she came out of it again—sobbing as she flew helplessly back through the air, snatched off her feet and spinning in midair, with a crossbow bolt right through her shattered shoulder.

Myrmeen Lhal looked up from the stack of decrees and dispensations she was rather wearily signing. That was the *third* alarm gong.

Three patrols called in as reinforcements? What by all the Nine Hells was going on?

Boots thundered in the passage, and she called out, "Asgarth? What's all the tumult?"

"Those stlar—ahem, those Swords adventurers! Men're firing crossbows all over Palaceside!" the lionar shouted, adding in his next breath, "Beg pardon, Lady Lord!"

"Granted," Myrmeen called, deep and loud. And shook her head in wry amusement. She'd expected the Swords of Eveningstar to get up to something after this day's gentle tonguelashing, but this quickly? And *three* patrols-worth of trouble?

"Gods Above, Azoun," she muttered, "you certainly can pick them."

Myrmeen turned back to the piles of papers. *Her* war was here, on this desk. As usual. Now where—? Oh, yes, the third request for an escort to Candlekeep . . .

Yet if that gong rang again, the Dragons would discover the Lady Lord of Arabel charging out of here at the head of the answering patrol. Oh, yes.

Myrmeen glanced down the desk at her helm, currently serving paperweight duty on the 'not yet seen' pile.

The look she gave it was a longing look.

Weeping freely—*gods*, it hurt, and she felt weak and sick inside, and kept falling, oblivion lurking like eager dark shadows to claim her—Pennae stumbled on.

Perhaps her foe had given up on cudgeling her brains from the outside, and was now riding the minds of this small army of men with crossbows who kept walking stlarned-near into her, acquiring looks of recognition on their faces though she *knew* she'd never seen them before, and firing at her.

If they'd been better shots, she'd have a belly bristling with bolts by now, or a hole through her middle large enough even for clumsy Purple Dragons to thrust their helmed heads through.

Instead, Pennae just *felt* like she had a hole like that in her, at about shoulder level. She'd spewed her guts out all over the cobbles twice now, and had nothing left inside her to heave.

Another stride . . . another . . .

Pennae wanted *so* much to lie down on her face on the cobbles and just rest—but that would mean swift death for her, with Agannor, Bey, and at least two myserious foemen in leathers now following her.

She was leaving a bloody trail as she trudged, and probably a solid line of tears, too. She'd given up clinging spiderlike to walls, because she'd kept falling from her perches aloft, tumbling helplessly back to the cobbles.

Yes, she was beginning to hate cobbles. Very solid things, cobbles . . . keep walking, Pennae.

"Hoy!" The face belonged to a bristle-mustached Purple Dragon, with a watch badge pinned to the baldric across his breast. Others, similarly garbed, were gaping at her from behind him.

"Evening, lads," Pennae gasped. "Never seen a lass with a crossbow bolt through her before?"

Strong hands caught her as she stumbled, and the Dragon attached to them growled, "So, maid, what befell ye, exactly? How came you to have a—"

"Florin!" someone distant called; it sounded like Islif.

"Hey, Florin!" someone—Semoor, for a handful of gold—even more distant chimed in.

"Pennae!" That nearby shout rang out like a war horn, cutting through a sudden hubbub of Purple Dragons calling "Ho!" to each other.

Sinking into the darkness that had been clawing at her for so long, now—the warm, welcoming darkness—Pennae smiled.

Florin Falconhand had come for her at last.

Horaundoon shook his head in weary exasperation. So many minds, fighting his.

He wiped his sweat-slick brow with a hand that trembled, sighed, and sat back. He dared not to stay linked—not with the very real risk that someone whose mind he was in would die, violently.

No, he'd dismiss the two Swords warriors as lost, and just watch things unfold through the orb. At the very least, it should be a good show.

"Lathander loves thee," Semoor's voice intoned, through the gurgling waterfall of cool, blessed release that was sweeping through her.

Pennae blinked, tried to cough—and gentle fingers stroked her throat as tenderly as any lover, quelling her gagging.

"Tymora loves you, too," Doust added, from above those fingers. "And—hrast it—I do too."

"And Florin *really* does," Semoor said slyly.

"Thank you, Stoop," Florin said firmly, from somewhere above them. "That's two potions, now?"

"We holy prefer to call them 'healing quaffs,' forester," Semoor said haughtily, and then grunted in startled pain.

"Ah," Islif said pleasantly, "just as we unwashed prefer to call *that* 'the toe of my boot, put right where it will do a pompous holynose the most good.' Clumsum, d'you think your healing spell worked?"

"Shrug," Doust said aloud, and there were several chuckles from above Pennae.

"Purple Dragons stand all around us, Pennae," Florin said, his voice drawing nearer. Pennae blinked through what seemed to be tears, and could make out that he'd hunkered down on his haunches to lean over her. "They want to know what befell you. So do we."

"Martess," Pennae gasped. "Murdered. By Agannor and Bey. Chased me here. Other men with crossbows . . . also chasing. Beware someone—wizard?—attacking you, inside your head. Made me . . . fall over."

"Blood of Alathan!" Doust gasped, at about the same time as Islif snarled, "Caztul!"

Then Florin said, "Swordcaptain, I must ask you to turn a blind eye to what we may do next. I am enraged, and am like to do my own murdering in your streets."

"Man," a gruff and unfamiliar voice replied, "three good men are down with bolts through them. An' that's just my Dragons; I hear there're shopkeepers dead, an' a little lad who was out playing in the wrong alley, too. Go do your murders!"

Departing boots thundered, and a surprised voice—Doust's—asked, *"Jhessail?"*

"Let her go," Semoor murmured. "As if you or I or anyone could stop her."

"Help—help me up," Pennae gasped. "I'm going, too."

"You, lass, are staying right here," the swordcaptain growled. "There's blood all over you, your leathers're sliced half off you, an'—"

"And my task stands unfinished," Pennae hissed, clawing her way up the man's arm until she could stand. *"My* task. I'm a Sword of Eveningstar, Swordcaptain. Mayhap you've heard of us."

"Trumpet fanfare," Doust announced helpfully. There was a moment of tense silence before Purple Dragons started to guffaw, all around them. When the swordcaptain she was clinging to started to shake with laughter, Pennae almost fell over again.

Chapter 24
FELL WIZARDS AND ANGRY DRAGONS

Again ye ask me which foe is worse, fell wizard or angry dragon? Well, I rather think my reply must be as before: that depends on how well ye can dance.

The character Hellflame
the Weredragon in the first act of
To Slay A Wizard
A play by Stelvor Orlkrimm
published in the Year of Moonfall

There!" Florin shouted, pointing ahead with his sword as they pounded along a back alley slippery underfoot with rotting cabbage leaves. A crossbow promptly cracked, followed by another.

Florin flung himself at the wall, taking Islif down with him, and the Dragon running behind them screamed and crashed to his face, bouncing and moaning, with a bolt quivering through his knee.

"Jhess," the forester growled, scrambling up, "you shouldn't be here! You've no armor—"

"Shut *up*, Florin," came the furious reply, at about the same time as two familiar voices cried, "Wait for us! We bring holy blessings!"

Jhessail rolled her eyes. "You're shunning *me?* What about them? The Happy Dancing Holynoses themselves?"

Islif flung her a rare grin, and Florin waved his surrender—then peered and cursed. In admiration.

A weak, pale, weaving-on-her-feet Pennae was running alongside Doust and Semoor.

Together once more, the Swords trotted on, the watch lionar beside them puffing, "We've closed the gates, and called every last blade out of barracks—the lady lord herself's out running around with her sword drawn, somewhere. So they can't escape us! 'Tis just a matter of time . . ."

Islif threw him a jaundiced look, but said nothing, until they ducked around a sagging, permanently parked cart to burst out of the alley, and she shouted and pointed. "There!"

"There" was the dark doorway of a warehouse, a refuse-strewn threshold where Agannor was just jerking his sword out of the throat of a reeling, blood-spattering Purple Dragon. Two crossbow bolts came humming past him out of the darkness, and one took down another Dragon. A war wizard stepped coolly sideways to escape the other, and went right on casting a spell.

Purple Dragons were converging from all directions. Agannor cast looks all around, saw the Swords and gave them a mocking wave, and disappeared into the warehouse. Another pair of crossbow bolts claimed another two Dragons.

Puffing along beside Florin, the swordcaptain growled, "Where're *our* bowmen?"

"Those murdering bastards could be just inside, aimed and waiting for us, know you!" another Dragon gasped as they sprinted for the warehouse door, keeping close to the walls of other buildings in hopes they'd not run right up to meet more crossbow bolts.

Islif gave him a wolf's grin. "I know. I'm rather counting on it."

Something crashed down right in front of her, exploding into shards and splinters as it bounced and cartwheeled away. A chair, or had been.

Islif looked up—in time to see a grinning pair of men launch a wardrobe over a balcony rail at her. " 'Ware!" she roared, launching herself into a full-length leap.

The crash, right behind her, was thunderous; two Dragons managed not even a peep as they were crushed.

Semoor, running hard, skidded helplessly in the sudden pool of blood, but kept his feet and came on. "What the *tluin* is going on? They're throwing *wardrobes* at us?"

A crossbow bolt hummed out of the warehouse and spun him around, laying open his arm at the elbow as it grazed him—and took a Dragon full in the face.

"Naed," Semoor gasped, and then shouted, two sprinting steps later, "Ho! Changed my mind! Let's have more wardrobes!"

"What *is* going on?" Jhessail gasped, as they neared the gaping warehouse door. "Who are all these foes?"

"Zhent agents," a Dragon grunted, from right behind her. " 'Least those two on the balcony were."

"Were?"

"They just got 'em," he growled in satisfaction.

Florin ducked down, plucked up the splayed shards of a smashed and discarded shipping crate, and turned. "Fire spell?"

"Done," Jhessail gasped, stopping and fumbling forth what she needed from her belt pouch. A Purple Dragon ran on, into the warehouse, warily ducking low—and promptly screamed as two crossbow bolts tore through him.

Flame flared up from Jhessail's hand. She caressed the rotten wood Florin held out to her, then another crate proffered by Islif.

Florin thanked her with a grin, turned, and hurled the blazing wreckage into the warehouse, where its merrily leaping flames showed all watching dusty shelves of sacks and coffers, a sprawled dead man, two men fleeing with crossbows, the Purple Dragon who'd stopped two bolts writhing in agony on the floor, and—

"Where're the hoist chains?" the ranger asked suspiciously. "Don't these high loft warehouses load wagons right there, just inside their doors?"

Islif tossed her blazing crate into the warehouse to add more light, but shook her head. "I see none. Come *on.*"

Emboldened by being able to see that no crossbowmen stood aimed and waiting, Purple Dragons were rushing the doorway from several directions. The Swords joined the streams of running warriors, but were a little behind the first men—the ones who shouted in alarm and then died, smashed bloodily to the floor, as someone unseen let fall the hoist-chains from above, in great thundering heaps that buried the men they slew or struck senseless.

Other chains came swinging out of the dark corners of the warehouse in deadly arcs, smashing men into broken things even as they were hurled back into the faces of their slower fellows.

By the time Florin reached the chaos of broken and struggling men at the warehouse threshold, things were brightening—in a familiar, flickering manner. He looked up.

"Get back!" he roared, catching Islif and swinging her around into a breath-stealing, jarring meeting with the onrushing Jhessail. *"Back*, everyone!"

A sword flashed above the burning crates and barrels atop the hoist-rack, severing a rope—and to the thunderous *clatter-clatter-clatter* of a winch going mad, the flaming hoist plunged toward the floor.

"Get out!" Florin shouted, waving his arms at onrushing Purple Dragons. "Fire!"

He was still shouting when the crash, behind him, shook him off his feet and made the entire building creak and groan. Tongues of flame spat past him, hurling shrieking, blazing men out among their fellows.

Purple Dragons cursed colorfully, war wizards threw their arms up to shield their eyes, and over the crackling roar, war horns cried fire-warning. Once, twice, thrice, and then the bellow of Dauntless could be heard, rising above all the tumult: "War wizards, quench yon fire! Swordcaptains, run to fetch every priest you can! *Get that fire out!*"

As the Swords rallied around him, Florin found himself face-to-face with a Dragon he knew: Swordcaptain Nelvorr.

"Sir Sword," that officer gasped, "put your blade away. The ones we're chasing are in yon warehouse." He waved his arm in a circle. "We have it surrounded, t'other side, and no one has tried to break out that way yet. If they do, they'll die."

Florin looked into the flames. The place was an inferno just inside the door, and the front wall was leaking plumes of smoke and swiftly climbing lines of flame, as lines of pitch that had been used to seal cracks in the boards caught alight. To either side of the door, however, the warehouse yet looked untouched, not even any smoke coming from its shuttered windows. "Are there any cellars? Tunnels?" he snapped.

"No," replied a voice from behind him. A voice he'd heard before.

"At least," the Lady Lord of Arabel added, a wand held ready in her hand, "none are supposed to exist—and my tax collectors look hard for such things."

"I'm going in there," Florin told her, as a war wizard finished an elaborate spell and the fire died down noticeably.

"You surprise me not," she replied with a half-smile, waving him forward. Florin gave her a smile and a nod, and ran, the Swords at his heels.

Smoke greeted them, thick and curling, as Florin ducked in around the eastern doorpost and led the way, sword out and keeping low.

Through the thinning blue haze the Swords hastened, peering this way and that in hopes they'd see the dreaded crossbows before a bolt found them.

The place was a labyrinth of open-sided floors, pillars with climbing pegs embedded in them, and stacked, roped-in-place sacks, barrels, and coffers. Ramps were everywhere, and cobwebs, and the motionless hanging chains of hoists.

Lanterns glimmered far behind the Swords as Purple Dragons entered the warehouse. The dancing lights of flames were gone now, leaving only the faint light of a few dusty glowstones, high up on the walls in their furry-with-webs iron cages.

Another pillar onward.

And another. With every cautious step the Swords grew warier; soon they'd reach this end of the warehouse. If the men they sought weren't back down the other end—and from the way the catwalks up in the roof beams ran, and where Florin had seen that sword slicing the hoist-ropes, that wasn't likely—they had to be somewhere here.

Close.

Waiting.

Of course, this was the lowest level; they could be anywhere behind the sacks up above, on all those dark, open-sided storage floors.

"How many warehouses like this does the city hold, again?"

Semoor muttered to Pennae. "Strikes me you could steal stuff by the wagon-load for years, and it'd not be missed."

Pennae gave him a fierce grin—then a fiercer scowl. "Later," she whispered into his ear. "We'll talk about this later. O high-principled holy man."

Ahead, Florin abruptly threw up his arm in a warning wave. Then he drew aside against a stack of crates and pointed.

The Swords looked out at what he'd already discovered: a sea of spilled grain, fallen from sacks sliced open in some accident or other, and now hanging limp and nigh-empty.

A line of boot prints ploughed through them, in a path that ended abruptly, in otherwise undisturbed drifts of grain. Men had hurried this way and then simply—vanished.

"Jhessail?"

The mageling stepped forward, her face set, until she was standing just on the edge of the grain. "Strong magic," she murmured, spreading her arms almost as if basking in the sun, embracing the empty air. "Like a fire, beating on my face." She took a long step sideways, shook her head, then did the same in the other direction, returning to where she'd first been standing. "Just here."

"Like a door," Doust murmured.

Semoor bent, scooped up some grain in his cupped hands, strode along the path of disturbed grain, and when he got to its end, threw his handful forward.

Aside from a little wisp of drifting dust, it abruptly vanished, right in front of him. "The way is open," he said, stepping hastily to one side.

No crossbow bolts came hissing out of the empty air, and after a tense breath or two Semoor rejoined them.

"Agannor and Bey went this way, you think?"

Islif nodded grimly. "I think."

Florin nodded too. "All right. We've not got our armor or gear, but if we go back to get them, I'm thinking the murderers will be gone forever. What say you?"

"Let's go get them," Pennae whispered. "I saw their faces, and her blood on their swords—and they tried to slice *me* often enough."

Jhessail nodded. "They know all about us. I don't want *that* creeping back at me unawares, some night while I sleep! After them!"

The Swords turned as one and started through the grain.

There was an angry shout from behind them. "Hoy! *Hold!* Stand and down weapons!"

The Esparran spun around, weapons raised, and found themselves looking at Purple Dragons. *Lots* of Purple Dragons. In full battle armor, these, wearing helms and shields, and hefting spears in their hands.

"Swords of Eveningstar, down weapons and surrender! *Now!*"

A hard-faced ornrion none of the Swords had ever seen before, who bore a flame-encircled red dragon on his shield, was striding to the fore, wagging a gauntleted forefinger at them. "We've heard all about you! I arrest you, all of you, for firesetting and—"

Florin regarded the ornrion incredulously. "What?"

"Down weapons, or we'll down *you*. And quick about it! Or I'll seize the excuse and save Arabel a lot of bother, by just butchering you like the mad dogs you are! Adventurers are always trouble—"

Trailing his sword behind him in his fingertips, Florin trudged to meet the man—who came on at him like an angry storm, wading into the grain and continuing his tirade.

"You're mistaken," the forester began, "and the Lady Lord of—"

"*Horsedung*, lying adventurer! 'Tis from *her* tongue we all heard of your villainy! Your crossbows have murdered a dozen Dragons this night, and if her orders to try to take you alive weren't riding me, I'd—"

Florin spread his hands to show his peaceful intent—and the ornrion's hand came up and took him by the throat.

For a moment the forester stared disbelievingly into the man's grimly smiling face. Then his fist came in with all the force he could put behind it, smashing up under the Dragon's jaw.

The click of teeth clashing on teeth was loud, and the ornrion was suddenly staring at the rafters, up on tiptoe and already senseless. His failing hand let go of Florin's throat, the forester twisted and snatched—and the flaming dragon shield tore free of the man's toppling body.

"Swords!" Florin roared, spinning around with his sword in one hand and the just-seized shield half-on his other arm. "To me!"

And he charged through the grain until he—wasn't there.

There was an instant of gently falling through endless rich blue mists ere Florin's boot came down on hard stone. Stone somewhere underground, by the coolness and the damp, earthen smell. The blue radiance faded—

At about the same instant as something crashed into and *through* the shield, slamming into him hard enough to shatter its stout metal.

And Florin's arm beneath it.

Triumphant laughter roared out from ahead as the fletched end of the broken crossbow bolt that had maimed him brushed past Florin's nose, into dark oblivion.

Stumbling back as pain lanced through him, Florin wondered how likely he was to end up following it . . .

The Purple Dragons charged, a shouting wave of deadly spear points.

"Get through!" Islif yelled at Jhessail and Pennae, swatting their behinds to urge them to greater haste as they plunged past her. "Stoop! Clumsum! *Get in there!*"

She waved her sword in defiance as she raced after them, grinning frantically as the foremost spear reached for her, perhaps the length of her own hand away from piercing her.

And then the world blinked, and she was falling through blue mist.

And blinked again, and Islif was standing in a dark stone-lined corridor with the rest of the Swords, who were clustered around . . . Florin? Hurt?

"Hoy!" she cried, as she spun around to face the blue glow behind her, "weapons *out!*"

Spears were emerging from it, thrusting out of the swirling blueness with grim-faced Purple Dragons behind them. Three soldiers whose eyes widened at the sight of their surroundings.

They widened still more when Islif struck aside two spearheads with her sword, and ran in past the third to backhand its wielder across the face.

He stumbled into his fellows, there was a moment of startled hopping and cursing—and Pennae came out of the dark with a startling shriek, daggers flashing in both hands, Doust and Semoor trotting behind her.

The Purple Dragons wavered, and Islif drove her knee hard up into a codpiece and then thrust her leg sideways, toppling that soldier into the one next to him. Pennae landed hard on their wavering spears, smashing them to the stone floor and splintering the shaft of one of them as she flung herself forward, her fists hammering down two dagger pommels into two helms.

The Dragons reeled, and Pennae jerked on their helms, tilting the metal down half-over their faces. They struggled under her, punching and kicking and trying to rise—and as Islif wrenched spears out of the hands of two of them, Semoor leaned in, plucked a mace from the belt of one Dragon, and crowned the man solidly with it, leaving him reeling.

"I've always wanted to do that," he remarked happily. "Are you going to start cutting pieces off them now?"

The Dragons were already trying to shove themselves back and away, and his words goaded them into frantic flight. Back into the blue glow, with Islif's and Pennae's chuckles trailing them.

"Now get away," Islif ordered, waving her fellow Swords to the sides of the passage. "Against the walls and *away*. I'd not put it past them to find some bows and start volleying right down this—"

A spear burst out of the mist and sailed down the passage, to bounce and skitter to a harmless stop beside Jhessail, who was helping a sweating Florin up, and easing the bent and ruined shield off his arm.

"Move!" Islif roared, as a second spear followed the first. The

Swords moved, in haste, as a third spear rattled past them.

"Florin says there's a crossbowman somewhere ahead of us," Jhessail warned, as they hastened on together.

"Broke my arm," Florin grunted. "Never saw him."

"When do we start having fun?" Semoor complained. "Pools of coins and gems, dancing girls, our own castles . . . when does *that* side of adventure kiss and cuddle us?"

Behind them, the blue glow burst into a wild, blinding-bright explosion that spat lightning bolts down the passage at them, crackling and ricocheting in a chaos that sounded like hundreds of harps being smashed all at once, metal strings jangling and shrieking. In its wake, all light faded; the blue glow was gone.

"A war wizard making sure we won't return," Jhessail said as darkness descended, leaving them all blind.

Doust groaned. "Now what?"

"Well," Semoor said, "we can sit down right here and pray, the two of us—and in the fullness of time be granted the power to make light to see by."

A dim glow occurred not far from his elbow, and brightened, as it was uncovered and held up, to about the same strength as a mica-shuttered lantern. "Or," Pennae told them all, holding what they could now see was a hand-sized glowstone, "we can use this." Its radiance showed them her sweet smile.

It was Jhessail's turn to groan. "Do I want to know where you 'found' that?"

Pennae shrugged. "I *imagine* the lady lord, or one of her staff, will eventually miss it. Yet I doubt, somehow, she'll now be able to chase after us to reclaim it."

"What happens if you drop it?" Doust asked. "Is it likely to break and go dark?"

She shrugged. "I wasn't planning on finding out."

"So where are we?" Florin gasped, his voice tight with pain. "And which way shall we go?"

"The Haunted Halls, of course. In the long passage just north of the room where we found the boots, pack, and pole. See yon cracks in the wall?" The thief gestured with the glowstone. "So the fastest way out is that way—and Bey might remember the route; I doubt Agannor ever paid that much attention to the maps—but the three we're chasing went *that* way."

"After them," Florin growled. Pennae nodded.

Islif took hold of her elbow, and steered her hand to hold the glowstone close to Florin, so she could peer at him. "Healing, holy men?"

"Not until after we pray for a good long time," Semoor told her. "We spent our divine favor helping Pennae."

"I'll live," Florin told them tersely. "Let's get after them."

The Swords exchanged nods, hefted their weapons, and set off into the chill darkness.

They'd gone only a few paces when they came upon a discarded crossbow on the floor. Pennae peered at it. "Not broken," she murmured, "so he was out of bolts to fire."

"Bright news," Semoor grunted. They hastened on to a wider chamber that offered them a door and three passages onward. Islif went to the door, made a pocketing gesture to tell Pennae to hide the light, and opened it.

Still darkness greeted her—then Pennae patted her shoulder, leaned past her, and pulled the glowstone out of its pouch again. Nothing. The room was empty—and across the door in its far wall was a fresh cobweb. Pennae shook her head and stepped back out of the room. "They probably went that way," she said, pointing down the passage that led to the feast hall, "but we'd best check this end way, just to be sure. I don't fancy them leaping out behind us and slicing Doust or Semoor into platter-slabs."

The end passage ran northwest, not far, ere turning west to a chamber that still held, along one wall, the collapsed and sagging remnants of ancient barrels and carry-chests. In the center of the facing wall was a door—a stone affair that lacked lock or bolt, and led to a room that had been empty when they'd explored it, days back.

As Pennae neared it, she tensed, stepped back, and whispered,

"A man's voice—unfamiliar—declaiming some grand phrases that mean nothing to me. I'd say he's working magic."

"Let's move!" Islif hissed. "In, before he finishes!" And she launched herself at the door with Pennae right behind her.

The Swords burst through the door and down the short passage beyond, startling a man who stood there into looking over his shoulder at them.

It was Bey, his drawn sword in his hands, and he shouted, "Get gone!" to someone around the corner, and ran that way.

The Swords raced after him, rounding the corner fast and ducking low, swords up in front of them.

They were in time to see Agannor's boot vanishing through an upright, swirling oval of blue radiance of the same hue as the glow that had brought them back here. An unfamiliar man in battle-leathers was keeping Bey from following with one outflung arm, but snatched it out of the way the moment Agannor had vanished, to let Bey plunge through.

Giving the onrushing Swords a malevolent smile, he followed, leaving behind the blue glow.

"Tluin!" Jhessail spat. "Where does *this* one go?"

"We'll see, won't we?" Pennae flung back at her, racing for the whirling portal with Islif right behind her.

Its glow swallowed them both before any of the other Swords could reply.

Ornrion Barellkor blinked again, his head still swimming. Strong hands were lifting him by his armpits, helping him to sit up.

"All right, are you?" one of his swordcaptains asked.

Barellkor put a hand up to his jaw and tried to shake his head—which proved to be a mistake. His head felt like it was splitting slowly open with someone's war axe firmly embedded in it. His chin felt even worse.

"I think my jaw is broken," he moaned.

"Idiot," the Lady Lord of Arabel said curtly, dragging the wincing man to his feet. "If that's all the hurt you took, Tymora must smile on you, Barellkor. Now get out of my sight before I decide to reduce you to lionar."

The ornrion stared at her disbelievingly. "But I—but they . . . they were the ones as murderered all our lads!"

"Horsedung, Barellkor, as I believe you're fond of saying," Myrmeen snapped. "Why don't you step over there and try throttling yon portal-blasting war wizard, instead of a gallant young forester? Perhaps you two stoneheads will succeed in murdering each other, and I'll be shut of the pair of you!"

Pennae was a little surprised not to be greeted by sharp steel stabbing at her the moment the blue glow faded before her.

She, and Islif, and a moment later all the rest of the Swords, were even more surprised by what they beheld in the large chamber in front of them.

On its far wall were mounted three huge, glowing and very vivid portraits of menacing, rampant monsters, all of them familiar to the Swords from bestiaries: a chuul, an ettin, and an umber hulk. To the right of them, stone steps led up to a passage stretching away elsewhere, and a coldly smiling, white-haired yet young man in black doublet, hose, and boots—looking for all the world like a minor courtier who might well be seen standing near the Dragon Throne—stood on those steps.

Floating in three green, swirling glows in midair, struggling to win free of them, were Agannor, Bey, and the man in leathers who'd followed them through the portal.

"These are yours, I presume?" the man on the steps asked the Swords. "Kindly slay them." He pointed at the man in leathers. "Especially that one, who had the effrontery to open one of my private portals and lead, it seems, half the adventurers in Cormyr here."

"Who are you?" Pennae asked, frowning in bewilderment. "And where's 'here'?"

"Ah. Well." The man waved a hand, and the glow behind the Swords winked out; the portal was gone. "As you've no way of ever finding this place again, there's no harm in your knowing that you stand in Whisper's Crypt. I am Whisper, one of the mightiest wizards of the Zhentarim."

"Oh, *tluin*," Jhessail said wearily. "When will all this running and fighting and killing end?"

The Zhentarim smiled at her. "When you die, of course."

Chapter 25
THE STORM BREAKS

See these hills, lad? So peaceful they seem now—but you'd not want to be standing here when the storm breaks.

The character Oldbones
the Shepherd in the first act of
To Slay A Wizard
A play by Stelvor Orlkrimm
published in the Year of Moonfall

Sarhthor snorted.

"Mightiest wizards" indeed. Whisper intended the intruders to swiftly wind up as food for his trapped beasts, of course, but was it really necessary to gloat like a reckless youth? Or waste the life of the best Zhent agent in Arabel?

Yes, 'twas time—well past it—to end the career of Whisper the mage. There were far more than enough reasons already, and unless Whisper did something truly surprising, he was about to hand Sarhthor a handsome opportunity.

With the thinnest of smiles, Sarhthor leaned over his scrying orb and started to cast a careful spell.

"Well?" Whisper asked the Swords. "What're you waiting for?" He waved at the writhing, whirling webs of green radiance, or at the cursing, straining men caught in them. "I told you to kill them."

"I—we—mislike the look of your magic," Islif told him, pointing with her sword at the racing emerald glows. "If I stick a sword into that, what will befall me?"

"Ah. Well." Whisper's smile was colder this time. "You ask the wrong question, wench. Your words should be: If I fail to stick my sword into that, what will befall me?" He gestured.

The air in front of Whisper suddenly sang and shimmered.

Though the Swords could still see him clearly, he now stood behind a wall of awakened magic.

"Know that I am less than pleased with you," he announced, and calmly cast another spell. The three green glows brightened.

Agannor was pleading now, crying to the Swords for help. Bey and the Zhent in leathers were saving breath for their doomed struggles to win free of the magic that held them.

And was now drifting across the room, carrying them toward . . . the three paintings.

Tiny green lightning bolts crackled a greeting to the portraits, stabbing forth as each mantrapping radiance floated up to a painting . . . and *into* it.

The emerald webs melted away, and the painted monsters started moving, reaching forth hungrily for . . . Agannor, Bey, and the Zhent, who tumbled across the paintings as if rolling and running across a room, silently shouting in fear as they desperately swung swords and daggers.

The Swords watched them die bloodily, ravaged and battered. It took but a breath or two, as Whisper watched with his smile widening. "Eat, my guardians," he murmured. "Eat, and be content. I promise you—"

At the sound of his voice, the three beasts turned, glared at him—and *boiled* forth from the paintings, emerging into the room.

Whisper's jaw dropped, but he stammered out a swift incantation, his voice sharp with alarm.

The umber hulk, foremost of the three monsters heading for him, shook itself as his spell washed over it, and turned toward the Swords of Eveningstar.

And charged, the club-waving ettin and the chuul following it.

"Naed," Islif whispered, hefting her sword. "We're going to die."

Jaw tightening, she raised her blade to launch a charge of her own—and the umber hulk stiffened, came to such an abrupt halt it tottered, and whirled around to face Whisper once more. And charged again.

Peering down at his scrying orb, Sarhthor of the Zhentarim smiled, and cast another spell.

Whisper the mage drew a wand from his belt and stood warily behind his shield, watching the monsters come for him.

As the umber hulk rushed closer, Whisper's shield grew brighter, until it looked like a solid wall of spitting, snarling sparks. The umber hulk shuddered and slowed, as if wading on into the magic was both painful and took great effort. Whisper started to smile.

Then the shield abruptly vanished, and the umber hulk was reaching triumphantly for the horrified mage, who gaped at it in disbelief. Its claws had almost closed on his face when he scrambled back and triggered his wand.

Fire splashed over the monster, leaving it staggering and darkening. As it shuddered and slowed, the chuul opened its huge claws and rushed at Whisper from his other side.

He whirled and fed it a burst of flame, retreating quickly as the umber hulk pressed forward. The chuul shuddered but kept coming; only the ettin hung back with growls of malevolent fear.

Pennae watched the Zhent with narrowed eyes, hefting a dagger in her hand—and when Whisper turned once more to bathe the umber hulk in fire, she threw her knife hard and fast.

It flashed back firelight as it spun, and Whisper saw it and shied back. The umber hulk lunged forward, its great forearms reaching; Pennae's dagger struck one of them and spun harmlessly away.

Whisper blasted the umber hulk again, a great burst of flame enveloping the beast—but even as he aimed his wand to unleash that fire, Pennae threw a second blade.

This one struck home, slicing Whisper's hand and sending the wand tumbling away. Which was when the chuul's claw caught at the mage's other shoulder, plucking him into an awkward, hopping turn.

Its other claw thrust forward, but Whisper hissed a frantic incantation and flung himself back up the steps.

In his wake, bolts of chain lightning arced and played the length of the chuul's body. It lurched sideways, wisps of smoke curling from its joints, its claws spasming with an eerie clattering. The umber hulk shouldered it aside—but Whisper was already fleeing.

He raced for three strides before the ettin's hurled club took his feet out from under him, and he slammed hard into the wall.

The umber hulk reached for him again, roaring—and Whisper plucked something dark and tiny from his belt and threw it down the monster's open mouth, throwing himself to one side.

The umber hulk exploded, spraying the reeling chuul with razor-sharp shards of brown body plates that tore it open in a dozen places, and snatching the ettin off its feet with the force of the explosion.

The ettin slammed into the floor, slid along stone twisting and roaring in pain, and when it skidded to a stop, staggered to its feet again and lurched forward.

By then the Swords were past it, trotting up the stairs with their weapons ready.

Whisper was on his feet, leaning on the wall and glaring at them.

Islif ran right at him, Pennae and a pale-faced Florin not far behind. The Zhentarim raised a bleeding hand to work a spell.

Snarling, Islif flung herself at him, waving her sword wildly, hoping to ruin his casting.

She landed *just* out of sword-reach, and threw herself forward again, her blade slashing viciously. Whisper's body flickered, vanished—and even as she cursed and hacked the empty air where he'd been, reappeared just a stride away.

He saw her and started to scream. Her first slash was at his mouth, to spoil any spell.

Then Pennae arrived, driving home a dagger hilt-deep under the mage's ribs, and following it with another into his throat.

Jhessail joined in the butchering, and the wizard reeled and slumped, fountaining blood in many places, to bounce once and lie still, his blood a pool of swift-spreading crimson around him.

Islif promptly sprang back across it to greet the ettin, Doust and Semoor whirling around with curses and ready maces to stand with her.

Frantic in their fear, the Swords swarmed the foul-smelling beast, thrusting, hacking, and clubbing it from all sides. It soon toppled like a felled tree, crashing down atop Whisper.

Who, forever staring, moved not a finger.

In Maglor's dusty back room, far away in Eveningstar, a gasping, bleeding man staggered to a bench, clung to it long enough to catch his breath, snatched a dusty cloth off Maglor's scrying orb, and passed his hand over it.

It awakened with a soft and silent glow, warming his face even as a scene from afar spun into sharp coherence in its depths.

Still breathing raggedly, Whisper the mage watched Maglor reel as blades struck ruthlessly home. He saw the screaming apothecary die in his place—and whispered fervent thanks to Bane and Mystra both for the long-prepared spell that switched his body with that of Maglor, and the even older spell that gave Maglor the face and appearance of Whisper.

As the Swords killed the ettin in the depths of the orb, Whisper turned his back on it and stumbled away, feeling sick and afraid. It was the first time he'd been truly frightened in . . . yes, years.

Pale, eerie radiance flared, banishing the gloom of the cold, dark tomb, as Old Ghost reared up, his eyes blazing in fury.

"*Now* you go too far," it whispered to the silence. "Maglor was a worm, yes, but he was *my* worm, his life mine to spend at a time and place of my choosing. Whisper, your life is forfeit."

The wraith stormed out of the tomb, chill fire moving with swift purpose.

The war wizard finished casting, let his hands fall to his sides, and sighed.

With a much softer sigh, a glowing doorway appeared in the empty air before him.

"That's where they went," he said. "Now I really must get back to the lady lord's side. By now, she could be halfway across—"

"Hold!" Dauntless was every whit as furious as he looked. His words snapped as fiercely as crossbow. "Is it safe to pass through?"

The mage shrugged. "Anything could await on t'other side—a dozen blades ready to stab, for instance. Yet unless the one who crafted yon portal commands magic so strong that the portal-enchantments can subvert my probing spells—unlikely, but by no means impossible—the portal itself is safe to traverse, yes."

Dauntless snapped names and orders over his shoulder, mustering particular Dragons by name to step through the waiting door, and ended rather ungraciously, "And Swordcaptain Draeth, I suppose."

Draeth swallowed. "Uh . . . hadn't we best clear this with Lady Lord Myrmeen Lhal?"

Dauntless spun around, his roar almost blasting the swordcaptain off his boots as he said *"Hang* Myrmeen, and her orders, too!"

"Ho, now! I think *not*, Lionar Dahauntul," a crisp voice said out of the darkness along the warehouse wall.

Dauntless peered, not seeing who'd spoken. "Who speaks? And I'm an ornrion, not a lionar."

"Disobeying superior officers, and speaking of bringing about their deaths, are offenses that may yet earn you more than a simple demotion, *Lionar* Dahauntul," the voice replied coldly.

Its owner strode forward into the lanternlight, and there were hoarse gasps and muttered oaths as the gathered Dragons recognized the king's cousin, Baron Thomdor, Warden of the Eastern Marches.

All of the watch went to their knees, Dauntless among them, sputtering, "Pray pardon, Lord! I must confess I—"

"Save it," Thomdor told him, "and tell me this: who went through that, and why d'you want to follow them?"

"Adventurers," Dauntless explained. "Chartered, but well on the way to becoming wildsword nuisances. Some here are saying they set this warehouse afire—but 'tis certain they fled through this magical way, to some unknown Zhent stronghold, in the company of known Zhentarim agents who've murdered more than a few Dragons this night. I'll be aft—that is, I *want* to pursue them with all the force I can muster, war wizards and all, and scour out the Zhents on the far end of yon portal, once and for all."

"No," Baron Thomdor said. "We'll let these Swords of Eveningstar handle things. That's what Crown adventurers' charters are *for.*"

"If he were trying to trick us," Pennae replied, "d'you think he'd try to do it with potions he'd so cleverly hidden away?"

"Keen thought," Doust said, taking one of the vials she was passing out.

Jhessail peered at hers. "What's this shining-sun mark?"

"A symbol for healing," the thief replied, watching Florin flick away the cork she'd loosened for him, and proceed to swallow the contents of his vial.

"It's working," he husked, holding out his hand for another.

Pennae grinned and slapped another vial into the forester's palm. "Good. Drink deep. Whisper seems to have stored his spellbooks and suchlike somewhere else—and the prospect of stumbling through his vile traps trying to find all of his other hidden magic is not one that leaves me especially eager."

Florin swallowed, sighed gustily, and leaned back against the wall, looking much better as pain drained from his face. He held up his no-longer-broken arm, wiggling his fingers gingerly.

The Swords were cautiously plundering Whisper's lair of what scant riches they could find and magic they dared touch. A room away, two glowing portals waited.

Not knowing where either led had touched off a halting debate regarding what they should do next.

Penny grinned. "I walked around rather more streets in Arabel than the rest of you—"

"Yes," Semoor interrupted, "and bedchambers, shop stockrooms, and back pantries, too, I daresay!"

There was a ripple of laughter, in which Pennae joined, ere she gave him a rude gesture and continued, "—and saw the same royal proclamation posted in five places: a screed promising the title of 'Baron of the Stonelands,' with a fortune and an army to go with it, to anyone who builds a castle in the Stonelands and holds it for two straight years, cleansing it of a certain count of brigands and beasts—the beasts' heads to be proofs of this."

Islif snorted. "Godhood, too?"

Everyone laughed.

"*Next* month, hey?" Semoor commented. "After we're whole and hearty again, and the priests back at the House of the Morning have granted me my god-name and told me what a great champion of the faith I am."

Giving Semoor a hard look, Pennae waved at the single small coffer of Whisper's coins they'd found. "And just how much coin out of this are you going to have to give them to get them to do that?"

More laughter ensued; mirth that was punctuated by Doust's loud throat-clearing reminder that *other* gods needed to be properly thanked, too.

+ + ✳ + +

"Sark them all," Whisper hissed, searching through paltry magics cached here so long ago that he'd half-forgotten what they were. "In fact, tluin all hrasted adventurers!"

What would he need to blast those darkblades? They'd butchered his three guardians, and Maglor too, and were doubtless plundering his magics right now. At least his hacked hand was whole once more, though it had taken *two* potions. Motherless bastards.

"May Mystra wither them and Bane maim them," he snarled, rummaging and peering. These were all baubles and battle-useless things—he needed the means to blast, melt, and humble!

Lost in his fury, Whisper never noticed the pale glow blossoming behind him, or gliding forward to plunge silently *into* him.

Then, with Old Ghost chilling his spine, it was too late.

The mage found himself forced upright with a strangled gargle, and reaching to pluck up a rod that "felt" metals and minerals from among his treasures.

Holding it stiffly, Whisper turned and walked, heavily and unwillingly, to his hidehold's waiting portal.

His hopes that whatever had him in its thrall would be stripped away during the translocation were dashed when the blue mists fell away and he was standing in a dim passage in his crypt.

Useless wand in hand, the helpless Zhentarim began the slow, unwilling trudge toward his storeroom, where the adventurers would almost certainly be by now. The walk to his own doom.

Other eyes widened in surprise over another scrying orb.

Then Horaundoon's eyes narrowed again.

Whisper's reluctant return had been astonishing enough, but his fareye was showing him more. The faintest of glows was riding Whisper: another sentience!

Grinning, Horaundoon leaned forward, not wanting to miss a moment of what was about to unfold.

This should be *very* interesting.

"Naed!" Doust gasped, scrambling to his feet. Whisper stood menacingly in the doorway, wand aimed at them.

The rest of the Swords looked—saw—and froze.

Slowly, very slowly, almost as if small segments of his upper lip were separately being pulled back from his teeth, the Zhentarim smiled.

And one of Pennae's daggers spun out of nowhere to stand forth, hilt deep, from his right eye.

The Swords erupted, weapons flashing out, but Whisper moved not at all.

Until, still smiling, he toppled forward to crash onto his face, limbs bouncing loosely.

As the Swords all stared, something ghostly and pale rose from him in wisps, to gather eerily in the air, ignoring the swords that thrust and slashed into it. When it had gained the strength and shape of a tall, broad-shouldered man, it turned its head slowly to regard each of the horrified adventurers. Though it had no mouth, it seemed almost to be smiling smugly, alight with glee . . . as it rose and drifted away, as lazily purposeful as a great shark.

Jhessail shivered as she watched it go, and none of the Swords said a word or lifted a hand to do anything until it was out of sight.

Whereupon, inevitably, it was Semoor who stirred. "What the tluin *was* that?"

No one had a reply.

Horaundoon reared back from his scrying orb as if someone had thrust dung in his face—then leaned forward again to peer intently.

The wraith-thing that had gathered above Whisper's corpse—and had come out of Whisper, he was certain—looked at all of the Swords of Eveningstar, slowly glided away.

As he bent his will to move the scrying orb's field to follow it, he realized what he was looking at and gasped.

"So the mindworms can be taken that far," he whispered, "and *that* is what their user becomes."

He shivered involuntarily, but it was the hargaunt that spasmed, squalling in fear, and wet his head.

There's a singing in the air here," Pennae said tersely. "Magic." The passage turned dark ahead of her, but in the light of the glow-stones the Swords had taken from Whisper's rooms, they could see dust-covered human statues standing clustered in the passage.

"The way on looks . . . unused," Florin mused. "Perhaps the magic is some sort of barrier, and yon is 'wild country,' for lack of a better term."

Pennae shrugged. "One way to find out." She strolled forward, despite his swift hiss of protest, into the singing magic.

Nothing befell her, and the magic did not change or vanish—but the moment Pennae stepped beyond it, the dusty statues moved, raising their arms to reach for her. She retreated hastily, watching them shuffle after her, and returned to the watching Swords.

"Zombies," she said. "Let's look for another way out."

"Six—no, seven portals back there," Semoor reminded her.

Pennae nodded. "I'm afraid we're going to end up stepping through one of them."

"And if one of them turns out to be a death trap, so we're stepping into fire or whirling lightning?" Islif asked.

The thief gave her a sour look. "I *really* wish you hadn't said that."

"I am the Lady Narantha Crownsilver," Narantha told the old, whitebearded war wizard, ignoring the lesser wizards who'd escorted her to this soaring stone chamber so deep in the palace.

Every chamber of this fortress around her was starker and more brooding and unfriendly than the rooms of the palace in Suzail. She was beginning to truly hate Arabel.

"You wanted to see me?"

The war wizard inclined his head to her. "Not me, Lady." He stepped aside, indicating the curtain behind him.

With an exasperated sigh Narantha stepped forward through its parting, into an audience room where a plain stone throne was flanked by two towering candlesticks. Two war wizards stood under those flickering flames, and one look at the seated man had her knee-dipping deeply.

"Narantha Crownsilver?" Baron Thomdor asked her.

"Lord Baron, I am she," Narantha replied. Aside from distant glimpses across rooms at revels and state occasions, she'd not seen the warden since she'd been a little girl. What interest could he have in her now?

"I regret the bluntness of this," Thomdor said, rising and extending his hand to her, "but your father stands in urgent need. Your mother has died, and Lord Crownsilver very much desires your presence, right now."

Narantha could only stare at him.

"These loyal servants of Cormyr stand ready to take you to him," the warden told her gently, indicating the war wizards. Narantha stumbled toward them, blinded by a sudden waterfall of tears.

Someone was weeping bitterly; she was burying her head in a stranger's breast before she realized it was her.

In their tenth dark passage, the Swords stopped—and stared. Disgustedly.

Whisper's tenth ward sang in the air before them. Beyond it stood the tenth silently waiting group of undead.

A dozen skeletons lurched forward, raising rusty swords. One overbalanced a handwidth too far—and fell into dust as the ward flared up through it, into a glittering wall of sparks. Beyond that deadly glow, something that might have been the skeleton of a giant came down the passage, hefting an axe larger than Florin.

"That's it," Islif sighed, as the Swords retreated. "Either we step into a portal to depart this place—or starve here, trapped."

There were reluctant nods.

"Should we try some of Whisper's wands?" Doust asked doubtfully, lifting the one he held.

"Triggering powers we don't know, into a spell that's holding back undead right now, but might well explode? Or shoot lightnings? Or turn us all purple? At undead that it *might* blast, but then again might make them grow, or come back to life? Or—?"

And with those words, Pennae turned to lead the way to the nearest portals: a pair flickering in what had probably been Whisper's storage cellar.

Everyone followed, without a word.

"Mine," Florin said, stepping into the waiting glow.

And through it, to stand frowning on its far side, still in the cellar. He stepped through it again in the other direction, toward the rest of the Swords—and found himself standing facing them, as if he'd been walking through nothing but empty air.

"Jhess," Pennae said, "doff your belt and try. Perhaps 'tis the metal that keeps it from working; I've heard of portals like that."

Jhessail handed over her belt and stepped through the first gate. Like Florin, she simply ended up on its far side, still in the cellar. She stepped through it again, in the other direction. Still in the cellar. With a shrug, she went to the second gate and tried it. With the same result.

"Could be we're lacking a password," Islif suggested. Pennae nodded.

Semoor sighed. "Well, Whisper's just a little too dead to ask, now, isn't he? Come on; let's try them all."

Much trudging and fruitless stepping through glows ensued, until they were back in the room of now-empty paintings and sprawled, dead monsters. Whisper still lay as he'd fallen, under the ettin. Rats scattered from the carrion as the Swords came down the steps and stopped in front of the glowing oval.

"Think it'll work for us, back to Arabel?" Semoor asked.

"Or will it take us somewhere else, I wonder?" Doust put in.

"*Thank you,* cheerful holynoses," Pennae said with a grin. "Well, there's only one way to find out."

Florin hefted his sword and strode forward. "Mine. Again."

Silently, the glow swallowed him.

"*Quick,* now," Islif snapped, trotting forward. "And keep those wands ready!"

The Swords hurried.

A spell cast long ago, that showed the watchful apprentices on duty who stepped through particular portals, flickered once more into life.

The master of those apprentices, crossing the room behind their desks, stopped in mid-stride to see who was departing Whisper's Crypt for Arabel. He nodded, saying nothing, as a succession of images flowed across that part of the wall.

"The Swords of Eveningstar," one of the apprentices reported excitedly.

"I am unsurprised, Alaise," her master replied. "Please take over doorguard from Thander now. You may soon be seeing the Swords in person."

He walked on, his mind already on scores of larger matters.

Not that the Swords lacked interest. Indeed, to an archmage who talked often with Dove Silverhand and betimes with Hawkstone the ranger, and at other times eavesdropped undetected on the minds of the herald from Espar, Lord Elvarr Spurbright, and Dauntless of the Purple Dragons—to name but three—these fledgling adventurers were interesting indeed.

Not just for who they were and what they were doing, but for who was trying to manipulate them.

The wizard ascended a winding stone stair to a higher level of his tower, passing many storage niches let into the walls. His gaze fell on a curious twisted pendant hanging in one niche, behind the warding that would sear all hands but his to the bone, and the Swords came back into his thoughts.

He had plans for the Swords of Eveningstar. Oh, yes, indeed.

Florin stepped out into—grain shifting underfoot, in a familiar warehouse that was now brightly lit indeed. Forty Purple Dragons, or more, were staring impassively at him over leveled spears, in a wall that extended around him in—yes—a ring.

A ring of Dragons at least two deep, that was broken in only one place: right ahead of him, where an officer stood with a drawn sword in his hand, looking both weary and profoundly unamused.

"Take them," Lionar Dahauntul ordered flatly, as the Swords emerged to stand with Florin.

"Alive?" a veteran Dragon asked.

"Take them," Dauntless repeated grimly.

Chapter 26
TRUE TREASURE

In life there are three real treasures: loving partners, true friends, and your brightest dreams. The trick is to avoid losing them along the way.

Elminster of Shadowdale
Runes On A Rock
published in the Year of the Morningstar

No," Horaundoon murmured, "I dare not use a mind-link now. Not when one of these fools is so likely to get slain while our minds are touching." He sat back with a sigh to watch what unfolded in the scrying orb.

If the gods smiled, he might not lose all of his tools this day.

If.

The orb glowed brighter, rising. In its depths, the Zhentarim saw Florin snap, "Jhess, behind me! Pennae, behind Islif! If they throw those spears—"

A spear sailed through the air, and his sword smashed it up and aside. Another flew, as the Dragons started striding forward.

"The wands!" Jhessail cried, reaching around Florin to aim the one she held. "Use them—*now!*"

More spears flew, Swords chanted strange words—and fire, lightning, ice, and dark tentacled shadows exploded outward. The gate's silent whirling built into a roar that towered over everything.

The air itself seemed to boil, Purple Dragons were flung in all directions like rag dolls, and Semoor screamed as his wand exploded, taking most of his hand with it. Doust's wand started to spit sparks and glow, and he flung it away and ducked, reaching out an arm to take Semoor to the ground with him.

The wand exploded against the nearest warehouse wall with a fury that sent everyone flying, timbers creaking and groaning, and grain and dust whirling up into a blinding cloud.

Horaundoon peered vainly at the dark roilings for a time, then shrugged. He could, after all, trace Florin at any time through the mindworm.

If, that is, the noble foolhead of a forester was still alive.

In a dark, chill chamber far underground, a lich turned in surprise as its crystal ball glowed into sudden life. How—

Something that glowed palely darted past its moldering workbench, darting among grimoires that had been old when the lich yet lived, and raced up into the lich's bony face before it could lift one withered hand.

The lich stood abruptly, overturning its highbacked chair, and flung out its arms wildly, bony limbs flopping and clashing together like the arms of a doll shaken hard by an angry child. It shuddered, bending over sharply and then arching back, and hastened across the chamber, babbling half-words that spilled over each other, sometimes rising into shouts. Parts of its body grew fur, or scales, or bulging muscles, and lost them again just as swiftly.

Then it shook itself all over, as a moose reaching a riverbank shakes off water, and stood still, an almost-skeletal lich once more.

The crystal ball, its aging cloth cover fallen away, showed a tumbling cloud of dust and debris. The lich waved a hand, and the cloud seemed to move, showing dark heaps—bodies—and a brightness with ragged edges. A hole in a wall that folk were stumbling through.

Folk who'd have been strangers to the lich, but whom Old Ghost, now master of what had been the lich, knew. He watched the one called Semoor swig a vial as he ran, fling it away, and hold out a ruined hand to watch it heal.

"Swords of Eveningstar," he told the darkness, his newly stolen jaw creaking. "You shall prove useful to me. Live a time longer, until I reach for you."

Then his jaw crumbled—and fell off.

The sound of a woman crying was sufficiently rare in the Royal Palace in Suzail that it made Vangerdahast turn his head from talking to Laspeera outside the tall doors of the Soaring Dragon Room, and look.

Two impassive war wizards were leading a weeping Lady Narantha Crownsilver down Longwatch Hall toward Vangerdahast.

The two highest-ranking Wizards of War watched her pass in silence. In the wake of that passing, Vangerdahast told Laspeera rather grimly, "I wish I had time to attend to this one myself, now, but . . ."

Laspeera gave him a look. "I'm sure you do," she murmured teasingly. "I'm sure you do."

"Down here!" Pennae hissed, pointing—and disappeared.

The Swords ducked after her, around a heap of rotting crates in the reeking alley and down a flight of worn steps that seemed carpeted in shrilly squeaking rats, into—a stone-lined, refuse-strewn room that Pennae had already crossed, to beckon them from a dark doorway beyond.

"Cellars," she called, low-voiced. "Come *on!*"

They sprinted across the room, through another, and were halfway across a third room when a cold light burst in the empty air in front of them. Out of it, almost touching Pennae as she fought to halt without falling, stepped a tall, dead-looking man who seemed to be holding his jaw on as tiny blue bolts of lightning encircled it. He was tall, bald, and strong-featured, and wore dark robes that left his pale, dead-white chest bare. He stank of death and mildew.

"Hold, Swords of Eveningstar!" he said hollowly, his half-healed jaw drooping. "I—"

Pennae launched herself from the floor into him, daggers glinting in both hands.

Before either of those metal fangs could hit home, an unseen magic had hurled her away. Her outflung body smashed Doust and Semoor to the floor.

"Hold, I say!" the lich snapped, raising his hands.

Florin and Islif were already moving. Hurling themselves against unseen magic that made them grimace with the effort of fighting their ways forward, they thrust their swords . . . right through the lich.

Its mouth gaped in pain, but no scream came forth. Instead, a teardrop of fell glow shot out of that withered maw, flying wraith-stuff that swooped, darted, and circled around the Swords—Doust missing it with a twisting swing of his mace from where he lay—as it grew.

The lich stood unmoving until Islif's mighty slash sent it toppling to the floor, where it lay still. The flying thing, however, ducked under Florin's fierce attack, shooting under his arms as he swung and swung again, only to soar up above them all long enough for Jhessail to set herself in a stance and raise her hands to lash it with a spell.

They could see through its glow a bearded, severe-browed human male head trailing away into a tail like a falling star. It glared at them, swerved suddenly to avoid Islif's reaching blade, then plunged down at Jhessail.

Who gabbled her spell desperately, and never knew if she'd cast the magic properly or not as the racing head plunged *into* her.

She gasped. There was no crashing impact, but merely a chill that stabbed up past her heart into her head, and left her breathlessly staring at inward darkness in something of a daze.

Behind her, Semoor shouted in alarm more than pain, and stiffened. The head tore right through him as it had through Jhessail—and as she watched, it did the same to Doust.

The wizard who answered to the name Amanthan raised his head sharply, as if sniffing the air. He'd been hearing the boots of running

Dragons, short horncalls, and shouted orders, this last little while, over the wall that kept all Arabel out of his garden, but this—this was something more.

Strong magic. *Strange* magic. Mother Mystra, what *now?*

In this city of folk who could smell as well as see, the lich was best abandoned anyhail. It had served his needs, and a living body would make a better host for several reasons.

Old Ghost soared down the alley, well pleased. He'd passed through all of the Swords, and worked two things on each of them in doing so: left their minds open to his return, no matter what shieldings might then exist, and—until that future visit—enabled them to perceive any nearby portal they gazed upon as a glowing "door."

A bearded head of translucent radiance, touches of white hair at his temples but with dark and scowling brows above storm-gray eyes, Old Ghost raced on, turning onto one street then another. He turned a corner where Lionar Dauntless was running along, shouting orders to the Dragons trotting behind him—and darted into that shouting mouth.

The lionar's eyes glowed eerily, just for a moment. Then Dauntless grew a crooked smile and ran on.

"This way!" Pennae panted, sprinting down another street. The far end of the cellars had been full of Purple Dragons searching for wayward Swords of Eveningstar. The Swords had been forced to flee up old and sagging stairs and through a bakeshop full of fat, shrieking cooks, out into streets where more Dragons were closing in from all sides. Arabel was roused against them.

"Shouldn't we?" Doust gasped, stumbling after her, "Be trying to get to a city gate, to get out?"

"No," Pennae shouted back. "Those three sharp hornblasts, same note in a row? That was them telling each other, gate by gate, that all was secured. There'll be no getting out that way!"

"Back to the wizard's underground lair?" Semoor suggested slyly.

"Go tluin yourself," Pennae told him crisply. "With a shovel."

Another horncall rang out, close at hand, and she erupted in swiftly hissed curses as she looked up at the tall, unbroken stone wall of a mansion compound beside her, a flood of invective that ended, "Mercy of Mask, if I but had one of those horns!"

"False calls?" Florin panted.

She nodded as they pelted around a corner—then pointed at a high-heaped cart groaning slowly along the street toward them. "Stop that one for us! Ask the driver if he knows Oddjack and can tell us where to find him!"

Florin frowned at her, but sheathed his sword and flung up his hands, stepping into the path of the slow cart. "Hoy!"

Running the length of the cart, Pennae didn't wait for the puzzled drover to haul on his reins. "Follow me," she hissed, and swarmed up the back of the lashed sacks of the cart's load, where the man couldn't possibly see her. From the height of that load she sprang over the frowning stone mansion wall—and through a mansion window beyond, with a horrific tinkling crash.

Jhessail stared up at that gaping window, her mouth open—then grinned, clawed her way up the sacks of the slowing, creaking cart beside a puffing Doust and Semoor, and plunged through the window in turn.

She found herself in a grand room of tapestries and pleated, neatly arranged draperies, its floor covered with fur rugs and a litter of broken glass.

Pennae stood in the doorway, listening to distant, fading shrieks. "The wealthy widow and all her maids, fleeing to the other side of doors they can slam and lock," she said with a wry smile. "Are the others coming?"

Doust came through the window, caught his heels on a rug, and sat down with a crash, skidding halfway across the chamber—which was fortunate, given that Semoor then landed like a full grainsack on the floor where Doust had just been.

"Gods above, our very own jesters," Islif observed, her boots slamming down on either side of Wolftooth's cringing body. She bent, plucked him up—more like a grainsack than ever—and sprang out of the way.

It was, however, a few breaths more before Florin came in over the sill to trample the same spot of floor. "Gods above, can yon drover curse!" he said admiringly. "So, whose grand house is this? Not a Dragon commander's, I hope?"

"Your sense of humor is even more twisted than mine," Pennae told him. "No, this belongs to a merchant's widow I robbed a tenday back. No place to hide here, even if they weren't all shrieking like banshees. I'm heading for the next mansion over; a reclusive wizard lives there."

"A wizard. *Splendid,*" Islif said cuttingly. "Oh, joy, even!"

"Your better alternative?" Pennae snapped. "No? Then come!"

And she led them on another run, this one down sweeping staircases and through grand rooms dripping with opulence, heading west. Dragon horncalls sounded again outside, close by, and Pennae answered them with curses as she plunged through a door, out into a garden of little fishponds, moss-covered modest mermaid statues, and artfully pruned shrubberies.

The Swords pelted after her, out of the gardens, past a stables where a startled horse awakened and tossed its head, and up an ivy-cloaked wall that had trees beyond it. As the last Sword—Semoor—scaled it, armored men burst around the corner of the mansion they'd just left, shouted, and started sprinting through the garden. There were splashes as the foremost runners precipitously explored the fishponds. Twisting silverfin flew into the air.

Grinning, Semoor turned away, clawed his way up the last torn ivy, and crested the wall, slipping once—which turned out to be a good thing.

The lightning bolt that greeted him raced past his shoulder, lifting every hair on that side of his body, and clawed harmlessly at the sky.

✦ ✦ ✴ ✦ ✦

In the light of the scrying orb Horaundoon smiled and sat back, ignoring the hargaunt's squirmings. This was becoming a superb show. Amanthan had once been an apprentice of the Blackstaff, hadn't he?

"Get out of here!" The tall young mage was so angry he was trembling. "I'm not afraid of kidnappers and thieves! I'll—"

"Live longer if you calm down and hold your tongue," Pennae said, drawing a wand from her belt and aiming it at him.

Behind her, the rest of the Swords all plucked out various rods, wands, and scepters they'd plundered from Whisper's hoard, and leveled them at the wizard. He need not know they hadn't the faintest wisp of a notion what the items did, or even if they dared to find out.

Their eyes were all fixed on his—except for the young lass with flame-red hair, who seemed to be peering with great interest across his gardens.

Amanthan swallowed, looking again along the line of wands. The lass in leathers, at the fore, was now hefting something more than the wand she'd trained on him: she'd produced a small metal sphere from somewhere, and was juggling it in the palm of her other hand. Her eyes were cool and uncaring.

Amanthan swallowed again. "W-what do you want?" he stammered.

"To pass into your house in peace," the tall ranger said, "and hide there. We—"

Jhessail put a quelling hand on Florin's arm and pointed across the garden, to where she could see a blue glow between two trees. "Where does yon portal go?"

The wizard blinked. "Waterdeep."

"Good. Let us pass unhindered through it, and say nothing of where we went. Do this, and I'll toss *this*—" She shook the scepter in her hand. "—to your feet as we depart. To be yours."

Amanthan blinked at her again, then shrugged. "Accepted."

The adventurers flowed past him like a hurrying wave, wands pointing at him all the time. The flame-haired lass lingered to do as she'd promised, bending to send her scepter skittering to Amanthan's feet.

He stared at it, then darted swiftly to one side, eyeing the portal warily.

Nothing came through it at him, as he drew three long, deep breaths in succession. Finally he sighed, took up the scepter gingerly—and whirled around as he heard the rustling of ivy tearing free of stone.

An armored flood of Purple Dragons poured over his wall.

Amanthan strode forward, finding he did not have to feign anger. "And just what," he snapped, "is the meaning of this?"

The Dragons landed with heavy thuds, panting and staggering. One of them, a lionar by his badge, dodged through the dozen or so who were busy drawing their swords, and growled, "Fugitives from justice—six of them—came over this wall moments ago. Where did they go?"

Amanthan smiled thinly. "Fugitives? Really? What *sort* of fugitives?"

"Lord sir," the Purple Dragon said icily, "three women and three men, attired for battle. You can hardly have failed to see them. 'Tis some good way from your house to where you stand, here, and we were *right* on their heels."

"Lionar," the wizard replied, in a voice every whit as cold, "I suffer *no* uninvited guests to trample my flowers—and live." He waved the scepter meaningfully. "Do I make myself *quite* clear?"

Some of the Dragons went pale. Behind them, the tops of ladders and many helmed heads appeared all along the wall, ropes were flung down, and a stouter lionar came puffing down one of them.

"Ah," Amanthan said pleasantly, "more for my scepter. Well, it *has* been some time since it was fed properly . . ."

A few soldiers ducked away, heading for the wall or at least a place behind their fellows, but Lionar Dauntless, hastening from the bottom of his rope, doffed his gauntlets and strode forward, extending his hand to the mage.

"Pray accept my apologies, lord sir. Amanthan of Waterdeep, is it not? I tender the apologies and beseechments of Lord Thomdor, Warden of the Eastern Marches, and Myrmeen Lhal, Lady Lord of Arabel. We hound six miscreants upon their orders, and they will stand coin for any damage we've done. I was about to ask if we might search your grounds, here, but if you've seen these six . . . ?"

Amanthan reached for the proffered hand. "I fear your time would be wasted: the six you seek are . . . no more. I was under attack—they thrust weapons at me—and defended myself with my scepter, blasting them utterly to dust, as you can see. Or rather, *not* see."

Their hands met, and the wizard stiffened as if someone had struck him.

"Ah," Dauntless replied, turning his head to look all around. "Well. Ah, I suppose . . . that's that."

Swordcaptain Nelvorr, standing near, noticed a wisp of something like mist drift from the lionar's mouth to Amanthan's.

The wizard turned his head to look at Nelvorr, and the sword-captain quickly looked away. And shivered.

"So, my king, this is about much more than tax-cheating and slavery."

Vangerdahast whirled around dramatically, robes swirling. "It concerns, once again, an eventual attack on your person; yet another attempt to seize the Dragon Throne."

Six faces gazed at him. Unhappily.

Azoun sat with his queen beside him, the sage Alaphondar in a lower seat nearby. A highknight stood guard behind each of them.

There was no one else in the Soaring Dragon Room but Lord Vangerdahast—until he turned and made the gesture that caused the life-sized images of two additional men to appear in the air beside him.

"It grieves me to report this, Majesty," the royal magician said, waving his hand at the image, "but here's the proof: Lord Gallusk meeting with the exiled 'Lord' Sorn Merendil. Note the room around them."

"The Swandolphin, in Marsember," Queen Filfaeril murmured, causing Azoun to blink at her in surprise. "Minus its usual dancing whores."

The king blinked again, as Alaphondar and Vangerdahast both glanced away to avoid showing their amusement. Safely behind the royals, two of the highknights grinned broadly.

"So the House of Gallusk," Azoun said, "are providing slaves to be trained into a rebel army?"

"No, Majesty. Lord Anamander Gallusk—we don't believe his kin know about any of this—has gangs who snatch peddlers, pilgrims, shepherds and hands from upcountry steadings, caravan-folk, and sailors they overcome with free drink in dockside taverns, and supply them as slaves to Rorth Torlgarth."

"Who is—?"

"A Sembian shipper who owns a sizable—and fast-growing—fleet of fast caravels. Torlgarth sells the slaves elsewhere about the Inner Sea, and in return recruits mercenaries and sends them to the Gallusk lands near the Sembian border, nigh Daerlun. Torlgarth's coins pay them for the season; in this manner, Gallusk's building a private army. We believe Merendil, here, is giving him both gold and orders, and is the brain and war-gauntlet behind this."

"And thus far, you've failed to arrange an 'accident' to befall Merendil—even when he leaves Sembia or Westgate to defy his exile, and slips back onto our soil?"

"Merendil has his own backers: three Red Wizards, led by one known as Klaelan, whose Art, I must confess, outstrips my own." Vangerdahast lifted a hand to indicate the floating semblance of Lord Gallusk.

"Anamander Gallusk, however, lies within our grasp even now. He's here in the city, and I can have him seized forthwith. I fear I must recommend his arrest and execution. Better one man's neck than an army on the march and hundreds—perhaps thousands—

slain. More, if others in Sembia and elsewhere see a chance to strike at us."

The king sighed reluctantly. "Every killing makes the people hate me more, and robs the realm of some measure—however fell—of drive, wits, and backbone." He turned to look at the highknights behind him. "Do it."

"Laspeera will meet with you," Vangerdahast added, "for you to choose which Wizards of War accompany you."

The highknights nodded curtly. "This will be no pleasure," the eldest one said. "Lord Gallusk trained and sponsored me."

"I know," Vangerdahast replied. "I have always known."

"What of the Arcrown?" Alapahondar asked. "I've heard folk in Daerlun are trading rumors that Gallusk has it, has discovered how to use it to pry into any man's thoughts and even, some say, has begun to winnow out all in the land who dislike him or bear him grudges. If he defends himself with it—"

"He'll be wielding a fantasy." Vangerdahast's smile was a wry, twisted thing. "There is no Arcrown, any more. The Blackstaff, Khelben Arunsun, came to hold it, and some years ago offered it up to Divine Mystra. She Herself destroyed it, as he watched, as an affront to magecraft everywhere."

Alaphondar's mouth dropped open. "But—but—all the rumors, your wizards scouring the realm . . ."

Vangerdahast studied his fingernails. "Falsehoods. Uttered by me, to shake the Wizards of War out of the complacency they are all too wont to sink into, and make them—to say nothing of the general populace—alert for treachery and unusual doings from end to end of the realm. I'll let them search for some time yet."

Filfaeril was smiling, but her husband seemed less than amused.

"Folk have died over this, Vangey! Confidence in the safety of the realm and the competence of the Dragon Throne has been assailed. And won't Holy Mystra have something pointed to say to you?"

"Words and deeds that enhance the real or apparent power of magic, and the regard all have for it, are encouraged by the Lady of Mysteries," Vangerdahast replied smoothly. "Their accuracy is beside the point. As for matters strictly Cormyrean, dangers to the realm are increasing. Wherefore I have made its citizens more wary and so stronger in their readiness to deal with any foe." And with those words, he bowed, turned, and departed, striding out of the Soaring Dragon Room in a swirling of robes.

"I noticed," Filfaeril observed, "our good Royal Magician failed to precisely answer your question, but rather offered Mystran doctrine."

"I noticed that too," Azoun agreed. "How many other direct questions does he evade these days, I wonder?"

The Swords of Eveningstar looked around—and blinked.

They stood in the midst of a noisy, crowded city, assailed by many stinks, with a mountain rising like a great wall ahead—and a scarcely less impressive fortress right in front of them, the cobbles under their boots less than a stride away from the stone steps that ascended to its closed front doors.

The curving stone wall of the tower looming above the Swords overhung the landing at the top of the steps, forming a porch of sorts—wherein a young woman in robes was rising from a chair and frowning down at them. She wore leather bracers, from each of which wands projected past her palms, held ready to be grasped in an instant.

"You stand before Blackstaff Tower," she announced formally, then added curiously, "I don't recall seeing any of you before. Were you apprentices of the master?"

"Yes," Jhessail lied boldly. "Please take us to him."

The young woman looked them over slowly, a slight frown on her face, and nodded. "Ascend and enter—but be aware that whoever's scrying you will see nothing once you pass these doors. If you desire to communicate anything to them, do so now."

"Scrying? We're being watched?" Semoor snapped.

As the woman started to nod, Jhessail spread her hands with a flourish. " 'Tis worse than I'd thought," she whispered melodramatically. "Hurry!"

The Swords hastened up the steps. As the doorguard-apprentice stepped smoothly back out of reach, wands ready in both hands, the doors opened by themselves.

Boldly, Jhessail and Pennae together stepped into waiting darkness.

Chapter 27

TITLES, RICHES, AND HIGH REGARD

For what have you gained, if you win fame, titles, riches, and high regard—and lose yourself?

Elminster of Shadowdale
Runes On A Rock
published in the Year of the Morningstar

Horaundoon of the Zhentarim cursed.

As the Swords entered Blackstaff Tower, his scrying was blocked. Its dark doors seemingly shut out everything.

He plucked a wand from a drawer, leaned over the scrying orb, and whispered the spell that would steal power from it—and fed the surge of magic to his scrying.

Blackstaff Tower remained a dark and solid wall to his scrutiny—but the doorguard's eyes narrowed.

Frowning, she sketched a circle in the air with her forefinger, raising one of her wands into it.

Hurriedly Horaundoon passed a hand over his orb, and departed the chamber that held it.

The explosion at his heels flung him across a passage, made the very floors and ceilings sway and shudder, and left him coughing in dust and clutching his head, his ears ringing from its roar.

He regained his feet and strode along the hall, hissing curses.

Only to stop, stunned anew. Reeling, he fell to his knees, clawing at his head this time and making the hargaunt chime in furious discordance.

It felt as if someone had just reached a fist into his head and torn something out. The mindworm link was simply—gone.

+ * ***** * +

The Swords blinked again. They could see nothing inside Blackstaff Tower but impenetrable darkness, with a faintly glowing flagstone path running away into it.

Running a longer way, it seemed, than it should have been able to stretch, given the size of the tower . . . or at least, the size the tower had seemed on the outside.

Pennae held up her glowstone. Its faint radiance was strong enough to show her itself—just—but shone nothing on the gloom all around them.

They stood tense, a darker menace settling on the backs of their necks: a strong, constant feeling of being *watched*.

"Naed," Pennae whispered. "Jhess, lead on."

"Me?"

" 'Twas your idea, lass, this marching right into the tower of the Blackstaff himself."

"But—"

"I'll lead," Florin said, stepping around them. "Keep your feet on the path, and don't reach out into the dark."

They watched him walk away from them. After only a few strides, he vanished, becoming part of the great darkness. All they could see of him were moving occlusions of the flagstones.

"Come," Islif ordered the others, setting off after Florin. "Holy men, *don't* go casting any spells."

They all walked the path, and soon enough came to Florin, standing on a small cluster of glowing flagstones. In front of him, the path ended, and steps climbed on, each one floating alone in an apparent void.

Frowning, Pennae climbed the lowest step and cautiously reached out to either side—only to draw back her hands. "Cold, hard stone," she murmured, "but I can't *see* it." She ran her hand over the hard nothingness to her right, seeing how far it extended—and then jerked her hand back with a hiss. Something small and unseen had bitten her, warningly.

"What is it?" Florin asked.

Pennae shook her head. "Just climb," she said, "and keep your hands in close."

They climbed.

The stair ended in darkness: a level, smooth stair stretching away they knew not how far. Cautiously Pennae advanced, tapping with her toes to make sure solid stone awaited her next step. "Keep still," she snapped over her shoulder. *"Don't* go wandering."

She took another two cautious steps—and suddenly, silently, without any fuss at all, vivid brightness sprang into being around her knees.

She was standing knee-deep in emerald green, dun brown, dark blue, and white-flecked gray: a glowing, incredibly lifelike map of Faerûn floating in the room all around her. It seemed as if she were a striding colossus, standing at the heart of . . . the High Forest, with Waterdeep just *here* and Cormyr over there, Suzail a tiny glittering on its coast, and Arabel . . .

"Gods above us," Florin murmured in wonder. All of the Swords were gawking at the splendor around them, walking with slow caution yet disturbing nothing with their movements.

"So, you are—?"

The voice was old, dry, calm, and male. It seemed to come from all around them.

They looked about uncertainly, still seeing only darkness where there should be walls and ceiling.

Florin cleared his throat. "I am Florin Falconhand, unseen sir, an—"

"I know *who* you are, all of you. I should have spoken more precisely; *what* have you become, you six? A destructive whirlwind that at least knows what it destroys, as it blunders across Faerûn? Or—wonder of wonders—a wind of destruction that begins to *care* about what it shatters?"

The Swords of Eveningstar looked at each other.

The voice spoke again. "Perhaps that's too much to hope, yet. Well, then: let me at least aim you, if you're the sort of weapon biddable to being aimed. How would you like to be wealthy lordlets and ladies of a beautiful backwoods dale, with a castle to call your own?"

Pennae drew in a deep breath. Here's where we get slain. "What's the catch?"

There was a chuckle, and the map faded around them—light stealing into the room to replace it, showing them no walls nor ceiling, but a faint, featureless glow.

Standing in it was a stout, burly shouldered man, muscled and vigorous, whose robes were as black as the staff in his hand. His bristling brows and unruly hair were black, his close-cropped beard was black but with a white tuft down its center, and the face above his raven-dark mustache was craggy and stern.

"Blackstaff am I," he said. "Welcome to Blackstaff Tower, Swords of Eveningstar. I've heard good things of you."

"Really?" Islif asked, startled into speech. "Who the Nine Hells from?"

Khelben laughed—a dry, rusty sound, as if mirth seldom burst from this particular wizard. "Surprising sources," was all he said, when his laughter ended.

Florin eyed him, waiting for him to say more.

Khelben merely met the forester's gaze and smiled.

Silence fell and stretched.

And stretched.

Finally Semoor sighed and said, "So tell us more of this lordlets and ladies offer . . . and as Pennae asked, the downside to it. We know full well: there always is one."

Khelben nodded—and there was suddenly a pendant floating in the air in front of Florin's nose.

An oddly twisted thing, hanging from a chain that floated in the air as if around a phantom neck.

"Behold the Pendant of Ashaba."

The Swords gazed at it in silence.

"The lordship of Shadowdale," the Blackstaff added. "Yours, if you'll take it. Meaningless, if you go not to Shadowdale, to the Twisted Tower of Ashaba that stands empty, and assert it. One of you can be Lord of Shadowdale—before the gods, one of the prettiest places I've ever laid eyes on, verdant farms walled in by a great greenwood, on the main trade road between the Moonsea and Cormyr. Your fortunes are made, if you but take it."

His words ended, and silence returned.

"I mean no disrespect, great Blackstaff, but I'm still waiting to hear the catch," Pennae said.

Khelben arched an imperious eyebrow. "Life," he replied, "is the catch. Life unfolding has a way of tangling and tripping up the best schemes . . . the brightest dreams. The gods play with us all—and I am no god, to have any skill at such games. So expect many catches, but be the bold adventurers you've been thus far, and they will fall before you."

The pendant glittered.

"Yon bauble," the Blackstaff added, "bears only magics that preserve it from time. It does no ill to him who touches it. Florin, will you take it?"

Florin shook his head. "I am a ranger. I want to walk the forests and be free, not sit on a stone throne. I need to feel the wind, see dawns and dusks standing under an open sky. I'd be happy enough to ride hither and yon, bearing Shadowdale's banner. Yet, Lord Wizard, my fellow Swords are all worthy folk. All of them would probably make good Lords of Shadowdale."

"The throne holds only one backside at a time," Khelben said dryly. "Choose among yourselves, then." All around him, the light started to fade.

Hesitantly the Swords eyed each other then bent their heads together.

"He can slay us just like *that*," Pennae whispered. "I'm thinking taking this lordship is the only way we'll leave this place alive."

"Agreed," Semoor hissed sourly. "So: who gets to be Lord High And Mighty?"

"Why not Islif?" Jhessail whispered. "Must it be a 'Lord'?"

"No," Islif said savagely, "I'll *not* take it. I might make a good tyrant, but I'd be a bad lord—and I'd hate myself so fiercely as to welcome death, even as I lorded it. I *will not* do this."

"Pennae?" Jhessail asked.

The thief grinned. "I'm too restless, and *much* too corrupt." She poked Doust in the chest. "How about you? Feeling lucky?"

Doust groaned, and Florin nodded. "The best lord is a reluctant lord."

"Yes," Pennae agreed. "Well?"

"He's got my vote," Semoor said.

"And mine," Jhessail added.

"Hold," Islif said. "Doust, how do *you* feel?"

The novice of Tymora shook his head, sighed, and said, "Well, if none of you want it, I'll do it, but don't blame me if—"

"We won't," Islif said, whirling him around by the shoulders and calling, "Lord Arunsun? We have our lord."

She shoved Doust a few unwilling steps forward.

The Lord Mage of Waterdeep looked amused. "Eager?"

Doust sighed. "Lord, I am—we are all—less than easy about this. We hold a charter from Cormyr, and some promises yet unfulfilled. We are nothing better than outlaws if we break our word."

Then he flinched, startled, as the pendant vanished from where it floated in the air—and reappeared, solid and heavy, in his hands.

The Blackstaff smiled. "I begin to think you *are* that wonder of wonders. Your coming was not unexpected—though you found your own way here and were *not* herded; I daresay Arabel is being turned upside down for traces of you right now. How's young Amanthan getting on, anyhail? He was one of my more promising app—but let us speak of him later; suffice it to say that your arrival was anticipated. Wherefore, as Alaise delayed you on my steps, I did what was needful. Step through yon door."

An archway silently appeared, outlined in soft radiance, beyond Khelben.

Hesitantly, the Swords went to it. The room behind them went dark, Khelben vanishing with it, even as the one ahead began to brighten.

By the kindling light that came from no source they could see, the Swords beheld a throne with a regal-looking crowned woman sitting on it, and a half-moon table beside it where a wise-looking man sat, writing furiously.

He looked up, set down his quill, and stood. "Kneel before your queen. Adventurers, behold Queen Filfaeril of Cormyr."

The Swords gaped at the smiling woman on the throne, and then hastily went to their knees.

Filfaeril waved her hand. "Rise, and be at ease," she said. "Enough of that nonsense, Alaphondar. Swords of Eveningstar, I propose a trade. I need a task performed, and in return I believe I can amend your charter. Cormyr would dearly like to have friends we can trust in Shadowdale, as a bright light on the road that brings so much Moonsea metal and coin to us, and sends our food and horseflesh thither. So turn thy back and open thy codpiece, Florin; the charter is needed."

Smiling at their startled looks, the queen said serenely, "Cormyr has many watchful eyes. Some of them make me quite confident the knighthoods I am now going to bestow are fully deserved. Florin, for example, made such fine work of the Lady Narantha that several scores of nobleborn mothers desire to send her daughters to him, forthwith."

"My, my," Islif murmured at the ceiling, "won't *that* prove diverting?"

In a room whose midair glowed with a life-sized, moving duplicate of the room where Filfaeril was now busily granting knighthoods, Dove Silverhand threw back her head and laughed aloud. "Ah, Islif," she murmured, "we might be sisters!"

Then she lost her mirth and murmured, "Not that I'd ever wish such a doom upon you."

Alaphondar had been busy writing the proclamations, it seemed—for he now spread them out on the table before the dumbfounded Swords.

"Knighthoods always come with a grant of lands," Queen Filfaeril added, "or a keep, or coins—gems, actually; 'tis hard to carry twenty thousand lions in one's hands—in lieu. Alaphondar, pay them."

The sage hesitated. "Your Majesty, one heraldic necessity must be seen to, first."

"Well?"

"They must be named knights *of* somewhere."

"Well, of Shadowdale, man!"

"Nay, good Queen, it must be the name of their granted lands in Cormyr—or, failing that, a legendary place."

"A legendary place?"

"Aye, such as 'of the Forest Eternal,' or 'of the Castle Unseen.' A place not of mere invention, but one known to heralds and loremasters, that's either lost or ruined."

"Well, pick one!"

"Nay, Highness—*they* must choose one."

Filfaeril shrugged and turned to the Swords, spreading her hands in an unspoken question.

The adventurers stared at her and then at each other.

"Uh . . ." Doust began, then ran out of words and fell silent. Pennae shrugged, and Florin and Islif stared at each other blankly.

High in the tallest tower of his mansion in Arabel, the wizard Amanthan smiled over a tiny crystal ball that held the room in Blackstaff Tower in its glowing depths, and cast a quick, deft spell.

A bell tolled warningly in Blackstaff Tower, the light in the room shivering in its booming echoes.

Khelben appeared behind Filfaeril's throne, eyes narrowed above a deepening frown . . . and *something* made Jhessail and Florin say together, "Let us be Knights of . . . Myth Drannor."

"Ah," Alaphondar said in satisfaction, dipping his quill in the floral-shaped metal inkwell before him. *"Perfect."*

The Blackstaff regarded the Swords thoughtfully as Filfaeril fished something on a fine chain out of her cleavage: a signet. Rocking it in an oval ink-dish Alaphondar held out to her, she applied it to all six parchments in turn, scribbled her signature in an oval around each signet-mark, and announced, "Done. The gems, Alaphondar."

The sage trailing behind her, the queen walked to the Swords, drew her dainty belt dagger, nicked each of them, leaving the tiniest of pricks on the backs of their hands, and said, "I dub thee all Knights of Myth Drannor. And now the task."

The newly made Knights held their breath, expecting the worst.

Filfaeril smiled.

"After being torn so precipitously from my husband's side, I'd prefer to return to Suzail with rather more dignity—with, in fact, a knightly escort. There's a royal remount stables on the Way of the Dragon nigh Zundle, and an easy ride home from there. If you're agreeable, my knights?"

Florin swallowed, seeking words, but Islif's tongue was swifter. "Command us, Highness."

As Alaphondar scrambled to pack his things, Filfaeril turned to Khelben. "Blackstaff?"

"Of course," Khelben replied. "I know the place." He raised one hand idly—and the Knights of Myth Drannor, the sage Alaphondar, and Queen Filfaeril of Cormyr were suddenly standing in strong-smelling straw, blinking at each other.

"I'll never get used to that," Filfaeril sighed. Then she gave the dazed adventurers a little girl's grin. "Knights, choose your mounts!"

A handful of hairs flared up in sudden flame. Horaundoon looked at them in satisfaction.

His spell had worked. Florin's hairs, torn from him on that moon-lit night above Starwater Gorge by Narantha Crownsilver's ardent hands, were now giving this particular cunning Zhentarim a way to reach Florin once more.

So the ranger was outside the wards of Blackstaff Tower, and in . . . Cormyr?

"Azuth mount Mystra," the Zhentarim cursed disbelievingly. Was the Blackstaff with the forester?

Horaundoon cast a spell over the bowl of water, watched it ripple violently then smooth out—and found himself gazing down at a stables, with three—no, all six surviving Swords leading forth horses . . . splendid beasts . . . and two others: a courtier and—

Queen Filfaeril.

"Mystra return the favor," he swore in astonishment.

And then clapped his hands, raced across the room for what he'd need, and set to work. Victory comes never to the mage who casts not.

Swinging his fire-tongs with all his strength, Amanthan shattered the crystal ball into a thousand shards. Just to be safe.

In life, Old Ghost had been a mage few could match, but the Blackstaff was one of Mystra's Chosen.

Poor doomed bastard.

Eyes glowing eerily with Old Ghost's riding presence, the young mage hurried into the next room, to fetch another crystal ball. 'Twas time to scry Horaundoon—before that Zhent fool got up to any more mischief.

"There!" Horaundoon beamed triumphantly, stepping back from the flying snake. It was frozen in spell-stasis, wings spread and head thrust forward, its body a graceful curve. He'd just placed the last of the eight mindworms around its snout. Six Swords were grand quarry, but a senior courtier of Cormyr now . . . and its *queen*!

He snorted in sheer glee, and worked the teleport that would snatch his serpent to the air just behind Florin Falconhand's head, whence it could easily swoop and strike.

Amanthan was feverishly working a spell of his own, glancing up betimes at one of the two crystal balls flanking him—the one scrying Horaundoon.

Done. Whew. The hairs he'd plucked from the vial that had appeared in front of him melted away, and the mage sat back in satisfaction.

Old Ghost would prevail. As always.

He waved the second crystal into life and looked from the first—Horaundoon—to the second: the newly minted Knights of Myth Drannor, riding along a road with the royal sage and the Dragon Queen of Cormyr in their midst.

To echo Horaundoon, this was shaping up into a superb show.

Radiance blossomed silently in the air behind the knights' heads, hidden from view in the lee of tree-boughs the knights had just ridden under. Out of that swift-fading light glided a flying snake. A single wingbeat took it over the boughs and into a long glide, its mouth opening, toward the back of Florin's neck.

Mindworms wriggled down the snake's pointed head to cluster between its fangs, dark and glistening . . .

Dove sat bolt upright in sudden alarm, eyes widening. *"No!"* she cried, silver fire kindling in her eyes as she clenched trembling fists. "Not Florin!"

The Weave howled with the frantic fury of her reaching.

Though he was too far.

And she was too late.

The snake struck, Florin grunting and stiffening—but no fangs sank into his neck, for at their touch the serpent vanished in a sudden burst of spell-light.

+ + ✦ + +

Horaundoon hadn't even time to blink as serpent jaws gaped, right in front of his face.

He did find time to scream as it struck, fangs biting deep—and the mindworms surged forward, to burrow in.

He went on screaming, reeling blindly around the room, clawing at the snake as the mindworms gnawed and devoured, sinking deeper.

He could feel the hargaunt fleeing from him, but was too lost in agony to care, raking at the snake until scales flew—and he finally tore it free, much of his cheeks and brow going with it, to dash it again and again against a wall, clubbing it into soft ruin.

Dropping it dazedly, he felt for the potions he knew were there. Six healing quaffs, and the others that were useless to him now . . .

Horaundoon gulped them frantically, feeling the hot wetness deeper and deeper in his brain as the mindworms gnawed on. Mystra have mercy, *eight* of them . . .

He was still blind, could in fact feel one of them gnawing behind his eyes, and vainly tried—with hands that trembled treacherously—to work spells on himself.

No. No.

"Not the doom I'm . . . looking for," he gasped aloud, clawing his clattering way across the table again, sending useless potions flying. Ha! He had it!

Snatching up the scepter he'd been seeking, Horaundoon turned it on himself and gasped out the word that awakened it.

A glow he could no longer see warmed his face. He writhed, shuddering helplessly, but locked his fingers in his lap, cradling the scepter, and nursed the beam that ravaged him, even as he curled up around it in pain.

He was, he knew, glowing and pulsing . . .

+ + ✦ + +

Between each pulse of his scepter, Horaundoon of the Zhentarim looked increasingly wraithlike. He was translucent now . . .

Looking down into the crystal ball that held the Zhent's image, Amanthan cursed softly, fists clenched. *"Die,* hrast you," he whispered. "As I did."

The husk of a body fell in on itself. With a ragged cry of despair and revulsion, a roiling glow burst up out of it.

Weeping and wailing, Horaundoon swirled around his rooms—then out of them, howling.

A fat, unshaven carter was tying up horses in the street below. Horaundoon plunged down through the man, savagely trying to slay.

The carter staggered, wheezed, stared at the street with wild, bewildered eyes—and fell on his face and lay still, his horses snorting and trying to back away.

It was that easy. That hideously easy.

And what comfort was that to him?

Howling anew, Horaundoon raced down the street, a pale and shapeless arrow, to slay again. And again. Purple Dragons, shopkeepers, alley drunks . . .

A lush-bodied woman in an upper window, preening before a mirror. He soared into the room and spiraled around her, not wanting to slay so much as touch . . . touch what he could no longer touch!

She screamed once then trembled, too fearful to breathe, tottering . . . He tried to hold her as she fell, but managed only to sink into her, passing not through her body but into her mind.

Which was both darker and more shallow than he'd expected, and faintly disgusted him, but which he found he could coerce . . . thus . . . and shape the thoughts of . . . *thus.* So he had no body, but could—yes!—live in the bodies of others.

Her mind was a small and cringing thing, flinching from him. Horaundoon lashed it scornfully even as he forced it to do this, then that.

She clawed her way stiffly back up from the floor, the gown she'd been trying on hanging half-off her, and went to the stairs, lurching and stumbling.

By the time she reached the street, she was walking more or less upright—stiffly, foaming at the mouth as her eyes rolled wildly. Horaundoon was still learning control.

"Ever the unsubtle, bumbling idiot," Old Ghost sneered through Amanthan's lips, as he scried the clumsy progress of the woman Horaundoon was mind-riding. "And as you stumble about, your schemes do the same—as clumsily as you do."

Yet they were now two of a kind, he and the Zhent. Possessing, mind-riding spirits.

Horaundoon just didn't realize, yet, what a great victory he'd achieved.

"Bitter laughter and applause," Old Ghost murmured. "For us both, I suppose."

The hargaunt was wriggling as fast as it could, flowing along the cold stone floor of a dark passage.

The flying gauntlets that pounced upon it, lifted it into the air, and expanded around it into a spherical prison were quite a surprise—but ignored its most belligerent chimings.

"You, little flowing menace, are going to come in quite useful to *this* war wizard traitor," the wielder of the gauntlets purred gloatingly, toying with a ring that bore a handsome, oversized carved unicorn head. "Yes, quite useful. When my time comes."

The war wizards had been gentle, even respectful in their questionings, and had left her some privacy to recover herself while they fetched her a meal.

That was why Narantha Crownsilver was sitting alone in a pleasantly furnished chamber somewhere in the palace in Suzail when horror burst open in her mind, unfolding with such awfulness that she could only whimper.

There was something called a mindworm in her head, linking her to this wizard—a Zhentarim!—the murderer of her Uncle Lorneth!

Who'd cold-bloodedly taken her uncle's face and voice to deceive her, using her to spread mindworms to Florin and others . . . so many others . . . nobles all across the realm!

"Gods deliver me," she gasped, when she could find words. "What have I *done?*"

This revelation was due to this Horaundoon's own misfortune. She watched the monster suffer under his own snake and mindworms, and she felt his sick pain—a dull echo of it, at least, as her own mind staggered . . .

And even as he shuddered and shrieked and wallowed in agony, her dazed mind stumbled through his dark plans, laid bare to her at last.

"No," she whispered. "Oh no."

He would survive this.

He would control her again, through the mindworm in her head—and through her, all she'd subverted.

"Gods!" she whispered, "so *many!*"

She must do something. Right now . . .

So this is what real fear tastes like. Fear for all Cormyr.

Weeping and trembling, she left the room and hurried through the palace.

"Failure, Lady Lord," Dauntless said bitterly. "Complete failure. The fugitives got clean away. I stand deserving of any punishment you see fit."

Myrmeen Lhal's eyes bored into his as if she were reading something written small on the inside back of his skull, but she said nothing.

And went on saying nothing as a curtain parted behind her, and the Warden of the Eastern Marches came into the room, stepped aside, and handed in an unfamiliar woman as if she outranked him. She was tall and muscular, her hair a long fall of silver—not silver as old folk go silver, but the shining silver of polished metal—and she wore green leathers, with the crescent moon badge of the Harpers at belt buckle and throat.

Baron Thomdor gave Dauntless a smile. "Well met this day, *Ornrion* Dahauntul. Be also well met with Dove Silverhand, of the Harpers."

Dove inclined her head in greeting. "Myrmeen, Dauntless: you share no failure. The fugitives you've been chasing have just been knighted by Queen Filfaeril, and are riding in triumph into Suzail right now."

Two jaws dropped in unison. Almost tenderly, Dove added, "When they pass through Arabel again, in a tenday or so, 'twould be best if they were made welcome, not hounded or imprisoned."

Stunned disbelief was clear on the newly restored ornrion's face. "And—and how can you know this?" he sputtered. "Forgive me, Lady, but words are easily said—yet more slowly trusted. Why, I've never even seen you before!"

"Ah, but you have, gallant Dauntless. That night at the Leaping Hart, when you danced on the tables, remember? And loudly admired the behind of a certain lass?" Dove turned and struck a pose. "Have your fingers forgotten this backside so swiftly?"

Dauntless reddened as words failed him again, and Myrmeen and Thomdor exploded into laughter.

Dove grinned and patted the ornrion's arm. "Ne'er mind. 'Bold to face the foe,' remember?"

The Horngate loomed high and impressive overhead. "Lady Queen," Florin murmured over his shoulder, "you should ride at the fore, and we behind you. 'Tis not right that—"

"Ride on," Filfaeril commanded, in a voice of sudden iron that sounded muffled. "Just as we are."

Florin turned his head and discovered that the Dragon Queen had cast a mantle over her head, and ducked low in her saddle.

He exchanged looks with Islif, they both shrugged—and an ornrion was stepping into their path, his hand raised imperiously.

"Hold hard, there!" he said sternly. "So large a company, and under arms? Who are you, who seek to ride right into Suzail?"

"We are knights of Cormyr, and chartered adventurers besides, and so are doubly allowed to bear war-steel into this fair city," Florin replied, as they reined in their mounts.

"Knights *and* chartered adventurers? On mounts bearing the royal crest on their harness?" The officer's voice was hard and incredulous. "Down from your saddle, sir, and furnish me with your charter—if you have one."

Purple Dragons behind him, in the arch of the Horngate, had already taken up cocked and loaded crossbows and were aiming them, their faces suspicious.

"I think *not*," Queen Filfaeril's voice rang out. "Stand aside, loyal Dragons!" She urged her horse past Florin, mantle thrown back, and raised her hand in a wave that set folk to astonished chatter—and sent the gate guards to their knees, their bows hurriedly pointed elsewhere.

"Diligently done, ornrion. Thy vigilance has our royal favor," the Dragon Queen said crisply as she spurred past the officer, leading the knights forward onto the Promenade.

Word seemed to spread like fire racing in a gale, and folk streamed out of shops and sidestreets to gawk at the passing riders.

"I wonder how many enemies she's making us?" Pennae whispered uneasily, as ragged cheers arose, the queen waved, and folk—so many folk—stared, faces upon hundreds of faces. "I mislike being seen so prominently in public."

"Get used to it," Alaphondar murmured. "And keep smiling. Every hamlet and realm, and all the folk in it, need their goats and heroes."

"Ah," Semoor asked wryly, as the tall iron gates of the Royal Court opened before them, "and which are we, I wonder?"

Alaphondar's smile was thin. "Learning how to find a way out of goatskins is the true mark of a hero."

As they rode across the broad and muddy courtyard, bright horns began to sound.

Epilogue

There was only one way to defend Cormyr.

Only one way to restore the honor of House Crownsilver.

Every god there is, give me strength to do this.

To do what must *be done.*

Rethendarr was the war wizard who'd been most angry in questioning her—the youngest, most eager and restless. To Rethendarr she would go.

After she made one necessary stop.

"I am the Lady Narantha Crownsilver," she told the startled Purple Dragon at the guardroom. "And I have need of—ah. This one will do."

Her sliced thumb told her the slender long sword was very sharp. Carrying it like a walking stick, she marched off before the guard could think of a pretext to stop her.

"Two things," she murmured to herself, "all the realm knows. The Wizards of War stand ever-ready to defend the realm—not the king or Obarskyrs or palaces, but Cormyr itself—and right now every last spellhurler among them has one peril uppermost in mind: the Arcrown, that can easily slay any mage from afar. They search for it day and night."

She stood before the door to Rethendarr's study for a long time, trembling, before she mustered courage enough to open it and step inside.

There had been a chair . . . and that high marble-topped table.

There still were. The table was too heavy for anyone to shift alone—good—but the chair Narantha dragged to where she needed it—and wedged the sword hilt in its back cushions, the blade angled up over the table.

Ah, he had a glowstone. Even better. She put it on the marble, just beside the sword with its jutting point.

Now, where did the wizard keep his wine?

Ah.

She chose the best, and his largest goblet, and it *was* good. She had a second goblet.

Yet found herself still trembling.

"Lorneth," she whispered, "guide me."

And she flung the goblet with all the force in her arm, at the closed door Rethendarr must be on the other side of.

He was, by the startled curse she heard through it.

In a moment he'd wrench it open, and she must be ready. Standing up straight and proud, she tossed her head, trembling so hard that she thought she'd fall over, and cried in as triumphant a voice as she could manage, "Ha! Face me if you dare, Rethendarr, for I wear the Arcrown—and I want to see your face as I slay you! You, and all who stand between me and the Dragon Throne!"

There was a moment of silence, then a swift incantation.

The glowstone on the table winked out—and several other things around the room changed, too.

"My, antimagic fields are wonderful things," she commented aloud, talking to keep her courage up.

The door crashed open—and Narantha hurled herself onto the sword.

Rethendarr's face was furious, his hands raised, but the jaunty greeting she'd meant to give him was lost in the sob of pain that burst from her.

The steel was so cold. So cold . . .

She slid down it, gasping. Blood was running from her lips like a waterfall, it was through her and must be thrust out through her back by now, dark and wet . . .

So this is what it's like, to die.

In a room far away in Arabel, Dove Silverhand's head came up sharply.

"What is it?" Myrmeen Lhal snapped.

"Something . . . bad," Dove said softly. "Oh, Mystra."

The knights burst into the study, a frantic Florin at their head, and ran right over the war wizard in their way.

Narantha Crownsilver was impaled on a sword, dying. "Highly overrated," she gasped, not seeming to see them, and her face twisted as she tried to laugh . . . and found she couldn't.

As Florin flung himself across the room, clawing at his belt for a potion, Narantha spat blood and turned to look at him, her face still twisted in agony. "It's *in my head,*" she sobbed. "Don't heal me, or it'll get out!"

"What, Nantha?" Florin cried, flinging his sword down and reaching for her.

Narantha drooled blood all over his hands as she shuddered, and let her head fall back onto his shoulder. "This," she whispered. *"This* is what it means to love Cormyr."

"What've you done?" he cried. "Why—why?"

The Lady Narantha Crownsilver peered up at him pleadingly through her mask of blood and tears to gasp, "Oh, Florin, I *had* to do it. You see that, don't you?"

And then she died.

*Here ends Book 1 of the tales of the Knights of Myth Drannor.
Their adventures are continued in* Swords of Dragonfire.

FORGOTTEN REALMS®

PAUL S. KEMP

"I would rank Kemp among WotC's most talented authors, past and present, such as R. A. Salvatore, Elaine Cunningham, and Troy Denning."
—Fantasy Hotlist

The New York Times best-selling author of *Resurrection* and The Erevis Cale Trilogy plunges ever deeper into the shadows that surround the FORGOTTEN REALMS® world in this Realms-shaking new trilogy.

THE TWILIGHT WAR

BOOK I

SHADOWBRED

It takes a shade to know a shade, but will take more than a shade to stand against the Twelve Princes of Shade Enclave. All of the realm of Sembia may not be enough.

BOOK II

SHADOWSTORM

Civil war rends Sembia, and the ancient archwizards of Shade offer to help. But with friends like these . . .

September 2007

BOOK III

SHADOWREALM

No longer content to stay within the bounds of their magnificent floating city, the Shadovar promise a new era, and a new empire, for the future of Faerûn.

May 2008

anthology

REALMS OF WAR

A collection of all new stories by your favorite FORGOTTEN REALMS authors digs deep into the bloody history of Faerûn.

January 2008